I0824528

# The Chronicles of Eorthe

## The Lance, the Key and the Door That Was Shut

# The Chronicles of Eoorthe

## The Lance, the Key and the Door that was Shut

BY

B.D. SUTFIN

ILLUSTRATIONS BY JUSTIN GERARD

NORTHERNNESS PRESS

PITTSBURGH, PENNSYLVANIA

FOR C, WHO RADIATES LIFE,

FOR E, WHOSE GAZE CAPTIVATES,

FOR A, THE BRAVE BOY WHO SLEW THE GIANT,

FOR G, WHOSE BATTY EYES BRING RAMPARTS DOWN,

AND FOR THE CROWNED QUEEN WHO LOVED A BROKEN PRINCE.



Northernness Press
www.northernnesspress.com

Publisher's Note: This is a work of fiction. Names, characters, places, and incidents are a product of the author's imagination. Locales and public names are sometimes used for atmospheric purposes. Any resemblance to actual people, living or dead, or to businesses, companies, events, institutions, or locales is completely coincidental.



The Chronicles of Eoorthe; The Lance, the Key and the Door That Was Shut/ B.D. Sutfin.
-- 1st ed.
ISBN 9780692988244

Printed in the U.S.A.

First American edition, April 2018

# CONTENTS

# CONTENTS

Many stories begin with long ago and by all accounts this story is no different. Our story begins with something like, 'a dark and stormy night,' but not in the way that you might imagine it. It was dark and stormy because *someone* made it dark and stormy. Dark in a sense that is really scary. At least it was for Valen Grimm, the boy (if you can call him that) who becomes—well we won't say just yet, what he becomes. It was the kind of storm that bent trees over and pushed you backwards as you walked along. Though, if you had been paying attention you wouldn't have ever called it a storm.

Anyway, it would be terrible for you if you knew what was going to happen to Valen or what did happen to him and so we won't say just yet what did. Valen was on an island and he didn't know he was on an island until he met some other boys who became his friends and told him. They were all alone on the island, too. The people on this island, though they had great ships and could navigate the sea better than anyone, never found any other land no matter how much they explored. They were completely and utterly alone on a great sea. The problem was, that everyone who lived on the island had memories of their ancestors who had been off of it—some never to return again. So naturally people believed that they could get off.

Though, they all were lost at sea is the truth of it. And no one visited or found them either. This island wasn't anything tropical if that is what you are thinking. Quite the opposite, actually. Giant rocky cliffs and tall fir and oak trees grew all around. Winding roads and stone cottages littered the landscape and one very large mansion, where Valen lived.. It was rumored pirates once buried gold there. The island Valen was on had fallen out of all knowledge (some said it disappeared below the Atlantic Ocean) while the history of our world continued on. But, it is still there if you went looking for it today. You'd have to talk to with someone wise who knew where it was. You can't find it any other way. But, I would be very cautious in ever going there. For the same reason it had disappeared, is the same reason to never go there.

Valen lived Far North surrounded by the Cold Northern Ocean (that is what it was once called)—in our world, but fallen out of time. Valen had disappeared out of time too, much like something which has been lost to history to you or me. It was after Valen's adventures with his friends that he realized it was *Something That Moved Through the Skies* which was responsible for the story Valen found himself in. Eventually this *Something* wasn't just *Something Which Moved*, but *Something Which*

*Rode on Something Which Moved* which caused *Deep Rumblings*. Valen eventually found out what that all meant, too. So, this is the story as best I can tell it and what he told me, when I met him. He was young then, just as he is now, but his memory is long and crisp as an old man. Though he never did grow old. In fact he never aged. The Rumblings which happened when this Something began to move shook planets and stars, bent flowers, trees and waves which caused the most peculiar things to happen which wouldn't have otherwise happened had Valen never been born. Of course, at the time our story begins; Valen didn't know any of this. How could he? To him it was just a horrible, awful, terrifying storm. *The Great Terrible Storm* as he eventually came to know it. It wasn't until long after this story, that looking back on it he learned what I am telling you now. But, before Valen enters our story, long before he was born some other creatures were up to some hideous plans and to that we now turn.

# The Chronicles of Eoorthe

## The Lance, the Key and the Door That Was Shut

CHAPTER ONE

# A MEETING OF MISCHIEF

A gangly man with sooty hair and a scruffy face, breathed heavily like a tired horse, glancing down at the valley below him. Cloaked under a swirl of snow, a tiny glowing village emerged in the night. The wind ripped across the hillside. He tightened his hands on the item he clutched. A white forest of evergreens pressed down on him. He crept down the icy slope and headed towards a decrepit manor that stood at the crossroads of a silent street. The wind and snow blew powerfully when at last it began to taper. A light snow continued to fall and his footsteps were outlined on the cobblestone as he hurried along. He stopped briefly and looked back up the hill. He turned, his heart pounding hard as his feet hammered the ground. A golden amber light emanated from the tops of the lamp posts casting their glow on the snow below.

Drops of glittering gold dripped off the man's hands. He darted across the street, slipping into another alley. At the end of it stood a shriveled looking figure covered in a tattered black cloak. Its face was sunken in and its bony hands which appeared to be long gnarled talons, grasped a tall and twisted, wooden limb. It paused, looked backwards then hobbled along. Leathery wings dragged in the white powder below, barely concealed by the cloak it bore. It turned the bend. The man who had been running stopped, blew on his hands to warm them, then slowly followed. He trailed the creature and stopped once more to think about what he was getting himself into or what he was already into. He stared at the frozen moss for a long moment and pressed his back up against an old high stone wall which cast long shadows. The darkness briefly hid him. At the end of the wall, just across the street, stood a small door. Two softly flickering lanterns cascaded rich warm light around the doorway. The hooded figure smashed them with his wooden staff and went through the dark opening. The man crept down the alley, hugging the wall desperately and fearing that the hunters which had been tracking him for the past several days, would appear at any moment. He moved cautiously, stuffing the item further behind his tattered coat and at last reached the end and darted toward the manor. He peered through the frosty glass panes. Inside he could see only a sallow candle with a sputtering, forlorn flame. Trembling, he knocked.

"Come in," came a raspy voice from the darkness.

The man slipped through the door. At a table in the corner of the room sat the hunched figure. A devious smile crept over the corners of its mouth. The man moved slowly towards the table. Cold sweat dripped down the side of his forehead as he followed the light of the dripping candle. He looked around. The room was full of shifting shadows. On the walls hung crumbling wallpaper.

"Has anyone followed you?" said the figure in a horrid whisper as the man reached for the chair.

"No, no, Prince," said the man his voice quivering. "I lost them three days ago."

"Lost them?"

"I was hunted for weeks," said the man. "I barely slept. I—"

"If anyone has followed you—if anyone uncovers our plans, I will let my beloved monsters have their way with you."

The shivering man dusted the snow off his head.

"Well, Bendy," said the cloaked figure boring its eyes into him over the faint light of the candle, "do you have it?"

"Yes." He cleared his throat. He reached from behind his coat and pulled out a large, worn and decrepit, dark reddish brown colored book, then slowly handed it over, his hands trembling. More bright, whitish golden drops slid off the edge of his sweaty hand. "I hope it is worth all of my trouble."

"Trouble?" said the figure who now held the book. "It would be trouble if we did not have it."

Bendy sighed heavily.

"You have done it then?"

"Yes, your Majesty. Though with much toil, I'm afraid." Bendy stuttered, moving uncomfortably in his chair; unable to see beyond the large tattered hood of his questioner.

The candle flickered and Bendy noticed the grin growing twice its normal size. A terrible pair of eyes appeared as it shifted its gaze away from the book towards Bendy.

He shivered in his chair.

"Death is only the beginning of our thievery," said the Prince with his smile continuing to grow. "You have done well and I am pleased." Bendy suddenly noticed a curious orange glow begin to swell around its neck.

"Now, tell me your tale, for I dearly desire to hear it," said the Prince taking one of his fingers which had a long gnarled talon that he now drug down the spine of the book.

Frightened and weary from traveling, Bendy stirred. Blinking timidly, he rubbed his frigid hands together. He watched the Prince move its finger up and down the book. More bits of gold dripped onto the table. The light of the dying candle flickered with the tiny bit of life it had left. Then, a cold draft crept through the room.

"I traveled for many, days," Bendy began. His eyes shot back and forth like a hunted deer. "I was alone the entire time. For I remembered how important it was not to divulge my plans. I tried to remain unseen, but it was nearly impossible. Great birds that fly faster than I could have ever imagined patrolled nearly everywhere. I tried to find the Road, but it proved harder than I thought. It almost seemed as if some other force was working against me," continued Bendy. "Days turned into weeks, and weeks into months. I followed the map as best I could. Then, one night when I was in the Twysted Forest near the border of the Land of Pantegon, I was approached by two soldiers."

"And—what did they ask?"

"They asked me what business I had in the Twysted Forest, where I was headed and what the nature of my travels were." His breath fell from his lips frigidly. "They seemed strangely suspicious of me—almost as if they knew of my plan."

"What did you tell them?"

"I told them nothing."

"Nothing?"

# CHAPTER ONE

"I swear to you!"

"You are loyal to no one except yourself. You are a pathetic creature—better to have never been born. Unborn would have been better as I see it, but now that you are here, I will make you trust me, I will use you for my purposes."

Bendy's hands twitched again. Shadows stretched up the walls of the room, spread up onto the ceiling and across the frozen glass of the window. Bendy watched the wax drip as the candle flickered.

"Your Majesty—I told them nothing of our dealings." Bendy paused. "Have I succeeded?" he said timidly.

"Not yet. You are forgetting that you have one more task!" Glaring eyes bored out from under the Prince's hood as it lowered the fabric down to its shoulders where two spiky bones showed.

Bendy glanced out the window. Snow was now dancing wildly in the steely air. He sighed desperately.

"I cannot go through with the second part."

"Do not speak of such things."

"But your Majesty, I cannot risk anything further. I do not want to—"

"To what? See our plans fully realized? Do not forget. You will be more than you could imagine now that you have joined us. You can be Treasurer if you'd like, for I know how much you love gold. Or, if you prefer; a Ruler of Cities or maybe even Head of Spins." The shadowy figure continued in a hoarse whisper then it changed into a low sort of growl. Bendy saw the glow around the creature's neck pulsate again. "Your treachery in stealing this is a delight to me. Oh the celebration! It was a sight to behold. Thousands of bells torn down in every city and village. Hauled away to make great machines and weapons of war. Our plans are coming together just as I imagined them."

"Spins?" said Bendy nervously.

"Spin-master, Chief of Lies," said the Prince. "You must love lying and keeping secrets, deceiving others. Which, I know you do. That is why I sought you out in the first place. But, you must lay aside all doubt and especially lay aside your own thoughts about whether or not this is a good idea, because your ideas about what is good is the thing that is so damaging. It is MY ideas which are good. You'll see. It'll take a while to train you. Though of course, as you know full well; we cannot ever really make anything as I have told you nor the others who have joined us. We are uncreators. It sounds so much better than 'Destroyers'. I grew tired of that name. Remember, our best work is unmaking things, bit by bit, person by person, thing by thing into what I want them to be."

"Once the task is accomplished we will be closer to our goal. Of course, then you must wait. Wait for when the time is right. Remember Bendy," the figure paused and a piercing darkness shot across its malevolent eyes. At that moment the light of the candle struck its face, revealing dark inset sockets and a hideously abnormal smile. Its skin appeared pale, dull, and lifeless. "Until our deal is complete, you are mine—for you have already given yourself to me." The Prince's tone became suddenly sweet. "So you found the Old Road?"

Bendy looked around nervously, his mind fretting over the possible sudden appearance of the hunters. Though he relied on the snow to cover his tracks, he knew better than to think that he had thrown them off his trail.

"Yes, your Majesty, it was as the map indicated. Only parts of it were left. I tried as best I could to follow it. But, I spent a few days on it before it wound its way through the mountains. Though, soon I lost the trail again. I do not mean to weary you—" said Bendy, twiddling his sweaty thumbs. The wind hissed outside like a striking snake. The floor creaked, popped, then let out a whining noise. "Yet, I must give you a full account. After all, you paid me to report all the details and so I have been revisiting them over and over again in my mind. Don't you want to attack The Beloved City of Dorodroos with precision? Didn't you tell me that you wanted to uproot it? Break its foundations? Seize all power? You came to me and told me to get this book and so I did. But there is something else; something about the creatures, the land. I hate retelling it, I hated the whole experience. I only continued to want to leave, but there I was. You paid me in gold and I don't take kindly to anyone sneering at my work."

"One more thing; you'll have to pay me extra," he began. "That place was, how do you say it, 'beautiful' and I couldn't stand it. The beautiful things there, were so ugly. I feel as though it has warped me, and I can't help hating my experience. Now, I can see why you hate beautiful things. Good things. The right things. The mere appearance of them turns you inside out and it is awful. Now this place, it has stuck in my memory and I can't very well erase it all can I? That's why I demand extra gold. Until I can start to think foggy again as I always have, I'll have to go and buy some things that'll dull my senses. Things that'll make it easier to steal."

"Mind your tongue," said the Prince. "We are both caught up in the same story and we need—I need you, but I will also get rid of you—if I must."

"Don't threaten me. It's been too long a journey and I am hungry and tired. Do you have anything to eat?"

"A few dead things," said the Prince. "Here—" He threw a satchel upon the table.

Bendy looked down at the dead animals and took out his knife.

"They're fresh?" he said.

The Prince's lips remained shut.

"As I was saying, days later I made it to the edge of Dorodroos. The Path was hard to follow, but I managed. When I arrived, the border was well protected. There were outposts all along the perimeter. I could see soldiers patrolling nearly every foot of it. At first it seemed impossible to penetrate. After much waiting and watching I finally found a way in. When I reached the interior I saw an old soldier, a creature from the Woods of Dorodroos. He dozed off regularly. I watched him for a few days from the safety of the woods. Then a strange thing happened; a wayward traveler appeared. I have seen many unusual folk on my travels, but this one unnerved me greatly. He came from the mountains and he seemed to have wind of something, but I knew not what."

"Tell me more of this traveler!" bellowed the Prince. "Tell me you followed him? Got his name?"

"He wore a dark purple cloak," began Bendy. "I did not see his face. I thought it was unusual seeing someone traveling alone near the Looming Mountains, so I watched and waited again. The old soldier talked with him for some time when without warning an argument erupted. The old creature seemed stubborn and distrusting, but finally after much debate let him pass. The creature watched the traveler as he walked back into the deep forest of Dorodroos. It was the chance I had been waiting for. His back was turned. As he stood there watching the traveler I decided to make my advance."

"So you made it in?"

"Yes, your Majesty."

"Just like that?"

"You did not hire a thief in vain," said Bendy feeling a bit of confidence regained. He coughed again. "I quickly hid in the thick trees and planned my next move. I hoped that I would find it soon, but I was watchful and on guard for fear of the man I saw at the gate. I waited a while longer as the sun set." Bendy paused as a strange sort of peace seemed to flood his eyes. It flickered then died out almost as fast as it came. "Now I know why they love Dorodroos so much and also why it's so detestable. All its beauty made me feel horrid, which in turn delighted me. I too want to destroy its foundations. I could scarcely bear being there. I felt I might die at any moment."

Bendy looked around for a long moment. Slowly, he gathered himself and continued. "Your Majesty," Bendy continued by making a strange gesture of allegiance. He raised his head, "I meant only to—" stuttered Bendy. The cloaked shape tapped its long shadowy fingers on the book that Bendy had given him—"to give you details. That's all. Thieves are good at that sort of thing. Good ones, anyway." Bendy paused. "Where was I? Oh, yes. The sun had set and I made my way to the heart of Dorodroos. Then I noticed something strange happening. I saw a small group moving hurriedly along the Path, full of serious and sophisticated looking creatures that were all dressed ornately, heading down through the streets away from the Heart of Dorodroos on up to what I gathered to be a sort of meeting place. The man who had the dispute with the gatekeeper, led them. The sky became darker. As I sat hiding behind a towering tree something troubled me, for it seemed they were somehow aware of my presence."

"And yet they did not see you?"

"I wasn't sure what they were up to in that chamber," said Bendy digging his dull, pale fingers into his chair. "But, I knew at once that I needed to find out. So, I concealed myself as best I could and made it to the Great Tree where the council was being held. It was there, that I discovered the worst news. I listened for a while with my ear pressed up against the side of it."

The cloaked shape recoiled as Bendy told his tale, wondering what kind of news Bendy had discovered.

"Well, speak fool!"

"They know!" shouted Bendy trembling with fear. He shivered and shook nervously.

"What do they know?"

"About you!" said Bendy. "They have heard of the Lost Tale. They know what you seek!"

"That is no matter! They will never know what it is that I truly seek."

"But it does, because I could no longer steal the book in secret. Don't you see? They know what we're after. Most of Eoorthe is on alert. There are soldiers gathering, seeking to destroy you. Oh, I should have never helped you! I should have stayed out of this nonsense. I am no murderer. I wanted only to steal this book." Bendy hung his head.

"Oh, but you are a murderer," said the figure as a smoldering aroma bore down on Bendy; unmoved at first, by the troubling news Bendy had delivered. He concealed his anxiety with a grin. "That is why you have the Golden Blood on your hands is it not!? The same beautiful poison runs in your blood—and there is no hope for you." The shape grabbed his victim by the throat. "Because you have one more task, I will spare your life."

"But your Majesty—theeey, knooow!"

"Quiet your tongue!" the creature's voice hissed throughout the room. Bits of paint fell from the ceiling. A patch of the new snow that had fallen slid off the roof above them. The figure tightened its grip on Bendy's throat, his frail neck on the verge of snapping. "Finish your tale and you may live to see another day."

"I—" wheezed Bendy flailing his arms helplessly. "But, I can't tell you, because I can scarcely breath."

The wispy shape loosened its grip and then assumed the form of a hunched, hooded figure. The figure Bendy had been talking to suddenly rose standing above him like a turret, dark and terrible, its face demented.

"I—" Bendy massaged his throat, gurgling to himself as he gasped for air. "Once I heard what was spoken in their council, I headed to the Secret Place. By that time it was getting darker. Then, up on the hill I saw it glowing. I slipped through more of the forest then up a long flight of stairs. I heard rustling and footsteps in the distance. I don't believe anyone saw me—but I believe someone knew I was there. Next, I saw torches and heard armor clanking and clinking as it came nearer. I hurried quickly up the stairs; but to my dismay, I met trouble. I saw the Keepers of the Book hiding in the shadows like statues. The voices from the trail became louder. Then something very interesting happened. At first I thought that I was seen. But, I realized something was cloaked over me as I started to slowly move down the steps with the Book in hand. I exited the trees. At first, the Keepers did not see me. It seemed I was invisible, though I do not know how."

"It was me you fool!" said Bendy's accomplice. "Did you not think that I was not aware of how to steal it?"

"Oh yes—well; I mean, right. Of course, you did. Uh, what do you mean?"

"The map made you invisible for a time. The moment you entered the place where it was kept, you became invisible."

Bendy stroked his scraggly beard. "That explains why I could steal it so easily and yet the Keepers did not see me—at first. But then how did they see me?"

"What do you mean how did they 'see' you?"

"The moment I was beyond the trees a whole army of them

descended on me. "

"Impossible! Are you saying my magic did not work?"

"No, I'm only saying that—"

"Do not insult me!" shouted the figure as its shadow suddenly engulfed the entire room.

"I'm only telling you the story the way it happened. So," Bendy quickly recovered, hoping to deter the Prince. "I ran into the forest. Soon, I was back near the gate. The old fellow was there. He stood silently in his tower, watching the woods, like a seasoned owl. Then he must have heard the Keepers behind me because he turned my way. I felt as if he was staring right through me."

"Oh, this is wonderful," the Prince grinned. "For I know what you will tell me next." He sneered. A sinister frown appeared on its face. "You have done something which is forbidden."

"No!" shouted Bendy. "It was an accident. I did not want to."

"Oh, but you did." An orange glow in the figure's chest suddenly flickered.

Bendy stirred anxiously in his seat.

"You wanted to do it did you not?" pried the Prince.

Bendy remained silent.

The figure laughed. Then, finally the candle died.

"The book is of little importance. What I really delight in is that you murdered one of those vile creatures. That was part of our plan. Never has their blood been shed." A sinister sound rattled the dark room, revealing a shape that Bendy could not quite make out, but one that made him shiver. "So, here I have in my presence, a murderer of one of the precious Creatures with the Golden Blood, and I finally have the Sacred Book of the Lost Tale in my own hands. I am satisfied my dear Bendy. You have murdered one of the Sacred Creatures and I am deeply, terribly, pleased." The Prince grinned. It tilted its head back unveiling jagged teeth. They shimmering in the light of the moon, which poured through the window that now stood frozen in the iron sky. The moonlight poured over Bendy's scruffy face which now had bits of Golden Blood smeared on it.

"I loathe weak men in my service." The figure tapped its long, pale fingers on the rotting sack of leather it clutched under its tattered sleeve. "Here is your gold."

"What will you do with me?" said Bendy, reaching out his trembling hand.

"If I find out that you have lied to me; you will wish that you were never brought into existence and I will be the one that snuffs out your sorry life!"

The wind hammered the window. A heavy moment of silence sunk in. The Prince looked out the window, then exited the tiny room. Bendy followed the figure towards the alley. Snow began to fall again. The weather had turned for the worse. Ice patterns began to form on the window. Voices floated through the brittle air. A small cluster of lights emerged down the alley where Bendy and the Prince now stood. The sound of hounds, clanking metal and hooves rumbled down the road.

"You fool! So this is the quality of your work?" groaned the Prince. "You would steal this and then lead those hunters here? I thought you were a skilled thief! Remember my monsters! I haven't the strength to match a platoon of Highmen from Dorodroos!" The Prince thought quickly. "When we meet again my monsters will have a bit of you! You would trade your sorry soul for a bit of gold? It is you they are hunting for and it is you I will leave. When you have achieved what I have required of you, you will get the other part I have promised."

"I will look for your sign, Majesty," Bendy nodded, bowing slightly.

"When I regain what I desire," said the Prince. "You shall pay a price for leading these men to us—for if I am caught, it will be my undoing and I will not fail now. We must depart. Go east through those hills," the Prince pointed, "there you shall find the stone road which leads through the clouds. Look for the Iron Candle which does not go out. There you will be given further directions."

The figure pressed his long talons into the book and drew the thick gray hood which hung around his shoulders, further covering his ghoulish face. In the distance near the other end of the alley there lay a bridge and beneath it, a large, frozen stream. A long sleigh sat layered heavy with snow. Ashen colored wood with jagged spikes lay all along the edges of it. Thirteen ebony wolves rose from the drifts of snow and stood at attention. Two iron bells hung around each of their necks. The Prince fled across the bridge and slithered up into the sleigh. The hunter's dogs howled as they approached, but it was too late. Bendy and the Prince had now made significant strides.

"Fly, slaves!" the Prince commanded. A hideous cracking snapped through the blustery air. Piles of snow lay on the backs of the wolves which quickly fell off. They gathered up their paws and dug into the mounding snow. The bells clanked and rung out across the land. Soon, the sounds faded beneath the swirling snow and the sleigh disappeared under a tunnel of trees that sloped down the high mountains which surrounded the village.

Bendy slipped between the shadows and disappeared down the frozen stream.

# CHAPTER TWO

# WHAT THE PROFESSOR LEFT BEHIND

Valen Grimm awoke to a bitter rain, sprinkling lightly as it hit the frosted glass of his large bedroom window. He watched the droplets dribble down. He moved his skinny legs slowly, struggling tirelessly to get out of bed. He put his weak hands on his knobby knees, got up, then walked over to the tall window he had been staring at and began gazing up at the ominous gray sky. The sun was trying to show its face through massive rolling clouds. A cold biting wind whipped through the trees which seemed to be bringing winter with it. Valen turned around, stretched out his arms, yawned, then went back to his bed and sat down to put his slippers on. His room felt as cold as the glass in the window. There were no pictures on his mantel. Cobwebs covered the walls of his room like an overgrown unkempt garden of ivy and weeds. He sighed, looking sadly at his barren bedroom walls. "A painting would help brighten this place," he mumbled to himself. He yawned again, got up, stretched and walked over to the sooty fireplace. He rummaged through the coals that remained from the fire the night before. He dragged a log onto it then walked over to a cracked mirror which spanned the height of his bedroom wall. For a moment he stared at his frail figure. His balding hair looked like an old a man who had seen many long and hard years. He gazed blankly at himself for a while, his groggy steel gray eyes glaring back. His face was sunken in. He shoved his hands into the pockets of his robes. His fingers were frail and grossly bony. It looked as though he had hands of a skeleton. Even though there was never anyone around to see his pathetic figure, he was often embarrassed of himself. He sighed heavily as he continued to stare into the mirror. A small beam of light trickled into his room and he watched it illuminate the wooden floor boards. His thoughts shifted to books he had read (for reading books was about the only thing he could do) where he would dream of adventures he wanted to go on. There he could explore and be wild. He wanted to go into one of the many stories he had read, where boys he admired fought and tamed wild beasts. Where mountains and rivers were as vast as the eye could see. But the thing that he wanted more than anything was to feel life in his body again. To feel healthy and free. Free from the dreadful place he was in now and free to walk as far as his heart would take him. The sunbeam disappeared and so did his thoughts of freedom.

"What's the use? This horrid house is where I'll be forever. Doesn't look as if I'll ever be able to leave. Just look at these wretched legs," he murmured scooting back from the mirror with a small sigh. "I can barely walk." It was true. As long as Valen could remember, his legs were unreliable, useless limbs. He gritted his teeth. His will was made of stronger stuff.

The One Rule that was laid down by his father, was that he was never to leave the Grimm Mansion especially with his "condition." At times Valen could walk normally, though it was a challenge even then. Other times, he had to drag himself to get where he wanted to go. Under no circumstances was he allowed to leave his house. His father insisted that if he did leave, he would surely be eaten by wild animals, especially when his legs failed him—which happened a few times a day. Lately though, it seemed to happen all the time. But, Valen could not help but long to be out of it. He wanted be in the forest—even if it was only for one day. He frowned, feeling downcast. His health was ailing as each day passed. It had been longer than he cared to remember the last time he felt good. His body ached. His heart ached. His mood was often somber. He stopped himself from despairing. "At least he's coming today," Valen said aloud. He couldn't quite think of the words to say, but he was feeling better suddenly—not in body, but in heart. A small bit of happiness squeezed in—the only thing that truly brought him joy—his beloved teacher. It had been long since he felt joy. Over the years his heart had become like a withered tree that had not blossomed in hundreds of years. Then, without warning, a towering grandfather clock which stood at the other end of his room, began to chime and bong. It struck eight o'clock. Slowly, he got dressed, then struggled his way through the sturdy oak door that guarded the entrance of his bedroom. "I'm late," he muttered under his breath. The clock continued to strike, booming down the hallway as he hobbled along. Valen struggled to move as fast as he could, but his legs felt like heavy logs. In a moment, he was standing at the top of the steep stairs which led to the long hallway which led to the library near the other end of the mansion. He had been here before. Though, he could not walk down them without falling and banging himself up along the way. Nevertheless, he tried his hardest to compose his thoughts and his legs, but he was soon barreling down the stone stairs and whacking his head, elbows, and knees. It hurt as usual and he had ripped his pants, but he had taught himself how to roll without getting too injured. Years ago, he would have broken bones and his father would be mending him. Now, he could withstand great falls, though it was still painful. A few minutes later, stumbling and limping, he found his way down the long hallway to the colossal library where books spanned three stories all along curved walls. A warm light from a large crackling fire situated in an ornate fireplace with exquisite carvings of faces and figures of ivory, emanated through an archway. At a small dark wooden desk there sat a wrinkled man in a bright white shirt and dark brown vest with matching pants.

"Time is passing quickly."

"I know. I had trouble this morning."

"Oh?" said the tall graying man as he raised his long forehead with suspicion.

"It's worse today than usual, Professor—sorry."

"Then tea and biscuits should warm you right up," said his tutor with a small familiar chuckle. "Besides, I found something that may lessen your suffering. Do you have the heart to try it?"

"Yes, thank you," said Valen slowly grabbing a chair. "What is it?"

"You might call it a fruit," said the Professor with a smile. "Though, this is from a tree which does not grow on this island. Of course, long before Had Wink was surrounded by the years of the Long Snow, the *Snow-Which-Melted-and-Filled-Up-the-Sea*. It came from one of my many travels when one could take ships anywhere one might imagine. I had sought long and suffered much to find it. The fellow who gave it to me—I trust him fully." Valen found it very pleasant.

Mr. Lewis had his books strewn about him in a perfect mess. His cane lay upright next to the hearth. Valen noticed for the first time that the handle was carved with the face of a beautiful head of a white horse.

His tutor was fiddling with papers and his glasses as usual. Valen looked down at the professor's shoes.

"I was wondering, sir," said Valen chewing on a warm biscuit smothered with honey and butter. "How do you manage to travel all the way here without ever getting mud on your shoes?"

"It's quite simple really."

"Oh?" said Valen.

"I bring a cloth with me on all of my outings," said the professor who was still sifting through stacks of papers and books.

"To clean your shoes?"

"Why, yes, of course."

"It's a lot of trouble if you ask me."

"Is it a lot of trouble?"

"Is what a lot of trouble?" said Valen taking a sip of his tea.

"What you just said."

"What did I just say?"

"What you just said before you said what you just said," said Mr. Lewis collectively.

"Oh, right," said Valen scratching his head. "I don't know."

"Well then how do you know that it *is* a lot of trouble?"

"I don't know."

"Then why am I asking you?" said the professor.

"I don't know," said Valen helplessly trying to get a bit of soggy biscuit out of his cup before it sunk. "Why are you?"

"Because *you* asked me."

"Right," said Valen with a small smile, "so I did. Now what's the first lesson?"

"You just had it—logic. Define your terms. It will save you a lot of trouble in the end. There are those that would manipulate words and twist them into all sorts of hideous things. Above all else you must learn to use your mind," said the professor as if he wasn't paying Valen any attention. He was still looking exhaustively through his things as he flipped through one book after another.

Valen watched the biscuit sink, then he slumped into his chair like a tired old lap dog.

"Here it is," said Mr. Lewis adjusting his glasses that sat on the edge of his nose. He pulled out a crumbling, battered looking book. "Have a look. Are you ready for the second lesson?"

"Yes," said Valen as Mr. Lewis slid it across the table."What is it?"

"A history of some sort I suppose—a diary is what I suspect," began the professor. "Open it."

"Whose is it?" said Valen feeling awkward and excited.

"Can't say really," said the professor as he got up to rake the coals in the fireplace, putting on a few more logs.

"You're giving me a diary and you—*don*'t know whose it is?" said Valen suspiciously.

"It's been in my family for centuries," said the professor sitting back down to pour a cup of tea.

"It looks ancient," said Valen handling it delicately as he inspected it. Then he opened it to the first page. "How am I supposed to read this? I don't even understand the language."

The professor looked at him curiously.

"I have done all that I could to understand where its origin lies," said the professor folding his hands and resting them gently on his knees.

"It has passed through the hands of common folk, peasants, soldiers, kings, queens, knights, princes—all esteeming it but never saying why," continued the professor stroking his worn face. "All of them unable to interpret it. So it seems they willed it to be given to those who remained. It has gone through the hands of the lowliest to the highest and yet no one knows why they keep it nor do they know why not to get rid of it. It is most mysterious. I myself am drawn to it. Though, I am unsure why. Any thoughts?"

"Maybe there's some terrible secret in it or something," said Valen smartly.

"The strangest thing that I have discovered is that all those who possessed it have vanished or disappeared entirely," said the professor. "None of them ever to be seen again and yet, always the diary is left behind. The bearer leaving it behind wherever they breathed their last breath. It has been found in pockets, under beds, left lying in fields, battlefields, cribs, high places and foul places. What do I make of it? The pages becoming fuller over the years adding to it certain unknowable things. In a word—mysteries. All of it is in the same language, but no language ever spoken in this world. So, how is it that I now have it and cannot glimpse into its secrets? It is a most fascinating riddle!"

Valen was sitting on the edge of his seat, his fingers dug into the bottom of his chair. His heart drummed with adventure. All these years he had been meeting with his professor and of all the meetings he had had, this was the most surprising one yet. He poured them both some more tea and then asked the professor to continue.

"Do you suppose there are other worlds out there?" asked Valen skeptically.

"Other worlds?"

"Yes, are there other places to go to besides *here*?"

"That's a most peculiar idea," said the professor. "I don't see why not. Of course any number of things are possible."

"So, if that's true," said Valen with an excited look in his eyes,"then it is possible these people you mentioned, who have disappeared, have gone on to other places?"

"Other places?" came an unexpectedly chilling voice. In walked a slithering man. His face was wrinkled and his eyes sat bulging largely out of their sockets.

"Father," said Valen in a shivering voice. He put another book over the diary. "I—ah—didn't expect you'd be here."

"What's this you're teaching my son, professor?"

"Good morning, Dr. Grimm," said professor Lewis confidently. "Any new patients?"

"The lessons—what lessons are you teaching him?"

"Oh, right," said the professor confidently. "Well, our first lesson this morning was a bit of logic. The second one, I suppose—we were just beginning to talk about history."

"Let's keep it that way shall we? I sought out your skills to further my purposes for Valen," said Dr. Grimm as he circled the table and wound his way over to the large window. "Now," Dr. Grimm sniffed, "I don't want you filling my son's head with nonsense. His education is to stick strictly to the content that he needs to become educated. I want him to learn all there is to learn. I must prepare him for this awful island and its horrid inhabitants. His condition is deplorable enough. No one is going to want a beast for company! So, he must excel in his mind. His intellectual capabilities must make up for his—*inadequacies*. His undesirable qualities."

"As you wish sir," said the professor.

"Carry on then," said Dr. Grimm. In an instant he was gone.

"He makes my skin crawl," said Valen. "I feel like he's always prowling about, eavesdropping and what not."

"The beast part is what I most despised," said professor Lewis.

"Professor?" began Valen after a few silent moments. "Do you think that I could ever get well?"

"I don't know my boy," said the professor. "I don't think there is a cure. But, if there was, surely your father would have cured you by now."

"If there was a cure . . . would *you* tell me?" asked Valen despondently staring at his bony hands.

"Certainly!" said the professor. "If I found a cure for you, then I would not withhold that knowledge from you. Though I don't know why you are in this state. Perhaps good will come of it?"

"Well," said Valen hesitatingly, "I'm pleased that you're my teacher"

"Now back to our lesson, shall we?" said professor Lewis.

For a while longer they talked about history and science and philosophy. Valen who was an excellent reader did not struggle with even the hardest texts professor Lewis had assigned to him. This went on for the majority of the day. They broke for lunch once the first lessons of the morning passed and then continued on until early afternoon.

"You have been extra attentive today, master Valen. You're ability to comprehend is most unlike anything I've ever seen before. It is almost as if you know of all the things that I am going to say to you before I say them." The professor smiled. His white hair was lit up by the light of the fire.

"Thank you sir," said Valen. "If only I could put it to some kind of use one day, that would make me happy."

"Use? Bah! It is this nonsense of the usefulness of knowing that sets me to itching. You must know for its own sake. Of course, you may *use* what you know, but do not desire to know for the sake of using it. None of us really know where our lives might end up," continued professor Lewis. "You were born the way you are for a reason you might not see just yet, and you may never see. But, there is *some* reason. And, even if you don't know the reason, there is still a reason nevertheless and that reason cannot itself be arbitrary! Reasons are still reasons even if we don't know the reasons!"

"Well," said Valen grinning a little, thinking about what the professor said. "Thank you. See you tomorrow?"

"As soon as the sun peaks its head, I will already be walking through the forest anticipating our next meeting. See you in the morning!"

In a moment, professor Lewis slipped through the large arched wooden door with his wooden cane in hand and was gone. Valen watched him through the window as he made his way down the long cobblestone road that led away from the old Grimm Mansion. Professor Lewis gave a final wave and then disappeared over the hill.

Once the professor was gone, Valen noticed that professor Lewis had left the diary. Valen looked at it curiously. It seemed to be thousands of years old. Then, his stomach began to rumble. He took the book and slipped it into his pocket. Valen made his way into the dining hall as best he could. Recently, his condition seemed to be getting progressively worse. During the day he was able to walk on a pair of crutches he had found several years ago buried deep in the basement when his legs first gave out. But at night his legs were almost entirely useless. He eyed his wheelchair that his butler had brought down from his room. He sat himself down in it and rolled himself over to a table in the nearby hall that seemed to go on forever. He positioned himself properly then picked up his fork and knife. That night, Charles had made him pheasant, paired with whipped potatoes and hot homemade bread. Valen sat quietly eating his food, until all of it was nearly gone. "The only thing missing I suppose are a few friends."

As long as Valen could remember he had eaten supper alone. No one had ever joined him, not even once. No one that is, except a few house mice now and then. But they were no use. They could scarcely hold a conversation. With the occasional company of mice and a large crackling fire all the way at the other end of the room that glowed brightly, Valen ate his lonely meal without any disturbance whatsoever. The fire cast its light freely on the massive stone walls that stood all around him. The stones were so colossal that he imagined them sometimes to look like sleeping giants who would wake at any moment.

"From what though?" thought Valen who was looking up at them. "I'm in Had Wink. Nothing ever goes on around here. I've never even seen anyone my age before. And the only friend I have is the professor." He pushed himself away from the table, took a final drink of his water and then made his way to the stairs. It was especially difficult this evening to drag himself up them, but he managed. Soon, he was back in his room alone with his thoughts, gazing silently out the window wondering what else was out there. Hours passed by and he sat there staring, thinking and wondering of the diary professor Lewis had accidentally left. He got it out to browse through it. Valen was looking at the strange writing when suddenly, it shut all on its own. Then, a very peculiar thing happened. For a few minutes or so, the edges of it glowed a silvery blue, then it fizzled out. But, something else very interesting happened that Valen could not quite explain. There were more written words that appeared. Valen studied it hard wondering what it meant. A magical book? Impossible. Then again, why not, he thought. He looked closer and his name began to appear very faintly.

Valen stayed awake a few more hours pondering the meaning of the mysterious light. Did professor Lewis know something that Valen did not? Of all the professor's travels, had he been to a place that he had not told Valen of before? Or was all of it just a dream? Valen didn't know. The next time he moved his eyes, the light of the new day was streaming through his window. He got up out of his chair that he had fallen asleep in, and went back over to the mirror as he did every morning. Normally, he spent a lot of time looking at himself, feeling lonely, but today sparked a new kind of hope that he hadn't felt before.

Excited to tell professor Lewis what had happened the night before, he struggled to move as best he could towards the stairs. He felt weaker than usual and looked down them precariously. Even so, he insisted on going down them. He was set on overcoming his condition. He moved down the stairs slowly. His determination didn't last long though and soon he was tumbling down the stairs. He fell nearly the entire length of them. Though this wasn't his preferred method of traveling, Valen was happy to have not struggled to walk down the entire flight of stairs. As weak as he felt, his bones had become stronger. Once he reached the bottom, he looked down the long hallway into the study area where he was to meet professor Lewis. For some reason, the hallway seemed particularly longer than usual. He rubbed his head, struggling to get back up on his feet. After a long while, Valen finally managed to get to the end of the hallway and soon enough reached the large double doors that led into the study. He sighed. He had the diary in hand and walked around to take his seat.

"Professor Lewis!" shouted Valen. "You won't believe it!"

"Believe what?" hissed Valen's father who was looking very much like a wriggling rat.

"Where's the professor?" said Valen concernedly concealing the book under his left side jacket.

"Disappeared," said Valen's father casually. Valen saw a shovel standing near the edge of the door. "I went looking for him this morning and I saw a bright light in the forest, just before dawn. Here—I found his walking stick." He threw it into the fire.

"No!" shouted Valen. "I want it."

"It's no matter to me," said his father coldly. "Fetch it before it burns, if you want it." Valen reached in and brought it out. He noticed that it was surprisingly cool. He leaned on it to hold himself up. His weight was nearly all on it.

"His walking stick?" said Valen perplexed. What's that shovel?"

"Strangers have arrived," said his father, ignoring his question.

"In Had Wink?" said Valen shocked. "But how? When?"

"There is no time for questions," sighed his father indifferently. "I'll get to the bottom of it soon enough."

"Does anyone else know?" said Valen. His mind wandered back to the shovel.

"The shovel what were you doing with it?"

"I brought it in for Charles. It was left outside near the garden." His tone switched. "I'm the only one who can detect anything!"

"Oh?" said Valen strangely. "Detect? What do you mean? How is it—?"

"Enough!" spat his father. "These Strangers can be useful in the preservation of Had Wink. They may very well have stumbled upon us unknowingly." His father glared at the fire.

"Never mind all that though. I will find out how it happened."

"Where did they move to?" asked Valen inquisitively.

"Just beyond the other side of town where one would least expect," said Valen's father, getting up to go to the door. "In the abandoned house near Had's Hollow." Valen remembered Charles mentioning Had's Hollow and he quickly committed it to memory. "What about professor Lewis? Where could he have gone?"

"Killed perhaps," said his father with a cold stare. "Charles has told me of a strange creature he saw the other night. A very foul beast, not from around these parts—*foreigner*. Though I doubt his analysis. Probably a wild bear or something. Though—it matters not what happened to professor Lewis."

"Killed! It doesn't matter what happened to him!?" roared Valen as his legs trembled violently. Then he fell, knocking over the tray on which his medicine sat.

"He was my friend!" shouted Valen looking down at the broken glass in humiliation.

"You'll get another professor soon enough," said his father agitatedly. "Now look what you've done! I'll need to go and get more medicine. That was the very last!"

"I don't want just any old professor," said Valen sadly. "I want to find out what happened to professor Lewis!"

"Enough quipping boy," barked his father who was walking away. "Charles will serve you breakfast momentarily. Read your books till then. I'll see about your medicine. I'll be back at sundown." And with that, he stormed out of the mighty house and was gone.

Valen was left in silence with his own thoughts. Charles came into the room a few minutes later to give him his breakfast, but Valen found he couldn't eat anything.

"Charles, what do you think happened?" blurted Valen, not realizing that his thoughts had made it to his mouth.

"I'm not at liberty to speculate," he said. "Orders."

"Right," said Valen. "Well, aren't you going with father?"

"No sir, Master Valen," said Charles tending the fire. "I'm staying right here."

"Oh," said Valen. "So, those are your orders? To shut me up in this place, like a caged animal?"

"Not an animal," began Charles nervously adjusting his bow tie.

"I don't need watched," said Valen defiantly gritting his teeth. "What I need is to find my friend! Will you help me?"

"I couldn't do that, no," said Charles apprehensively. "If Dr. Grimm found out—why I'd be in a heap of trouble."

"Argh!" roared Valen in a rage as he shoved his food aside. "But it's only logical to go and try to find poor professor Lewis. I mean—suddenly he's disappeared and now all we have are his shoes? I'm positive he'd want me to come and find him."

"Your condition does inhibit you though," said Charles lightly. "How could you look for him when you can scarcely walk?"

"Well, that's what you'd help me with," said Valen feeling as though he was nudging his butler into a place to accept his offer.

"I'm under strict command from your father not to let you leave the house," said Charles.

"But, I should be able to help find the professor too," said Valen. "I don't see what the trouble is. You care about the professor too, right? What better time than to go now—to find him—then to come back here before father ever knows?"

"I have my honor to protect—" said Charles. "And my work, too. I have worked with your father for a very long time. He trusts me."

"So do I," said Valen sorely. "But we can't just leave the professor out there."

"Yes, but we don't even know if he *is* out there," said Charles.

"And we don't know if he isn't either," snapped Valen. "The point is to *try* to find him.

A short silence fell into the room.

"Father said you saw a beast in the forest?"

"I'm not sure what I saw—" said Charles.

"But it was a beast, right?"

"I saw a strange silver light glowing and an odd creature," said Charles. "It was probably only my imagination. There are many odd sorts of animals in the surrounding forests."

"We should hunt it down and capture it," suggested Valen.

"Capture it? Hunt it down? Have you gone mad?" said Charles. Valen was finished eating. Charles reached down to take Valen's plate away. "We don't even know what *it* is. Or, even *if* it is. All we know is that the professor is gone and it's safe to assume that whatever creature is in our forest has killed him—" Charles' sentence fell off.

"Killed him! What in Had Wink do you mean?"

"Something your father said."

"Whatever he said—we're wasting time!" said Valen angrily. "My friend is out there. You aren't a coward are you?"

"I am not!" said Charles feeling his face turn into a raging fire.

"Then prove it!" shouted Valen.

"We'll leave at once," said Charles. A spark seemed to grow in his eyes that Valen had seen once or twice before. One time, Valen recalled, Charles had killed another beast that was very much the size of a grown grizzly bear, with his bare hands. "I'd very much like to find the professor myself— But, you mustn't be seen by anyone. You have to stay in the carriage."

"Thank you so much Charles," said Valen. His eyes lit up. "I certainly will!"

Once they were outside, Charles held open the door of an old, wooden carriage with glass panes in the door. The sky was dimly lit. Charles helped Valen into it graciously. Valen sat down and looked back at the mighty Grimm Mansion. He sighed. It was a very lonely place. He had lived there his entire life. The mansion remained silently still, like an ominous storm towering over the horizon. The wind brought leaves and bits of twig whipping across the road. Valen shoved his hands into his pockets and felt the diary, then sat down. A gust of wind ripped through his jacket and a chill shot through him like an icy arrow.

In a moment, Charles snapped the reigns and the horses began trotting forward. Valen continued to look out through the now fogging panes of cold glass. He moved his crutches to the side. The wind howled and screamed as they wound their way up through the forest to where there stood a solemn château that looked as if it had been thousands of years old. Giant trees stood guarding the entrance. He looked down at his hands for a moment. They were trembling as usual. He sighed. Where had his father gone? Would he have enough time to get back before him? He sat gazing up at the giant fir trees that surrounded the château. He was twiddling with a piece of thread from his jacket inside his pocket, thinking intensely about what his father said about those who had recently moved to Had's Hollow. "I wonder where he's gone to? Probably not to find anything out about Professor Lewis." His shoulders sagged. Valen had been through more professors than he cared to count. His thoughts faded when suddenly Charles opened the door.

"Master Valen," he said stepping down off the carriage, "shall I go and make an inquiry at that school there?" Charles looked and pointed to the building they had just pulled up to. I suggest we put out a search party."

"Yes," said Valen gazing out through the door. "I suppose."

"You'll stay here then?"

"Of course," said Valen with a slight nod. "I'd only hold you up."

"Well," said Charles, "I'm off. I'll be back in a minute. Stay out of trouble." And then he was gone.

Charles dashed down the stone path leading to the school. He fumbled with his hat as the wind howled, tearing through the area. Valen sat staring out the window. A few minutes had passed and no sign of Charles had yet come. The windows of the carriage glass had fogged up almost entirely. Then, without warning, Valen heard a few voices.

"Golly," said a boy,"you don't suppose this is the Grimm carriage do you?"

"How many other people could afford something as extravagant as this?" said a second boy.

"Oh, whoooo cares," said another. "I mean what does it *really* matter."

"It would matter to you if you were poor Jude," said the second boy smartly.

"Speaking of poor—I don't know why we hang out with your type anyway Henry," retorted the short squatly boy who said 'whoooo cares' and began to shove him into the side of the carriage. "It's bad enough you wear those same clothes everyday."

Henry looked down at has ratty pants, and holed shoes.

"Shut up!" he retorted. "At least I have *real* parents."

"Make fun of me one more time," snapped Jude, pushing Henry in the chest.

"Stop it!" said the other boy who hadn't said anything in a while.

"He started it Jack," said Jude with a smirk.

"You dirty liar,"roared Henry. "You did! I don't even know why we are friends!"

Angry and frustrated the boys gave up and resolved to ignore each other for a bit. Henry had a scowl on his face and Jude grinned back reveling in his antagonistic tendencies. Valen was listening to all of this anxiously. He put his finger up to the fogged up window and moved it around in a slow circle creating a tiny hole to see out of.

"Wait! Shhhh!" hissed Jack. "I think there's someone in there."

"What if it's that creepy old man Grimm," said Henry with a shutter. "I heard he eats children."

"That's a load," said Jude confidently. "Do you really expect us to believe that?"

"Yes, as a matter of fact, I do," said Henry. "He's half giant you know?"

"Giant?" said Jude who was now laughing. "What ridiculous books do you read?"

"They exist!" stammered Henry. "I know they do!"

"Riiiiight," said Jude with an indifferent attitude. "The only things that exist are things that you can prove."

"Well, that is a preposterous statement, given that I cannot see your words," said Jack moving his glasses up his nose. "Not to mention, contradictory. It's just your type that will ruin civilization itself—at least Had Wink will suffer at the hands of your illogical reasoning."

Jude looked troubled as he worked this over in his mind.

Valen was watching them intently as he stared out the window.

"You do realize that we could take this?" said Jude maliciously, trying his best to ignore Jack's comments.

"Yes, and be eaten on a stick for supper," said Henry sorely.

"Getting in there would be a really foolish decision," said Jack who was now standing up on his toes trying to peer through the window. "First, we don't know whose it is and second we should be in class now."

"Let's get in," suggested Jude. "Just until someone comes."

"Fine," said Jack. "But, I'm warning you. If anything comes of this—"

Jude slowly opened the door. He glanced over his shoulder to see if anyone was looking. "All clear," he said deviously. "Come on, let's go!"

Valen sat in silence curiously waiting for them to get in. Then the short boy said the strangest thing Valen could have imagined.

"It's empty," said Jude. "Come on!"

"Empty?" said Valen out loud, glancing down at his hands and feet. He wiggled them around for a few seconds just to make sure he was still alive. "But I'm here. I'm here!" He yelled it again and again. But, no one heard him. He lunged for the door to open it. He grabbed hold of the handle and pushed it open.

"How in the world did that door just open?" said Jude with a hint of fear in his voice.

Even though Valen was feeling extremely weak, he made up his mind to get out of the cab, but the wind outside was too powerful for him. The door slammed shut as a sudden gust of wind pounded the side of the cab rocking it back and forth.

"Well," said Jack scholarly, as the cab settled back down. "It was obviously the wind. It's shut now."

Valen looked at him with dismay.

"This thing is impressive," said Henry excitedly. "I have never been in one before."

Jude sat down next to Valen.

"None of us have ever been to the Grimm Mansion before," said Jude putting his hands behind his head. "I say we go exploring."

"It's private property," said Jack.

"The Grimm Mansion may be guarded, but who cares," said Jude. "This is our chance to get in."

"We'd get into too much trouble," said Henry cautiously. "I don't think it's a very good idea."

"How is it that they can't see me?" thought Valen who began wondering if he was dead.

"Look," said Jack quietly peering through the window. "Here comes the driver."

"Looks like he's driving us today," cracked Jude.

"We can't stay," said Henry. "Haven't you heard?"

"Heard what?" said Jack.

"A man went missing in the forest today up by Grimm Mansion," said Henry his voice trembling.

"Oh?" said Jack. "Who was he?"

"Well, no one knows for sure," said Henry with a gulp. "No one knows where he came from or what dealings he had with Grimm, but whatever happened to him it's evil. Nothing good ever comes out of that place."

"So they know about it too?" thought Valen.

"He was probably murdered," said Jude looking out the window.

"There is no way I'm going to the Grimm Mansion," said Henry with finality. "Besides, my mother and father will want to know where I am."

"As will mine," said Jack thoughtfully.

"Well, I don't give two whips about my dad, ever since he left me.

Though, I like my mother sometimes. Cooks me what I want. Anyway, don't be a wimp," said Jude. "What could possibly happen?"

"Do you really know he left you?" said Jack. "Maybe he got lost at sea. The storms are ferocious, you know. Especially down near the cove where the tall rock is. Men get lost at the sea, that's the nature of being a whaler."

"Well either way he left." Jude became suddenly, visibly upset.

"I'm not a wimp," gritted Henry standing up for himself. "I love my father very much and it is a shame you don't."

"You *are* a wimp," muttered Jude paying no real attention to Jack.

The boys had been talking so intensely that they did not hear Charles come back and shout from his seat up above the cab. "Well, I've told all of the staff. No one has seen the professor. Now we'll go through town and look ourselves." Then, without warning, the carriage began to move forward. It jerked at first, then it slowly picked up speed, moving faster down the long hill that wound its way down from the château which was the school.

"Wait!" shouted Henry grabbing for the handle of the door, having just realized that they had left. He was seething so much at Jude's comments that he did not realize what was happening. "We have to get out! I don't want to go!"

"See, I *told* you. You're a wimp," said Jude with a crooked smile.

"Shut up!" snapped Henry reaching over to punch him, but Jude deflected it and Henry knocked his head against the side of the window.

"Enough Jude!" shouted Jack. "Why do you always have to start trouble?"

"Me?" said Jude. "I didn't do anything."

"You called him a wimp," said Jack. "You've been calling him a *wimp* all morning. When are you going to learn?"

Henry was rubbing the side of his head with a terrible look on his face.

"Looks like we have no choice," said Jack slouching back against the cushioned bench. "We're bound to get into trouble now."

As the boys talked, the cab whipped its way down the long and winding road that went into Had Wink. Time traveled swiftly as they had gone several places that day. The boys got to see most of Had Wink that they had never seen before. It was an exceptionally old city. Crumbling buildings stood next to each other throughout most of the streets. There were wealthy parts and poor parts, but most of it was poor. Massive structures once boasting power and might had come to their end centuries ago. The boys looked on in amazement. Valen sat quietly, still unable to discover why he could not be seen or heard.

Had Wink was practically abandoned and the townspeople hoped that one day it would be restored, though in their hearts it was only a faint hope. Winkers as they were called, said things like, 'One day our town will be back to the way it used to be,' and, 'we don't know why we can't seem to make things right, but one day all of Had Wink will be back to normal.' This was a common belief that the people had. At one time, they held their city to be the most wonderful city around. They held festivals and parades and celebrations as the years went by. Some despaired, saying their city was cursed. Some said it was their location, the fact being that it was an island. It had giant oaks and pines and it was littered with enormous stones and rolling hills. Stones gathered from the nearby shores were constructed into walls that lined quaint country roads. The houses were fit with tall chimneys, wooden shutters and giant windows that clung with time, stuck out all over the town.

Charles whizzed down the streets looking for anyone that could help find the professor. Occasionally he found someone who was willing to talk, but not often. Men were out working as usual. Year after year they tried desperately to restore Had Wink. But, all the work that was done to try to improve the city only continually failed. Something would be fixed one day, then immediately following the next, would break again. A lamp post would be erected only to appear that it had been there for a hundred years after only a day. Some windows were cracked and shattered glass lay strewn over sidewalks and streets.

Caved in roofs and collapsed buildings passed by as Valen peered through the window. He yelled until his throat was hoarse, but no one heard him. His heart plunged into despair. Here was his chance to finally meet boys his own age and they could not see him.

The boys he was with on the other hand, had never been so excited. They nearly saw the entire town that day. Jude was thinking very highly of himself as usual and grinned proudly as he stared out the window. "One day I'll be king over this town," he said. Henry was worried they'd get into trouble as usual and Jack was making careful observations of all that he saw. Of course, they had explored Had Wink several times before, but not in such a grand way.

The day went by quickly and many stops and visits were made to folks Charles knew; yet still they had no luck in finding so much as one clue about the professor's whereabouts. After some time, the horses were tired and began their journey back to Grimm Mansion. The sun dipped behind the trees. They rolled down the road with leaves churning out from under the carriage as the horses galloped steadily along. Soon, the forest became thick and dense when at last they began to climb the steep road that led back to the mansion, deep in the distant forest. Shadows clung to the trees as the horses trotted along, when suddenly, Henry started yelling with a terrible terror in his voice.

"There's someone in here! Quick! Get out!"

Valen didn't know it, but he was gradually reappearing.

"Come on, let's go!" continued Henry trying to get back out. "Hurry!"

"What are you yelling about?" said Jude.

"N-next to you," said Henry with a white face. "C-can't you see him?"

"See what?" said Jack.

"It's a g-ghost," said Henry, finally able to get the word out.

Then Valen realized that Henry was pointing at him.

"I'm not," said Valen who wasn't sure why they were suddenly able to see him.

"He's talking," said Henry nervously. "He's talking." His eyes were bulging. "He's still talking."

A few more moments had passed before Valen appeared entirely.

"W-what are you?" said Jack who now saw him too, trying desperately to be brave.

"Are you *dead*?" asked Jude who scooted away from Valen.

"No," said Valen who's voice came back to him at once. "I'm not a ghost and I'm not dead."

The Grimm carriage came to a sudden stop. Charles stepped down. The boys could hear him coming closer.

"Valen my boy," said Charles as his voice came closer. "Are you okay?"

"I'm fine," said Valen locking the door. "I'm just going to sit out here for a while."

"I heard some voices," continued Charles. "Are you *sure* you're all right?"

"Yes, Charles," said Valen. "I'm quite fine."

"Okay, but you mustn't be out here long! Your father is probably on his way. I'll see you in a moment?"

"Yes, see you in a moment."

"Okay then, I'll just go in and start supper. Do you need your chair?" said Charles.

"No," said Valen feeling slightly embarrassed (even though the boys he was with didn't know he had to use a wheelchair sometimes). "I, ah—think I can make it in okay."

Valen waited, looking out the window after Charles. The sun had finally set and darkness shrouded the mansion.

"Let's go!" hissed Henry. Jude slapped his hand over his mouth as Henry tried smacking it away.

"We're staying," snapped Jude glancing at Charles. "Now, shut up!"

A few moments of silence passed. Valen waited for the door of the mansion to shut. When he finally heard it, he began talking.

"My name's Valen Grimm—in case you didn't know," he said scooting awkwardly back on his seat.

"You're the son of the old man?" said Jack.

"Yes," said Valen. "You didn't know?"

"Know?" said Jack. "We thought that the only person who lived here *was* the old man."

"Oh," said Valen. "Well, that makes sense. Today *was* the first day out of that house in a very long time."

"You don't go outside?" said Jack with his eyebrows raised.

"I'm not allowed," said Valen sheepishly.

"Oh," said Jack, shocked. "You're out today though."

"So if you're not a ghost or *dead* then what are you?" said Henry his eyes still popping.

"A boy, just like you," said Valen just as confused by the event himself.

"Then how do you explain appearing out of nowhere?" said Henry again suspiciously.

"I—am not sure really," said Valen. "It's never happened before, as far as I know. I mean—at least *I* see myself everyday."

"Yes," said Henry,"but how do you explain appearing out of nowhere? Things just don't—you know—merely pop into existence."

Jack raised his forehead.

"I'm really sorry," said Valen,"but I seriously don't understand what happened."

Henry frowned.

"Actually," continued Valen, "before we started driving through Had Wink it was I who opened the door. Then, as we were driving through town I tried to get your attention by yelling several times—obviously, it didn't work."

"Okay," said Henry frustrated because he felt Valen to be lying.

"Then what about the professor?"

"That is interesting," agreed Jack. He looked over at Valen. "He's gone missing?"

"Yes," said Valen. "That was the reason for my outing today—we—well, Charles and I were looking for him."

"Do you think he left?" said Jack as he glanced from Jude to Valen.

"Left? No—wait—you can *leave* Had Wink? Why would you say that?" said Valen.

"It's a logical possibility is all," said Jack glancing down at his watch. He sniffed.

"I think he must have fallen off one of the cliffs near the sea or something. Father tells me, that they're dangerous. Though, I think he's in the forest somewhere. My butler said he saw a strange creature the other day. Well, whatever the case, I do hope to find him soon. He was a close friend to me."

"I heard there was a body found—" began Jude.

"Body?" said Jack. "Well, why didn't you say so before?"

"Yes," said Jude. "I dunno."

"Body?" repeated Valen. "Something is going on here. I hope it is not the professor."

"Me, too," said Jack. "It has the townspeople very worried—" He paused then added, "We could help you. I mean, *we have* explored the woods around here so much that we'd probably be able to find him. What do you think? Jude, Henry?"

"Sure," said Henry sarcastically. "Why don't we go and get ourselves eaten too—or drowned!"

"Does that mean you'll help?" asked Jack.

"Of course," said Henry with a slight nervous grin. "I don't want to miss out on any adventures."

"And you?" said Jack looking at Jude.

"Sure," he said dangerously. "I don't have anything better to do."

"Thanks!" shouted Valen. "What do you say we meet at midnight tonight behind my house, by the old oak tree? Do you know where it is?"

"Yes," said Jack. "I know exactly where it is."

For a moment Valen had almost forgotten about his father, when without warning, the sound of hooves came rushing down the road.

"It's Father!" he shouted. "Quick! You must leave now! If he sees or knows that anyone has been here, I will be in terrible trouble."

Jack threw open the door and rushed outside.

"See you tonight!" hissed Valen. Then, the boys darted into the forest that bordered the lawn of the massive Grimm Mansion just in time.

The trotting horses came closer and closer to the cab that Valen was sitting in. He watched the cab come to an abrupt stop. Out stepped his father. Valen watched nervously in the shadows as his father walked up to the giant arched doorway. "He's up to something," thought Valen waiting quietly to see if his father would go straight in or not. A few seconds passed then he turned his head side to side as if to check on things before going in, and just as he was about to go through the door, he stopped. Slowly, he turned and looked in Valen's direction. Did he see him? Valen wasn't sure, but he wasn't taking any chances. He scooted back as far as he could onto the seat he was sitting on. His father approached the cab slowly. Then, he looked into it. Valen felt his blood pumping wildly through his veins. His father circled the carriage suspiciously. Valen shrunk out of sight, his heart still pounding his ribs. Then, his father turned and went back to the house.

Valen didn't have long. Charles had probably finished making dinner and Valen had to make it back inside before his father realized that he was missing. He opened the door as fast as he could, then made his way along the edge of the house. He stumbled as usual and his legs seemed weaker this time. He clutched the stone sill of a low window and inched his way along. After a few minutes or so he finally reached the door on the side of the house.

Breathing heavily, Valen stuck out his hand to turn the door knob. Once it was turned the entire way, he pushed the door slowly open. He glanced inside. A dim light shined down the corridor. It was deathly silent. He stumbled into the entry way shutting the door behind him. The light hardly helped him see at all. Trying to make it into the dining room before his father knew where he'd been, Valen reached out to grab the side of the wall. No sooner had he done this and a powerful hand suddenly grabbed his wrist.

# THE DARK LIGHTHOUSE

Shhhh!!" said Charles clasping his hand over Valen's mouth. "You mustn't let your father hear you. Here, I've brought your chair. Now it's obvious you're struggling to walk. Sit down and I'll take you into the dining hall."

Valen was extremely relieved that it wasn't his father. He grasped the edge of the wheel chair and managed to sit down. His legs trembled.

Charles whisked him speedily down the long dark hall.

"Wait!" exclaimed Valen as they passed through the large arched doorway before the stairs leading up to his room, "I don't care to eat tonight. I'll just retire now."

"Not eat?" said Charles. "You must eat."

"I'm not that hungry. I'll be fine."

"Alright," said Charles turning his chair around. "But, if you change your mind—just let me know."

Charles helped him out of his chair.

Charles always felt sad to see him drag himself around, but Valen insisted on not being helped; unless he was feeling especially ill. Once Valen got to the top, he got into his other chair, and pushed himself down the winding corridor that led to his room. He rolled past several windows on his way, looking out of them, nervously. The sun left wisps of reds and oranges in the sky as it slipped below the horizon.

Soon, he was in his room thinking about the meeting he was to have by the old oak tree. He was excited about his new friends. Valen sat, waiting quietly for any sound of his father. But, no sign came. He gazed out his window, listening to the clock tick away. He was getting sleepier by the moment. His head tilted to one side. His eyelids felt heavy as stones. The sky became darker. Suddenly, he heard something. The sound got closer. "Footsteps," he thought, as they came closer and closer until finally they were right outside his door. A knock quickly followed.

"Hello?" said Valen.

"Open this," came a familiar voice as the door handle rattled. Valen obeyed. Immediately, his father stepped in. Valen couldn't help but notice that his father had an unusual amount of dirt on his shoes and under his nails.

"Did you find Professor Lewis?" said Valen looking suspiciously at his father's feet.

"No—I, well, never mind," said Dr. Grimm as he moved towards the window, "but I do have news. Dr. Grimm moved towards the window.

"What news?" asked Valen.

"A cure," said his father with a strange smile. In his hands he held a bottle that was black with specks of dark green.

"A what?" gasped Valen.

"I have been working on this cure for many, many years," said Dr. Grimm.

Valen was trembling now, partly from his illness, partly from excitement. His sickness had disabled him severely for so long and he was tired. His thin, sick, malnourished legs, were no bigger than his arms. His bones were showing and he scarcely had any energy at the end of nearly every day. His eyes had sunk far back into his head and his face hardly had any color left in it. He seemed close to dying.

"I can't believe it!" shouted Valen. "I'm *actually* going to get better?" Then, Valen felt suddenly wary. Why was his father suddenly acting kind? As long as Valen could remember his father was never particularly caring.

"Yes," said his father shortly. "Soon." He moved over to a small table that had a candle flickering softly on it and set the bottle down.

"This is one part," said his father placing the black and green one down. He pulled out a small red bottle with an **M** painted on the side. "This is the other. There are three doses. You will take one as soon as I leave and one at midnight. I will give you the other part in a few days time."

"Why can't I take them all now?" asked Valen nervously; he wasn't accustomed to being in the presence of his father for more than a few seconds at any given time.

"It doesn't work that way," said his father turning around, his eyes concentrating heavily on the bottle he had in his hands. Valen noticed his hands trembling.

"Are you all right?" said Valen who was still sitting in his wheelchair watching his father's movements.

His father took the cork out of it ignoring the question. A small puff of smoke spurted out. Valen was watching earnestly as the cloud slowly disappeared. Then, for a moment, he thought he saw a strange face in it.

"You must take the black bottle at midnight exactly," his father continued. "If you should fail, it will prove disastrous. You must not fail *me*. Here—take this one now." He slid Valen the red one.

"How long until I feel better?" said Valen, looking at the bottle curiously.

"I do not know!" said his father seeming to get angry.

"Well, how much of it do I drink?" Valen yawned wide as he took the bottle his father had just given him.

"All of it!" snapped his father angrily. "You *must* drink every last drop!"

"Okay," said Valen still leery of his father. "I will." Then, he yawned again and stretched his arms widely.

"Three hours," said his father. "*Three* hours precisely. That is all you have. You have one dose tonight and the next at midnight. Do not miss your chance."

"What if I fall asleep?" said Valen yawning.

"DO AS I SAY!" roared his father suddenly, pacing back and forth across the front of the window.

"Okay," said Valen noticing the strangeness of his father's face, watching him as he shifted back and forth.

"Once the clock strikes twelve, you must take it at once. Do you understand? It is very important that you do exactly as I say." Then, Dr. Grimm walked to the door. " Once you're better we'll go see about the Professor. I think I may have a clue as to what happened to him. But, I cannot divulge what that is. *Now*, I must go and entertain my guest. I will come to you in the morning to see how you're feeling."

"Can I meet him?" said Valen.

"No! He has had a long journey. Now, good night!" He turned and swung the door open marching loudly down the hall and slipped down the stairs.

Valen looked tiredly at the clock. The big hand was about to strike eight o' clock in the evening. How could he possibly stay up late enough? His body ached all over. He felt extremely tired from the day. He could scarcely move. Even though Valen hardly had any energy, he moved over to the window sill. He looked back at the clock. "My friends!" he said out loud. "I have to go. They're waiting for me!"

He got up as quickly as he could and went over to grab his pack and scarf that was hanging in the closet. Then he grabbed his coat and lantern. For a moment it sounded as if someone was coming down the hallway again. He grabbed what he needed and made his way over to the window. Valen looked down at the bottle his father had given to him.

"I have to take this before I go," he said picking it up. But would this truly cure him? His thoughts abruptly transformed into doubt and fear. Why was his father so adamant that he took it? He had been taking medicine his father had given him all his life. His thoughts whirled around his head like a flock of direction-less birds. He looked down at the bottle. It sat quietly, as if *it* wanted to be drunk. For a moment Valen was so taken by it that he felt as if he didn't have any control over himself. He stared at the bottle again, rolling it back and forth in the palms of his hands. "If it makes me well. . ." he said. Then, he put the bottle up to his mouth and just as he was about to take a drink the wind suddenly whipped so hard against the side of the house Valen stumbled. The bottle slipped out of his hands onto the floor spilling everywhere.

"Oh, no!" he muttered, his heart racing. "How am I going to explain this?" He sat down, stroking his hands through his thin ragged hair. The wind pounded the house again. Valen looked at the clock. The time was near. He picked the bottle back up. It still had a small amount of liquid in it. He put it up to his mouth and drank the remaining drops. Then, the wind whipped furiously against his house again and again as if it was trying to get into Valen's room.

"I must go," he said getting back up. He walked over to the window, and looked outside. It was pitch black. Not so much as one star was out. He knew his father forbid him to leave the house but at last he had friends and Valen determined when he first met them in the carriage that no matter what, he would meet them by the old oak tree.

Valen tried lifting the latch. The giant trees beside his house swayed back and forth like mighty swells in the ocean. He tried opening the window again. But, there was no use. It had never been opened before. He stared outside despairingly. How could he possibly get outside without someone noticing all the noise? He would have to go downstairs.

But, how? The wind blew again rattling the window. The window burst free. Valen walked back over to it. The wind grabbed the shutters and slammed them into the side of the stone wall of the mansion. Valen looked around frantically for a moment, thinking that again someone was coming. Feeling very weak but determined, he sat perched upon his window sill three stories high, staring down wild eyed at the large swath of yard. It was a long drop, but Valen knew he must leave. There was no other way. If he went through the house, he would surely be caught. The way down was equally frightening. Valen could scarcely walk, much less climb down the side of a giant mansion. What was he to do? He looked out across the tree line. The forest seemed darker as he glanced over at it. After several more moments passed, he made up his mind. Just as soon as he did, his body surged with a strange sensation that gave him new strength—strength enough to climb. There was no time for waiting.

He scurried to the very edge of the window. Slowly he put one foot down on the ledge of one of the stones which made up the mansion's walls. He struggled for a moment. His foot slipped as he tried to manage his balance and for a moment nearly lost it. He clung to the side of the house and regained his composure. His frail, wobbly legs knocked together with each step. Every few moments he looked down to find his next footing. The rocks of Grimm Mansion provided sure footing all the way to the ground. He took his time traversing here and there until after five or so minutes he reached the bottom. His hands were sweaty and cold. The wind howled at his back. Then suddenly he felt a surge of energy and stamina that he had never felt before. Hours ago he felt pathetically weak. Yet, again he felt a small bit of strength surge through his achy muscles. The medicine seemed to be working.

Still not possessing much strength, he hobbled away from the mansion and made his way to the forest. Suddenly, he saw something dart quickly across the yard into the trees.

"Hello?" mumbled Valen to himself. But just as soon as he said the words, he realized it was probably better not draw attention to himself; especially with the condition he was in, which made him defenseless. But his imagination went wild with what it could possibly be. Was it the creature Charles claimed he had seen, or was it some kind of animal—the animal that killed Professor Lewis? He pulled the hat tight over his head, put his hands up to his mouth to warm them and then limped his way under the looming trees to meet his new friends.

Frightened at what might be lurking in the dark, he walked slowly, trying as best he could to pay attention to any strange noises. He continued along at a slow pace. Soon he discovered a worn path that zigzagged back and forth through the forest. For a moment, Valen thought he saw a figure on a distant ridge slipping between the trees. Rubbing his eyes, he squinted and looked again. "Maybe it's just Jude or Jack," he thought, trying to reassure himself. He pulled the scarf more tightly around his neck. He continued to walk, but it proved harder as it became increasingly darker. Finally, he reached the old oak tree. There sat Henry, alone and yawning. Valen stepped on a branch that snapped in half loudly.

"HELLO?" he said launching to his feet as if he had a firecracker in his pants.

"Hi Henry," said Valen not paying attention to Henry's jitters.

"Geez, you scared the daylights out of me."

"Sorry," said Valen indifferently. "Have you seen anyone else yet?"

"No, why?"

"Because I think I've seen someone else we have not invited," said Valen setting his bag down on the ground.

"It's probably your imagination," said Henry looking even more frantic than before.

"I don't think so," said Valen with certainty. "I know what I saw."

"What did you see?" said Jack who had just arrived. He reached into his bag, pulled out a few lanterns to give to the others, then lit one.

"Put it out!" hissed Henry trying to grab it.

" Relax," said Jack compliantly. " What are you so skittish about anyway?"

"It's nothing really," said Valen combing the distant ridge again. "I'm not even sure what I saw."

"He said he saw someone else," blurted Henry looking more terrified than ever.

"Oh," said Jack. "Well, maybe it was Jude."

"It's not me," said Jude striding up without a care in the world, chewing obnoxiously.

"Seriously, pie?" said Jack matter-of-factly. "Must you always be eating?"

"Shut up!" said Jude cramming the rest of it into his mouth.

Jack began polishing his glasses with an annoyed look on his face.

"Well, I brought you some, if it makes you feel better," said Jude shooting out his hand sharply.

Valen was looking around still.

"Valen you made it—" said Jude loudly, coming over to him.

"Shhhh!!!" Henry hissed. "He thought he saw someone."

"Honestly," said Jude. "Do you really think there's someone out here besides us?"

"I don't know," said Valen strangely. "But, if there is, I don't want to stay here any longer to find out."

"Well, what's the hold up?" said Jude happily.

"Nothing," said Jack.

"Let's go then," said Jude licking one of his fingers.

The four boys gathered their things and began walking through the forest. There was no definitive trail, so they walked side by side instead, dodging branches along the way. The wind picked up a bit and brought with it a nasty chill. In the distance, the ocean could be faintly heard crashing against the jagged cliffs.

An hour had passed before they reached a small clearing in the forest. Jude sat down first; Jack and Henry followed suit.

"We can't stay long," said Valen. "I have to be back before the sun comes up. We only have a short amount of time."

"Sure," said Jude breathing heavily.

Valen suddenly felt exhausted and sleepy.

"Are you all right Valen?" said Jack concernedly.

"Yes, it's just that I feel a little light headed," said Valen sitting down. He sighed heavily.

"Why didn't you just stay home?" said Jude.

"What and let you guys have all the fun?" snapped Valen. "I don't think so."

"I didn't mean it like that," said Jude exasperated. He stood up.

"Leave him alone," barked Jack.

"Here we go," said Jude irritated, "always defending everyone."

"I don't need anyone defending me," said Valen standing back up.

"Look!" said Henry pointing back into the forest.

"It's your imagination . . . I'm telling y—" began Jude. But, his words fell silent for he saw it too.

Valen looked to where Henry was pointing.

"I see it too," said Jack squinting through his glasses.

Henry was right. Far away in the forest a tiny black shape darted back and forth between the giant trees. Then, two soft glowing silver lights appeared, but quickly faded into the blackness of the night.

"What is it?" said Henry frightened.

"Probably a deer or something," said Jude stupidly.

"A deer?" said Jack. "You can't be serious Jude."

"Can't I?" said Jude.

"Deer have nothing solar about them," said Jack hotly.

"Who said anything about the sun?" said Jude sharply.

"Did you not see those lights?" said Jack. "I mean even I can see them and I have spectacles."

"Why do you have to call them spectacles?" said Jude. "Why can't you call them glasses like the rest of Had Wink."

"Come on," said Valen still staring into the forest. "I think we should head to the lighthouse now."

"What if that thing is the one that does the haunting my grandfather told me about?" said Henry nervously. "Or what if it is the creature that murdered—"

"It's not," said Valen angrily. "The professor is not dead. I won't believe it. And—there's no such thing as ghosts anyway. It's superstition. Hauntings always happen when people are alone. Ever wonder why?"

Henry scratched his head for a second.

"You have a point," said Henry.

"I don't see it anymore," said Jack.

"Yes, me neither," said Valen. "Come on, we're wasting time."

Valen thought that maybe his father and the visitor he mentioned earlier was following them. They wouldn't be wandering through the forest at midnight, thought Valen, as he walked towards the distant trees. At first, Valen thought he was imagining things. Now he was sure. Even his new friends saw it. But, what did he see? Was someone following them? Or were they supposed to be following someone? Perhaps it was the professor?

Another hour passed before they came to the coast. The ocean raged. The wind howled. Thick black clouds swirled above them veiling the stars above. The moon was full, but Valen could not see its light.

"Look, another light!" said Henry excitedly staring into the murky night. "Do you think it's what we saw earlier?"

"No, it's too big," said Valen decidedly.

"But what do you suppose it is?" continued Henry wandering toward it aimlessly.

"Henry, stop!" shouted Jack, grabbing him before Henry had almost fallen over the edge of a giant cliff. "Well, that was close."

All four of them turned, making their way to an old, crumbling staircase that wound its way down to a quiet beachhead. The light became brighter. They hurried along, hearts pounding in their chests. Valen still felt weak, but he found a bit of strength to carry on. After a few slips and falls they finally made it to the bottom. The ocean crashed in its fury. They looked out onto the sea and far into the distance on a tiny island sat a towering lighthouse.

"Do you suppose it's abandoned?" said Valen trying to make it out.

"From what I know, it hasn't been used for hundreds of years," said Jack staring at it curiously.

Henry's eyes bulged out of his head like giant eggs as he walked backwards. Then he stepped on someone's foot, shouting.

"AAAAAHHHHHHH!!!!!" shouted Henry.

"Relax," said Jude calmly giving him a shove. "And, ah—you're standing on my foot. Do you mind?"

"Sorry," mumbled Henry, his teeth chattering.

Then, something strange happened that none of them expected. Instantly, the ocean became as still as a pond. The moon began to emerge from behind black rumbling clouds. Suddenly, Valen saw something crawling out of the water onto the rocks surrounding the lighthouse.

"Look!" he hissed. "That thing! I think it's going into the lighthouse!"

"Do you think it sees us?" said Jack, polishing his glasses for the tenth time that evening.

"I don't even know what *it* is," said Valen. "Much less know if it sees things."

"I told you it was haunted," said Henry proudly.

Then the ocean began to roar and spit its furious waves back onto the beach. The moon disappeared and gloomy clouds resumed.

"I guess we're not going out there tonight," said Henry again.

"We aren't?" said Jude. "Do you think I hiked this far to go back? Well, you're ridiculous."

"So what about this boat of yours, Jude?" said Jack sitting down on a protruding rock that stuck up out of the sand.

"Uh—" said Henry timidly shoving his hands into his pockets. "I think we should head home."

"Whatever," said Jude. "Don't be such a coward!"

"So, Jude . . . where's this boat of yours?" interrupted Valen again.

"Follow me," he said trudging down the rocky coast.

"More hiking?" complained Henry.

"Yes, more hiking!" barked Jude into the wind, but Henry couldn't hear him because his voice was completely muffled.

The four boy, heads down, drove into the ferocious wind. Valen followed behind Jude with Jack at his feet and Henry in the rear. They plodded along, like devoted soldiers. Then the temperature plummeted drastically and Valen suddenly felt weaker than he had all night. His whole body ached with icy chills. Occasionally, he tripped over a rock but Jack and Henry grabbed him before he could fall.

Any other night Valen would have been confined to the Grimm Mansion in his rickety, horrible wheelchair. But, for some reason that he could not quite explain, since the moment he opened the window, he felt strength periodically surge through his frail muscles that he had never felt before. Indeed, he felt more alive than he had in many, many years, but it continued to surge and plummet erratically, almost as if something else lay hidden beneath.

Jude quickly got ahead of everyone. Valen tried to keep up as they walked about, twenty minutes before he began yelling to get Jude's attention. But Jude didn't hear him. Instead, he kept walking towards an inlet that lay far away in the distance. Valen struggled, following along, gazing around the coast at the giant, thick pines. This was the first time Valen had ever seen trees this large before. They stretched far into the sky like turrets of a mighty castle. He stared at them wild eyed. For a short moment, Valen became enthralled with them and lost sight of Jude as he disappeared into the night. Suddenly, Valen slipped on a mossy rock.

"Are you hurt?" said Jack trying to help him stand.

Henry grabbed his other side.

"Yes, I'm fine. I'm just tired. You walk on. I'll wait here."

"We're not leaving you," said Jack. "We should stay together."

"Really, I'm fine!" said Valen sharply into the wind. "I can look after myself!"

Jack loosened his grip.

"I'll go and find Jude then," said Jack loudly, as the wind carried his words away.

"Can I stay with you?" said Henry.

"You go on," began Valen, but he was quickly interrupted.

"I'd rather stay here," Henry continued.

"I'M FINE!" yelled Valen.

Their argument was short lived when Jude unexpectedly came up out of the inlet in a small row boat, navigating it proudly.

"Where on earth did he get that?" said Jack curiously.

"That's so amazing," said Henry leaving Valen to himself.

Valen followed them over to the rocks that made stepping stones out into the water.

"Ahoy, there!" joked Jude with a large grin on his face. "Welcome to me boat."

Jack was the first one in, followed quickly by Henry.

"Come on Valen! We have a lighthouse to get to," yelled Jude.

"I'm coming," he said hoisting himself into the boat. Jack lent him his hand.

"Thanks Jack!" said Valen sitting down in the back of the boat. The wind died down somewhat as Jude tried to manage the pounding waves as they bobbed up and down on the sea. Waves rolled and tossed, spilling into the boat.

"So who'd you steal this off of?" said Jack sounding like a private detective.

"Now why do you have to go accusing me first thing?" said Jude with a bit of laughter in his voice.

"Because I know for a fact that you didn't buy it for one," said Jack smartly. "And two, I know that there isn't anyone stupid enough to let you use their boat."

"Yes, well you have a point there," said Jude rowing along dangerously. The three of Jude's passengers held on tensely expecting to be dumped into the ocean at any moment. Henry grabbed the back of Jack's coat as they rowed towards the shore of the lighthouse. It was still very dark and the only thing they could see was each other. Jude grabbed an old lantern that was lying on its side under one of the seats.

"Here!" he shouted to Jack. "Light this!"

Jack laughed. How could he possibly light a lantern, as windy as it was?

"Very funny!" shouted Jack, once he realized that Jude was joking.

"Seriously," said Jude laughing. "We can't see a thing."

"Here," said Valen reaching into his bag. "I brought a lantern too." He lit it. Valen shined the light in front of them giving them some guidance, but it went out momentarily.

The boat rocked and shook for the next several minutes until they finally reached where they had first come in. The ocean gurgled and swirled violently as their boat bobbed up and down like a giant bobber.

"Are we going out *there*?" said Henry nervously as he clutched the sides of the tiny boat.

"Of course we are," said Jude grinning widely.

"I think he was asking Valen," interjected Jack furrowing his brow as the ocean lapped up against the boat.

Jack threw his hands under his arms to keep them warm. Jude slowly moved the boat forward. The lighthouse stood up out of the water like a tremendous tower of an old castle washed away long ago. Gigantic waves crashed over the base of it. Jude guided the boat with increasing difficulty as the swells of the ocean impeded their boat. Henry frowned despairingly as he pulled a piece of seaweed out of his hair.

"I think it would be wise to head back," shouted Jack over the rage of the sea.

"I agree!" barked Henry.

"We're not going back," shouted Valen. "I want to find out what that thing is."

"Maybe it's the lighthouse keeper," shouted Jack.

"This lighthouse is abandoned," roared Jude. "It hasn't been used for centuries . . ." Then, a sudden jolt sent the boat rocking. Jude grabbed the oars tightly and threw over the small anchor that sat at his now wet feet. "It's probably smart to hold on at this point," he began. "Just as soon as I can get this boat under con—" But it was too late. The powerful hands of the sea dragged them further out, then threw them back as the boat slammed into the side of the lighthouse as waves pounded the other side of it.

"Quickly! Let's get out of the boat," shouted Valen as he got up trembling. He was becoming increasingly weak as the spray from the sea spit up cold salt water, hitting his face mercilessly, sending a chill over him like icy electricity. The boat was being hammered by violent swells and the waves looked like huge gray arms with mighty fists, pounding away at their tiny boat.

After five minutes of ruthless waves, the four of them safely managed to get out of the boat and onto the slippery wet rocks that surrounded the bottom of the lighthouse. Jack pointlessly wiped his glasses again as the sea continually made them foggier and wetter. Henry grabbed Jude's arm.

"Come on! Let's get inside," said Valen urging his friends along. "Jack, do you have the other lanterns?"

Jack rummaged through his bag to get them. In a few moments four lanterns were shining under the moonless sky.

Valen quickly found the door knob, but to his surprise and disappointment, it was locked.

"It won't open!"

"What should we do?" said Henry.

Valen examined the door. It was made of old wood that had a layer of moss growing on it.

"Let's all push it together!" he shouted.

Henry, Jack and Jude came rushing over. The wind blew violently at their backs bringing with it a cold wet whip.

The boys pushed and dug their shoulders into the door and shoved with all their might. When they realized their efforts weren't working they threw their backs against it instead. But, that didn't work either. Frustrated, tired and exhausted, the door had defeated them. Suddenly, Valen noticed a large ornate key which seemed to grow as he looked at it protruding out of the keyhole. It was covered in seaweed. Jack tried turning it with all his might, to no avail. Then, Jude took a crack at it. The key was quite large, but no matter how hard he tried it would not turn. Henry, feeling at once that he could prove his strength to Jude, also failed after minutes of twisting, turning and grunting.

"What should we do?" asked Henry nervously, his teeth chattering.

"I'm thinking," said Jack.

"Well hurry it up," said Jude abrasively.

Then Valen reached up, his cold hand trembling and gave it a turn with a minimal amount of effort. Minutes passed by. The temperature dropped steadily.

"Look!" shouted Jack utterly surprised. "The door! It's open!"

"How on earth?" said Valen nervously peering into the blackness.

"It must have been stuck," said Henry. "Great work!"

Jack pushed the door slowly open. It was in bad shape and creaked loudly. In seconds they were all inside. It was eerie and substantially warmer than outside. Valen shined his lantern around looking curiously at the decrepit place. He looked out again at the inky swirling eddies, before going through the door, then thought it might be a good idea to pocket the key just in case they got caught on the inside. Before he did, he gazed at it long and hard for it struck him as odd. It looked ordinary, but mysterious too as if it had a long tale to tell. Valen wondered why it was in the door at all.

Finally, Jack got out a few more lanterns, which luckily were dry; he pulled them out of a small compartment from under one of the seats on the boat. Jack pulled out some matches from under his hat. He always kept them in the brim of his hat in a tiny pocket he made especially for them. Soon, the lanterns were lit and Valen, following Jack, hobbled up the steps. Spiderwebs crisscrossed the stairwell. The other boys hugged the sides of the walls tightly following Valen along. The sound of the ocean was muffled by the thick stone walls of the lighthouse. Soon they were at the top. Valen walked cautiously along, sensing someone was there. The air hung thick with something foul.

"I feel like I'm in a graveyard. Do you think this place is haunt—" but Henry was cut short by a sudden noise coming from above the room they were in.

"Did you hear that?" hissed Jack.

"Shhh!!!" said Valen.

All of a sudden they heard a loud—poof! Instantly, the eerie feeling vanished. Valen rushed through the door where the noise came from and up a small flight of stairs. When he arrived, he saw on the floor, a glowing silver bottle with a note tied to it that read,

*Valen, Keep this safe. ~V*

Valen bent down to pick it up. The bottle was extremely tiny, and yet when he picked it up, it felt like a block of iron. Many strange things had been happening that evening and just when Valen thought that things couldn't get any stranger, Henry started yelping like a wounded animal. Valen turned and walked back down the stairs. He entered an adjacent room where the other boys had gone into. Jude, Jack and Henry stood, peering down, where there sat a man face down on a table covered in dust. The old man was covered in cobwebs and his tattered shirt and pants had holes eaten in them.

"Who is this?—" began Valen as his sentence fell.

"He's sleeping," said Jack. "Look at his chest! It's moving. But he's not—how is he breathing, but not conscious?

"I don't understand why he doesn't hear us?" said Henry.

"Maybe he's deaf?" said Jude.

Just then, a lantern lit up on the desk that sat in front of the man.

They all jumped back like grasshoppers.

"I'm really beginning to think this place *is* haunted," said Henry frantically.

"No, you think?" said Jude sarcastically.

Valen was over at the desk rummaging around. It had near an inch of dust over everything.

Valen glanced back at the man. He was still breathing.

"Who do you think he is?" said Henry.

"Looks like the lighthouse keeper to me?" said Jack.

"What's happened to him?" said Henry.

The other boys did not answer. Valen wrapped his sweaty fingers around the bottle, twirling it around in his pocket. He didn't want to mention it for some reason. Partly because he was confused about everything himself and partly because he thought it would merely complicate things further. The lantern flickered for a second and then came back on a moment later. Once it was on they noticed written in the dust,

**"Under the window sill"**

"This is creepy," said Henry.

But the other boys were very interested and went over to it.

Valen looked around for a few seconds before running his hands over the edges of it, but couldn't find anything.

"What is it supposed to mean?" said Jude looking down at the floor.

That's when Jack discovered a loose brick underneath the sill. Behind it was stuffed a ragged and worn looking book. He pulled it out and was about to open it when suddenly the lanterns went out.

"Ah, maybe we should go now?" said Henry.

"Seems like a good idea," said Valen as he pulled his hand out of his pocket letting go of the bottle he was still fiddling with.

Once outside, the weather was much different. The moon was out shining on the surface of the sea, its light chasing away shadows. The wind was warmer now. In the distance, clouds loomed, but they were blowing away from the coast gathering over the island. Valen smiled. He had just had the most exhilarating night of his life.

The four boys walked along the bottom of the lighthouse until they came to where their boat rested. It sat almost perfectly still as if it was sitting in a giant bath tub.

"The weather sure is strange," said Jack squinting up at the pale moon. "There is something awfully weird around here, that's for sure. I think Henry's right, maybe it is haunted."

"I suppose he is," said Valen getting into the boat and sitting down. "But what he's right about, I'm not exactly sure."

The four of them were in the boat within a few minutes. Jack was trying to read the book they found by the light of the moon. Valen still had the bottle he'd found held tightly in his hand. Jude grabbed the oars and headed for the beach. Once they arrived, Jude and Jack pulled the boat onto the sand, gathered their things and headed back up the trail. It was getting earlier by the minute and in two more hours the sun would be up. As they walked into the forest Valen had a strange sense that someone was following them, but instead of telling his new friends he kept it to himself. An hour or so later they finally reached where they had started out.

"Okay," said Valen. "I think it is probably better if we keep this to ourselves until we figure out anything else. Jack, whenever you find something out about that book let us know."

"You can count on me," he said polishing his glasses methodically.

"Jude, Henry," said Valen looking at them dead in the eyes, "don't tell anyone about what happened tonight."

"Yep," said Jude half paying attention, sifting through his pockets, as he looked for the remaining pie he had saved earlier.

"I promise," said Henry yawning.

"Good," said Valen watching Jude chew with a slight chuckle. "Though it's not you I'm concerned about."

"What's that supposed to mean?" said Jude with a bit of cream slipping down his chin.

Jack glared at Jude for a second before he said, "Dear me, how can you ever be trusted if you can't even be decent?"

"I'm just gonna pretend I didn't hear that," said Jude.

"Goodnight," said Valen and he struggled his way back across the lawn and slipped in through the door of his house.

Henry, Jack and Jude bade goodnight and parted company.

The next morning, Valen woke to the sound of what he thought to be a trumpet of war.

"GET UP!" shouted his father. "UP! NOW! DO YOU HEAR ME?"

"I'm up," said Valen groggily as he dragged himself out of bed, staring up into his father's face.

"YOU HAVE BROKEN THE ONLY RULE I HAVE EVER DECREED!" said his father in a vicious rage. "I FORBADE YOU NEVER TO LEAVE THIS HOUSE!"

"What do you mean?" asked Valen yawning confusedly.

"DO NOT PLAY DUMB WITH ME BOY! DID YOU NOT THINK THAT I WOULD KNOW?"

"I—" stuttered Valen.

"SILENCE! FROM NOW ON, YOU ARE HEREBY CONFINED TO THIS ROOM!"

Valen watched his father pace the room frantically. Then, a sudden kindness came over him.

"Have you taken the medicine?"

"Yes—" said Valen lying, as he looked over to where the spill occurred the night before.

"This is very good news," said his father with sudden change in his voice. “Charles will bring you your food. I’ll return this evening.”

Then, he turned abruptly and stepped through the doorway and slammed the door.

Valen listened as his father locked the door behind him. An hour or so passed and before Valen got the idea to escape out of his window his father had a ladder up to it and shut the shutters. Valen sat in silence as a sadness settled around him like a fog. A few minutes passed when he heard a ‘click!’ The window’s shutters were locked. He was trapped, stuck in a dark room with nowhere to go. He sighed, lit his lamp and looked up at the ceiling gloomily.

Time passed and Valen became terribly hungry. His stomach rumbled around like a thunderstorm. Judging by the waning light from the cracks along the edges of the window where there was a gap in between it and the shutters, the sun was well on its way to setting. It had been hours since he’d heard anything from downstairs. Annoyed and angry that he was shut up in his room, Valen got up off his bed to get the bottle he had found in the lighthouse last night. When he did, he felt a sudden surge of energy. In the other pocket sat the key. He pulled it out and lay it on the table. It seemed quite large and unusual. He stared at his curiously. He picked it up again and suddenly became overwhelmed by an urge to try and unlock the door. He felt as though he was unable to control himself when he had the key in hand. He stuck it in the lock and opened his bedroom door. The door flung open and instead of the landing and the stairs, which he normally saw, he was looking down a long stone path which wound its way through a medieval forest. The trees were stooping. Dead animals lay everywhere. Tombstones with moss on them were spread under the gray bark of trees. Fearsome looking creatures never before seen—wolves with human bodies, pigs with human bodies, spiders and all sorts of other foul things and beasts stood etched out of stone, some out of wood, all along either side of a long tall wooden door. It was the largest door Valen had ever seen. Suddenly he felt quite sad. Tears filled his eyes. Then they fell away from the door and he looked again at the many figures all around. He saw in the forest what looked to be a white stone figure of a little girl—a statue lying on the ground—her neck was crumbling. Lying next to her feet was her head. In the distance, a mother and father, also made of what looked to be white stone had vines covering their legs. Their faces were buried in their hands and they lay prostrate together. Then he saw a man that looked to have been working on something but had fallen. A ladder spanned the high wall, also made of black stone. It reached into the sky and disappeared. There was no way over it. The door in the wall was shut, too. The man lay face down in the dirt. Valen heard the wind suddenly and put his hands on his head for a moment thinking that he was dreaming. He took the key out of the door which was in front of him and then the scene disappeared and the landing and stairs appeared, but the door slammed shut and the lock clicked again. Suddenly, he remembered that he had dropped the bottle. He took the key and put it back in his pocket. He stumbled forward to reach for the bottle and on his way down to pick it up, he heard a tapping at the window. For a moment he thought it was his imagination. Then he heard it again. Rap, rap! Valen walked over to the window. He opened it and sitting between the shutters was a letter with the same writing on it that he saw in the lighthouse which read,

*Valen Grimm,*

*You must leave at once! You are in grave danger!*

*~V*

Valen was utterly confused. Who on earth was V and how could Valen possibly leave? After all, he was locked in his room! He sighed heavily recounting the events that had just happened. Valen looked through the crack. He could hear the wind hissing wildly as he watched swirls of leaves dance through the air like beautiful red, yellow and orange wisps. The light of the sun was fading fast. Then, the shutters his father had shut, suddenly sprung open. Valen tried as fast as he could to grab his things. He threw the diary, and the rest of his things into a leather bag he kept in one of the drawers of a tall dresser that sat up against the wall. He quickly looked around for his jacket, but it was not to be found. He saw his father's jacket. It lay on the chair just next to the fireplace. He must have left it when he had come to give him his medicine. It was certainly too big for him to wear, but it would do. He would have to wear it despite how ridiculous he looked in it. He still felt weak, but then a sudden burst of energy revitalized his frail body. He looked down, hung his leg over the window sill and in a few moments his feet were on the ground.

Valen looked around. His heart thumped fiercely. Should he really leave? He thought about the prospect of being confined to his room indefinitely. Was the creature who had been communicating with him trustworthy? His chest tightened. He looked into the black forest behind the mansion. If he left, his father was sure to find out. Always he monitored Valen, watched him. Valen felt trapped. And now that Valen thought of it, his father seemed to have been acting unusually strange. What was he up to? Valen felt torn. He looked up at the flapping shutters, then turned and decided to go.

The air had a nasty chill clinging to it. The wind bit at Valen's neck as he darted between the trees that marked the boundary of his property. He stopped and looked back at his house one last time. Things seemed quite odd. All his years living in that gigantic mansion and things never seemed quite right. And what of the lighthouse and the strange letter he received there? Or the one sticking in the window moments ago? He turned and stepped into the forest. Moments later he was standing under the mighty tree where he had met his friends a night ago. The night was silent and all Valen could hear was the pounding of hundreds of horses in his chest. Then something else stirred in the darkness.

"Who's there?" he said squinting his eyes, frightened. He could barely make out the figure coming towards him.

"Hello? Is there someone there?"

The figure was getting closer and closer.

"Who are you?" he said again.

A girl stepped into a splotchy patch of moonlight. The wind whipped her long golden hair around her face. Valen looked closely at her as the light of the moon reflected her emerald eyes.

"Oh, hello. I'm Murrin Voors."

"I'm Valen Grimm," Valen said noticing a strange scarf upon her neck and what were two extremely sharp spears which were thrust through a belt around her waist. Murrin had long glorious golden hair. It was pulled back with a crimson band. Her skin was white as cream. Slung over her back was a very large and ornate silver shield. She had on a light blue hood which hung around her neck. Upon her arms lay a pair of greaves and tall brown leather boots.

"I know," said the girl squatting to adjust her laces on her boots.

"You *do*?" said Valen taken aback. He looked at her long and hard. "How do you know my name?"

"We've been looking for you for a very long time?"

"You have? We?"

"I can't tell you all you desire to know—not now anyway," said Murrin. "You know your father has been acting quite strange lately, no?"

"How would you know that?" said Valen.

"There's much more I know," said Murrin. Valen noticed she was looking intently at the trees. Her eyes continued to look above. "We have known you for hundreds of years. A message, a rider on a silver steed brought word that you were alive."

"Hundreds of years?" Valen's eyes grew with disbelief. "I am sure you are mistaken. I am only thirteen."

"And *I am* sure you are not," said Murrin looking up at the sky. "Snow is coming. "Soon, you'll *have* to trust us. They're coming."

"Snow? Who's coming? Are you V? Are you the one who's been trying to contact me?" said Valen awkwardly.

"V?" said Murrin. "Who's V?"

"Didn't you open my window?" said Valen strangely.

"No," said Murrin.

"Well, if it wasn't you, then who was it?"

Murrin was quiet.

"*Who* are you?" said Valen after pausing for a second.

"I have come from Somewhere Else," said Murrin looking up again. The wind shook the trees.

"That's obvious," said Valen nervously grabbing his bag tighter. "But what for?"

"I have told you once—to find you," said Murrin.

Valen scanned the ground for a moment. He had the thought that he should tell her about the events that had been happening lately, but he thought better of it.

"Where did say you are from again?" Valen stuttered.

"I cannot tell you that now," said Murrin. "Follow me and you'll have answers to some of your questions."

"I will?" said Valen distrustfully.

"Quick! We must go! You have to trust me," said Murrin crossing her arms. "You can't go back to your home."

"I can't?" said Valen partly relieved.

"Yes! Now come on! You must trust me!" shouted Murrin.

Valen would not move.

"Look, I know what it is like to be trapped in a house all alone," she said.

"You do?" said Valen rather surprised.

"Yes," said Murrin. "I'll tell you all about it if you come with me. But, we must be quick," she said looking down the path between the trees where she had come from.

"You have not given me any real reason to believe why I should go with you," he said forcefully. "Though you are quite enchanting, you could just as well be *untrustworthy*—a sorceress or something far worse. I have read all about children who lose their way in the woods."

"Not all tales from those meetings in gardens, forests, or even caves end as you might imagine," said Murrin. Murrin looked thoughtful, and after a long pause finally said, "I know what you have in your pocket."

The color fled Valen's already pale face. "You do?" He moved his hand over the key, which felt quite large and heavy. Valen knew the key was something magical, but how did Murrin know he possessed it?

"The bottle you have," said Murrin, "It must be taken away from here. I dare not speak of what is in it, for it is a long and sad tale. Is it enough, that you should know that I was aware that the bottle had been found? Is it enough that I have sought you and found you and that I knew that you had it in your pocket? A most peculiar place to set up a—Duargian—a Chain from the Deep. I think it's best we get out of here before . . ." Murrin trailed off with her thought as she looked above at the gathering storm.

"Forgive me," said Valen his legs beginning to quiver, "the bottle? "I don't understand. I haven't the slightest idea—"

"What do you take me for? Do you think I would have guessed something else?" said Murrin. "Even you know things are not as they should be. Tell me, did the ocean rage and quiet suddenly? With your clever mind do you really think that you can slip your deception past mine?"

"Yes—I did not mean—"

"The choice is yours. There is no point pretending," said Murrin. "Even you are affected by what you carry. All have been since the Beginning—since the Tremendous Tree fell thousands and thousands of years ago." Murrin paused again and grabbed the long shafts of her spears. "We haven't much time. The bottle has been found and taken, as it was planned. *You must bear it away*. It is the first one."

"Bear it away?" said Valen. "The first one—I—"

Valen's words fell away as Murrin turned and began walking away. Valen gazed upon her golden hair. The moon caught it for a brief moment and it looked as though it was a waterfall cascading down her back; with bits of starlight catching it. He looked back once more through the trees at the Grimm Mansion. It rose up out of the darkening, blustery sky. That was how Valen at last came to his decision. It was that place, grand though it was, that he wanted to leave. Now that he was honest with himself, he remembered his father. He did not know where he was going, but he slowly began to follow Murrin. At that moment she picked up her speed twofold. Valen's strength seemed to be increasing by the hour. His mind raced wildly as they dodged branches and jumped over logs, tearing through the forest. Snow started to fall softly. What was the hurry? Did Murrin know about the events that had been happening recently with the professor? Was she the shadow that had been following them the previous night? Whatever or whoever she was, Valen followed closer. An owl hooted above them, then flew across the path swooping down near his head. A deer darted through a nearby grove of trees. Then, the sky grew black and an eerie silence penetrated the forest. Valen felt cold, almost dead inside. He clutched his side, feeling as though he was going to pass out. Without warning, as if he had used up all the energy he had gained before; he felt his strength vanish and the last thing he remembered was seeing Murrin running down the trail ahead of him before finally collapsing.

Hours later Valen woke up in a house with a warm, rich smell of chocolate permeating the room.

"Where am I?" he said looking wildly around the room, standing to his feet as he knocked over the fire tools next to the flew of a fireplace that looked a few centuries old. Murrin was nowhere to be seen.

"How do you do?" came a cheeky and lively voice. "I am Mr. Voors. You can call me Voors if you'd like." He moved towards the light. "You look quite pale boy. Dear me. I don't suppose you'd want some chocolate right about now?"

"Chocolate? Sure, I guess," said Valen sizing up the room where his eyes fell above the fireplace where there hung an old picture. "I have to go!"

"You've only just arrived boy," said Mr. Voors putting down a plate of cookies.

"Ah—yes. You're right," said Valen trying to hide his nervousness. "It's just that I'm not supposed to be here."

"Not supposed to be here?" asked Mr. Voors suspiciously. "Come now boy, surely you can entertain the Voors' who are new to Had Wink.

Valen looked at the picture above the fireplace again. In it the sky was gray and dull and Mr. Voors' grin was large and cheerful. His wife (Valen assumed, though he'd never met her) had a tiny smirk on her face. Murrin looked mischievous as she had her arms crossed and was barely looking at whoever painted the picture. Valen took his eyes off of it for a moment to an endless amount of books that scaled the entire length of the twenty to thirty feet of wall. Everything seemed suddenly bigger than his home and Valen felt entirely dwarfed.

"Then you're staying?" suggested Mr. Voors happily.

"Not really," said Valen now being lured in by the smell of warm chocolate cake as it wrapped its arms around the frame of the door, nearly grabbing him by the nostrils, dragging him into the kitchen.

"Oh dear, dear, dear, snik, snok, nik, nok," said a woman walking speedily towards him, snapping her lips and tongue together in an odd sort of way. Valen looked at her for a moment with the light flickering off her soft pale skin. She was taller than most men. Her hair was short and blonde and her arms were long and gangly, but she was well composed. Valen immediately recognized her as the woman in the picture.

"I am Mrs. Voors," she said boisterously. "You must be Valen Grimm. Ah! My dear. Are you cold? Hot? Hungry? Here have some chocolate cake won't you?"

Valen bent over the table to try a piece. He was terribly hungry for it had been hours since he had eaten anything at all. He felt for a moment as if a real lion was in his stomach ready at that moment to come charging out of his mouth to eat the cake for him. Then, instantly, he felt light and free and somehow healthier and normal.

"I have to go," he mumbled to himself feeling a bit strange. But in seconds Valen abandoned his idea of having to go.

"Sorry?" said Mrs. Voors putting a hand up to her ear.

"Uh—never mind," said Valen rubbing his head.

"These chocolates are special," she said, grinning oddly. "They're from an old family recipe and the ingredients . . . oh dear me . . . very special indeed."

Just then the front door flew open and in walked Murrin with a giant black dog.

"Arf! Roofff!!! Arrwww!!" The dog tugged and pulled at Murrin's coat.

"Stop dragging me you nasty beast! This dog is hopeless!" she screamed. "He doesn't know a thing! He doesn't listen to a word I say!"

"That's obvious. Now, calm down dear," said Mr. Voors with an exasperated look in his eye. "He's very capable you know. Those animals are amazing creatures." Mr Voors pulled a piece of meat from his pocket and threw it to the dog. Valen couldn't help noticing how strange the meat looked. But the dog chomped on it happily and then plopped down on the ground. Murrin walked over to the fire place frustrated.

"Snow?" said Valen in amazement feeling better by the moment. "You have snow on your shoulders. But, how is that . . . it wasn't nearly cold enough earlier."

"The weather does change rapidly around here I've noticed," said Mr. Voors coming over to sit on his brown leather lounge chair. The dog was sitting at his side gnawing on what was left of the meat Mr. Voors had given him. The fire cracked warmly in the background. In a few short moments almost all the chocolate was gone and Valen felt as if he might float away on a cloud of delight. Mrs. Voors was now reading seriously in her chair that sat next to Mr. Voors. Murrin came and sat down with two steaming cups of hot chocolate. Valen got up to look out the window where sure enough it was snowing fiercely.

"Strange," said Valen grinning with excitement. "I've never seen it snow like this at this time of year."

"Here," said Murrin putting the tray down, "this should warm you up."

"Thanks," said Valen.

"More chocolate? Voors' best," said Mr. Voors. "Comes from my very own collection of fine chocolates."

"I'm really thankful," said Valen looking down at the cup as steam billowed out of the top of it."Honestly, I can't eat anything else that's sweet or else I think I might be sick."

"Oh really you must," said Murrin happily. "It's the absolute best!"

"Okay," said Valen as he grudgingly gave in. "But, I think I'll wait a few minutes."

Mr. and Mrs. Voors sat intrigued by Valen although Valen didn't know why. Murrin sipped quietly on her drink. The Voors' dog licked his lips quietly as he lay close to the hearth. The fire gave its light away proudly, illuminating the room with bits of orange and red. Then, Valen caught a peculiar look in Mr. Voors' eye.

"Tell me about your father," he said lighting up his pipe before taking a giant drag. "What does he do?"

"He's a doctor," mumbled Valen.

"What sort of doctor?" said Mr. Voors taking another puff.

"Ah," stuttered Valen, "he's a family doctor . . . I guess?"

"You mean you don't know what kind of doctor your father is?" said Mr. Voors his eyes glowing for a moment as the fronts of his eyeballs flickered from the orange ember resting in the end of his pipe.

"*Mr. Voors,*" snapped Mrs. Voors.

"Well, surely he knows," said Mr. Voors as he turned and gave a little smirk.

"Actually, I don't," said Valen feeling more stupid by the minute. "I've never asked."

"How many patients does he have then?" asked Mr. Voors sensing that he might have been a bit too rough with his new guest.

This question proved even harder for Valen to answer. "How many patients?" Valen repeated to himself in his head.

"I'm not exactly sure—'"

"You don't know that either?" asked Mr. Voors skeptically.

"Yes—ah—why would I?" said Valen abruptly. "I don't know and I'm not sure I care." He paused for a second, "Why would I care anyway?"

Mr. Voors uncrossed his legs and sat up in his chair puffing his pipe like a locomotive.

"What about your mother?" asked Mrs. Voors taking her focus away from the book that she was somehow reading at the same time.

"Mother!!" said Murrin so loudly, Mr. Voors spilled his chocolate on his jacket.

"Of all the—" barked Mr. Voors.

"My mother?" said Valen feeling hot in his cheeks and tiny beads of sweat rolling down his temples. No one had ever asked him that before. Ever. He flipped back through the pages of his mind for a second only to feel more stuck than he had seconds ago when Mr. Voors asked him about his father. In fact he had always wanted to know where he had come from, but really only ever heard the word mother a few times. He heard about it in his education mostly, but no one ever talked about *his* mother, least of all his father. His jaw hung stupidly open for a moment or two before he talked again.

"I never knew my mother," said Valen feeling awkward. "I ah—" he stumbled over his words again. "She died when I was little." But Valen knew this to be false for Dr. Grimm had never spoken of her.

"She died when you were little?" the Voors said almost in unison.

"Yes, it was snowing too," recalled Valen gazing out the window, "or at least I think it was." His mind was now foggy and gray like a morning with no sun. "My father said she died in her sleep. One morning he woke up and she was gone. Just like that."

"And the really strange and creepy thing about it is," Valen continued now, feeling silly and embarrassed about lying and not knowing why, "at night when it's frigid and snowy I remember what seems to me like a dream." Then he stopped. "Why I am telling any of this to you. I've only just met you. Where am I?" His reason came rushing back. "Who are you? What do you want with me? Get me out out of here!" He took another drink and as if he could not help it, then he began to speak freely again. "There I am sleeping soundly in my mothers arms. Next to her stands a tall, handsome man with black wavy hair and hazel eyes. The sky has a quiet purring sound and then it begins to snow wildly, much like it is tonight. Then it gets cold and dark and I try to wake up but I can't."

Mr. and Mrs. Voors we're listening intently. The fire had dwindled down at that point and all that remained was a pile of coals. Murrin's eyelids kept fluttering as she tried to ward off sleep. The dog's tale twitched.

Mr. Voors got up and looked out the window, the wind lashing against the house. He shoved his hands in his pockets. "Well, son, looks like you're staying here tonight," he said smiling. "We're in for a nasty storm."

"Will you be okay staying here?" asked Mrs. Voors as her lips curled upwards.

"No, I'm sorry I can't," replied Valen. "I must get back home. My father believes I'm locked up in my room at this moment. If he finds out that I am gone—it would be for the worst."

"Locked up in your room?" said Mrs. Voors. "Goodness. Why on earth would he lock you up?"

"I don't know," said Valen stammering. "He's been acting very strange lately . . ." He paused.

"Is that so?" said Mr. Voors surprised.

And that is when Valen realized he had said too much, but part of him was greatly relieved to have told the truth of the situation he was actually in.

The candles that were lit in the room provided the only remaining light. Silence set in rather quickly after Valen had shared this fact. No one said anything for what seemed to be ages. Valen felt his heart beating in his chest like an old clock clunking loudly back and forth. He looked at Murrin, then his eyes flashed back to Mr. Voors'. The fire breathed softly. Valen felt as tense as a wound up spring.

Mr. Voors sat back down in his chair. Mrs. Voors put a few more logs on the fire and light returned to the room. Then Mr. Voors took a long drag from his pipe, and leaned forward, looking Valen dead in the eyes. Valen tried to move further into the tall lounge chair he was shifting uncomfortably in.

"I have some very bad news for you," Mr. Voors said. He let the smoke out of his mouth slowly as he made the statement. "I'm afraid your father has been lying to you for many years and that a great secret surrounds your life, that he has kept hidden from you for a very, very long time."

# SHIPS AND STRANGERS

I don't believe your father is a doctor," continued Mr. Voors as he leaned forward further.

"What do you mean?" said Valen. "How do you know?"

"Have you noticed anything strange lately?" said Mr. Voors getting up to stoke the fire.

"Strange?" asked Valen thinking back to the lighthouse incident and the figure he'd seen the past few nights.

"Has your father spoken of someone coming to visit him?"

Valen thought for a few seconds.

"Yes! But—*why*? Who are they?"

Mr. Voors became suddenly still and quiet. Mrs. Voors peeped over her book. The dog put his paws over his snout looking frightfully up at Valen. Murrin looked white as the moon. The fire glowed brightly.

"He's more cunning and clever than I thought," said Mr. Voors taking a puff on his pipe again. "Indeed, he is."

"Who are you talking about?" asked Valen skeptically.

"It would not matter much to you now. But, in time you will see." Mr. Voors crossed his legs, adjusted his jacket and then took another drag.

"See what?" asked Valen feeling awkward and curious.

Mr. Voors got up suddenly and began pacing the room, smoking his pipe like a fiery locomotive.

"I'm terribly sorry to disappoint you," began Valen with a shakiness in his voice, "but none of this has to do with me. My father *is* a doctor and that is all there is to it. He often has guests that come over and visit." Though Valen knew this to be false and wanted to leave. "I must go at once. I'm sorry, but it's getting late and my father is probably worried about me." Valen got up in an instant and made for the door.

The Voors looked taken aback as they looked at their new guest before them. Mrs. Voors looked frightful and nervous as she slowly slid the book down to her lap. Murrin remained quietly unmoved, like a cold stone statue.

"It's very strange here," thought Valen getting up from his chair.

"I will walk you home," said Mr. Voors. "It's unsafe to be out there all alone at this time of night."

"I don't mean to be rude sir," said Valen as he adjusted his scarf around his neck, "but this is *Had Wink*. It's the safest place in the world. Nothing dangerous or suspicious has ever happened here until now—and I think you're the ones that are unsafe. I don't need assistance from you either. I can walk myself home." Valen grabbed for the doorknob, thanked the Voors kindly and entered into the swirling snow.

In minutes he was deep into the forest. Snow poured down on his head like someone up above was shaking giant bags of flour on him. He could hardly see an inch in front of him. As he walked and grumbled to himself about all the news the Voors told him, he then suddenly realized that he could see exceptionally well and hear clearer too. He could hear so well in fact, that despite the wind, he noticed the voices that were being carried with it, but could not quite make them out. At that moment a very curious thing happened. Valen saw the glowing lights he had seen the other night and then . . . wham! He ran right into something warm and very fury.

"AAAAHHHHHH!" came the voice that Valen immediately recognized as Henry.

Valen looked around, amazed to see his friend standing like a stranded animal in the middle of a snowstorm.

"What are you doing out here?!" shouted Valen into the wind and snow.

"It's Jack," bellowed Henry. "He said we need to meet him at his house right away."

"What for?" asked Valen turning his back on the raging snow.

"There's no time to explain," yelled Henry. "Your father is furiously hunting for you! He said you went missing! He's got the whole town practically looking for you."

"Why the whole town?!"

"I don't know," said Henry getting a mouthful of snow. "But, I don't think there is much they can do about it now, with this dreadful weather."

Valen looked back through the snow to the trail he had just come down. The snow was drowning any available sight and now the jacket he had taken weighed heavy like a saddle for it was thick wool. Though very warm, he became suddenly aware of how big his father was. The jacket drooped over him and covered him like a large blanket. Valen rolled up the sleeves and made it fit the best he could to make it look like it was his.

Hours had passed and Valen and Henry were nearly frozen to death when they arrived at Jack's house. Jack was waiting for them outside, standing with his head tucked under his thick wool hat. The wind whipped his scarf around his neck recklessly.

"Are you all okay?" asked Jack uncrossing his arms to reach for the basement storm doors.

"Yes, we're fine," said Valen and Henry simultaneously, practically shivering to death.

Jack had to move quite a bit of snow before he could find the handle.

The three boys quickly headed into the cellar away from the icy snow and howling wind. Jack disappeared for a moment up the stairs. Valen and Henry took off their wet clothes and hung them near a fire Jack had made. The basement was warm and inviting. The walls were strewn with old round stones. The quiet fire hummed snugly in a nearby wood-stove. To the right of Valen stood Jack's father's workbench. On it, lay many tools that he used for fixing and making things. Jack came back quickly with a plate full of ham sandwiches, three steaming mugs of hot chocolate and a container of extras.

"I hope you're hungry," he said placing the plate on the table, then putting more wood in the fire.

"I'm *really* hungry," said Valen grabbing a sandwich immediately, then feeling a twinge of weakness followed by a surge of strength. He was beginning to get used to this new sensation he had been feeling the past couple of days.

"I am too," said Henry reaching down for one.

"Help yourselves," said Jack sitting down. Laid out on the table were all sorts of decrepit news paper clippings of Old Had Wink. A few tattered looking books were stacked next to a dripping candle that sputtered with a steady stream of smoke. Valen sat down exhaustedly. Henry followed suit.

"We must try to keep quiet," said Jack after he took a sip of his drink. "Mother and father are sleeping and I do not want to wake them. Soon, father will have to get up and work the night shift in the mines." Jack paused to polish his glasses as he regularly did. "Valen, your father sent Charles looking for you earlier. He told my father that if he saw you that you were to come straight home, despite the weather. What on earth did you do?"

"I broke out of my room," said Valen taking a bite of his sandwich.

"Broke out?" said Jack throwing his hands behind his head with a raised brow.

"Yeah," said Valen as he finished chewing. "He locked the door, including the window, in a fit of rage. The next thing I know is that there's a note tucked in near the edge of the window."

"What did it say?" asked Henry taking a sip of his hot chocolate.

Valen pulled out the note that was crumpled up in his pocket. He gave it to Jack. Jack squinted his eyes, moved his glasses up his nose much like and old man, then read it aloud,

*Valen Grimm,*
*You must leave at once! You are in grave danger!~V*

"Now what on earth does that mean?" asked Jack inquisitively.

"It's the same person who wrote to me in the lighthouse," said Valen. "The writing is the same and all. Look, see the "*V*?" He pointed to the end of the note.

"Well, who is *V*, I wonder?" said Jack very thoughtfully.

Then, without warning, the door they had come through, opened.

"Quick, blow out the candle," shouted Henry frightfully.

"It's quite fine," said Jack looking over at the doors. "It's Jude."

"Hey fellas," he said strolling up as if he regularly hiked through mountains of snow. He noisily sat down.

Valen nodded.

"Hi," said Henry with a slight huff and puff of his chest.

"Aw, don't be too down to see me," he said, grabbing the last sandwich. "What's all this about anyway?"

"We were just about to find out," said Valen anticipating what Jack was about to say.

Jack grabbed the newspaper clippings that he had laid down on the table earlier along with the journal they'd found stuffed behind the old brick in the lighthouse.

"I went to the town library earlier today to try to dig up some information on the old lighthouse," began Jack excitedly. "While I was there I looked for hours in all sorts of books and didn't come up with anything until I finally asked if there were any history books on Old Had Wink. After finally persuading the old Mrs. Stoork that I had a project for school due next week, she reluctantly let me peruse some of the old books that had been sitting in the basement for years."

"Once I went down there, I found to my surprise, that there were never any books even written about Had Wink."

Valen, Henry and Jude looked at Jack curiously.

"Do you know that Had Wink isn't on any maps that I came across?" continued Jack enthusiastically.

"What do you mean?" asked Valen skeptically.

"Just that," said Jack clutching a book he had apparently gotten from the library. "*No one knows we're here*?"

"You mean because we're a small town?" said Jude looking at him and cramming a bit of food in his mouth.

Jack reached behind him and plopped the book down on the table. A plume of dust rose as he fingered through the pages.

"This book I have here is the only book I could find about Had Wink," said Jack proudly. "And in it is a very peculiar piece of information."

"What is it?" said the three other boys loudly.

"Shhhh!!!" hissed Jack and just then they heard a noise upstairs.

"It's your father!" said Henry looking wild eyed.

"No," said Jack. "It's my house—it always creaks. Besides, my father's nothing to worry about. If there's anybody at all that would encourage our adventures, it would definitely be him."

"Finish your story!" prodded Valen excitedly.

Jack had his one hand on the book from the library and his other on the journal they found in the lighthouse.

"Look at all these dates and times," said Jack as he pointed to the journal. "Here it says, **'Ship sighted 1625, 1 October ... arrived safely at port ... 10:30 p.m.'** And here it says, **'Ship sighted 1650, 1 October .... arrived safely at port... 10:30**

**p.m.**' and here it says, **'Ship sighted 1675, 1 October . . . .arrived safely at port . . . .10:30 p.m.**' and look here," Jack pointed his long finger on the final entry. "All the way up to 200 years ago in *1725* was the last sighting of anything—but then that's it. The writing ends." Jack paused for a moment looking flummoxed. "So why is it that two hundred years have since passed and not one ship ever made it to port again?" He flipped to the back of the journal and found a spot that was stamped with the name of the lighthouse keeper in it. "As I was looking over it for any clue, I found inscribed into the letters of this man's name, a message. Jack pulled out his magnifying glass and moved the journal over to the light. "See here?" he pointed. "It reads,"**–Go to basement–HW library–statue.**"

"I don't understand," said Henry with a wrinkled brow.

"Once I went downstairs, I found that nearly everything was covered in dust. I found some old books here and there. A few paintings propped up against the walls and then lastly in the corner, tucked beside a bookshelf, stood a statue that was holding this book! Whoever put it there did a very good job at concealing it." Jack flipped the book over. "When I searched the statue, I could barely make out the book, because it was practically the same color as the statue. But after I searched around for a while, I saw carved carefully into the back of the statue, a compartment for a book. It blended in almost perfectly."

"I don't see what's so exciting," smirked Jude rather nonchalantly.

"This book explains what happened here long ago," said Jack excitedly. "I wondered—Why did the journal entries end so abruptly? As I thought about it for a while, searching through the pages of it over and over again—well that's when I discovered the hidden message—that the man who wrote this journal was trying to communicate something! Don't you see? For some reason he wanted someone to find the book that he hid away in the statue. He couldn't risk writing anymore about the strange events that were taking place, so he encrypted a message in his name so that whoever found his journal would also find the book—which records the remaining history of what happened in Had Wink long ago."

"But—he was *breathing* when we saw him last," said Henry.

"I know and that's the really strange part," said Jack lighting another candle, then getting up to put another log in the stove. The wind and snow outside sounded like a new widow.

"*Something* happened to him," said Jack curiously. "Clearly, he's still alive. But, how? Yet, this is not what is most striking. Here, I'll read this—" Jack flipped through the pages of the book he had found in the library, then pointed to the cracked and faded handwriting.

"September, 21, 1725

Had Wink is a fine place to be. It's buzzing with life and people. New faces from around the world are showing up nearly everyday. But, today a very strange man appeared. Strange man and creepy too. The sort that makes your hair stand up on edge. Didn't look like he was from around here or like any of the new people I had seen. Had a strange thing about him. In town when I saw him. Traveled alone. Never seen the likes of him in Had Wink before."

Jack continued,

"September, 25, 1725

The strange man bought the Old Grimm mansion today at an auction. Said he wanted it for a vacation home or something. Lots of wealthy philanthropists detested the idea and scowled at him as he slithered through town peering through shop windows as if he was invited to come and live amongst the likes of Winkers."

"September, 26, 1725

"The days are ever darker. The sky is full of black clouds. No ships. The strange man is still at Grimm Mansion. Not a good time to holiday. I wish he'd leave."

"September, 27, 1725

I think I'm going to sleep in the lighthouse tonight and see if I see anything strange. I've heard he visits the shore line late at night. I'll watch him from there...... Finally arrived and it's quite dark out. He came to the lighthouse this evening asking if I was its keeper. Evil man indeed; made my bones shake."

"And this is the really fascinating part," Jack said excitedly. "Look!" Jack read it aloud again, pointing to the book. "A very strange thing happened this evening. An odd looking creature, that looked much like a human, but possessed foul shaped wings appeared tonight. At first there was only a few, then hundreds of them appeared. Foul beasts, beasts with smoldering flames under their wings, flying everywhere. The strange man is here again. I shall tell him where he should go tonight! Over my dead body if he'll stay in Had Wink any longer!"

"September, 28, 1725, stranger things are happening. Indeed stranger than I imagined. Where shall I go if what he says is true? Had Wink, disappeared? How do whole towns disappear? Who will help me? I have to do something, but what?"

"What does it say next?" asked Jude acting as if he wasn't at all interested.

"Nothing," said Jack with a sigh. "That's all I found."

"Do you mean to tell me that the journal entry has a couple entries, there's a hidden clue and that's all?" said Jude skeptically.

"Yes," said Jack. "And you could come up with something better?"

Jude sighed, slumping back in his chair.

"What do we do now?" said Henry putting on his already dried clothes.

"There are people who recently moved to Had's Hollow" said Valen after a few moments of silence. "Perhaps they know."

"People have moved here?" said Henry.

"Wait! That's it!" said Valen. "Jack you said no one knows we're here right?"

"Right," said Jack. "What are you on to?"

"Well, then how did those new people get here?" said Valen smartly. "Either you're wrong about all this or they've found another way in."

"What should we do?" said Henry.

"Let's go to their house and find out!" said Valen invigoratingly.

"Are you feeling different?" said Jude.

"Different?" said Valen putting his dry clothes back on.

"Last time we saw you," continued Jude, "you didn't seem well."

"Yeah," said Henry in agreement. "You look—uh . . . *healthier*."

"Well, that's because I've never been on such an adventure before," said Valen though he did feel better physically. "Ready?"

"Don't you think it's too late?" said Jack concernedly.

"Late!?" said Valen. "There is no time to waste. Come on now. Get your stuff and let's go."

The four of them were ready and out the door in moments. The snow was still pouring down. It was knee high at that point and quite hard to walk through. They trudged on. After quite some time they managed at last to get to the Voors' house.

The boys stood in front of a towering wooden door with a shabby archway looming above. Valen looked in through the tall windows to the left of the door. The lamps were all out.

"Don't you think it's too late to knock?" said Henry looking nervously around as he rubbed his arms desperately trying to stay warm.

"Look at this?" said Jack bending down in the snow. "There is blood here on the ground."

"It looks like there was some kind of struggle," said Henry.

"It was probably some animal," said Jude indifferently.

"These are a man's footprints," said Jack peering through his glasses as if he was an experienced detective.

"Look!" shouted Henry pointing to the forest behind the Voors' house. "There is a bunch of people coming towards us on the path!" The boys looked in the direction Henry was gesturing and sure enough he was right. A crowd of men and women, children and dogs were all moving slowly but steadily towards them.

"They're shouting something!" said Jack putting his hand up to his ear.

"It sounds like they're chanting something about kidnappers!" said Valen.

And he was right. As the mob moved closer and closer it was quite evident what they were yelling.

"Kidnappers! Kidnappers! Kidnappers!" they shouted as Mr. Grimm led an angry mob of Winkers, wielding clubs, knives and farm tools.

"Quick! Into the forest!" shouted Jack who knew the forest best. The boys followed him through the trees.

They watched from a distance as the mob, angry with torches and still chanting, stormed the front door of the house. A few burly men went inside. Mr. Grimm watched from his sleigh. His giant black horses snorted loudly as they tossed their coarse black manes in the icy night.

Minutes passed and nothing happened. Valen sat, watching from behind a huge fallen tree. Henry, Jack and Jude sat next to Valen as they too watched intensely, waiting for the men to come back out.

"They're not here!" shouted the men who came back out minutes later. "Someone must have tipped them off. What should we do now Grimm?"

"Anyone who finds these kidnappers and brings back my son," gurgled Mr. Grimm, "will receive a hefty reward from me. These Strangers have brought trouble upon us! You all know very well that we have lived in peace and quietness for many years, and now we have these cruel and vile people moving into our town, stealing our children! Corrupting our way of life! They should be arrested! Find them and bring me home my son!" Mr. Grimm turned the sleigh around and disappeared. In a moment he was gone.

Jude looked on at the sleigh as it faded away.

"Come on," said Jack grabbing his arm, "we have to go."

"Valen, you have to tell him the truth!" said Henry blowing warm air into his hands.

Valen looked back at the crowd of people, his heart beating fast. The flames from the torches lit up the wintry night.

"No!" he hissed.

"Why not?!" retorted Jack. "They think you've been kidnapped."

"Well, maybe I want that," said Valen miserably.

"What do you mean you want that?" said Jack oddly.

"It's something the man said," Valen said, his face looking paler than ever.

"What man?" said Jack.

"One of the *Strangers*,"said Valen. "I've been to see them already."

"What!?" said Jack, his eyes popping.

"Yes," said Valen. "I met a girl in the forest earlier—she brought me to their house." He put his hands up to his mouth to warm them. The snow above pounded them into the mounding piles.

"Well," said Jack uncertain of Valen's information. "What did he say?"

"He said my father is not my father," said Valen with confusion.

"What on earth do you *mean* he's not your father?" shouted Jack equally confused. "*Everyone has a father.*"

"I didn't stay long enough to find out the story," said Valen calmly.

"Well, it's all quite odd this whole thing," quipped Jack. "If you ask me, I'd say they're connected to the book I found in the Lighthouse."

"None of it makes sense to me either," said Valen. "It's just—" His words fell." My father—he's been acting odd—*very odd*." He paused and stared. The wind snapped at his face. "Oddly enough," said Valen at last, "I felt safer with the Strangers than I ever have."

"Well," Jack said. "It seems *somethin*g is going on. Something no one here has seen in a very long time, least of all me.

"Valen?" said Jack after a long pause. "Do you trust your father enough to go home?"

Valen paused for what seemed to be several long minutes."I guess I don't."

"I had a feeling you'd say that," said Jack quickly. "Now pay attention. We need to go warn my father, and then get out of sight for the night. He's down in the mines. Come on! Near the Cove at Old Man's Hat, just up the hill there is a hiding place," said Jack. "We're going to need all the help we can get." He pulled his hat over his head, stuffing his ears under the brim.

The boys bound through the forest like rabbits. They leapt over rocks and logs. Jack, who was leading the way, suddenly stopped, looking back to where they had come. Valen wasn't anywhere to be seen. In Jack's excitement, he had forgotten that Valen did not know his way. Suddenly, Valen and Henry tumbled down a small embankment and landed right at Jack's feet.

"Where did Jude run off to?" said Jack holding up his lantern. "This is no time to fool around. Where are you?" Jack held his lantern high and its light grabbed at the white splattered trees. But Jude was nowhere to be found.

"Never mind him," said Jack suspiciously. "He's funny that one. I never trusted him ever since we met down at the wharf last summer, when we went looking for the lost pirate ship. We are better off without him—at least for now."

"Pirate ship?" said Valen.

"Wailing Woman's Bluff," said Jack with great enthusiasm in his voice. "An unsolved mystery from long, long ago," said Jack. He turned saying, "Cargo—*Dragon's gold*."

The boys made their way down the edge of the coast line. The waves hammered the rocky shore. In the distance the moon was high above the horizon. All Valen could see for miles was the clear sky and a dark mass of frigid water, though a huge front sat hovering above the island dumping snow heavily. All of the sudden, a ship appeared in a cove a hundred yards or so from where they climbed. The other boys didn't see him, but Jude was listening eagerly behind the bushes about the gold.

"Look!" said Jack who was leading the way. "That's strange, isn't it?"

"What?" said Henry quite distracted as his foot was temporarily stuck in between two rocks. Valen reached down to help him.

"There," said Henry wiggling it a bit, "I've got it."

Henry bound towards Jack who stood on a mass of boulders which fell downwards spreading out and around towards the crashing surf. Then out of the churning waters a shadowy ship emerged. The moon glowed brightly and it was enough to reveal the color of the wood. Valen saw at once the inky color of the hull of the ship. The waves rocked the boat to and fro. Suddenly a tiny light began to glow at the bow of the ship and a sinister figure who held it walked about, alone. Soon more figures joined him. A dim light flashed near the shore.

"If this is still Had Wink," said Henry eager for adventure, "then I can't imagine what is at play."

"Agreed," said Jack then he pointed, "Look, there in the distance. Do you see that dark mass making its way towards the ship? Now! They have signaled each other. Something funny is going on and we are going to find out what it is! We had better continue on though as planned—for the moment" said Jack cautiously. "I am all for risking it, but we don't know what we're up against. Father is working deep below the surface tonight so I'll have to leave him a note with those in charge. We might need grown men to help us if it starts to get dangerous. We'll do good to have his protection. We have to go back up through the woods and stay on the trail. Better not to be seen by whoever these strange arrivals are." Then Jack took a long moment before saying, "There is a spot up off the trail on the other side of the cove where there is the entrance to the old abandoned mine. Below where the surf hits the rocks, we have our old fishing boat."

"Golly!" shouted Henry at once. "I forgot all about it! It's been since the summer that we last were in it. Seems like ages ago now."

Valen who hadn't seen much of the coastline of Had Wink before, imagined that there was all sorts of hidden gold in the cliffs and the caves. He had read enough that he knew very well that pirates had for thousands of years, loved hiding their gold on islands and the ship he saw now, *was* none other than a pirate ship.

They climbed down the mound of boulders they were standing on then back up a small path which wound its way past a few logs which had washed up centuries ago. Valen climbed on top of one, then walked the full length of it. The trail was much more concealed as the trees were quite thick. It was warmer too, Valen thought, as the wind from the sea weaved through the green pines. The path they were on wound up and down and made sharp right turns, then sharp left turns. It climbed high, then plummeted down near the shore line. Occasionally, Jack found a small opening in the trees where they could peer back down to where the ship was. Soon, they made it all the way around the cove and Jack took one last look where the ship was anchored before everyone agreed that they were safe.

"Now we are getting closer to the mines," said Jack adjusting his glasses. "Further up in the distance is the mouth of the Long Caves where my father is. Come on."

Valen followed Jack and Henry at once, up the long hill to where a small light began to emerge. Soon, the sound of men rang out. Horses whinnied and the noise of wagon wheels crunching rocks echoed through the trees. Men with flaming lamps seated on the brims of their hats were sitting around large fires. The smell of ale and roasting meat filled the air. Valen watched the men. They sang songs of family and of Had Wink. They sang songs of the women they loved and the strange things they found hidden in the secrets of the rocks. Valen felt his legs tremble for a second, before at last he could stand no more. The shaking became fierce and he started to sweat. His stomach turned viciously.

"Are you alright?" said Henry as Jack came over too."What is it?" he said.

"I don't know. It has been going on for some time," said Valen who felt he might collapse at any moment.

"You stay here then," said Jack. "You'll be alright for a minute?"

"I'll be fine," Valen grinned as much as he could bear it. He found a rock just off the path where he sat down. The snow started to fall harder. Jack and Henry were soon just shadows in the distance. In moments they disappeared into the mouth of the cave. Valen wriggled with nausea for what felt to be days. Really it was only a few minutes. Jack knew all of his father's fellow miners and it didn't take long for him and Henry to reappear. Valen started to feel miserably cold.

"I have given him a note to let him know about this ship," said Jack reappearing. "His break for the night comes soon. If something should happen to us, he'll come to our aid. I am sure of it."

Valen's nausea subsided and he began to feel normal again.

"Come on," said Jack. "We are going to find out what is happening on that ship."

Henry and Valen followed Jack back down the trail. This time they didn't go all the way back to where the mound of boulders lay. Jack found the old entrance to a mine which wound its way through the tall cliff below where they now stood. The moon shined brightly off the surface of the sea, then without warning, a mass of clouds covered the ocean and joined up with the snow clouds above them. The snow picked up in ferocity. Jack entered the cave first. Henry and Valen followed next.

It was pitch-black, but Jack still had his lantern and currently it grew brighter and brighter. "We don't have much oil left!" he shouted. "We need to at least get to the end of this shaft, just over there." The lantern went out with a gust of wind as they entered. Jack relit it and held it up to survey the mine. Valen saw the cave was dry. Old wooden boxes and bottles were stacked all around. A rusty railway track went down around a bend and disappeared into the thick blackness.

"Come on!" shouted Jack. "This way! We'll be able to sneak through down here. I've been down here a hundred times. The exit side of this cave goes out onto a cliff concealed above by a few trees. We have to use this ladder. My father has a boat down there, which we use for fishing. That's where he'll meet us should we find ourselves in trouble. Come on."

Valen felt better than he had, but he continued to wonder what it was that was making him so sick. He stepped over the rail and followed Henry and Jack down the long shaft. The lantern lit their way, which exposed a sharp drop. It was precarious, but the journey was over before Valen knew it.

Once they arrived at the bottom, they went outside and stood on the edge of a smaller cliff. Where they were just walking moments ago was now hundreds of feet above their heads. The snow pounded the sides of the tall white cliffs. In the distance the ship bobbed up and down in the swelling surf. Out of the noise of the crashing sea below, rose a chorus of voices. Valen heard a hideousness arising and he thought he heard his name with each crash of waves.

Without warning, Valen saw something else smeared on the edge of the side of the cliff. Some kind of foul smelling liquid. The voices grew. At last, Valen could make out what they were saying.

"It was that creature," roared one. "I saw him in the forest. It isn't as easy as we have been told. That foul thing cut me down to the bone. They're protecting him. Our orders are to kill him should the old man fail. It is our only chance."

"What is it Jack?" said Henry curiously bending down beside him.

"I'm not sure," said Jack looking at it very intently. "I've never seen anything like it before."

"That's because it's not from around here!" came a man's voice.

"What? Who?" said Henry looking around frantically. "Did you hear that? Where are you? Show yourself!"

All at once the man Valen was talking with earlier, appeared out of thin air.

"Wow!" said Henry awestruck. "How'd you do that?"

"I'm an Unseen," said Mr. Voors kneeling down next to Jack. "Your friend is right. This is not an animal from around here and those creatures moored out there are no friends either. Your friend Jude, where is he?"

"Jude?" said Jack. "I haven't the slightest clue."

"If those foul beasts have gotten to his mind before you," said Mr. Voors. "There isn't much you can do. It is so easy to believe their whispers. Bludblax." The name was horrible to hear. Valen felt as if he had just heard news of someone's death. "They are preparing to invade your island."

Poof! Someone else appeared. This time it was Murrin.

"Murrin!" said Valen. "But how?" Then—poof! Mrs. Voors appeared. Jack gazed up at her for a long time for her beauty was deep.

"How'd you do that?" said Henry extremely interested in how three people appeared out of nowhere."

"Oh, I hate explaining," said Mrs. Voors.

"Well, be thankful that we are on a mission—it's been a while now—and be kind. He doesn't know," said Mr. Voors standing back up.

"I don't know what?" said Henry.

"As I began to say earlier," said Mr. Voors, "we are Unseens."

"Yes, but would you explain to me how you can appear suddenly out of nowhere?" said Henry excitedly. "What I mean sir is, could you tell me exactly how to do it so I can learn too?"

"It's not something you can learn," said Mrs. Voors who had finally adjusted her coat and hair to her liking. She walked back into the cave.

"This is all very odd," said Jack scratching his head. "You people appear out of nowhere and . . ."

"I know it's very strange," said Mr. Voors. "I'll explain it all later when I can. First, we need to get back to the top. We have limited time. Quick! We had better go and prepare ourselves for battle. There are more of these foul creatures out there."

"There is a cave, a hideout," said Jack thinking quickly, "just beyond. Come on. Over here." The path was narrow and they all hugged the cliff tightly. After a hundred feet or so and many looks down towards the crashing sea, they finally found the opening. Valen immediately understood why it was a hideout. Once they were deep enough inside the cave, the lanterns were lit and all around lay bones and skulls. Murrin jumped. When they journeyed in, Valen did not notice at the time, but they had many several turns so that once the lanterns were lit the light was concealed from the outside.

"Can we light a fire?" said Henry blowing into his hands. "I'm freezing."

"We can barely even see each other," said Jack trying to squint through his glasses. "Our oil is nearly gone."

Instantly Mrs. Voors lit a fire and the entire cave was filled with a warm gust of heat.

"How did you do that?" said Henry intrigued by the powers they possessed.

"All right," began Mr. Voors. "Now listen to me. We have limited time. The mob will return momentarily, though I'm not really worried about them too much. I'm worried about the Bludblax and Grimm—Grimm especially. His power has grown beyond what we may be able to control. He has called that ship since Valen escaped. I have placed an invisibility shield around the mouth of the cave, but it will only last so long. The power that these creatures have is terrible. They are hunting for us all now, but what they want most of all is you—" He peered at Valen.

"Me? An invisibility shield?" asked Valen.

"It is sacred magic given to us by the King himself, magic which can only be used in desperate times. It is a magic beyond your world."

"King? Magic? What about the lighthouse?" said Jack. "Do you know about that?"

"Yes," Henry jumped in. "And do you know anything about why no one knows about Had Wink?"

"Sit down," ordered Mr. Voors. "We are here to help you. Valen your death is near but not if we can help you. Grimm has purchased your grave."

"Grave?" said Valen wondering why anyone wanted him dead.

"Yes," said Mr. Voors. "He has been digging one for you. And you'll be in it soon enough, unless we have something to say about it. We come from the Golden Woods of Noroth if you want to know. A land far, far away, but closer than you might think." He paused. "Now you boys listen carefully to me," he continued matter-of-factly. "I cannot explain everything to you in this short amount of time, but you have to trust me. You *must* trust me. It is crucial that you do! At this moment Dr. Grimm suspects us as being from another world. He is right!"

"Another world?" said Jack with a raised brow.

"Yes, another world," said Mr. Voors. "Now I need to tell you something that is very important. So, no more interruptions, please; time is not on our side." The boys nodded. "As I was saying—Valen, your father—well not your father, rather Mr. Grimm—he is not who he says he is. He is a liar! And a murderer! We believe he has just murdered your professor."

"What? How? When?" said Valen.

"You know when," said Mr. Voors. "Did not your father bring the professor's cane back to the mansion?"

"Yes, you are right," said Valen sitting down. "I can't believe I didn't see it. I have grown more and more suspicious of him . . ."

"He has plans for you that are too horrible to imagine. If you want to live, you'll come with us. You are no longer safe here in Had Wink. You must leave at once! You must follow my instructions, precisely. The only way out of Had Wink is through the barn behind Grimm Mansion," continued Mr. Voors.

"*That* old barn!?" blurted Valen. "That hasn't been used for a hundred years."

"Ordinary things are not always what they seem. Now," quipped Mr. Voors. "You must go and find the stone horse in the barn of the Grimm Mansion. When you reach the door you will be met by the creature Veeps. He will guide us the rest of the way. We have to get there before more Bludblax return! Quick! We have very little time!"

Presently, they heard a voice at the entrance of the mine.

"The mob!" said Jack rushing over towards the door concealing his face just enough. But, as Jack turned towards the light, he saw the mob they had seen earlier coming up the path.

"They can't have gone far!" shouted one very gruff man. "Grimm's got gold waiting for us! Search in there!"

Jack hid in between two very large wooden beams which supported the ceiling. Without warning, he heard another familiar voice which he knew at once to be his—

"Father!" said Jack greatly relieved. Jack decided to protect his friends and draw them away from the cave.

"Jack? What are you doing out here in weather like this?"

"Did you get my letter?" said Jack.

"That's what we've been wondering, too," said a gruff voiced man. "We heard he was with the Grimm boy. Someone seen them with your boy they did."

"I don't know what you are talking about," said Jack straight-faced. "I have been looking for him just like you."

"My son is an honorable boy," said Jack's father stepping in between Jack and the man. "You aren't accusing him of foul-play are you, Dag? You lay aside your personal grievances with me in this matter."

"I'll lay aside what I want, when I want Thore," said Dag. "I've been waiting for this moment for a long while."

"I have no quarrel with you," said Thore tightening his fists. "But if it's a fight you want you can have it."

Dag put down his lantern in the mounding snow. The first fist from Dag flew through the air and Thore dodged it perfectly.

"Get him father," said Jack, "Hit him! Hit him."

Another barrage of punches flew at Thore, one landed on his forehead, the other on his chin. Thore, not as big as Dag, but quick on his feet and quite lean from working in the mines for years, had the strength that Dag did not. Dag was big from too much ale and his waist showed it. Thore threw a fist square in his chest and Dag nearly lost all his wind, but then he came rushing back.

The mob, with their clubs, lanterns and swords rang out into the night. Wind and snow swirled around the glowing torches. Jack winced at the brutal noises which echoed down the abandoned mine.

Then, Jack remembered Valen, Henry and the Voors. He stepped back into the tunnel and went back to where he last saw them. Jack's father protected the entrance.

"If we are going to escape, now is our chance. The Bludblax are coming. They are preparing their invasion," said Mr. Voors. "We need to move fast! I placed a shield near the coast too, but it will not last long. The Bludblax know we are here. They are busy hacking away at it this very moment. Hurry! How do we get out of here?"

"Can you take out that mob?" said Jack.

"We cannot," said Mr. Voors. "We have our allegiances—our rules, they have been laid down for us. We cannot harm a human; not now anyway. If our powers come close to you, if we battle with the Bludblax now, we may have casualties. It would be too terrible a day, should even one human fall on our account. We must find another way out. Do you know another way?"

"There is another passageway that leads back up into the forest," said Jack. "It sits higher up above Had Wink. From there we can navigate our way towards the barn behind Grimm Mansion."

"Lead the way," said Mr. Voors.

"What about my father?" said Jack. "He is out there fighting alone. He is a strong man, but he cannot fight all of them on his own."

"You must decide," said Mr. Voors. "We must leave at once. Grimm is hunting for Valen. There is no time left." Jack started to speak when Mr. Voors picked up a skull which lay at his feet. He ripped the jawbone off and a strange gray light began to hover over it. The bone grew twice its size. Jack went back to where his father was. He was still standing—enduring the blows of Dag. Jack peered his head out. The light from the lanterns did not illuminate where he stood. Suddenly, Thore fell headlong and landed at the entrance to the cave. Cheers rang out. Everyone was focused on Dag. His fat stomach bulging out from under his too small vest. His beard matted down with blood. His long hair fell behind his head. He raised his fists again. The wind grabbed the cheers of the mob and sent them rushing into Jack's ears.

"Father?" said Jack. Blood brightened the snow. "Father?" Jack took off his glasses. Hot tears welled up, but he fought them back. He remembered what his father taught him about crying, about being a man. It wasn't that crying was bad, it was what to do about it once the pain had happened. Jack had to make a choice. "Father, I brought you this." Jack threw the jawbone to him, then he began to move. First it was his leg that came up, then it was his hands. The crowd died down. Dag turned around. Jack saw what he thought was a grin and what he heard as, 'go'. The last thing Jack remembered was his father picking up the jawbone and smashing it across Dag Weezol's head. He didn't have time to see the rest of the match, but was sure he would be alright now that he had proper defense.

Valen, Jack and Henry led the Voors down the mine, past the shaft which went down to the beach where Jack's boat was docked. The tunnel grew quite dim, but the Voors' clothing seemed to glow. Mr. Voors lit a torch of sorts. Jack, Henry and Valen lit their remaining oil. Valen began to feel an intense bout of nausea. The tunnel was long and the air was frigid. They climbed up the long shaft. The air was dense. Soon, the night sky appeared above them and Valen's ears tuned to a fell cry which he could not make out at first. Valen could scarcely bare it. He covered his ears. Soon, they were near the top. The sounds became more unbearable. A gust of wind slammed the company. Valen shuddered. The screams grew. They made it to the top at last. Down below, Had Wink glowed like a tiny crown. Giant clouds swirled above their heads. Snow hammered them this way and that. Strong gusts of wind grabbed, pulled and tore at their clothes. Valen was feeling horribly weak. The Voors' giant black dog was outside sniffing earnestly. Suddenly a long howl rose into the night. Valen saw at once that he was no ordinary hound. Indeed he seemed to be nearly as big as a bear.

"Into those trees! Now!" shouted Mr. Voors. "They will provide some protection for a little while. Bludblax hate all living things."

The three boys hurried along the trail as best they could, considering the immense amount of snow that surrounded them. Mr. and Mrs. Voors and Murrin followed behind looking to the sky. Then, without warning came the pinnacle of the scream Valen had been hearing—a horrid screeching, squealing noise.

***"HHHHREEEEKKKKKKK!!!
HHHHREEEEEEEKKKKKK!!!"***

Valen covered his ears in agony. Jack and Henry did too. The noise intensified.

"What is that!?" shouted Valen looking back to Mr. Voors for an explanation.

"Go!" he said picking Valen up by the back of his coat. "We need to be moving faster. There is great evil here tonight. Foul beasts and creatures are hunting you!"

"Hunting me?" said Valen.

"I told you —*you are wanted*—dead," said Mr. Voors. "Now—*run*!"

The sickness fled. Instantly Valen felt his body surge with energy. He felt as though he could run over anything and run forever. His feet picked up fast and light and he began to see clearer than he had seen before. He saw hideous shapes above the island. Monstrous beasts with horns and claws and thick robes with pale fingers and lanterns which burned dark ink. They were consuming all light, the moon and the stars, and the tiny lights below. His heart pounded. Then another wave of sickness swept over him and he nearly fell off a cliff. He stumbled as Jack came to his aid. Yet, again he felt another surge of strength. His ears could hear the fell creatures calling his name.

"Vaaaallllleeeennnnn," they hissed. "Vaaaallllleeeennnn."

Jack and Henry were soon far behind as Valen ran powerfully through the thick snow. Moments had passed and soon he could see his house. He continued on through the forest, walking slowly and cautiously now as he waited for the others to catch up. He leaned up against a tree that had a layer of snow splattered up and down the face of it. His heart beat fast and his breaths were deep and heavy. Then, at that moment, two giant glowing, silver hands appeared out of nowhere and snatched him and pulled him behind a tree.

CHAPTER FIVE

# BRIDGE THROUGH THE SKY

Valen tried to scream but could not find his voice. He looked around frantically. Then the Voors suddenly appeared by his side. Moments later, Jack and Henry came heaving heavily through the trees, clutching their sides.

"Where's Valen?" asked Henry practically looking right at Valen.

Valen was looking right at them, but couldn't say anything. Giant hands were wrapped around him. Just then, someone was heard in the distance. Someone was following him with a lantern hung high above their head.

"Oh, it's only Jude," said Henry despondently. "Just the person to ruin a good adventure."

"Where did you go?" said Jack.

"Yes," said Henry, "where did you go? Strange, you showing up now."

"I slipped on the edge of the cliff," said Jude. "If one of you had come sooner, I would have been with you the whole time. By the way, a ship has docked. Might be our best chance to get off this dreadful island."

"That ship is no friend. Shhhh! Bludblax!" hissed Mr. Voors. "Stay low! They don't know we're here." Without warning another eerie screech penetrated the cold winter night.

*"HHHHREEEEEEEEKKKKK!!!"*

Five hideous creatures with hoofed feet and a nasty stench landed not far from where they stood. Mr. Voors grabbed Henry and Valen by the coat and Mrs. Voors snatched up Jack and Jude. In an instant they vanished.

"You know the rules," said Murrin boldly. "We cannot bring them into our dimension."

"Quiet!" shouted Mr. Voors. "We must protect them!"

In a twinkling they disappeared. Jack could see as if behind a great veil that covered the whole town. Shadows of the beasts surrounded them. The air became thick and menacing. Suddenly, a huge blinding silver light flashed like lightning on the distant horizon and lit up the forest. The snow looked like meteors. One of the creatures howled and was sent flying face down in the snow. Then it happened again. Another massive flying silver ball that looked like a comet, crashed loudly into a nearby tree. It was a magnificent sight. A plume of smoke billowed up into the air. Bits of silver streaks painted the night sky. Splinters from the vast tree shot out everywhere like a barrage of artillery. Snow came crashing down to the ground, burying two of the other creatures. A strange short creature with the largest hands Valen had ever seen, scolded himself.

"Confounded!" he spat, looking at his humongous hands which glowed like the moon. "I hate missing!"

"Who are you?" said Valen.

"I am Veeps of Dorodroos." He bowed.

Mr. Voors and Murrin suddenly reemerged out of thin air. Jack and Henry dropped to the ground. Mr. Voors who had two small spears drawn, which he now wielded as swords, dueled viciously with his enemies. The creatures had snow which fell from their wings. An icy fog curled up from under their nostrils. Valen thought that as the snow poured down they would all surely freeze to death, but a very curious thing began to happen instead. All over golden spirals began leaving the trees, deer fell over dead. Rabbits went to sleep. Foxes got stuck in their holes. Valen heard the growl of a bear and it too stopped. Valen saw a golden bear flying through the air. As each tree stooped over, everything became the color of bone. Valen reached down and felt a squirrel which had fallen out of the tree. It was hard like bone too!

"It *is* bone," said Mr. Voors as if he had read Valen's mind. "They steal all good things and whatever they touch, it becomes bone, cold hard, unbreakable bone."

"How did you know that is what I was thinking?" said Valen.

"Just a guess," said Mr. Voors. "We have seen this since the Beginning. It is part of the *Deep Poison* that has infected your world."

"The *Deep*—?" but Valen did not finish his sentence.

His attention was now on Mr. Voors who responded instinctively as he set up a small glowing shield. The tiny creature who was protecting Valen, sent off another blinding silver comet into one of the creatures again. But this wasn't enough to stall the Bludblax.

"I'll set up another shield!" shouted Mr. Voors. "But we need to get to the horse and wagon! Go!"

Then immediately Mr. Voors drew out a long shiny dagger and thrust it into the ground. Suddenly a giant umbrella shape of silvery dust burst into the air creating an impenetrable wall. The rest of the group began to run back through the forest following the little creature as he waddled quickly along. They ran fervently through the snow, dodging branches and jumping over downed trees and rocks. The Voors' dog howled. Valen, Henry, Jack and Jude, tried hopelessly to keep up with the creature as it continued to shoot fiery silver comets out of his hands. Within a few moments they reached a high stone wall. Round the side of it was a creaky arched wooden door, which the creature quickly opened.

"Quickly!" shouted Veeps pointing with his massive hand. "Get in!" Out of nowhere appeared Dr. Grimm. Bright lanterns illuminated the night and the falling snow. He had a staff which was shooting black wispy streams of smoke into the night. It was unbearably dreadful as it seemed to be giving the creatures some kind of fortification, enabling them to carry on. Veeps deflected it as best he could, but Grimm was getting closer to Valen and as he grew closer Valen became weaker.

"Go!" shouted Veeps. "We must lock this gate! We must have time. Grimm is coming."

Valen looked around and just in the distance stood a large old weather beaten barn. The trees from the forest which went down to the sea lay just beyond. The bright white snow and deep green moss hung over the wooden planks. It leaned slightly to one side. They opened the large barn doors as quickly as they could and soon found themselves shrouded in shadows. Veeps' hands glowed brightly enough for them to see. For a brief moment they had lost Grimm. The snow had been howling and whipping so hard that as quick as they forged tracks they were filled in.

At the far back of the barn stood a shovel near a hole which was uncovered and sticking out of the ground. In it lay a beautiful stone horse. Valen noticed that someone had been digging it up. His mind raced back to the day he saw his father with dirt on his hands. The horse was majestic, having an ornately carved mane. It was missing one hoof.

"Do you know how to ride a horse?" said Veeps. Valen observed he had on a funny hat, a vest, bright golden bracelets, long fleshy goat ears and what looked to Valen to be quite an angry, miserable face.

"Do you mean *that*?" said Valen as he clutched his side looking over to where the horse lay. "It's a stone horse lying in a hole." He scowled.

"There is always more to things than they first appear," said Veeps. "Now can you ride or can you not?"

"I'll try," said Valen bravely.

"Good, quickly," said Veeps. " There is no time to waste. Voors, fetch the wagon."

Mr. Voors went over towards a wagon that looked very rickety. He picked up the pole which was connected to the harness of the horse and pushed it from the back and drug it over to where the horse lay, but it proved too heavy. "Boys," he shouted, "if you want to live to see another day, you had better come over here at once and help me push this thing to where the horse is."

"But," doubted Valen, "what *are* we doing? An old wagon about to fall apart and a stone horse—"

"Enough blabbering," said Veeps as the wagon moved closer. Mr. Voors began connecting the horse's harness to the wagon.

"This is peculiar," said Jack, "or ridiculous. I do not know which one. I have to agree with Valen." And just as soon as he said this the horse began to move. It slowly got up out of the hole and all the dirt that lay upon it fell off. It made a crunching and popping noise. The horse went from stone to a shining white. A long white mane appeared. The wagon which moments ago looked as if it was going to collapse looked now as though it had just come out of a carpenters' woodshop, its wood bristling with golden grain. The idea to throw the bag he had been carrying over the horse was an easy one. Valen could not bear its weight anymore.

"How on earth?" said Henry in a stupor.

"What is going on I wonder?" said Jack inquisitively.

"Just get in! Let's get out of here!" said Jude.

"Is it real?" asked Valen quite shocked.

"It could not get any more real, now could it?" quipped Veeps adjusting his hat. The horse let out a giant snort.

"Yes, but—" said Valen suddenly, clutching his side. He writhed with a massive pain and stumbled. "I—"

"Valen is fading," said Veeps jumping up onto the wagon. All the boys jumped up, too.

Valen stumbled backwards and Mr. Voors caught him. Suddenly, fell voices rang out across the windswept roof.

"They are coming closer," said Veeps. "The fool did not even know where to look. It was here all along."

"What?" said Valen.

"Yes," said the boys in unison. "What?"

"I cannot explain everything at this moment," said Veeps. "Nor can the Voors." Veeps looked over at Mr. Voors. "Lock the other doors. The Threshold can only be crossed for a little while longer; if we do not make it, it will be our certain end." The creature looked to where they had come in. "I will go and open these ones," he continued and went to the other side of the barn. Suddenly, the voices outside rose. The same violent screeches they had heard before, rang out.

Valen held onto the horse as best he could, though he struggled a bit. He had never ridden a horse before and he was feeling sicker with each minute that passed, but somehow he managed.

"Slowly," said the horse.

"What did you just say?" said Valen.

"Slowly," said the horse again.

"Do you mean you talk?" said Valen.

"Well, if you mean by my saying 'slowly'," said the horse, "why then yes, of course, but we haven't time to have a proper conversation as it were. Best be off. My name is Fin."

"Nice to meet you," said Valen feeling very strange to have just had a conversation with a horse.

Everyone was now in the wagon, except Veeps. The voices that were calling Valen's name, grew louder. The wind whipped harder and harder. Fin whinnied and snorted and stomped its feet once or twice and slowly, steadily, brought the wagon out of the barn. The snow howled and poured into their faces. Valen shook from the frigid air. Snow pounded his sunken face. He held on tight as he could to Fin's mane but nearly fell off. He heard at last Dr. Grimm enter the other side of the barn. Mr. Voors having locked the doors did not work. Fin pulled the wagon and all his passengers as quickly as he could, but deep frozen ruts gave them a fight. Finally, they made headway and all at once a shot of warm air and Spring blew across Fin's great back. Valen looked ahead. A long curving road behind to large doors, which went up into the sky appeared out of the tapering snow. A beautiful ornate and mighty stone bridge spanning a long valley below, also came into focus. The warm air blew gently and pushed back the cold and bitter wind. A little light appeared, but still it was dim. They were between a sort of half light. Fin pulled one more time as powerfully as his stiff legs could (he hadn't used them in hundreds of years) and at last the wagon began to climb up the long bridge. Veeps dismounted and headed off Dr. Grimm as the wagon rolled on. Valen glanced back and saw at once, not his father; but a desperate, frightened, and skittish man. A panic shot across Dr. Grimm's eyes as though he were losing more than his son. And it was also in that moment that Valen wondered if what Mr. Voors said was true. As he looked back to where Veeps stood fighting Dr. Grimm, he didn't see his father at all; only a man who kept wishing to *do* something to him or with him. His thought slipped away. He continued to look over his shoulder and could see Veeps fighting Dr. Grimm and the Bludblax. It was struggling terribly. Finally, Veeps unleashed a volley of silver comets which all at once sent Dr. Grimm soaring down the road where he landed into a thick tree. Dr. Grimm lay still but only for a moment.

Fin pulled the wagon up the cobbled road. Then out of the clouds two giant doors appeared. Mr. Voors got down and opened them. Screams still floated towards them.

"We must cross the Threshold before it is too late! Quickly, Grimm is still coming," said Mrs. Voors, scanning the clouds. Fin pulled hard and soon they were through. The creature shut the doors and ran after the wagon. Fin ran too, picking up great speed and suddenly his foot regrew. Valen grabbed at the reins, for even though he had never ridden a horse before it seemed the most natural thing to do. He pulled hard and the horse nearly came to a stop but then Fin decided to keep moving, onwards and up, into the sky. Veeps had finally caught up to the wagon and jumped onto the back of it. They were now in the sky above Had Wink. Valen looked down. Fin's hooves trotted along the stone road. "A road in the sky?" wondered Valen aloud. The huge doors stood closed behind them, but now the sky grew thick like fog and the doors faded. Everything felt heavy. Then what appeared as fog at first was really some kind of layer between Had Wink and where they were now. The bridge went on for some time, before at last they came to a cliff. Valen forced Fin to stop. But, Valen's strength was weakening and he was unable to hold Fin back—Something was drawing Fin onward. As Valen's strength faded, he yielded to Fin's lead and the entire company fell headlong over a cliff. As the wagon descended, it was as if Valen was on a ship taking on water in a wide and deep ocean that was now all around him. As they descended, Valen still on Fin, the light and dark thickened. Several items they had stowed away in the wagon fell all around. It looked as though darkness lay over a thin layer of light. Valen could scarcely make out where they were going when all at once they nearly fell out of the misty ocean they were now in. They traveled through a thin layer of light, then thick darkness, more light, then darkness again. Valen thought it felt like a large veil of some sort which he was all tangled up in. What appeared to be the bottom was actually the top of where he now looked. And what looked to be a veil was actually the sky. Below them appeared bright blue flowers that layered the fields as many as the stars. The flowers were a deeper blue than Valen had ever seen. They looked to be capturing starlight as they pulsed with light. Fin galloped briefly and Valen found they were quite near a hill. Actually, they were right on top of it. The wagon's wheels quickened and they soon touced down. Valen looked down and saw in the middle of the field an dark gray colored candle which had a bright flame flickering above it. He saw it was made of metal. The weather was cool and refreshing. It was certainly springtime or something very like spring. The smells which filled the land, smelled as if they had always been there.

Still feeling weaker and feeling at once that he might fall, Valen grabbed Fin's mane and dismounted slowly. More bright glowing blue flowers spread out around his feet. Valen looked over to where Jack was. He was stooping down to pick some up. The shore of a large lake appeared in the distance across the darkened landscape and the moon shimmered off of it. Valen looked up at the moon and that was when he noticed something quite strange. It was the moon, only it was the *other* side of the moon. It was the Otherside of the sky.

"Where are we?" said Henry rubbing his head stupidly, but feeling rather relieved.

"Eoorthe, a world just beyond yours, not to be confused with earth. It is the Place Above. The Hovering World. The High Heaven. The Deeper Realm. It has many, many names. Very few know about it, very few know it exists. Those who do not know it exists, only believe that *they* exist, but it exists whether or not you want it to exist and whether or not you believe it *to* exist. Though, it is known as Fairee by my people," spouted Veeps, blowing lightly on his hands. "You can call it Eoorthe."

"What are you doing?" asked Jack inquiringly.

Veeps eyed him suspiciously. Then he smiled toothily. His eyes were big and a little droopy, but a deep kindness was in them.

"My hands are hot," he said.

Valen noticed the bottle that he had picked up in the lighthouse, had fallen out of his bag. He rummaged through the bag, but couldn't find it.

"What is it?" said Jack noticing Valen's frantic face.

"Nothing—just this—" his sentenced fell off. There was no more hiding what he had taken. Valen stood staring at the bottle where it lay just below the grass. Jack walked over to it. Valen bent down and picked it up. Then, he spotted the key in the grass, but for a reason he couldn't explain, he drew attention to the bottle instead. He didn't know why he was unwilling to reveal the key too. Somehow he felt it was very, very dangerous. Instead he drew attention to the bottle. The diary Professor Lewis had given him sat undisturbed in the bag draped over Fin's majestic back.

"Stay away!" said Veeps, but no sooner had he said this than Jude who had seen it too, ran towards it. He picked it up and tossed it into the air as though they were about to play a game. That's when it happened. The bottle came crashing down onto a rock, bounced, and landed on its side. Veeps went over to it. Valen, Jack, and Jude stood around him. Henry came rushing over. The Voors too.

"Stand back at once!" said Veeps. The bottle began to spin and it seemed to grow. The glass expanded as though it was soft and not glass at all. It appeared an invisible glassblower was blowing air into it. Suddenly a wispy shape rammed and knocked itself against the inside of the bottle. The blue flowers surrounding them dimmed. Veeps knelt down. He picked it up cautiously. Everyone stood transfixed. Valen's heart thumped. Then all at once, whatever the thing inside was, broke the glass and a deafening scream rang out. It rose into the night, cracking trees and splitting rocks in two. The wind grew steadily and a storm suddenly swept in and thunder rolled through the thick clouds. Valen felt at once a shot of fear, like an arrow run through him.

"Arm yourselves!" shouted Veeps. But Valen and certainly his new friends, had no weapons. Then the being went from a wispy shape of smoke to take on the form of a body. Veeps shot at it at once and it soared across the meadow several paces. The Voors came nearer, their weapons drawn. Valen wished there was something, anything he could do, but he felt weak and the weakness seemed to grow. His energy plummeted and he nearly fell. The creature now grew to hideous proportions. Valen clutched his frail body. Henry came to prop him up. Veeps was now dueling with the creature. He fired again and again knocking the creature back into a high cliff at the edge of the meadow. Silver light lit up the night sky like a meteor shower. Veeps shot one comet after another, but then the creature drew out a thick iron chain and snapped it as an angry horseman. It fell down to the ground and shook the very ground where Valen now sat, his hands clutched to his sides. This creature had an effect on him which crippled him further. Veeps fired again, this time the comet which flew out of his hands was ten times the ones he had shot moments ago. Veeps whole body convulsed. The power which Veeps possessed shook him mightily with each shot. Valen saw that it was a great struggle for the tiny creature to conjure up so much energy. Valen saw what Veeps had seen all along and which he had been laboring to break. The creature wore a dark thick metal breastplate. Veeps fired at it again and again and as he hit it in that spot repeatedly, it slowly began to crack. The creature stirred just as a tree about to fall. The crack appeared small at first, then spread. Mr. Voors' shield shined bright and again an umbrella of massive proportions guarded the boys. Murrin and her mother stayed near where the boys sat. Mr. Voors and Veeps battled the creature bravely. Valen peered closer and saw two shining silver javelins which Mr. Voors wielded impressively. Mr. Voors jumped high and stabbed the creature in his neck, then again in its belly. Again he used it as a powerful club, lopping the creature across its piggish face and it shook the creature so hard that it nearly sent it crashing down. Then Veeps knelt and his hands, hot as they were, rung out a comet of such power that it blasted the creature nearly to pieces. Its breastplate shattered with a terrible *boom*! Mr. Voors thrust both his spears into the creature's chest and drew them out. It staggered, then at last fell with such a force that the small lake shook with waves.

Valen lay still, relieved that the creature was dead. He felt his energy come back a little, but he also felt as though he was fading quickly. It was odd, except for the creature Veeps and Mr. Voors had just killed—

"Who are you?" said the boys simultaneously in disbelief.

"WHAT was that?" cringed Henry.

"I have told you my name already," began Veeps. "And you should know that I am a dwundlegob from the Woods of Dorodroos. I am here to protect you." He bowed. "That is the first of the many thousands of wicked beings, which have been hidden all around your world since the Beginning. Now, it has finally begun. For now, I cannot say more. Please, if you will, follow me," he said gazing up at the sky, and slung his bag over his shoulder. He began walking. "We must be going."

"Wait!" said Jack. "How do we get back? And, what do you mean, 'it has finally begun?'"

"We must get back to our fathers and mothers!" said Henry suddenly. "They will be wondering where we are."

"Yes," said Valen. "What's happening? Where are you taking us?"

"You will not see them for a while," said Veeps solemnly. "I am very sorry, but you are needed now. You cannot go back until it is all over. It began with this pitiful creature. Many chances he had to turn away from evil. He hungered for good things, but only went round the wrong way to get them. He has lost his reason. His soul has become permanently twisted. His imagination, darkened. Though, there is always hope and love conquers even the darkest things; but for him, I cannot say where love or hope will end for him. I am no judge. Can you help him?"

The boys looked over at the creature. It had a pig's head, a massive spider abdomen and the legs of a man. Then the creature who seemed so powerful and terrible a moment ago stood up into the shape of a hunched bird—but Valen noticed he was not alive at all, not in any real sense. He was a dead man. A hideous, evil man. He hissed and snorted, then crawled on all fours through the neighboring trees, south-east of the Iron Candle.

"What in Had Wink was that thing?" said Henry. "What's happened?"

"I cannot tell you all at this moment, only that it is time," said Veeps.

"Can you please tell us what this is all about?" said Jack. Valen would have spoken more, but his pain had intensified.

"The War has begun," said Veeps. "That creature you just saw, it was because of Valen taking that bottle which has set these course of events into motion. There is no stopping it now," concluded Veeps.

"You caused this?" said Jude curiously.

"What?!" said Jack.

"Yes," agreed Henry. "What *are* you talking about?"

Valen felt he would pass out at any moment.

Veeps stood there, his impatience growing by the minute, but Mr. Voors spoke first.

"We *must* go!" said Mr. Voors. "I agree with Veeps. I fear something else is coming."

"Valen?" said Veeps calmly. "Did you drink something that Grimm gave you?"

"Only a few drops," said Valen. "I dropped the bottle."

"A few drops of the potion Grimm gave you is enough to kill any powers you have left," said Veeps.

"Powers?" said Valen awkwardly.

"You have tasted the fruit of the Forlin Tree," said Veeps intensely. "For the moment you feel fine, but ruin will befall you if we do not go quickly."

"Forlin Tree?" said Valen confusedly. "What are you talking about? My father was a doctor. He was trying to cure me!"

"Enough! There is no time to discuss this! We must fly! Come, I know who can truly cure you," stammered Veeps. He glanced around. "But, if we do not go quickly, you will die. We had better be out of sight if the Bludblax or Grimm come from somewhere else. He and they are nasty business. Eoorthe is a mysterious place full of many creatures. We would not do well if we were caught by the Othoritees."

"What are the Othor—?" but Henry couldn't finish the word. "What exactly do you mean sir?"

Suddenly Mr. Voors came rushing over to Veeps.

"We must go!" Mr. Voors shouted. "We are safe, but only for a little while."

"All of your questions will be answered soon enough," said Veeps. "Now, move!"

"We need to go at once!" said Mr. Voors forcefully. He was looking around the edges of the long ridges in the distance. "The Othoritees will be on the move before too long."

"Just as I have said!" exclaimed Veeps, heading for the dim forest North of the Iron Candle. Valen looked and saw its branches with gnarled and knotted looking trees.

"Follow me. We have someone to meet."

Veeps dashed across a long field and disappeared under branches. Valen felt wonderful at points, for the past several hours and that awful excruciating pain racked his body. He knew something was not quite right. Then, all at once he began to feel as if a poison was spreading through out his entire body. The weakness he thought he had finally been rid of suddenly returned. But this time it was much worse. He clutched his head. But, he pressed on. Slowly, he followed Veeps. The others followed, too.

"We are not safe," began Veeps once they joined company under trees. "There is an Evil in our land that has taken up residence. The Lightlessness is all around us. Long ago your world was whole. For many thousands of years your world and ours has been split. Elves, Dwundlegobs, Hagbags, Mightys, Men, Knights, all are scattered, some have betrayed the King."

"Do not despair," said Mr. Voors as he moved a branch out of his way. "Not all of us are wretched."

"That is true," said Veeps who was walking steadily along a trail that had long been unused.

Looking down, Valen noticed that there were stone slabs covered over by dirt and vines.

"This was once a real road?" he said, stepping over a fallen tree. He suddenly felt a wave of the most excruciating nausea he had ever known.

"Yes," said Veeps with a sadness in his voice. "We are at near the once mighty City of Sorothgar, home of the Seven Rulers of the Western Kingdom. There are few left now who are alive to speak of its glory. It has faded into legend mostly."

Veeps kept walking. Massive stone statues laid crumbling in the forests surrounding them. The others followed closely behind. Mr. Voors was at the back of the group, looking around cautiously for anything suspicious.

"Where are we going?" asked Henry curiously.

"We cannot stay here," said Veeps. "Othoritees are sometimes hard to detect."

"Why should we trust you?" said Jack suddenly. "I mean, it seems reasonable to infer that we should, given that you saved us already, but;—"

"Your concern is understandable," said Mrs. Voors who hadn't said anything for quite some time. "There are many things to say of course. In fact, there are many questions that we have ourselves. There are many things that we or you, do not understand. In time you'll see. We are going to visit—"

"We hope it is true, but it is not who we are meeting now. The man Mr. Voors speaks of? I dare not speak his name just yet," said Veeps sharply. " Though, in my heart, I have longed hoped for the day—"

"What?! What's true?" asked the boys in unison who were walking closely together in a line, as they followed the creature Veeps closely.

"Someone This Realm has been waiting for, for a very, very long time. Someone who will put Eoorthe and the Other World to rights again! It's what we have been expecting for thousands and thousands of years. He is the One. A King, a real king, *the King*—come to take all the wicked rulers, tyrants and their minions far away to the Lonely Planet. Though it will break his heart to do it. It is said the gates to that hideous place is locked from the inside."

"But what does that have to do with any of us?" said Valen clutching his side again as he stepped over a mossy log.

"Everything," said Veeps and the Voors at once. "You'll see. The fact that we found you. The fact that it might all be true. The fact that you were there, all along, on that island, right under our very noses," beamed Murrin. She gave a little squeal and a dance.

"We must keep our voices quiet," said Veeps sternly. "All of us have questions and I do not know the answers to them all. So—no more for the time being!" He turned abruptly and pressed onwards, through the thick forest.

They marched on through the trees, over fallen branches and twisted, knotty roots. The sky became darker. The wind blew lightly, rustling the leaves above. Veeps walked quickly, careful not to make too much noise. After a short while they reached a more obvious path. Above them stood gigantic walls that went up as high as the eye could see, towering over them like brutish giants. Their journey continued long into the night. It was darker than any place, the boys had been before. Strange noises fell on their ears as they walked limberly along the now scant trail. Then Valen began to notice that he had become more attuned to the sounds around him. He could hear whispers as if they were conversations he was directly a part of. Valen looked at Veeps who was mumbling something to himself.

"I don't believe it!" Veeps hissed to himself angrily. "I've come all this way and for what?" he continued. "He is wrong. I know it! The line is broken. It was severed thousands of years ago."

"What are you talking about?" asked Valen interrupting the silence of the company.

"No one is talking about anything," said Jack suspiciously. "What are you talking about?"

Valen suddenly realized that what he could hear, others could not.

"Sorry!" he said yawning and feeling sicker by the minute. "I think I was beginning to fall asleep and I was ah—."

"Well, you'd better keep it to yourself," said Mr. Voors. "These woods are not safe and any unnecessary noise is sure to stir up trouble."

Mr. Voors' words were the last for some time. The moon went in and out of the thick night clouds above. Bits of stars could be seen in between breaks. The night air had a sweet bit of summer clinging to it. The towering trees above had a bright green moss growing on them. Hours had passed when finally they came to a clearing in the woods.

"Shhhh!!!" hissed Veeps.

"What is it?" said Mr. Voors clutching his spears.

"I hear something," said Veeps, his large ear perking up.

The company peered into the dark, behind an old tree, where there came a little light that glowed softly and brightly amidst the thick blackness of the forest.

They all watched curiously.

"This is where he said to meet them," came a little voice. "Yes, I know this is it. The tree with the face. I'm very good with directions you know. Of course you are. Yes, well I'll have to greet him first and then ask him. But you can't just ask him. There is a lot that he doesn't even know. And of course there are lots of problems everywhere. What makes you think that your problems are any more important that anyone else? You're quite right. I guess I'll just have to—AHHHHHH!!!!!"

"A Dysapier!" said Veeps.

"Funny you are sneaking up on me!" said the strange creature that was fat and furry who stood on two legs, and looked very professional. It had on a bowlers hat and bifocals, a large green tweed coat. It had beady eyes and giant whiskers, though his bifocals made his eyes look nearly as large as saucers. In its hand it carried a scroll and a walking stick.

"Who are you?" said Mr. Voors as he approached the creature.

"I don't see how my name is of importance. Of course, are names important at all? Oh, yes, I guess they are indeed. My mother has a name and my father has a name. Of course if they didn't have names then they'd be very confusing to get in touch with in large crowds. Though we really aren't ever in large crowds, so I guess names aren't that important."

"Dear me," said Mrs. Voors. "Just when we're trying to be quiet we have one of the most talkative creatures in the world in our midst."

"Tell me," said Mr. Voors calmly, "what are you doing here and tell us your name?"

"My name—ah yes," the creature looked perplexed, scratching his head as if he had forgotten it. "Thomas Tiddle is my name . . . what am I doing here?" The creature looked around. "Well, I was having a conversation with a close colleague of mine where we were trying to sort out some of our business dealings, and all the sudden I popped into this place here—with you folks. That scoundrel has to pay too. He's been badgering me nearly everyday. He's been bothering me for months now, asking me all sorts of strange questions. Ah, tis no bother though. I will make him pay if I have to take him to court. I am a man of principle. Honor! Justice! Now those are fine concepts indeed. Let's take a look at them for a moment shall we. Ahhh . . . sweet books. I was reading this book just the other day, on philosophy, and oh how good it was!"

"Enough!!!" shouted Veeps, whose hands were glowing with a fiery silver. "We don't have time to keep talking. We *must* leave!"

"Well, there's no need to be rude," said Mr. Tiddle adjusting his hat.

"We don't have any time to sit here and chat about—oh whatever it is that you're going on about! Now—" Veeps looked behind him. Everyone had been listening very intently to what Mr. Tiddle had been saying, almost as if—he *wanted* to stay and talk longer. Even though the creature was clearly annoying Veeps. It seemed as though his voice could keep captive those around him at will.

"Everything is fine!" Mr. Tiddle said casually. "We're only having a polite conversation."

"Nonsense!" interrupted Veeps in a fit of anger. "Come! We leave at once!"

But Mr. Tiddle kept talking.

"I don't know who you are exactly," he began, fiddling with his giant buttons on his coat. "As for me, I'm a bookseller. My life is books. But, I suppose we can discuss that in further depth later; since you are all so obviously in a rush." Finally he stepped out from behind the tree. "This isn't exactly a good time to be traveling in these parts of this world you know? It isn't safe. No—in fact, it is the least safe it has ever been." He looked around suspiciously as the light of the lantern he now held was glistening off his eyeglass.

Valen adjusted his collar nervously. He was still feeling ill. Henry got nearer to Jack as he awkwardly stepped backwards. Veeps was furious at this point as he scowled at Mr. Tiddle.

"Excuse me sir," he began gritting his teeth, "I don't mean to be rude or anything, but we must go! We have an appointment."

"Tell me," said Mr. Tiddle abruptly. "What exactly is a lone dwundlegob doing near Hallowell?"

Veeps' face was sparking like a hot raging fire. For a moment it looked as if red smoldering coals were in his eye sockets ready at any moment to shoot out of them and burn off all the hair on Mr. Tiddle's face. Then it happened, like a small silver sun which lit up the forest for a fraction of a second. FOOOMMM!!!! Veeps sent a *silverslugg* flying through the air. It landed in a tree that was several feet away, exploding and sending pieces of limbs, bark and leaves everywhere.

"A dwundlegob with *silversluggs*? Now that is rare," said Mr. Tiddle totally unfazed by Veeps' recklessness.

Veeps head was smoking with anger, almost as much as his hands.

"Confounded!" he stomped.

"Look," began Mr. Voors, "we really must be going."

Mr. Tiddle looked thoughtful.

"You're right," he said stroking his whiskery face. "I know a very good shortcut. Won't you follow me?"

"If you don't mind me saying, Mr. Tiddle—it seems reasonable to me that we could have gone quite sooner than you have allowed." Jack spoke up suddenly. "So, though it is not certainly true, it does seem peculiar to me that now you are listening to Mr. Voors and that before you were not listening at all."

"Well, this passageway is not open all the time you know," said Mr. Tiddle going over to where he had come from. "I have not used this way of traveling since I was a young. So, yes, you are quite right. I was stalling you so that you did not go anywhere that you would later regret. Where we are going I assure you is exactly where we need to go. Look!" He pulled a letter out of his pocket and handed it to Veeps who looked quite distraught. It read,

> *My dear faithful Veeps,*
> *Trust Mr. Tiddle. He will guide you safely to meet me. Do not tarry.*
> *~G*

"There, you see?" said Mr. Tiddle. "I mean you no harm. I am a friend and an aid to you. Darkness need not prevail on account of your honor. I respect your race indeed. Yet, I must warn you that since you left there has been evil that has taken some of those even in Dorodroos."

"Now you insult the dwundlegobs! This is a disgrace! I cannot hear any more of this! How do we know to trust you?" griped Veeps as his hands glowed again as his level of annoyance rose.

"Well," said Mr. Tiddle lifting his nose quite high into the air and adjusting his hat, "*I have just given you a letter.*"

"Alright!" shouted Mr. Voors at last. "We must be off. I sense things are becoming stranger." He looked around the thick blackness of the trees.

"We will go with Mr. Tiddle," he said.

"I will not!" said Veeps. "I promised him, I would deliver Valen safely. I gave my word—my honor! I will not have my good name drug through all the mud of this world should my small quest end in the ruin of the—" Veeps almost said it.

"We don't know if it is even true!" said Mr. Tiddle. "That is what this meeting is all about! Keep your head about you now won't you?"

"And safe he will be Master Veeps," said Mr. Voors patting him on the head.

Veeps swatted his hand away. Mr. Tiddle moved in for an equally patronizing swat which Veeps, using his other hand also swatted away.

"We will now follow Mr. Tiddle," said Mr. Voors as he moved toward the tree."Come, there is no time to waste. If what he says is true, then we will all be better off by getting out of this eerie place." Veeps at last relented and his hands cooled.

Mr. Voors was standing next to Mr. Tiddle who was now unlocking a door that was not visible to the naked eye. He held his lantern over his head as he fiddled with his rather large set of keys.

Everyone was now standing anxiously around the tree.

"Now," began Mr. Tiddle putting the keys back into his pocket. "I'm sure that most of you have not done Treetravel before, but I assure it is safe and entirely painless. It is one of the best kept secrets of Eoorthe. Now all you have to do is hold onto the lantern above your head like this." He held it high above his head and glanced around at his audience. "Then, you step back into the doorway like this." He put his foot back into the trunk of the tree."And when that happens the lantern will stay where my hand is now and the next person grabs it to do the very same thing." He smiled. "Quite simple I assure you. The last person to go will have to bring the lantern with them." Mr. Tiddle began fiddling with a contraption on his wrist, mumbling to himself. "Now all I have to do is set the number for nine." He looked down at a strange looking dial that he had on his wrist that looked to be an old clock, with Roman Numerals on it. "There we go! That's it. I was afraid I wouldn't remember! It's set now. I'll go first and then the rest of you can follow. See you in a moments time." Then, he stepped back and in an instant disappeared. The lantern flickered in the darkness as it remained firmly floating in the air just as Mr. Tiddle had said it would. Jack went next, followed by Henry, Valen, Veeps and then the Voors and their dog.

Moments later, they all arrived, one by one. Mr. Tiddle sat quietly on a bench staring at the wide trunk of the tree his guests appeared in. He looked to be enjoying himself as he sat puffing on a long wooden pipe. It wasn't long until everyone had made it through. Minutes passed and finally the entire company had arrived.

"Come, we must be going," said Mr. Tiddle. He took a long drag and blew a tiny ring of smoke through the air.

They set out at once. The road was windy and small. To either side was a small stone wall that lined it all the way into the village. It wasn't long until they reached the town. Once they did, Mr. Tiddle opened the gate quickly. Lightning flashed wildly behind them. The company stepped beyond the gate and into the village. All the streets had houses wrought with small smooth stones. Plumes of wispy smoke curled up from a tiny little building away in the distance into the approaching darkness of an ominous storm. Chimneys reached to the skies that looked as though they stood guard over the town for ages. The wind blew the shudders of the houses as they passed by, pounding them against the building. The wax of the candles in the windows looked pale and cold. Not a single one was lit. Nothing stirred. Valen scanned the old houses looking for any sign of life.

They hurried along the streets, weaving their way through the village as speedily as they could.

"Come," said Mr. Tiddle. "We mustn't be late. Hurry it up!" He moved along quickly. His large glasses reflected the light of the now fading moon. Giant clouds moved above their heads like an ocean full of gray cotton. Valen followed closely. Henry, Jack and Jude followed swiftly behind. The Voors were last.

At last Mr. Tiddle arrived at a small shop just on the other side of town tucked away down a small side street. A sign hung above the store window that read,

***"Thomas Tiddle's Tattered and Timeless Tomes"***

It was dark. He reached inside his pocket and pulled out his large set of keys again. He fumbled around for a while before he managed to find the one he was looking for.

"There it is," he said plunging the old key into the small wooden door that was barely half the size of a full grown man. "Watch your heads humans," he said. In a moment they all managed to make it in. Inside the ceiling spanned high above them. Darkness clung to the walls. Moments later Mr. Tiddle came waddling out of one of the nearby rooms with a bigger lantern in his hand. Slowly, he moved around his shop, lighting candles as he went. After he lit several different ones, he went over to a small fireplace that stood between two huge bookshelves at the far end of the room where the company had just entered. Thousands of books spanned the surrounding walls. Valen looked around, fascinated by the massive collection of them that Mr. Tiddle possessed. It wasn't long before a fire was snapping brightly.

"Now for a sophisticated ale—" said Mr. Tiddle. "Won't that be pleasant?"

"They're children,"said Mr. Voors stepping forward.

"Ah yes," said Mr. Tiddle, "That's right. Soon to be men. It's not drink that destroys a fellow, but a fellow that destroys a drink," he grinned. "What'll it be?"

"Perhaps another time?" came a deep soothing voice.

"Hello?"said Mr. Tiddle looking around the room inquisitively.

Everyone turned suddenly, when at that moment, an exceptionally tall man, who looked to have lived for a thousand years, and who had more wrinkles on his face than any one person could ever possibly have, emerged from the corner of the room where he sat quietly. Though, strangely, they didn't appear to be wrinkles at all; rather a face that seemed to have seen many ages forming a majestically carved face of a mythic statue. He moved graciously across the room to greet the newcomers, like a powerful lion. In his eyes there flickered a flame that seemed impossible to extinguish. Around his back hung a sword that looked as though it had been passed on by powerful kings, its hilt as large as a man's leg. He stooped his massive head down as he approached the boys. Valen looked up, terrified by the sheer massiveness of the man.

"Oh dear," said Mr. Tiddle. "I did not realize you'd arrived sir."

"Valen Vanderbolt," the man said in a low, deep, voice. "It is a pleasure to see you again."

"Valen Vanderbolt? To see me again? You must be mistaken sir,"said Valen oddly. "I don't know you. That is my first name, but the last—it's wrong."

The colossal man stepped out from the shadows. Valen watched him curiously. Then, he began to notice something familiar about his face.

"Professor?" said Valen. "Is that you?"

"It is," said the man extending a hand to Valen. But, it was useless. Valen's hand was so small in comparison, that the professor's hand nearly made Valen's disappear entirely.

"Actually," said the professor with a huge grin. "My name is Potus Gawdspelle and I am not a professor."

"Not professor Lewis?" said Valen. "Then, Po—tis—Got—however you pronounce your name—who—what are you then?"

"You'll see in due time," said Gawdspelle. "The question we should be concerned with now though, is not who am I, but rather, who are you?"

CHAPTER SIX

# WHAT HAPPENED LONG AGO

"Who am I?" said Valen clutching his side with a sudden excruciating pain. Gawdspelle looked at him curiously and almost as if he had read Valen's mind said, "Still feeling horrible?"

"Yes—terrible," Valen replied as his eyes began to water, looking pale and gray as a winter sky.

Gawdspelle reached into his pocket and pulled out a dark brown flask with an engraving of a tree imprinted on its side.

"That's because you've drank Moorbad Elixir," said Gawdspelle. He pulled the cork out of the flask he had in his hand.

"Drank, *eh*, what?" said Valen feeling as if at any moment he was going to die.

"Here," urged Gawdspelle.

"Why should?—" his sentence fell off. Valen couldn't finish his thought. He collapsed on the floor with a loud thud. The other boys gasped. Gawdspelle bent over him and placed the flask upon his lips and poured the liquid slowly into his mouth.

"Is he going to be okay?" said Jack rushing over to where Valen lay.

"He'll be fine," said Gawdspelle reassuringly.

Jude, Jack and Henry watched curiously. Valen wasn't breathing at all. Mr. Tiddle buzzed around the room as if he was used to seeing dying boys lying on the floor of his bookshop.

"But sir?" said Henry. "He *isn't* breathing."

Gawdspelle said nothing.

"I hate seeing dead people," recoiled Jude, looking away.

"Dead?" gasped Henry.

Gawdspelle's lips did not move. He hovered over him.

The Voors watched quietly as Valen's body lay limp on the dark wooden floor. Veeps stood silently in between Jack and Henry, staring at Valen's stiff body. Then, a strange golden light appeared around him that looked like a distant galaxy, swirling around his frail, sickly thin figure and pale corpse like skin. Then, it began to change. Slowly, his grayish dead hair turned to a refulgent silver-yellowish hair and then it grew longer, reaching down to his shoulders. His physique instantly changed too as his once emaciated body turned into a fit healthy, muscular one. His ears turned into pointed ones. Straightaway, his eyes flung open and a bright blue flashed out of them like a burst of sunshine on a dark and rainy day. Valen stirred groggily.

"What's happening to him?" said Jack. "Is it that—*that* stuff you gave him?"

Valen moved, slowly, rising to his feet.

"What happened?" he said uncertainly. "Why did I fall over?" He stood up. Everyone gazed at him in amazement.

"Oh, it's true!" shouted Mr. Tiddle waving his hands in the air, knocking over a tray of tea cups that sat on the edge of a small table which Veeps stood next to.

"My goodness it is true!" whispered Mr. Voors in a hush.

"A riddle unraveled right before our eyes," said Veeps walking closer to Valen as he reached his massive hand up to touch him.

"What's going on?" said Henry."What's true?"

"Yes," agreed Jack. "What did you do to him?"

Gawdspelle laughed as he rocked back and forth in his chair.

"My dear boys," he said. "There is much you do not know and much that I need to tell you. Sit down for I have a very long tale to tell." Valen obeyed, massaging his head gingerly, still feeling slightly disoriented.

Everyone else followed too.

"Well, to start," said Gawdspelle stroking his face after some silence. "How shall I put this?" he mumbled to himself. "You are—well—an *elf*."

"An *elf*?" said Valen awkwardly rubbing his head. "But I'm *human*."

"Partly, yes," said Gawdspelle,"You are what a human could be or should be. I'm sure you're elf-kind. There is a bit of elf even in your friends, though they aren't aware of it. A great thing has just happened to you, but now you must become a full elf."

"A full elf? We have elf in *us*? What do you mean? We don't look like elves. Valen didn't look like an elf minutes ago," said Jack looking in bewilderment at Valen's transformation. "But you do now—I guess. I mean I don't know what an elf is supposed to look like. But you—ah—have pointy ears and everything."

"I want to be an elf!" shouted Henry jubilantly.

"Do not shout for joy yet," said Gawdspelle. "The road Valen must go on now is one that will, dare I say be full of trouble, danger and suffering and he will need friends, too. Can you help, Henry?"

"Well," said Henry as bravely as he could, "I'll stay the way I am for the moment. Valen can be an elf all he wants, but probably I could help."

"Yes, to answer Jack," said Gawdspelle with a grin. "You are quite right."

"But how is it even possible?" said Jude who was eating an unusually large piece of cake that Mr. Tiddle had given him. Unsightly crumbs dangled about the corner of his mouth.

"Well," began Gawdspelle, "the answer to that lies in the pages of our history from long ago. But, we don't need any books to help us here, for I know it quite well." He placed his sword down.

Quietly, everyone gathered around anticipating what Gawdspelle had to say as they held their breath eagerly.

"There are many different kinds of beings in Eoorthe," began Gawdspelle. "Two of them are called Seryfim and elves. The Seryfim existed long before. They were gifted into seeing into the minds of their kin, elves. This is how they ruled them. Though the elves knew not how they were being ruled, only that they sensed there was something in their minds that made them "see" things in a certain way. They knew someone watched them, but could not quite explain who.

"In the Land of Iddling where elves once lived, existed a beautiful place that no one has ever seen. The beauty of this place was unparalleled and utterly unmatched in splendor. A place of unimaginable bliss. It was here that there grew Trees, revered above all the other Trees of Eoorthe—the name of the land it was called before Iddling.

"The mandate as laid down by the Seryfim, thousands of years earlier, were that they were supposed to protect the Hallowed Trees and preserve their powers, never to touch them and one Tree in particular—the Tree of *Wragog*. They were forbidden to leave the Hallowed Forest—for that was where their home was—in the Land of Iddling. For if they did, they unknowingly abandoned the protection of the Hallowed Trees as well. For, just beyond the Trees was a vast unknown, uninhabited land, never before seen by anyone and in the middle of the forest beyond, towered the mighty Tree of *Wragog*. As they honored this mandate, the lves lived in peace for many thousands of years. Always though, conversations took place under the shadows of those Great Trees. Conversations that consisted of the elves' desire to know what lay beyond the borders of their land and in particular what the Tree of Wragog was, which glowed mysteriously in the dark of the forest. Nights slipped by and the elves continually desired departing, until finally the ones who wanted to find out could no longer bare not knowing. So the elves, understanding that they were not to go beyond the Hallowed Trees, one night became deceived. They succumbed to their desire for what lay beyond and traveled to the Tree they longed to behold. What they did not know was that an army of foul, hideous creatures lie in wait. An abominable army led by a white dragon. A beautiful dragon that changed shapes and could in a moment appear as the most beautiful queen. Oh how beautiful her voice was the elves said. Oh how they desired her beauty. Her voice sounded like the very wind of the sea. Though at the back of it was a devilry and sorrow, none of the elves would have ever imagined had they stayed under the Great Trees. When they met this creature, Murkus is its name, it whispered to them many things. It takes the shape of a hunched hooded king at times; though he is a false king. And it is a cunning trick—for hidden away is a terrible, foul dragon."

At this point, all the boys were listening eagerly. Mr. Tiddle was tending the fire when he saw something go past the window outside.

"Othoritees!" he hissed loudly.

Gawdspelle stood up quickly. "As the falcon flies, put that fire out!" Mr. Tiddle threw a bucket of water on it. Mr. Voors stood at the window, his twin spears at the ready. Gawdspelle peered through the thick glass. A shadow moved through the streets. Then they heard stomps and growls and metal clanking. Then everything went deathly silent.

"He's gone! I knew it." The voice echoed with a roughness and hideousness.

"He's got it! I know," said another nasally sort of one.

"If he does, Dorgg? What then?"

"I don't know what it means," said the other. "And I don't care what it means. I've got my orders. We don't question orders. We do what we have to do and by whatever means possible. We are just following orders, that's it. I'm not responsible for what happens. These are the orders." Dorgg, the fat, thick, pale, creature which looked to be half rat and half bull (he had a bull face and massive horns and a thick fat rat tail) gripped his sword. Valen listened eagerly to what was being said as he sat still as could be.

"I'm telling you," retorted the other, "I met with him the other day. I posed as a customer. He's gone. He's probably got it with him. When I find him I am going to pull those whiskers off his face." Mr. Tiddle winced.

"Very well," said Dorgg. "Let's move on. If I find out he never left, it'll be your head I cut off myself. You'll be made an example for your stupidity."

In moments the tiny platoon of soldiers marched away from the streets. Their torches lit up the night as Mr. Voors watched through the windows.

"What were those?" said Valen standing up.

"It has begun," said Gawdspelle.

"What has begun?" asked Jack and Henry nearly at the same time.

"Murkus has sent out his cronies, brutes, beasts—Othoritees," said Gawdspelle. "They are on alert. I thought we would have longer, but he knows you have escaped. The Light is beginning to fade. Rescuing Valen is the Beginning. Murkus was holding him captive to try and prevent This Realm and the Otherworld from joining. Now that Valen is here war is imminent; Darkness is descending and Light is leaving, but it will not always be this way."

"What do you mean?" said Valen.

"It is the other part of the long tale to tell," said Gawdspelle with a worried countenance. "Though there is much more. Those creatures are hunting you. They are already aware that you have come to Eoorthe and now they are hunting Mr. Tiddle for they know he is one of the last to decipher the meaning in the Verustome; the book Bendy Grimm stole. Murkus is aware of me too." Gawdspelle's solemnness hung over the room with a heaviness. He sat down again. Mr. Tiddle relit the fire and refilled everyone's tea. He drew the shades on the windows and Gawdspelle resumed his tale.

"Murkus told the elves of riches and pleasures beyond the wider world of Eoorthe; a place where they could indulge themselves with every desire, enslaving them in the end; though they were deceived for they were not truly riches or pleasures at all. This day is called the Day of Great Sorrow. They would travel far into the North after Murkus promised treasures and dominion over places far away, fellow-rulers, Kings and Queens of a place Murkus would rule one day. Murkus built his Throne of Dark far away in the cold winters near the Moors of Moon. The White Dragon lives in the heart of Pestyphooris. A land with only the moon to lend her light. The road of the elves would always and only ever be dark roads which led to misery and death. They sought gold and silver under the Deep Moors, shipped on great vessels and brought to lands where giants and beasts, in obedience to Murkus stuffed it in their mountains and built cities that soon were given to decay and ruins. All around the Moors, lay a frozen wastleland, full of swamps, and bogs.

"When the White Dragon raised its kingdom, any sign of life had fled; then things grew colder and soon snow, ice, mist and fog would only ever be. It is a truly hideous place. Not one single thing grows there now. No bird sings any song. No golden leaves blown by the wind. Only trees which are barren. Spiders and crows, ravens and wolves and many other beasts; far too sad to name, are there now. It is a dreadful place."

"But," said Valen. "What happened to the elves?"

"As the elves aged, and after many wars, they slowly faded and became withered, some of them beasts, slaves of Murkus, journeying ever deeper into the Moors of Moon. They soon would leave all the Light they had ever known. The White Dragon would become a great sorcerer, but we are getting ahead of the story."

Everyone at that point, including Mr. Tiddle who would normally be fluttering around, was listening intently to every word that Gawdspelle spoke; for even he did not know all the histories of Eoorthe despite his love for books.

"The Seryfim created the Hallowed Trees to keep the elves from evil, destruction and darkness. The Hallowed Trees provided enough Light which always glowed and knowledge about their land and what lie beyond which kept their minds and hearts pure. Only the elves didn't know that. All they knew was that they were supposed to stay within their borders. For what purpose they did not know, but it was their own desire that they fell by the power of the Tree of Wragog. So, the Hallowed Trees," proceeded Gawdspelle, "which once gave unending life to the elves, now stripped them of their powers; for they immediately began to die, though it took a very, very long time. The Hallowed Trees which once gave them their life, now to them were darkness, and the power the Hallowed Trees had, which once possessed the Pure Light of Eoorthe, began to dim. They lost their Light, because the elves left their borders. After their departure, the elves now lusted for the power another tree gave—the Tremendous Tree, though it was hidden from their sight. For now they felt its power in their hearts, and their imaginations became darkened. They now longed for the Tremendous Tree's beauty and power which they had dwelt with for thousands of years before. Though they desired it, they could no longer see it, for they were now cut off from the Land of Iddling. This Tree remained in the midst of the Hallowed Trees, hidden, until one day it was found again." Gawdspelle stood up and took a sip of tea and paced the room.

"There were some, though, who never participated in their rebellion. These elves, resisted the powers of the Wragog and soon a mighty war ensued. This was after the Nyfarius Elves, as they are now known, rose up against the Luminous Elves—the elves who stayed in the protection of the Hallowed Trees. The Nyfarius Elves had left, gone away in search of treasure and returned as vicious marauders. A bloody battle erupted and the Nyfarius Elves, being mighty in number; destroyed all their fellow elves—or so they thought. These battles are now known in the legends of Eoorthe. Once the War ended, the Nyfarius Elves left the borders of the Great Hallowed Trees of Iddling, only to settle in a far away land to build new, dark and terrible cities."

Gawdspelle stopped and looked around at the tiny room. His eyes shimmered off the orange glow of the fire on the other side.

"You said, 'Or so they thought'," said Jack listening keenly, watching the giant man with reverence as he placed his cup back on a nearby wooden table.

"You listen attentively," grinned Gawdspelle. Then, all at once a massive wind blew outside and heavy rain began beating hard against the roof above, rattling the walls of Mr. Tiddle's tiny bookshop.

"What about Valen though sir?" said Jude staring at the walls as they creaked. "You still haven't told us why he looks like an elf?"

"He doesn't look like an elf," said Gawdspelle, "he *is* an elf. You have answered Jack's question. He is descendant of one of the Luminous Elves who lived long ago."

"Amazing," said Henry with wide eyes gawking at Valen. "He's one of *those* elves?"

"I don't understand," said Valen who felt uncomfortable with all the new knowledge that he had just heard. "If I'm from Had Wink how can I be an *elf*?" The word seemed to stick in his throat.

"That is the other part of the story," said Gawdspelle raising his eyebrows.

The wind whipped loudly outside. The candles flickered and the fire crackled in the room the company sat in.

"I must have more teeeeaaaaa!" blurted Mr. Tiddle suddenly. He got up from his lounge chair making a stir and made his way into the other room. Before long, he was back with another tray of cups and more delicious looking cakes. He set it down, served everyone second helpings; then went over to the fire and threw a few more logs on.

"As you've discovered," said Gawdspelle taking another sip of his tea, "you are an elf. And contrary to what you've believed, Dr. Grimm is *not* your father. All the things he ever told you were lies. Terrible, terrible lies. Your real parents are Thayne and Eleanore Vanderbolt and they loved you with all their hearts. Indeed that is why I called you Valen Vanderbolt earlier—"

"Lies?" said Valen in shock and anger. "And—*love*?"

"Yes, lies and love."

"Not my father? Lies?! A mother?! A father?" asked Valen doubtfully, yet somewhat relieved that Grimm wasn't his true father.

"Who are they?" said Valen. "What I mean is—ah—are they *elves* too? Can I go see them? Where do they live?"

"They were elves, long, long ago, but they have fallen away from any semblance of elves or the world where elves once lived. A shattering, a splitting apart of This Realm or Eoorthe if you prefer, and your world, what we call the Other World, has taken place and it has shaken both severely. What I mean is, they are connected—only you can't see This Realm from the Other World, because it is veiled. It is where a great many dreadfully dark battles have taken place for thousands of years. Both worlds are intimately connected, closer than you can imagine. Things that happen in your world affect Eoorthe. Things that happen in Eoorthe affect what happens in your world. The Long War. There is deep mystery to it, though and I cannot plumb their depths if I wished, least of all now.

"Anyway," resumed Gawdspelle. "Your mother and father were elves, but they were *de-elved*. Their elvishness was taken away, but not entirely. All the beautiful things that they ever made, their people, their trees, all of it has fallen under Murkus' foul words which he has spread over This Realm like a thick spidery web which has blotted out the sun. Your world is a pale phantasm that groans and aches for its ruins to be remade. It is *This Realm* though, that shall play the part in setting the Other World to rights again. Of course, now that you have arrived, the arrival of the King is imminent. How this will happen and how the news that you are a real flesh and body elf will reach the ears of those who are out fighting on different fronts, is yet to be discovered. You will understand more of this in due time." Gawdspelle turned his head and glanced at the fire. "I do not know where your mother and father are." He looked away, his face suddenly full of sadness. "I *have* looked everywhere for them but they are in hiding. Though, it isn't safe. I imagine they want to get to you as much as you now want to get to them. In my heart, I believe he has always been looking for you, ever since you were stolen from him by the Othoritees—Murkus' henchmen. I have discovered the tale, of the day when you were taken and I can say that it broke, and crushed his heart when you were taken, more than any loving father could bear."

"He is looking for me?" said Valen hopefully. And it seemed that Gawdspelle knew he'd ask this because he said, "Yes, your father loves you more than you could possibly imagine." Gawdspelle gazed around at the faces in front of him, crossed his hands, then continued. "In time you shall find him or he you." Gawdspelle paused again. "Where was I? Ah, yes, your mother. She bore you and as she carried you, her husband, your father, was busy trying to decipher a book that he found long ago. Knowing that you would soon come into the world—the Other World—as we call it, he looked frantically for any clues to decipher the meaning contained in the book."

"You mean the one I have!?" shouted Valen, "Is that the one?"

A smile spread across Gawdspelle's face. "The Tale of Knells, the one I left you—do you have it?"

"Tale of Knells, do I have it?" repeated Valen, "Of course I have it! You left it for me?"

"To come here," said Gawdspelle with a smile. "It is a passport so to speak. It was the only way to transport the man in the bottle here, to break the chain, the spell over Had Wink. It is only one chain, but the one who holds all chains, Murkus; he will be the one we must reckon with."

"This book helped me to get into Eoorthe?" said Valen. "That is how the bottle was able to travel here?"

"There is only one way to get here in a manner of speaking," said Gawdspelle. "And yes, I found out through Thomas here, that the Tale of Knells was the way to begin the withdrawal of the Deep Poison, which has infected your world.

"But how?" said Valen.

"There are many magical things in your world and in ours and we do not have time to explain it all," said Gawdspelle. "Rest assured; all your questions will be answered. Though, I knew that if it was true that the line of Luminous Elves had not been broken, as many had longed believed that it was, then giving you this book would prove it. You bringing this to Eoorthe was the only way it could have ever arrived and it proved undoubtedly in my mind that you are indeed the Beginning of what many, many people for thousands of years have been waiting for."

"I wish I understood," said Valen, "his hands propped under his chin.

"What have they been waiting for?" said Henry.

Gawdspelle smiled and a deep joy filled his eyes.

"The trees are going to wake up," he said. "Flowers, the sea, the stars, the mountains all will be free at last from the Deep Poison which has filled them all for so long. Wolves, bears, badgers, foxes, great beasts and monsters of the deep will lose their cruel vicious teeth. Food will begin to grow and never stop. Storms will never destroy another home, another tree. Trees will never rot. Fathers and mothers and sons and daughters, brothers and sisters, friends separated from one another will come to The Great Feast and we will go and eat with the Hidden King in his New Kingdom which he has been working on for a very, very, very long time. Rumor has it that a Great Wedding is to take place. But the road before us is long and full of much more sorrow, I fear. But, do not worry your hearts. We will find our way."

"What Kingdom?" said Henry. "What are you talking about? Are we in a dream?" Henry began to feel very tired and was yawning.

"You are in no dream," smiled Gawdspelle. "You have arrived here at precisely the right time. Or I should say that you have left your world at precisely the right time. Time isn't the same as it is where you were. There is waiting—do not misunderstand me, but it wouldn't ever be waiting as you understood it. It is a bit like reading a story. The author of the story knows the end in his mind and as a reader you have to continue reading until you get to it, but once you arrive, you say to yourself that now the author is showing you what you didn't know. That is certainly true in one sense, but he isn't *actually* showing you. He already told the story, now you are only seeing it as he saw it when he wrote it. Now," Gawdspelle took a sip of tea, "you are going to see what has always been. You are stepping into the Long Story of your world. Though that was already imagined long ago, before any of you ever existed. You have all been summoned."

"Well," said Mr. Tiddle, "now that they are all bewildered beyond buttons. I will make some more tea and fetch some more cakes."

"But my father," said Valen,"how did he get it?"

"I was hoping you'd ask," said Gawdspelle. "Thayne Vanderbolt—your father, found that book in a cave. Long ago he was a soldier, dispatched to give orders to one of his commanders many miles from the camp of the army he fought for. One frigid and snowy midnight, with no choice but to go and deliver the message of the enemy's activities to another officer miles away, he headed out in secret. Along his journey, he encountered danger. That night he met spies of the opposing army. But, being resourceful and clever, he quickly outwitted them. Veering from his main path to evade his enemies, he made his way instead to the nearby mountains, where he stumbled upon a cave. The snow was heavy that night. So, he set up camp and made a fire. As he was gathering wood he discovered a raggedy crumbling book sticking out of the cold ground. Curious, he dug it up. Unsure of what to make of the book he opened it up slowly and tried to read it. But, he could not understand the meaning. Thinking he found something valuable, he stuffed it into a tiny opening he discovered in the side of the cave wall, placed a rock in front of it, then fell asleep. Not long after though the spies appeared again. During the night, they picked up his trail and followed him back to his cave. He woke up fighting valiantly, but was quickly outnumbered. His enemies cut him down with their weapons and left him for dead. Thinking that they had killed him they left him then headed back to their camp. He lay in a pool of blood, stranded and helpless for many days. As his eyes closed, thinking he was dead, one of his friends, a man from his regiment, found him. The man brought him back to their camp. But, he knew he had to return and get the book. So he vowed that he would one day return. Soon he healed, the war was over, and he retired to a quiet life.

"A simple soldier, your father had single handedly won the war. People everywhere said that it was because of his mission that dangerous night that the war ended. In gaining the information necessary for his country to triumph, your father was decorated with all the adornment and prestige a country could give. But, for many years he could not understand why. For he knew that he had lay dying in that cave unable to carry out the mission he was responsible for."

"What happened?" asked Valen confused.

"For years, his country maintained that it was your father that won the war," continued Gawdspelle, "because you see—he had provided information that was unbelievable. What, he wondered, were they talking about? Confused and feeling as though he hadn't really done anything significant, he resolved to find out the truth. Maybe, your father reasoned, the book he had found years ago would provide him a clue. Remembering the cold nights he had endured, he decided to go when summer came. So, he made his plans and packed his things. Summer came and he set out at once for the cave. But once he got there he could not find the book. He searched frantically, but without any success. Frustrated, exhausted, and confused, he finally gave up. And right at the moment when he sat down, it wasn't the ground he found but the book! He got on his knees and examined the ground. But, how he wondered, did it get there? For, he had placed it in the cave wall. In his excitement, he picked it up and instantly something phenomenal happened to him. He was transported into This Realm—Eoorthe. Suddenly, he remembered everything. He looked back on the day that he had found it and saw how he could "see" from this world to your world. He recalled the battle that took place several days after he had thought he was dead. He remembered that he had recorded everything that would happen in the future as if it had *already* happened. But, this world he was in was not a figment of his imagination. It was more real than anything he had ever known.

"After your father visited Eoorthe, he took the book and brought it back to his home. From then on he would use it to come here. For years and years he did this. He realized that, by using it, he could gather information and accurately predict the outcomes of wars. As he did this he regularly received large sums of money for his service to his country; which eventually the army successfully managed to dominate the Other World or your world—through his help. This is why his country loved him in the beginning, but it is also why they despised him in the end. For one day, the predictions stopped. He tried to go back, but could not do it. Eventually, the empire that he helped build, began to crumble. And so he hid the book and himself. His country had turned against him and he knew he had to disappear."

"What happened to him?" asked Valen worriedly.

"Several more years passed," Gawdspelle proceeded, "before something else strange happened. At that time, your father and mother were getting old and before he went into hiding he buried all the money he had made by the sea, only to have returned years later and it was dug up and gone. One day your mother went to your father to tell him that she was pregnant. Oddly though, your mother could not bear children and your father naturally, was shocked. Now an old woman, your mother bore you for nine months until finally you came. And to your father's dismay, he knew that the kingdom where he lived—that you would be wanted by the Judges for their evil purposes. For they taxed the people heavily and controlled everything to serve themselves. It was a most hideous time! They took little innocent ones and did horrible things. Your father saw you the way you are now—as an elf, who knew you would be unwanted in his country. He had to report that you were born and hire an artist (which he and your mother did not have any money for) and give the painting to the Witchqueen who served Murkus. She came up with the clever plan of the artist to ensure what the children looked like. That was the law. When a baby was born, it had to be immediately reported what they looked like. This was a tremendous burden for parents. Not only were the people heavily taxed and unable to provide for themselves, they had to pay the Witchqueen's artist's fee, which of course, was very expensive. She did not care about her people. Only herself did she feed, while the rest starved. But, how deeply your father loved you. Being a good man he never would have given you up, unless by death first and never would he ever let you be offended by the Witchqueen. And so, he set it in his heart to hide you—to keep you safe. You were strangely curious to him at first, being an elf, but then he understood how special you were. Knowing a thing or two about hiding things, your father made every provision to keep you safe; which he did for a few years with lots of hiding and traveling (your father sought the Land of Fen, where some of the good men still live). But the Witchqueen's spies had been following your father and after a few moons appeared by the marshes (bear in mind that your father told me this for that is how I gathered all the clues and it is why you are here now). The spies knew that the painting your father produced was a fake, for the Witchqueen's artist told her. Your father tricked them and made it appear that you were a girl. But, he did it to protect you. For the Witchqueen was busy rounding up all little boys under the age of two and slaughtering them. Sometimes disguising or pretending to be someone you are not can be used for good or evil. The spies reported that they saw you do strange things from when you were very young—powers that the Witchqueen wanted for herself. Soon, your father found out that the Witchqueen had sent word to Murkus far away, for she was under his rule. A few years after your were born, hunters appeared and took you from your beloved mother and father. They took your father and put him in the Witchqueen's dungeons and did twisted things to him which should not be named. They came in the night, for those who served Murkus the dragon, and the Witchqueen did their deeds in the dark. They hated all beauty, especially your family. That was the last time your father or mother ever saw you."

CHAPTER SEVEN

# ANOTHER RIDDLE UNRAVELED

"You say his name so—confidently," said Valen with a shudder. "I mean—you don't seem afraid of him at all."

"There is only one name to fear and it is not his. No, the Person whom we should fear—His Power defies understanding." Gawdspelle swallowed. "There are many things to be feared in our world and in yours, but at the moment all that matters is that you are safe," continued Gawdspelle reassuringly with a smile. "Nothing evil will befall you—at least not now."

"But what's happened to my mother and father?" said Valen. "Where are they now?

"I found them long ago near a quiet place on the Longriver, which feeds into the Glass Boot—a beautiful clear blue lake which has golden aspen trees and white rock all around. It is a good, sacred place," Gawdspelle replied. "Your father is very old, but has a stout and steady heart. He has endured much and they are constantly on the move. Especially, since Murkus believes your father had a part to play in failing him."

"Does he know that I am alive? That I have been found?"

"It should be known that some of my flying friends have told him," answered Gawdspelle. "I visited with your father and mother months ago.

The journey is a long, hard, and cruel one."

"Well," said Valen, "I should like to see him and my mother presently."

"That is out of the question," said Gawdspelle. "Othoritees are on the move."

Then, a solemn mood fell upon the company and time seemed to stand still. The fire in the room cracked. A mouse scurried across the floor.

"What happened after I was kidnapped?" said Valen after some time.

"Ah, yes. The other part," Gawdspelle sat up in his chair. "Several hundred years ago, indeed long before the one who kidnapped you, there existed an island known to you as Had Wink. At one time this village was a quiet community of people who had lived in peace for many years—until *He* showed up. Murkus, the Lord of the Nyfarius Elves, whom I mentioned earlier found this island and turned it into a place that would eventually be used to imprison you, placing a curse on it that bound you to it. His plan, as I've discovered was so deceptive that the island he used would one day disappear and no one would ever know it ever existed. Indeed that is exactly what happened."

"The book in the library!" said Jack leaping up off his chair.

"And the lighthouse!" shouted Henry. "There was an old man in the lighthouse that we found alive who had a book!"

"Yes," said Gawdspelle, "he was one of the first to take note of Murkus' activity."

"But he wasn't dead," said Valen.

"Yes," agreed Jack. "And if Murkus is so dangerous," he continued,"why didn't Murkus just kill the lighthouse keeper?"

"That is one thing that Murkus cannot do," said Gawdspelle,"kill humans—at least not in your world. He can do far worse, far more evil things than simply 'kill' you."

"That's why he was still breathing!" said Jack exuberantly. He paused, thinking hard, trying to piece together the mystery. "But, why just him? I mean we have never found anyone else like that."

"Exactly," said Gawdspelle. "That's because Murkus did not *want* you or anyone else to ever uncover his secret. He wanted things to appear as normal. The man in the lighthouse was the only one who knew there was something going on and Murkus decided to put him into a dark sleep."

At that moment, Valen remembered what he had felt before in his pocket. And, no one else noticed except, when Jude had gotten up and made his way to the window. Valen watched him curiously. It looked as though Jude was waiting for someone, for he peered out the glass in the door. Then Jude quietly slipped outside as Gawdspelle's attention still lay heavy on the fire as he churned the events and stories through his mind. Curious, but remembering what he had found Valen reached into his pocket.

"What is this?" he asked.

"A *key*?" said Gawdspelle cautious yet with great surprise. He took it and cast a suspicious gaze over it. "Where did you get this?"

"I found it in the door of the lighthouse," said Valen. "It is *strange*."

"*What is it?*" said Jack looking curiously at Valen.

"This evening has become filled with more mysteries than I could possibly have imagined!" Gawdspelle glared again at the key for a long riddled moment. "This may be the Fallen Key. *The Key* that was forged when the last piece of Sacred Fruit had fallen. In it is kept Life itself, some believe." Gawdspelle took a long deep pause. "I was looking for you, dear elf and in finding you I have found *the Key*. It opens *The Door That Was Shut*—a gigantic door—the Door in the West—the Door Which Brings Two Worlds Together. No one has ever been able to open it, though One and only One has ever been through it. It is said he is a Great Builder who left long ago to build a City Which Will Never Ruin. Some said, they saw him long ago." Gawdspelle folded his hands and with a large, slow and deep voice and began to sing,

***'Now wrinkled life, now olden, withered tree of death. Gone from heights above, below to depths. Gone morning, evening gone, now darkness forged.'***

"That is a small part of a song that I remember. Thousands of years ago, *Eoorthe* had fallen into what is remembered as the *Deep Dusk*. The day that Murkus and the Nyfarius Elves had succeeded in finally killing the Tremendous Tree. The tree he attempted for thousands of years to find and finally having found it, only to murder it. He lit infernal fires at its mighty trunk, hacked and hewed at its beauty, its uncorrupt long past, poisoning its roots. Yet still, it remained. Then one day he gave at last, birth to a profane, vile act. *The Year of Sorrow,* as it is known. For that is how long it took to die. One night, as the fires raged at its mighty trunk, Murkus took a powerful bow, forged by the hands of the Nyfarius Elves and its quiver full of deathly arrows. Made from the wood of the Withering Wragog—the Forbidden Tree in the Land of Iddling, the tree which possessed the knowledge the Nyfarius Elves lusted for in the Beginning. They shot into the mighty tree's heart, a volley of arrows containing a terrible pestilence. Soon its fruit turned to frighteningly heavy stones which broke off from its beautiful branches and fell from the sky with terrific force. After the Year of Sorrow, the Tree, so massive in size, finally fell, shaking the heavens with a mighty thunder, mountains crashed into seas, whole new lands emerged from the deep."

Gawdspelle paused and then began again. "Yet, there was something that he did not account for in his blasphemous plans. After the mighty fruit which had become stones had fallen, there was one very small piece that had also fallen that became black as death—unseen by Murkus' blind malevolency. As he departed with his despicable joy trailing him, his eyes passed over it. In time though, after the Luminous Elves of *Eoorthe* had grieved the death of the Tree, the lone blackened piece of fruit had withered and transformed into beautiful golden key." Gawdspelle held the key in his hand which seemed to cast an enchanting spell of mystery over the company. "Its powers may be too great or too simple, one does not know. The great mystery behind The Door That Was Shut." Gawdspelle paused again and looked down at it, then lifted it above as all eyes in the room became suddenly transfixed upon it.

"How do you know this is it?" said Henry.

"It is in the *Great Foreshadowings*," agreed Mr. Tiddle proudly, holding an ancient looking book up to the light of the fire. He read,

***'When once the Fallen Key reforged,***
***Has found its way to home reborn,***
***Lost its life, by death it came,***
***Beyond ruin and decay,***
***Night and day, a world reborn***
***Light was lost but unending life regained***
***Safely bear it into darkness***
***Light will come if love shall give it.'***

"This key," began Jack, "what does it do? Does Murkus know of it?"

"We are fortunate. Murkus does not know it was ever crafted," said Gawdspelle

"Do you not know of the *World That Went Away*?" said Murrin, unexpectedly.

"Much knowledge, mystery, truths, great laws and most especially stories, have fallen away out of all memory," Murrin lamented. "It is all very solemn. I am afraid that when the King does at last appear, he will be mistaken as an imposter, a trickster or even worse a magician."

"It wasn't until many years later that Murkus discovered, that something had been found near where he committed his grave evil, near the Tree's great roots which stuck up out of the ground," continued Gawdspelle looking at his audience. "But, he never knew it was a key. Because of the *Great Foreshadowings,* he knows that something, some item is supposed to exist which is supposed to give life forever, but that life was not meant for him. Yet, in his fury, he could never find it. He does not know what it is, and therefore, does not know what to look for. There are things that the wise have hidden from him." Gawdspelle examined his sword meticulously. "This key may be it, I do not know. But, when I saw it moments ago a deep joy flooded my heart, which I have not felt since I was young and I first came across its history." Gawdspelle paused and took a deep breath. "The key to unlock The Door That Was Shut. Long did Murkus seek a way to harness the Tremendous Tree's life and power when he and the Nyfarius Elves captured the power of the Withering Tree of Wragog in the Land of Iddling. Murkus murdered the Tremendous Tree in his quest for unending life *through* the Withering Tree. Yet, Murkus deceived the elves, for he persuaded them in his wicked heart he would live forever, by having the power of the Tree of Wragog alone. But he was wrong, for Life remained in the very tree that would have given him the life he desired—the Tremendous Tree, if only the Nyfarius Elves had never left the Hallowed Trees. It was the Dragon, Murkus, who was whispering to those elves who left, beyond the edge of Iddling with the power from the Tree of Wragog. He could tempt, mame and murder most creatures he pleased, the Nyfarius Elves and anyone who was loyal to him could do the same so long as they remained in his service. In time they became his slaves, ruthless, vicious slaves of death. Slaves to a foul King of Darcnis and all their hearts became corrupt by him, the Prince of Death, Ruler of the Terrible Armies of Darcnis." Gawdspelle looked around then went over near the fire, his figure filling up the room. A silence fell like soft snow before he spoke again. "I must try and decipher more answers to its past."

"Well, that's a light story," cracked Jude who suddenly appeared in the corner.

Jack, Valen, Henry and Jude felt a twinge of adventure in their hearts coupled with a great fear and were about to ask something, when Gawdspelle turned, dropped the key in his pocket and continued in a different tone, but not before Jack's analytical mind went to work again.

"But, this Key?" piped Jack."What are we going to do with it?

Shouldn't we investigate if it is really, truly it?"

"Yes," said Henry nodding, "shouldn't we make sure?"

Valen remained silent.

"Yes, but there is nothing to *do* with it—at least for the time—until we find out its ultimate purpose. It does more than open a door, that I am sure. A key has many powers and does many things. Though, there are strange powers unknown to me—powers that I am unsure I want to discover, even if this key does open *The Door That Was Shut*. Though, if it is the Key, then I would go to whatever lengths to open the Door, even if I cannot see the end." Gawdspelle looked agitated, troubled and worried. "It seems it has an evil cloaked over the tale it is to tell—a gloomy tale, but also a glorious glimmer of hope clinging to it that I cannot make out in my mind." He paused. "We must keep it hidden—until we know more. We must bring it to the Fair Princes, they will know what to do."

Suddenly, a somber mood soaked the room. Gawdspelle turned to the rest of the story, but everyones' minds still lay with the tale of the key.

"If it is *the Key* it will be the very thing upon which our journey will hinge, for it will lead us deep into a dark country. And, the road before us will be a very long one." Gawdspelle paused again and took a swig of ale. "Where was I before the tale of the Key?" Gawdspelle looked pensive, his eyes ruminating. "Ah yes," he said after some time, "I remember now. After you were kidnapped, you were taken to Had Wink," he began."There you would live for the next several years of your life, where your powers would slowly diminish and you would remain under the watchful eye of a man by the name of Bendy Grimm."

"Dr. Grimm?" said Valen.

"Yes," said Gawdspelle, "only he is not a doctor. He merely acted as one. It has come to my knowledge that he was recruited by Murkus, long ago to capture you and hold you as a prisoner."

"Why hold me as a prisoner?" said Valen.

"Draining an elf of his power is no easy task," said Gawdspelle. "A Luminous Elf, least of all."

"But why not just kill me?"

"Kill you!?" shouted Gawdspelle his voice sounding like the thunder outside. "If he could not kill the man in the Lighthouse, surely he could not kill you. Besides, Murkus will only murder. It is soldiers who kill. You are far too powerful for him to simply try killing you as someone falls in battle. Don't you see? Murkus is terrified that you exist! You've descended from the line of Luminous Elves! A true elf! He desired to rid you of powers that he knew he'd never have and after they were entirely depleted he planned to bring you here to *eventually* murder you—to rid This Realm and Eoorthe of the last of the Luminous Elves—but even he did not have a completed plan. He had to take you out of This Realm to kill you because he does things in secret and he knew that there were others hunting for you too. There was more than just his plans at play. I think though, Murkus wants you dead because he knows what you are capable of and he will stop at nothing to destroy you. Life from the Tremendous Tree runs somewhere in your blood. Just as he failed in possessing the powers he desired from the Tremendous Tree, he failed in murdering you. Yet, his will is set and his imagination is darkened. His blood is black and poisonous and will begin hunting for you soon. Of that, I am sure. Though there is something else I fear he wants with you but I have not yet uncovered the answer."

"What else do you think he wants?" said Valen feeling a heavy sense of despair as he felt the awful gripping fear that someone whom he never met wanted to murder him. He gazed down at the floor, tracing the lines in the grain of the wood back and forth nervously. Gawdspelle placed his aged hand on Valen's shoulder.

"Won't he try to find me and bring me out of This Realm back to Grimm? Won't there be a worse end for me, now that he knows I have escaped him. Most stories I have read about prisoners escaping, hasn't ended very well for them," said Valen solemnly.

"Do you not see?" said Gawdspelle. His eyes twinkled with kindness. "Already his plan has foiled. He did not succeed in stripping you of your powers. Grimm's attempt with the Morbad Elixir has been thwarted; for he intended to give you another potion, which would have surely destroyed you." Gawdspelle sat quietly then said, "Do not easily be deceived. Now that you are here, Murkus can appear in many forms and present all sorts of horrible things and ideas as good. Only when you are so far down a road, will you then realize it—*if* you realize it, that it is the wrong road and then, it may be too late. But, do not fear for help is never far away."

"But what do we do now?" said Valen trying hard to process all the new knowledge Gawdspelle had just told him.

"We will make our way to the Moonhouse in the morning, then onwards to the Southern Post," said Gawdspelle. "Further up and into the high country where the Castle of Cylvirstone resides, then on towards Hyddenne, the Old City. Summer will soon be over in your world, but that is when our summer begins. It will last twelve full moons. In one full moon cycle, The Festival of the Two Wandering Stars begins. But, this one is especially important and historic for this festival has not happened in a very long time. Armies of This Realm and Kingdoms and Dominions have been dismantled and weakened for thousands of years, and they have wandered away from their homes and lands after Murkus scattered them. These great warriors were exiled, lost and wandering; soon they will gather from all over This Realm to take the journey to the High Places to plan the War to siege Murkus' Kingdom. But, as you now know, the Lightlessness is spreading and dusk is closing in. I only hope that those who are being summoned, will come. This Realm grows dim. Soon, all color will leave the stars and fields of both our worlds. We are now just past the stars in your world, somewhere near the edge of your universe. Once the Great Festival begins, which is accompanied by a Grand Feast, there are the Fair Princes which I must meet with. We must bring this Key to the Fair Princes and find out more of the history of its passage down through our history. But, first there is someone at the Southern Post I must see to first. There are certain places in This Realm that the Othoritees, or the Hidden Patrol as they're also known are watching and so we must be ever careful. They are loyal to Murkus alone and we should not be fooled into thinking they will not be all around. They will be watching the roads, inns, cottages along the way. We will take to the forests and rivers. It is there that we can be safest and have clear minds."

"Soon, portals all over your world will begin to open for the first time in thousands of years and monsters of every kind will have full access. Before they do though, many things must come to pass in This Realm. Slowly, with the help of our allies we will capture them and hunt them down one by one and take them away forever. But, I fear, what will follow is a time of gloom that our worlds have not seen since before the Year of Sorrow," Gawdspelle continued. "A Foulness is at work and I do not know how much hope we have to gather up an army capable of resisting Murkus. Already, cities that were once good have betrayed us. Murkus' plans are set. He is a Destroyer and he will use all of his power to make our worlds forever dark. What's worse are the Othoritees. I have seen them. The have already begun trying to rid This Realm of anyone who would stand in their way. They are just as all tyrants are—afraid of words and thoughts and anyone who resists is hunted down and silenced by death or prison. We must avoid them at all costs. Until we get to Hyddenne where it is safe, I do not know what lay beyond. There we shall find wisdom beyond ourselves."

As Gawdspelle said these words, the company became hushed. Jack sat back timidly. Jude, who had come back when he thought no one noticed, picked some more cake up and wiped his mouth. But Valen had seen him and remembered how long he had been gone. Henry gripped the arms of his chair in terror. Valen remained fixed like a statue.

"Will you let this trouble you to the point of despair?" said Gawdspelle. "Evil and suffering will not last the night. Besides, you are now in the company of friends. And however grim our journey, we will not be cast down. You should be very encouraged. I will do all that I can to protect you. In time you will see that you will find the courage to believe when all seems lost. Do not despair yet! For the road is long and our hearts must be light! We should rest."

# THE SOUTHERN POST

The morning sun climbed to the top of the forest that surrounded the tiny village of Hallowell. Streams of sunlight steadily filled the quiet forest. Birds flapped their wings gracefully, gliding through the cool air effortlessly. A gentle wind swept across the lush green meadows, rustling the long thin blades of grass, making it dance elegantly. Insects buzzed about performing elaborate, artistic air-shows as they crisscrossed through the muffled morning sky.

Valen and all his friends, including Mr. Tiddle, Veeps, Gawdspelle and the Voors had gathered outside of Mr. Tiddle's bookshop. Mr. Tiddle lavished them with a giant breakfast consisting of eggs, sausage, cakes, berries, tea, biscuits, beer and several other desserts, meats, drinks and fruits. This was all of particular enjoyment for Jude who surreptitiously filled his pockets with an assortment of cakes, biscuits and sausages.

Mr. Voors, Paltrow and Murrin Voors stood under a tree talking to Gawdspelle with hushed voices. Then, Valen noticed Murrin's face go pale. The boys and Valen were staring.

"It's impolite to stare," said Mr. Tiddle waving their gazes away.

"But she's crying," said Jack. "Why is she crying?"

"They're leaving," said Mr. Tiddle.

Without waiting a moment longer, Valen raced outside into the cool morning air, where Gawdspelle stood commandingly, facing Mr. and Mrs. Voors. Murrin looked the other way, her arms crossed stiffly, the wind gently combing through her hair.

"Murrin?" said Valen kindly approaching her slowly. But she tore off into the woods.

"I don't understand—" said Valen. "What's going on? Why did she leave?"

"We are leaving," said Mr. Voors. "We have brought you safely here. But now we must be going, my daughter feels—" His words fell off.

"What if we meet another one of those things?" said Valen thinking back to the terrible Bludblax.

"You have Veeps and Gawdspelle now," said Mr. Voors. "He will accompany you on your journey. We will soon meet again," continued Mr. Voors, nodding to the boys who now stood beside Valen. "Goodbye." Then he and Mrs. Voors disappeared into the forest without another word.

"Where are they going?" said Valen.

"They are going back to their people. I believe that perhaps we will meet Mr. Voors again," said Gawdspelle. "He is a very skilled warrior and I desire him in battle should we need him when the time comes, but he will have no place in our journey. His cares lie elsewhere, whatever happens with the Key and Murkus."

"Will we see them again?" asked Jack.

"I do not know. Come! There is no time to waste! We must be going. Gather your things boys. We make for the Moonhouse. We must not tarry. We need to hurry!" Gawdspelle threw his mighty sword over his back and waited for everyone to gather their things.

"I suppose you're not coming either?" Henry said turning towards Mr. Tiddle.

"Nonsense! Of course I'm coming. You'll need me," he said. "I've read almost every book that has to do with any topic that you might find interesting and I'm a natural navigator. I know this land as good as the whiskers on my face! Plus, I'm very sociable and you'll need someone like me— to bring—you know—happiness to your journey." He took his glasses off and gave them a quick polish.

Gawdspelle laughed.

"He's very talkative indeed. You'll serve us well Mr. Tiddle. Everyone ready?"

"Oh dear," said Mr. Tiddle. "I almost forgot. I need to lock up my house. One never knows what kinds of beasts and creatures might come through one's town, while one's away."

He took off his pack and reached into his coat for his key.

"Confounded!" he shouted. "I can never keep up with any of my things!" He stormed inside his house and was back outside in less than a minute with a tea pot and several cups.

"This is no time for tea," said Gawdspelle scowling. "No, we must leave now."

"I know, I know," retorted their furry friend adjusting his hat. "It's for when we stop. There's nothing better than a hot cup of tea after a long day's walk."

Veeps tapped his foot irritatedly, his arms crossed. Valen noticed his hands beginning to glow.

"Come," said Gawdspelle. "We make our way to the Moonhouse."

The company followed obediently. Valen walked closely behind Mr. Tiddle who was talking rapidly. Jack, Henry and Jude followed Valen closely. Veeps walked behind everyone else keeping watch on anything unusual.

The road leading out of Hallowell took them far into the distant forest where it wound its way up over hills and across rivers and bridges for miles and miles. As they walked along, the road began to slowly fade. The small round stones etched into the ground beneath their feet began to slowly disappear under wild vines and weeds. The day wore on and soon the sun had set. In the distance the moon rose slowly. The company pressed on into the darkness of the night. When at last they came to an open meadow, before finally, in the distance, appeared a small house.

"That is our destination," said Gawdspelle. "Come, we are almost there."

Soon, they reached it. The house was small and insignificant. The roof was caving in and the porch was falling apart. Grass grew up in between the planks. But, the front door remained fixed and solid, boasting gloriously almost as if it had a life of its own. It stood resolute. The company approached it cautiously. Then, Gawdspelle took his staff and held it up to the light the moon emitted. His staff funneled the light and made a perfect circle of white light in a carved circle on the front of the door.

"Now what?" asked Valen skeptically. The house sat still as ever and it seemed that at any moment it might collapse into a giant heap of wood and rubble. Then a strange thing began to happen. The house seemed to come to life. Slowly all the oldness and abandoned feel it possessed slipped into the fading night and the house became a bright glowing structure. The windows let out a golden light and the door glowed a soft red. Then it creaked open slowly, revealing a wispy, white, see-through curtain.

"Now we go in," said Gawdspelle stepping in first. The entire company followed.

Once inside, the boys stood, perplexed. Their eyes moved around suspiciously as they watched the twinkling glow of stars that covered the sky. Then, turning their attention downwards, they saw a river that wound its way through the nearby colossal green hills like a huge silver snake glistening gently in the surrounding darkness. The moon reflected off it gingerly. Valen looked up to where it hung, high in the sky. Walking further, he discovered as he glanced down and found not wooden floor boards, (as one might expect in a house) but jagged, lifeless, withering grass that had not seen rain or sun in far too long. Gawdspelle walked steadily onwards, his grayish white hair wrapping gently around his worn face. Veeps followed behind, pushing the children on. Mr. Tiddle followed, hurrying.

"Come," said Gawdspelle. "We must make it to the gate, before the light of the moon fades."

It wasn't long before they reached a grove of bent, withered trees. They stooped down, avoiding the low hanging branches. The bark on them looked cracked and worn. Through the trees ran a disappearing path that wound its way to the bottom of the valley. "This way," shouted Gawdspelle as they all followed, continuing on down the hill.

"We must hurry Valen," said Veeps pulling him along. Veeps looked up into the night sky. "The moon is fading quickly."

"This really is a strange place," said Henry gazing intently around. "It seems, in a way, more real than Had Wink. But, I sense darkness too. I don't know, I just can't seem to put my finger on it."

"I know what you mean," agreed Jack. "Seems as if it was here all along, but we just couldn't see it."

The company didn't speak another word for some. Everyone was exhausted and hungry. Mr. Tiddle wobbled down the hill with his sack slung over his shoulder, speaking quietly to himself. Gawdspelle walked at a smooth steady pace in front of them. After some time, the company arrived at an old cobbled road that bottlenecked into a small stone bridge where a tiny trickling brook ran under it. Beyond it lay a town lined with a towering stone wall which surrounded the entire village. Scattered intermittently along the tops of it hung massive lanterns, their flames absent.

“Valen, above all we must get you to the Cylvirstone quietly,” said Gawdspelle as they reached the town. “That is our task. Do you understand? Our Adversary’s agents will be hunting you, for I am sure word has reached Murkus' ears that you have escaped *Had Wink*.”

Valen looked into the face of his wrinkled guide, his eyes glowing with friendship. Valen nodded, quietly with understanding.

“Your identity must be concealed for a time,” said Gawdspelle placing a kind hand on his shoulder. He reached into his bag and drew out a dark blue cloak. “This will keep you from any dangerous eyes.”

Gawdspelle turned and stepped forward slowly. The moon was sinking fast. Then, as Gawdspelle ventured towards the gate a sudden heavy silence fell on them like an ominous storm. The others followed cautiously.

Finally, they arrived at the gate. Gawdspelle approached it slowly. Then, without warning, he stepped back, as the gate began to slowly open. It creaked and popped and swung gradually backwards. Gawdspelle entered the village cautiously. Things seemed deathly quiet as he crept forward. The company entered. Then out of the gloom emerged a stout and sturdy, squashed man with a dull and faded, crimson velvet vest on. In his hand he carried a lantern. His face, though human, seemed to look very much like a lion. He walked with a hunch. His hair was coarse and golden, flecked with gray as it hung in his face, like a wild overgrown garden. His hands were covered in fur and his feet were the feet of a lion with claws that gripped the ground. He had a sword clutched to his side and a rusty silver shield that hung over his back.

“Hullo,” he said, clearing his voice. “Who goes there?”

“I am Gawdspelle.”

“Eh?” said the creature putting a wooden looking horn to his ear.

“GAWDSPELLE, SON OF GUTHENNE OF DINGILF THE GREAT!”

“So you are,” said the furry creature indifferently.“What business are you on? Eh? There hasn’t been anyone in these parts in thousands of years."

“Yes, I know,” said Gawdspelle looking at the creature intently.

“We don’t have anymore work to do,” said the creature. “The armies have diminished. They have been overtaken—” He couldn’t bring himself to say it. “Hope has long since faded.”

“Since when have the Rikrooturs of Koratikoom given up hope?”

“Are you not aware of the Flight of the Silver Knights?” said the creature angrily, looking at Gawdspelle uncertainly, then he crossed his arms impatiently.

"I know more about the long history of Eoorthe and your own history than you yourself know," said Gawdspelle seriously.

"The world is dark," spat the creature. "Great evil has taken shape in many forms. They say," he paused and looked around suspiciously, "*Pestyphooris* is bristling with darkness again. I heard just the other day from a fellow Spy that the Factories of Darkness are in full force. Their fires go on all through the night, never ceasing—foul creatures come out of them that are beyond description. It has been told to me also, by Travelers of the Dark, that there are Beasts multiplying in the North and mighty ships have been seen moving up the swift rapids of the Doobglash—*the Dark River.*"

He paused, thoughtfully, then sighed.

"What you say is true," said Gawdspelle. "But—might we come in? We are weary from travel and are in much need of rest."

The creature grumbled.

"Very well. But you mustn't stay for long. I've things I must see to. Come. Come." He waved them in with a hurried hand. "Quickly!" he hissed, glancing up at the sky with a shudder.

"Follow me."

He turned and disappeared into the inky night.

Gawdspelle's troupe followed the embittered, furry creature, through the abandoned town. He moved swiftly and easily through the streets despite his age. They followed him closely. All the houses were made of old stone that looked to have been salvaged from an lost kingdom long ago fallen—for the stone did not seem to be in keeping with the lay of the land. Shadows hung like strangers around every turn.

The creature moved down the middle of a desolate street, then far into a thick forest of trees beyond the edge of the village. Then it found what appeared at first not to be a path, but looked to be instead some secret trail, for it was well hidden. The path veered left and then right and before dropping sharply down a steep slope, then flattened out at the bottom where a swift stream flowed quietly through the black forest. A small path outlined the edge of it as the creature, turned left and then followed it down for quite a while before they finally came to a small cascading waterfall.

As the group waited for the creature to guide them further, they glanced around. The water crashed down headlong into a quiet lagoon where small eddies formed on the sides of the banks. The forest didn't say a word. As Valen looked at the surroundings, he couldn't help but notice how rich in green the trees seemed to be. Suddenly the creatures lantern was aflame and he slipped into a concealed doorway tucked behind the swift, frigid cascading water.

Inside was a long corridor of dirt and rock that was cool and yet there was also a sense of warmth and homeliness to it. Before long they came to a small set of stairs that were made of felled trees. The stairs wound there way down the side of a deeper cave. The company moved slowly along as they climbed along the edge of the large underground cavern.

Finally, they came to the end of the stairs and a locked door. Here the creature reached into his pocket and pulled out a set of keys. In moments, he had the door open and they entered down a wooden hallway where there hung fat, flickering candles. This led them to another door and then at last to the creature's dwelling place.

"Sorry for all the trouble," he said. "But Rikrooturs can't be cautious enough in these Dark Days, for we live in perilous times and the Southern Post has seen what I believe to be the Lightlessness spreading. Dusk is falling"

The boys entered first, followed by Mr. Tiddle, Veeps and Gawdspelle. Valen looked around. The room was small and squashed. The walls were made of a fine dark reddish wood. Scattered about, sat wall sconces where tall bright candles burned brightly. A fire crackled in the far corner of the room. In the center, sat a short table where three other creatures just the same as the one that had led them in were prattling amongst themselves.

"Francis," began an older one, gazing up from the inside of his mug. "Guart duty wearying u tonit? Been out makin' trubl?—What'sis? Strangurz?" He stood up and looked alarmed.

Francis didn't speak a word as he went over to the table to pour a mug of golden colored ale, placing his bag, lantern and shield down on the floor.

"How'd you get past the Othoritees?"

"Hello, Frump," said Francis finally.

"They must not've been watchin' good," said Frump dismissively. He sighed.

"Itz tru?—youmans?" He glared suspiciously at them. "Thes'r strange times."

"They came in through the Moonhouse," said Francis trying to be more precise.

The Rikrooturs immediately began blabbering amongst themselves again with growing eyes and nervous hands.

"There asn't been anyun to come through dem doors in sum time—

hundreds—thouzands of yers. And what might I asx are these?"

Mr. Tiddle and Veeps stood quietly in the shadows.

Veeps stood with an annoyed look, his back pressed hard against the wooden wall, arms crossed and hands flickering with a soft silver glow. His mouth remained glued.

"Actually," began Mr. Tiddle suddenly. "We're from beyond. Through the House—if you've ever been there."

"Ben ther? Yu kant jus go through," said Frump. "Thoz dors are one way."

"Right," said Mr. Tiddle happily. "Actually, I don't prefer too much travel personally. I'd rather read about it in my books."

Veeps sighed.

"But," proceeded Mr. Tiddle,"I am rather enjoying myself—if you want to know."

Veeps rolled his eyes.

"It's not often that I get out," continued Mr. Tiddle.

"Come," said Francis with a bit of an uncomfortable, obligatory tone. "Let's talk over some food. Gather round the table and get yourselves something to eat. We've plenty—bread, honey, ale, cheese . . ."

Mr. Tiddle talked for a while longer, before realizing that no one was paying him any attention. Veeps was deeply pleased at this.

Francis introduced the newcomers to his friends as they gathered round the table.

"It's been far too long," said a plump one named Oswald, taking a swig from a large wooden jug, "since anyone has passed through the gates of the Southern Post. These are strange times."

"Dwundlegobs, Dysapiers, and *children* from the Other World?" said one of the quieter ones after some time, his eyebrows raising steadily. "What business do you have here?"

"Eoorthe has become darker," said Gawdspelle placing his mug on the table. "Lightlessness is spreading as you say—the Other World grows darker." He paused. "I've heard talk during my recent travels, that Murkus the Dragon is gathering armies—for what purpose I cannot see."

"Nutin' but talk," said Frump obnoxiously, "We'ven't seen any one in a long while. Mark my erds. Jus a nuther rumor if u asx me."

"What brings you here?" pressed Oswald.

"Yes," said another one named Ivan in a raspy voice who looked very thin. "What? And—how'd you get *them* here?" He took a deep look at Henry who gulped.

"Do you know of the Sacred Tree of Falling Stones?" said Gawdspelle.

"Sounds familiar," said Oswald.

"Familiar!" blurted out Mr. Tiddle who hadn't spoken anything in a while. "How can it only sound . . . *familiar*? It's known all over in the Great Books of Eoorthe, in the legends and memories of all—except in yours, I suppose—that it is *the* Tree—the Tremendous Tree that Murkus destroyed long ago."

"Oh, right," said Oswald stupidly. "I seem to have remembered now."

"So it's—*regrown*?" said Francis lowly, his voice concealed by a small hope.

"Not quite," said Mr. Tiddle bubbling. "You see, we have this key and someone has broken into Dorodroos—"

"SILENCE!" roared Gawdspelle. "Fool!"

The room flooded with murmurs.

"Dorodroos?" began Francis suspiciously.

"It is the Verustome, I fear," said Gawdspelle solemnly. "I am—"

"There are many magical items," interrupted Francis. "A key, too?"

"It is true," said Gawdspelle. "And this one—I do not know for sure."

"But," said Francis curiously, "where did it come from?"

"From a door in the Lighthouse in Had Wink!" blurted Henry.

"Fool!" shouted Gawdspelle angrily. "Announce it to all of Eoorthe while you are at it."

"And a book?" said Oswald.

"Yes," said Gawdspelle solemnly. "I am concerned, but my heart has begun to thaw a little—at least as far as the Key is concerned. I have always had faith and trepidation that this time would come. I only did not want to be too presumptuous. The Verustome—this is a grave matter. But, I do not want to be hasty and rush to conclusions."

"There are many books which predict all sorts of things," began Francis. "There is no one here that is a foe," he added and paused. "Why are you so reluctant to tell us what you have found in the lighthouse? A Key, and the Verustome? This is no coincidence, Gawdspelle. Surely, you know this." Francis paused then spoke again. "You haven't visited me in hundreds of years and you don't expect us to ask any questions? I have paid attention to the signs too. I am no fool, Gawdspelle Son of Guthenne of Dingilf."

"I admit," said Gawdspelle settling down, "I too am overjoyed, though, should it be true my heart dreads what lies ahead. For this journey, should this be *the Key*, will be long and full of hardships none of us yet know." He stopped and took a long deep swig of the ale which Francis had given him. "Thankfully, Murkus does not know it was ever forged."

"Tell me it has something to do with the *Foreshadowings*?" Oswald jumped up with eyes lusting for battle. "This means that we will raise an army again!"

"Do not be too quick to rush off to war. The Foreshadowings—yes, indeed," responded Gawdspelle. "The mighty arrival of the King and the Cracked Throne shall be remade." Suddenly there were many mutterings in the room, including that of the boys. "Though, I do not want to give anyone any false hope. The door which Valen came through is no longer open. Veeps and the Voors bound a chain to it and Murkus' cronies are crawling like snakes in the land of Had Wink. Yet, it will only last for a time—they grow in terror and power."

"No sense in waiting around. If they are festering like they stench they are then we will go and crush them!" shouted Oswald with a voice booming like a war drum.

"No, no, my friends," said Gawdspelle. "The time is not right. We need to plan secretly. We must have a council. So, I do not mean to trouble you," he continued calmly. "But there are too many questions. What is first and foremost is—" His sentence fell off.

"*Why* did you come here!?"said Oswald suspiciously looking suddenly in Valen's direction.

Valen stood quietly in the corner, concealed under his blue cloak.

"Who is that?" said Francis glaring suspiciously in Valen's direction.

"My companions only seek to make it to Hyddenne the City High Above," interjected Gawdspelle trying to evade Francis' question.

"I am no fool," spat Francis. "Who have you brought with you?"

Francis got up and moved toward Valen as he remained fixed like stone. Valen, feeling he would be discovered anyway, began to feel a burning nervousness hanging round his neck. He stepped forward.

Francis neared.

"I am Valen Vanderbolt," he said, taking down his hood.

Gasps rippled through the little room.

"It can't be!" said Oswald getting up off his chair. "An elf? Descendant from the Luminous Elves! I have heard of you in myths and stories from when I was young, but never did I in all my life think I'd actually see one right before my very eyes." His mouth flung open like a blossoming flower at the first sign of spring.

Gawdspelle was watching anxiously as Valen stepped further into the light.

"How do we know this isn't just some trick?" said Francis with a raised brow. "Show us your powers."

"The Key could only be brought here by the Elf himself," said Gawdspelle firmly. "I am sure of it." "Besides, there isn't time for shows." "There is enough evidence and with that, you must believe. Soon you will see. We must keep him secret and guarded. We are in need of the great speed of the Mighty Falkose." He paused again. "We need your help, that is why we have come."

"We owe no allegiance to anyone for we have no king. We do not believe in such, tomfoolery—" Francis paused with a bitter scowl. "Myths," he mumbled. "Elf or not. What you ask cannot be done. The Falkose are all together wild and are often away or do not want to be approached by anyone. Elves least of all."

"Perhaps it is because they have lost their purpose?" said Gawdspelle.

"But Francis!" snapped Oswald. "It's an elf—a true elf. Before our very eyes. Can't you see what that means? You know of the *Great Foreshadowings*."

"I don't care about elves or the *Foreshadowings*," spat Francis.

"You're a stubborn fool!" shouted Oswald. "The Elves—it means that This Realm is ready to fight the *War Between*—ending it once and for all..."

"What do you mean, *end it*?" asked Jack curiously.

"Yes, what does he mean?" followed Jude.

"I don't know if it is true," said Gawdspelle. "None of us do."

"But, what?" began Henry just as excited.

"I cannot say," said Gawdspelle. "It must wait—for now. The story must wait. We have to be very careful during these times. The important thing now is keeping Valen safe—keeping him away from Murkus at all costs. He will know soon enough that his plan has been foiled, but I want to keep the elf protected as long as we can. What do you say, Francis? Can you help us?"

"Cannot say?" said Oswald.

"Yes!" said Frump. "We are no foolz. We know what Murkus haz dun."

"We have heard Something Rumbling in the Heavens too," said Oswald. "We watch the seasons and the skies. Many things are happening now. It is just as those before us have said it would be. Just before the Festival of the *Two Wandering Stars* and an elf appears. You speak of a mysterious Key, Lightnessness is spreading—what more evidence do you want?"

"I agree with some of what you say, but I do not know the answers to all the riddles which lay before us," said Gawdspelle. "It may be as you say." He paused and took a long breath. "I am troubled though. There are things which I don't know. If this is *the Key*, where do we go? Where do we take it? What does it open? Keys open many things. Murkus does not know it was crafted, nor would he know what it opened if he did know it existed. I fear it will open something far more hideous or terrible to imagine should it fall into his hands. But I could be deeply wrong. It could be the Key which those long ago said it would be. So, we travel to meet the Fair Princes in time for The Festival of the Two Wandering Stars. We will arrive at the beginning of Autumn."

"Yes," said Oswald pounding his fist. "But suppose it does open the *The Door in the West*, *The Door That Was Shut*? None of us have ever been there. The land is full of eerie creatures too many to count. If we did manage to open it, would it not be the most joyful day in This Realm and in the Otherworld? We have been stationed here to wait and to guard and that is what we have done. But, it has been too long. Generations of my family have held this post for many ages. Their graves line the city walls and hills. The Lanterns are not lit and have not been lit because long ago they were snuffed out by the Foul Wind from the East. I want them relit. Don't you? I want the Falkose to return more than anyone."

"No one knows what is behind that Great Door. It has been shut for thousands of years. Perhaps something beautiful, perhaps something hideous. And what will we do if it is hideous?" Francis took a deep breath. "Long ago the Falkose aided in battle freely. They will have nothing to do with the cares of This Realm. Now, they cannot be tamed. The Falkose will never return."

"How long has it been since you have spoken to them?" said Gawdspelle.

A steel silence fell upon them.

"Though, I want them to return," added Oswald coming to Francis' aid, "Can't you see that he does not want to speak of it!?" Oswald stood up and waved both his hands in the air.

"Oswald," said Francis placing his hand in the air commandingly. He looked towards Gawdspelle. "They are gone now. I cannot help you."

Oswald sat back down.

"There may be a time before long that I'll need the strength of the Rikrooturs. The Light is Fading." Gawdspelle ripped some bread off a large loaf which sat in the middle of the table. Then he spoke again. "It was foretold long ago in the great myths. The *Fading of the Light*, then the *Long Lawlessness*. The Light Thieves are coming. A dimming as you know, is spreading through This Realm. Dusk has begun to fall. I have many questions and not enough answers. Murkus the Magnificent, as he calls himself, is up to some malevolent mischief, some evil, darker than any of the Wisest know—that is what I see in my heart."

Francis stood, arms crossed.

"I believe in what you say," said Oswald with a shaken face and wide pupils. "I feel it now in the air or have felt it lately. Something has changed. It is the same feeling after a terrible battle has happened and death is in the air. Or, one who was once thought to be a good man, went suddenly wrong. Though, is there is hope? Only, it feels the same way even though no battle has been fought. What are we to do?"

Finally Veeps who had not said anything for a very long time, spoke.

"Before I left my Beloved City," he began, placing his mug down on the long dark table, "my father told me that the Verustome had been stolen. A thief had broken in and stolen that which is sacred to my people. Shortly thereafter, Gawdspelle arrived and said he had found another strange book. A book which had many names in it. A book which had survived war and fires, famine and winters. Something which had been lost and guarded. Something which was held a secret for a very long time."

"I love books!" piped Mr. Tiddle. "When can we read it?"

"There are two books. Veeps is right. The Verustome has been stolen by Grimm. *One book to be stolen, one to be found*," said Gawdspelle. He sighed heavily. "The Tale of Knells has been found. Its tale is a long sad one. One book, Valen has brought here." Gawdspelle paused. "I am sorry. I did not want to speak of it for its tale is too long to tell. I am sorry to be the bearer of it," concluded Gawdspelle solemnly.

"Many riddles which have remained for an age are coming into focus. *Light fades as Light shines*," said Oswald. "That is the riddle."

"Yes," said Gawdspelle. "The Light of the Elves comes as the Light of This Realm fades."

"What other news do you have?" said Ivan worriedly.

"Other *news*? What other possible news could you want?" said Oswald hotly. "Can't you see what this means?" his face became gripped with ferocity. "Many, many people have believed in the Verustome. They believed that it was safe, deep in the Land of Dorodroos, where those old warriors protected it for thousands of years."

"Yes, but I am a young warrior," said Ivan, "and I do not know the things which you do, Oswald. Forgive me." Ivan bowed.

"It means we have work again!" shouted Oswald. "War! Many, will come to us who want to be a part of our cause and the ones that do not—bah!—we will go to battle without them!"

"Patience," said Gawdspelle his hand lowering. "War is part of it, yes, but that is not all of it. And war is not something any of us should want, unless there is no other way."

"But—if it iz *the* Book," spat Frump. "Then it *iz* troo!"

Then a great sorrow fell upon everyone for Francis who had looked to have seen the most wars and whose face was greatly aged began to speak again. Valen looked upon him and noticed for the first time gray tips of fur which lay upon his face and an old wrinkled scar which jutted up above his cheek bone traveling west on his face. His face sagged with sadness.

"The Verustome and where it lay is something which has always filled my heart with hope, but I am weary Gawdspelle. Especially now that it is stolen. I have always had hope, always believed that it was immovable that its secret was safe and that if it was stolen the King would never come and all would be cast forever into darkness and despair if it was ever lost. I thought those words in the Verustome were safe from anyone, especially Murkus." Francis paused. "I cannot go to war anymore. I am too old. My mind and sword are heavy."

"I know your bravery and your concern and your fear," said Gawdspelle. "You are considered by many, including your enemies, to be of a certain valor which was once known all throughout This Realm." Gawdspelle nodded. "Do not lose heart now." Gawdspelle took a chair at last for even he could not bear all the weight of the news that the Verustome brought, though he had long known it.

He sat before them quietly. Valen watched him, his sharp blue eyes ruminating over this truth. Everyone wanted eagerly to know what this news meant, then after a good long while Gawdspelle at last spoke.

"It is true. Murkus—Conjurer, Deceiver, Liar, Fell Dragon," began Gawdspelle, "has stolen it. The power of Murkus, Lord of the Nyfarius Elves breached Dorodroos with his puppet Grimm, not too long ago. Together they *stole* it." The words fell like lead. "Murkus is planning something in secret. He now possesses the *Verustome*," said Gawdspelle.

"So it is true. He really does possess *the Verustome*? *The Sacred Book of the Dorodroos*?!" gasped Ivan after a while who seemed to be asleep or deep in thought. "This is the worse news I have heard in a very long time."

The other creatures murmured and whispered taking deep drawls from their mugs.

Francis' eyebrows raised with a deep suspicion.

Whispers and terror filled the room at least in part. For the boys did not know what this all meant and Valen felt he had stumbled upon the deepest sort of mystery that ever an elf could and he was not sure at all he wanted to be in the story he now found himself in.

"This Grimm?" said Oswald. "The name reminds me of someone."

"He is a treacherous, duplicitous man," said Gawdspelle, "and a betrayer."

"Surely," said Ivan, "Murkus cannot take something so beautiful and do anything good with it."

"That is precisely the doom which lay ahead of us," said Gawdspelle solemnly. He bowed his head as though he bore a sorrow too deep to be uttered, but then he spoke. "Murkus, will try to twist This Realm and the Otherworld up into a nightmare. Murkus will take the beauty of all the long, lovely fair words of the Verustome and make it hideous and ugly. Some of his foulest work is the perversion of words. Murkus will try in the end to destroy every leaf and tree, every flower and bird, every kind and noble idea, every beautiful and joyful thought, streams, and rivers, mountains and every race or being in This Realm and the Otherworld. Murkus is a beast maker. He turns children when they are grown up, into wolves, monsters. He makes you *want* to serve him, so that in the end you are a slave, believing you had no choice. He will Unmake all things if he can. He will blot all things with a Dark Stain which will will not be able to get rid of on our own." Gawdspelle continued to speak and his words fell heavily, like cold wet snow and an eerie silence filled the room. A heavy burden and a deep sadness hung in the air and gripped everyone's heart.

"Where is it now? What do we do?" said Francis after what felt to be a very long time.

"I do not know what to do—yet. But, that is why we shall seek those wiser than I." Gawdspelle paused again. "I have come to enlist your good will, to see if you will aid me in this quest. We must go far and deep into Murkus' Kingdom and take it back. If you should come, know that it is a long and cruel journey. It is a voyage over mountains and under them, over seas and rivers and deserts, through forests which feel as though they will never end. I cannot see the end, but I have hope, always I have hope and so must you. But, should we recover it we may very well change the course of This Realm and the Otherworld forever. For Murkus also seeks *the* Key, though he does not know it is a key at all. But he shall not have it!"

"Do you mean the Golden Key which was formed after the Tremendous Tree had fallen?" asked Ivan. For even though he was young the story was told to him and he knew it all by heart and it lay deep within his memory.

"Yes," said Gawdspelle. "That is the one."

"The Key has been lost," grumbled Francis. "It will never be found. There have been those who have tried to find it and have failed time and time again. The idea of suggesting that it is even *possible* to find it, unsettles me. That Key is no good to anyone, least of all those who would try to unlock the Door in the West. No one has found that either. It has grown over and has been hidden away." He took a swig of his ale and thunked it on the large wooden slab which made up the table.

"It is true about the Door, but I have seen it when I was young. It is possible to find it even though it may be quite difficult, if not impossible." Gawdspelle reached inside his deep pocket and pulled out the Key.

Whispers, as though a King that no one had ever seen erupted as the Rikrooturs gazed in fascination at it.

"This is the Key?" said Francis skeptically. "How can you be sure?"

"I believe it is," said Gawdspelle. "The story is that merchants from the far South found it long, long ago. It was kept because of its distinct characteristics. At times it has had healing properties. Stories which surround it have woken up some which have fallen asleep. It has brought those in famine food. It has cleared floods which have decimated towns. It does more than open doors. But, there is something else which it does that Murkus wants it for. And I do not know what that is. For this reason, I believe it needs taken to the Fair Princes where they will be at the Festival of Wandering Stars. Silflam of Seavenbell is going, too and I desire to speak with him. He knows more about Eoorthe than all the great minds of This Realm, save a few. It is his council I seek." Gawdspelle paused again. "Never has there been a key which was cast such as this. I looked for the threads of all the stories that surrounded it to be woven together into some meaningful tale, searching all the libraries of castles and kingdoms all about Eoorthe and even in the Other World and I believe it is *the* Key."

"You say the *Verustome* has been taken and you say have patience?" barked Oswald. "This is no time to wait. I have waited long enough for work. My job is a soldier and to war I will go."

Gawdspelle remained silent staring at the flickering lantern on the long table.

"For what?" said Ivan.

"Yes," agreed Oswald. "If we wait, Murkus will crush us! We must gather fighters, quickly! Sound the Warbells."

"*WE CANNOT GO MARCHING OFF TO WAR*!" boomed Gawdspelle at last, the furs of the Rikrooturs blowing as though they were caught in the beginning of a storm. "The Warbells will have their place and I will need one of you to sound them when the time is right. Wait, is all I am asking, until you hear from me. If things align as they were foretold in the *Great Foreshadowings*, then—never mind all that for the time. There are many things that still need to be known. War," sighed Gawdspelle, "is the least desirable thing. Though, I do not believe it can be avoided in the end. Nevertheless, the Southern Post must be prepared," he continued. "I have come here to also ask you to unite the Outer Posts. Do not delay and do not get caught. If the Othoritees are policing the forests and lands surrounding the Southern Post, exercise utmost caution."

"Any enemy of yours is an enemy of ours! We'll spread the word like a raging fire," said Oswald with his hoarse voice rising. "We'll go at once. Come Ivan, Frump, Francis! Put down your drink. We've work to do. If you can use us Gawdspelle, we're at your service!" He bowed low.

"Rikrooturs have always been faithful and dependable creatures," said Gawdspelle kindly. "But our plan must not be known. The elf must remain hidden for the time. Gather your kind, but do not divulge to anyone that you have seen us. We make our way to the Cylvirstone, then we are off to the City of Secrets and Mysteries—Hyddenne."

Francis nodded his head reluctantly.

"Where is Jude?" said Henry suddenly.

"Gone!" said Mr. Tiddle looking at his coat and half eaten plate.

"Find him, quickly!" said Gawdspelle worriedly.

"Goodness," said Mr. Tiddle nervously adjusting his buttons. "It's been a while."

"He's gone!?" said Gawdspelle angrily, looking out the door into the long wooden corridor. "How could he have gotten past my watch?"

Suddenly they heard something. Then, a long shadow stretched across the flickering torches in the hall.

"Show yourself," said Francis commandingly. "Who are you?"

Up strolled Jude, walking carelessly into the company's midst.

"Where have you been?" said Gawdspelle.

"Just out having a walk," said Jude casually.

"Out having a walk?" said Jack. "This isn't a time for walks. It's dangerous out there."

"Calm down," said Jude. "I'm here now."

"So he is," said Gawdspelle. "And I only hope he hasn't led any Othoritees here or any other spies."

Gawdspelle turned and looked at Francis who had a troubled look on his face.

"I'm very sorry," said Gawdspelle. "Humans are very curious creatures."

Francis looked away displeased, before saying, "I will bring you to the edge of the Southern Post."

With that, he turned and headed out the door.

"The hour is late," said Gawdspelle. "We must be going."

Valen turned to Jude watching him carefully for a moment, before gathering his things. He looked different somehow, thought Valen, but unsure why. Jude ate the rest of his food and gathered up his things. Valen noticed at that moment a curious look in his eyes.

At last, the creatures gathered their belongings and headed for the door. Gawdspelle followed closely behind Francis and the other Rikrooturs, followed last by the boys, Valen, Mr. Tiddle, then Veeps. They made their way down the hall, back up the long stairs, out through the tunnel and then out past the waterfall. It was still dark when they arrived in the forest.

"Gawdspelle is right, you must leave at once. Come, this way," said Francis. "Follow me." He headed left and then north up a small, obscure trail that carved its way ruggedly through the crowded trees. It wasn't long until they came to the end of the trail, to a place where an abandoned pair of white stone stairs led them from the bottom of a deep ravine, up to a wide open grassy field. Slowly, each of them began making the long ascent to the top. It was longer than expected and by the time they reached the top, most of them were fatigued.

At the end of the trail, they came to a large stone boulder where a little creature wearing a tall pointy hat with a very official looking face stared at them with a large grin.

"Strange times these are," said the creature. "We have not had visitors in quite some time. Nevertheless, welcome to the Forest of Fogmore," he said. "My name's Piddlefoot Magoon. Though you can call me Piddlefoot. I am the Keeper of the Flying Falkose. Atleast I was when they were around."

"Come along," said Piddlefoot as he rummaged through his tiny coat pocket. "Oh, where is it? Where is it?" He panicked as he searched frantically. "Ah, ha! Here it is! Quickly!"

Piddlefoot pulled out of his pocket a glasslike sphere and mounted it on his head as if he was a little lighthouse. Without another word he marched off hurriedly beneath the ever darkening sky. He was fast and it proved hard to keep up. The company trudged along, through the thick high grass of the field. Above them, billions of stars illuminated the night, like glimmering snowflakes, unwilling to fall. Piddlefoot's head was bobbing up and down like a wandering bottle in a vast ocean. Time wore on until they came at last to a vast, open meadow, stretching deep into the dark land.

"Here at last," said Piddlefoot. "Welcome to the Threshold of Fallenne. Beyond Fogmore," he pointed to the west, "lies one of the last kingdoms of This Realm—Cylvirstone, the City of Kings—an old city with a Withered King."

"What do you mean, withered?" said Jack.

"You'll see soon enough," said Piddlefoot. "The first thing is to get you there."

The troupe assembled, slowly, pouring out from their path onto the bending blades of the field that seemed to Valen, far, far away. He scanned the silence. At first, all he could see was a never ending field of grass. Then, in the blackness emerged colossal, white trees. Their limbs barren, cracked and dead.

"What is this place?" said Henry with a shiver.

"This is the Sanctuary of the Mighty Falkose," said Francis stepping out from behind, standing solemnly next to his brother.

"What *are* Falkose?"said Jude.

"They are the Guardians of the Sky—the Mighty Wings of War," said Piddlefoot, his arms crossed, glaring into the darkness.

"This is useless Ivan," spat Francis. "We all knew that they were not here. We should return."

"Return?" said Piddlefoot, turning to face his brother. "This is the only way to the Cylvirstone. You know that."

"I know," said Francis. "But, I do not think they will be aiding us this night." He walked away from the group and Piddlefoot followed him. Valen watched and listened from a distance, his friends and Gawdspelle, standing quietly behind him.

"Why do you not believe?" said Piddlefoot, his eyebrows raising.

"You know why," snapped Francis. "I do not wish to speak of it." He turned away.

"That is in the past," said Piddlefoot. "Don't you see what's happening?"

Francis glared, then his eyes softened, as if a thousand years flashed suddenly across them.

"That was too long ago," said Piddlefoot. "You cannot go on like this."

"It is not a matter for your concern! I shall go on as I always have! They are not here!"

"But you can't—" said Piddlefoot his words falling. "Don't you see what's beginning to happen? We still have a part to play! The Rikrooturs can aid those who need our help."

"What ever is happening," said Francis adjusting his vest. "It is no longer my place to do anything. What ever happens in This Realm is none of my business."

"You do remember the Oath we pledged?" shot back Piddlefoot. "You are bound to it!"

"Of course I remember!" roared Francis. "Do you forget your age? I am five hundred years older than you and I will not be reminded of oaths and bindings!"

Then, he tore off into the night and left the company alone, shrouded in the murky night. Piddlefoot crept back to where Valen and the rest of them stood.

"What's going on?" said Veeps looking into the shadows where Francis passed.

"My brother—" he began, nervously. "Ah, well, it is too long a story to tell."

"Do tell us," said Mr. Tiddle with a nervous smile. "I love stories. They absolutely delight me." He grinned happily.

"Well," said Veeps annoyed,"It's obviously not a very good one. Don't you have any sense?" He shot dagger eyes at him.

"That's no matter," said Mr. Tiddle placing his bag down. "A story is a story no matter how it ends."

"Yes," said Veeps. "But, don't you think Francis would stay and tell it, if he thought it worth telling? Some stories are tragic, you know."

Mr. Tiddle looked thoughtful.

"Yes, but not everyone knows *how* to tell a story," said Mr. Tiddle thoughtfully. "You've got to *really* tell it, no matter how long it takes to tell. It does not matter how bizarre it may seem or how many strange characters are in it or...."

Veeps sighed, then walked away.

"It's got to have an ending worth some weight in gold, too!" finished

Mr. Tiddle staring at the back of Veeps' grayish head.

Jude chortled.

"Piddlefoot?" interrupted Gawdspelle. "Our time is short. I will talk with your brother. Do you know where he has gone?"

"Back to the caves I presume," said Piddlefoot.

"Then I will go and retrieve him," said Gawdspelle, clutching his sword.

"And I will go with you," said Veeps, rushing to Gawdspelle's side.

"You will serve better here," said Gawdspelle placing a kind hand on his shoulder. "I will be back as quick as the moon rises."

He turned and disappeared into the night.

CHAPTER NINE

# AN UNEXPECTED WELCOME

He'll be gone forever," sighed Jude, plopping down in the grass, placing his hands behind his head, gazing up at the stars. "What do we need him for anyway? Why don't we just go and get one of these beasts and make them do what we want them to?"

Piddlefoot stood on the fringe of the company, staring off into the wild, giant, devouring forest in the distance. Henry walked over to him.

"Piddlefoot?" said Henry bringing Jude's question to his attention. "What do we need Francis for?"

"We need him because he is the only one who knows how to speak the language of Falkose," said Oswald quietly.

"But we've been here for a while now and I haven't seen anything," said Henry, after a long moment.

"That's because they're gone," said Valen suddenly.

"Gone?" said Henry.

Piddlefoot turned at once.

"How did you know they were gone?"

"They used to live in those trees, right?" said Valen.

"Yes," said Piddlefoot in amazement. "But how did you know?"

Valen didn't answer. Instead, he stood thoughtfully, staring off where the giant barren white trees stood.

"Do you know where they are?" said Piddlefoot.

"They are a very long way from here," said Valen. "They have gone on to another place."

This alarmed Piddlefoot even more. He gulped, looking at Valen mysteriously.

"So what they say of the elves is true," he said staring at Valen curiously.

"I don't know," said Valen. "What do they say?"

"Well, many things," said Piddlefoot excitedly.

Mr. Tiddle, listening from a distance, came over expectantly. Veeps followed. Then, the boys came too, trailed by the Rikrooturs.

"What's going on?" said Ivan as he wagged his walking stick, rattling it like a snake.

"Valen—ah—the elf here," swallowed Piddlefoot,"seems to know where the Falkose are."

The Rikrooturs immediately began whispering among themselves.

"How can this be?" said Oswald.

"H'd ju no where they are?" said Frump.

"Yes," said Ivan. "We've only been looking for them for the past several hundred years. And suddenly you know where they are?"

"I've seen them too," said Valen.

"Seen them!?" said Oswald seeming agitated.

"Yes, though I don't know where."

"You know where they are, and you've seen them but you don't know where you've seen them?" said Ivan waving his stick around as if he was spelling something with it. His eyebrows ascended. "I don't follow."

"Well, it's simple," said Valen. "I have *seen* them, in a manner of speaking. But, I have never seen them with my eyes. Rather, I can *see* them in my mind."

"Ohhh," said Oswald. "That clears things up."

At that moment, Gawdspelle appeared with Francis at his side.

"The Elf!" shouted Ivan. "He seeees them!"

"Hmm?" said Francis with a deep rumble.

"Valen—the elf," said Piddlefoot, "says that he can see the Falkose."

"This is very strange," said Francis, thoughtfully. "I do not know how you can 'see' them, nor does it matter."

"Doesn't matter?" said Piddlefoot nervously. "You said yourself that we need to find them again and that if you didn't, you would—"

"I know what I've said!" snapped Francis. "Save your reminders for yourself." He turned to face his guests. "I am sorry," he said trying to recover his words, bowing graciously. "I should not have abandoned you."

"Where did you go?" said Henry.

"I ah—it's no matter presently," said Francis dignifiedly. "What is important though," he began, clearing his throat, "is that you need the power of the Falkose to aid you, but," he stalled, "they are not here."

"We'll just walk," said Jack helpfully.

"Walk!?"snorted Francis.

Ivan laughed out loud.

Oswald snickered and chortled obnoxiously.

"You do not understand," said Francis in a low voice. "Fogmoor is *ripe* with evil. You cannot simply *walk* through it. Not with the greatest of armies!"

"Oh," said Jack sheepishly.

"Secret Othoritees and Spys of Murkus rove about This Realm and have taken up residence in *Fogmoor*," said Francis sternly, turning and facing the ominous trees beyond. "Go into that forest and you will never come back!"

"Is that were the Falkose live?" said Jack.

"Fool!" snapped Francis. "Do you know nothing of Our World, This Realm? Don't you see?"

Jack furiously began to scrub off something on one of his lenses, sheepishly, ignoring Francis' intimidating glares.

"The Falkose are not here!" Francis stammered. "They have been gone for hundreds of years. There is no way over the Forest of Fogmoor, without the Falkose. The Southern Post is as far as you'll be able to go. I am sorry."

"You assured me that you would be able to help," said Gawdspelle.

"Ivan was hopeful as we all are," snapped Francis.

"But only a moment ago you said—" began Gawdspelle.

"Do you not think that I understand?" sighed Francis. "That we would not aid you if we could. We are Rikrooturs! And I have been commander of the Southern Post for most of my life. I know that there is only one way across those trees. If there was another way—"

"Oh, why don't you just tell them!" bursted in Piddlefoot. "Tell them the story?!"

Francis sighed, his head cast towards the ground as if a giant stone hung about his neck. Then he gazed up at the night sky. At last he could bear it no longer.

"Do tell us!" piped Mr. Tiddle getting ready to dig into his bag for his tea cups.

"I don't think it's a very good story," whispered Henry into his ear.

"Oh," said Mr. Tiddle unaware.

Francis looked out at the sea of faces before him. Piddlefoot was clutching his hands nervously.

"Look!" said Francis in a melancholy tone. "The Falkose are gone and they are never going to return." He sighed heavily yet again, then looked off. "They have seen their days in battle and they will see no more." Then suddenly his voice began to get soft and kind as if he had been remembering some fond memory. "The Falkose will never return." Then, he turned abruptly.

"They are dead," he said solemnly. "We will not see them again and you will not be able to ride them."

Everyone was watching him fixedly, their eyes burning.

"Where's Valen?" said Jack suddenly looking around.

"I thought he was here with us," said Henry.

Gawdspelle turned his head like a large owl, looking in various directions for Valen.

"Can Othoritees get past the gate?" said Gawdspelle.

"Not in this age or in any other," said Francis certainly.

"Quick," said Gawdspelle. "We must find him! Spread out into groups! He could not have gone far."

Veeps and Jack set off at once. Henry went with Oswald, Jude with Frump and Mr. Tiddle, Francis, and Gawdspelle went together into the trees. Minutes passed by, which seemed like several slow never ending hours. Where had he gone? Would the company see him again? Gawdspelle, Francis and Mr. Tiddle walked slowly through the giant withering white trees.

Silently, they walked. Then, a sudden thunderous noise rang through the eerie night. The ground shook softly. In the distance Mr. Tiddle spotted an ominous figure. Below it, at its yellowish scaly legs stood Valen, calm, and gazing up at it.

"Falkose!" hissed Francis, "they have returned. Impossible. Do not go near!" he shouted. "He could kill you with one swipe!"

But Valen took no notice of Francis' warnings.

Gawdspelle and Mr. Tiddle came closer.

"So it *is* true," said Mr. Tiddle. "The legendary Falkose are no myth."

At that moment Francis pulled off his shoulder a coil of golden colored rope he had been carrying. It dangled gently below his hands, nestling into the wet grass underneath him. Then suddenly as if the creature became spooked, it lifted its mighty wings. Huge gusts of powerful wind fell down upon them. Then the creature stood up from its stooped position.

"Stand back!" shouted Francis. "Stand back!"

The other Rikrooturs rushed over, followed by Henry, Jude and Jack. Veeps trailed at their heels, his hands a silver radiance.

"Falkose," whispered Oswald to his friends. "Can you believe it? They have returned."

"Stand back I say!" said Francis again, this time more forcefully. "Falkose are wild and untamed."

But the creature stood, majestically, powerfully, quiet. It flapped its wings fiercely, but otherwise did not move. And neither did Valen. Francis moved closer to it with his rope, dangling limply around his stumpy legs. Then, suddenly the creature flew up in the air, hovering above the crowd below. As fast as it went up it came back down. Then it pulled its head back and looked wildly at Francis, before it shot its face forward, screeching loudly as if it was indeed angry with him. Francis recoiled. Then, it did it again. Valen watched in astonishment.

"Stand back," repeated Francis ineffectively. Taking his own advice, he shrunk away. Valen stayed. Then, he walked closer to it, bravely. The Rikrooturs looked on, their mouths dangling like broken flowers still attached to their stems.

Valen stepped up to the side if it, his hand outstretched. But the creature backed away and then without warning it turned and flew into the night.

Valen followed it with his eyes as it flew upwards. Its feathers shimmering in star light.

"Great! Foolish elf! Now, he's gone and he shall never return," roared Francis heatedly. "I have been waiting for hundreds of years for them to return! And suddenly you, a ridiculous elf, show up and now they've disappeared again!"

"It is your fault they are gone in the first place," said Piddlefoot stepping in to defend Valen.

"You do not know of what you speak!" retorted Francis throwing down his rope. "I was there! I know what happened."

"It's because of you that the Southern Post is dead!" said Piddlefoot. "We have no work! You brought this on us!"

The other Rikrooturs stood by quietly watching the feud unfold.

"Our bond was sealed!" shouted Francis. "I *cannot* and *will* not be held responsible for the exodus of the Falkose. They left of their own free will."

"And now they return," continued Piddlefoot, "only to leave once they've seen you? Clearly, their memories have not lost the pain you brought them."

"It was not my fault," said Francis crestfallen.

"It was!" said Piddlefoot. "We will never see them again! The Southern Post has lost its purpose—because of you!"

"Enough!" countered Francis his face looking like a ferocious lion. "Do you want to know what really happened? Do you want to know the truth?"

"That would be most welcome," snapped Piddlefoot his arms fixed like a tree. "It's only been a few hundred years."

Francis recomposed himself. Frump, Oswald and Ivan gathered round. The children's ears perked up.

"Well, I'll tell you," said Francis softly. "If I must."

He traced the blades of grass with his eyes, nervously, slowly, collecting his fragmented thoughts. He gulped. The memory weighed upon him like thousands of rocks.

"Where do I begin?" he paused looking around at his audience.

"Yes, I remember. It was spring time," began Francis calmly, after some time. "Everything was alive. The trees were growing, stretching winter. Deer moved in the nearby forests. Birds soared through the warm spring day. The memory is burned vividly in my mind, but the wonder of it is not without pain." He drew a deep breath. "War was imminent. The Southern Post hummed with soldiers. The Falkose were preparing for battle." Francis looked around despondently. "But, we could not go to war without the King's youngest son. He was taken a few days earlier. So, I received the blessing of the King to be the one who went and reclaimed him. I was to fly on his oldest son, the Prince of the Skies. I would ride him into battle. Our mission was short and secret, but crucial in turning the tide against our Enemies in the East. By order of the King we would go and rescue his beloved son, who was being held for ransom by the wicked Krowz. So we prepared. Our confidence was set and our courage was unmatched. That day, we traveled hundreds of miles south, before finally turning East. After a long flight, we landed at dusk." Francis paused momentarily. "From the moment we arrived I have not been able to arrest the memories of the Trees near the Blackwitch's Dominion, for they have been seared deep into my mind. They were twisted, malevolent trees. Trees that watched what went on in the night. They were despicable. Guardians of the Blackwitch's kingdom. So, we stayed the night, under cover of darkness, just across the River Hid. We made camp and were in much need of sleep, so we set up a patrol and rested until first light. In the morning we rose and prepared for what would very likely be an inevitable battle."

"The Battle of the *Blackwitch*," hissed Ivan frightened, clutching his cane tightly. "I have waited to hear this tale since I was young."

"I'm afraid it is not a glorious tale, Ivan, my friend," said Francis solemnly.

"But Francis, to hear any story about a battle between the Mighty Falkose and the Foul Krowz of the East is exhilarating," said Ivan, coughing. "It has been far too long since I have heard the history of our people."

Francis remained silent for a few more moments before speaking again.

"That morning, the sky was gray and gloomy," he continued. "The Rikrooturs and the Falkose all knew what to expect for that day—but none of us knew how tragic it would be. Battle was brewing. We felt it in our bones. Smoke rose above the Blackwitch's tower."

"Excuse me," said Jack kindly. "But, *wouldn't* it have been better to have attempted a rescue at night?"

Francis turned towards Jack staring at him with contempt.

Jack immediately felt an icy electricity shoot up his neck as if he had said something unforgivable, his mouth suddenly became dry as a cotton ball and wondered if Francis might, at any moment seize him and be thrown into a dungeon never to be heard from again.

"That's a very good question," said Francis as Jack smiled awkwardly, surprised at Francis' response.

"It was?" said Jack sheepishly.

"Krowz hide themselves during the day," said Francis ignoring Jack's remark. "At night they are workers of mischief and they are everywhere. They hunt, murder and steal when the light of the sun fades. Yes, that is when they do their deeds. You see, they are terrified of the day and hide themselves, for that is why we decided to do our mission then. So we set out that morning certain that we would be back at the Southern Post by nightfall. But that was not how the events took shape." Francis' eyes were heavy as he looked off into the night across the dark fields. Valen thought he saw a tear fall from his cheek.

"Francis?" spoke Valen.

"That morning the Falkose were prepared as they would ever be. They were the Warriors of the Air—unstoppable, invincible, and I was proud to ride on the backs of such valiant creatures. Within moments we were airborne. We flew low, undetected. The King's son, the Prince, was imprisoned high up above, in a cave, near the Trechoris Mountains, the range bordering the Blackwitch's Kingdom. So, our band of Falkose flew, with the speed of all good-willed creatures and we descended like mighty warriors upon that cave. Within moments, the Falkose seized and slew the guards while others headed for the King's son. Soon he too was rescued and we made our way back to the Southern Post. The mission was nearly over, or so we thought."

Francis' audience listened intently, anticipating each word that came out of his mouth.

"We were a mere league from the Dominion of the Blackwitch when our troop was suddenly attacked. We thought we had slipped past our enemies gaze, but we were wrong. They appeared out of nowhere. And a fierce battle ensued. We were caught off guard to be sure, but ready to battle. And, though the Krowz of the East are fearless, that day they met veterans that they had not encountered before. As the Krowz descended, the Falkose tore through the air with the speed of ten thousand horses. The powerful talons of the Falkose slashed through the thick armor of the Krowz as if they wore nothing at all. Black blood from those vile breed of beasts spilled through the air, as their bodies crashed back down to land lifelessly."

"The Prince was swift and brave, possessing all the traits of a valiant soldier. We flew through the air as if a stallion with wings. My heart soared as I witnessed his unmatched valor. Then, all at once, everything became suddenly slow. The very air was silent. The Prince's wings went limp and was cast down out of mid-air, plummeting, like a stone falling from a giant peak into an endless chasm below. I descended with him, and as I watched him fall, his life slowly slipped away. We crashed into a small grove of trees and were quickly surrounded by the rest of the Falkose. I gazed down at his body where one foul black arrow had pierced his heart and blood poured out onto his glistening white chest. The Prince was dead. They gathered him and myself and we flew, all the way back to the Southern Post. It was the first and only time a Falkose has ever died. All the years we served together, and not one of them ever died."

"That is because it was from no random bow," said Gawdspelle.

"Come again?" said Francis.

"It was an arrow from a powerful bow that is known by the name of the Darkfeather," continued Gawdspelle. "They knew the only way to stop you would be with a weapon so potent there would be no room for error."

"Darkfeather?" said Piddlefoot. "I did not know the Krowz possessed such a thing."

"The Krowz stole it long ago," said Gawdspelle. "I do not know all the creatures of our world, but I know the story of the Darkfeather and I believe that it was perhaps the only way to kill such a beautiful creature as one of the Falkose. The death of the Prince was not your fault, Francis. Take heart, it could have happened to any of us. And yet, it happened to you and I do not think it chance." Gawdspelle paused.

"What happened when you returned?" said Henry after a few moments.

"The King was enraged," said Francis recalling. "'I sent you to rescue my son and you return with his corpse!'" Valen listened to Francis' sad tale. He continued. "He stripped me of my armor, which was made only for a rider of the Falkose. It was not long after that, that the Falkose began to distance themselves. The bond we had had for thousands of years dissolved over night. Within a few years they were gone and the Southern Post has been abandoned ever since."

"The King blamed you for the death of his son and he has not forgiven you . . ." said Gawdspelle thoughtfully. "I knew there was a great mystery for why this Post was abandoned and now I know why."

Francis looked away.

Piddlefoot too, looked remorseful. Then nervously, he went over to his brother and placed his hand on his shoulder.

The Rikrooturs, Veeps, Mr. Tiddle, Gawdspelle, Valen and the other boys watched intently as Piddlefoot started to speak.

"Brother," said Piddlefoot. "Forgive me. All these years and I never knew. If there is room in your heart, I beg for your kindness."

Francis stared, blankly, into the night. Then, he turned and spoke.

"Nothing more needs to be said," he began. "You are my brother and will always remain as one."

Piddlefoot smiled.

"Well, that's a relief," blurted out Mr. Tiddle wiggling his whiskers. "Dysapiers are not accustomed to anger, least of all between brothers."

Everyone laughed.

Gawdspelle walked away from the company and climbed upon a tiny knoll, where there grew a small flourishing tree. He placed his hands on his mighty sword, like a king before a coming war, seeming to gather that world into them all at once, pondering what course his army should venture. Then, his thoughts were interrupted, a sound like a rushing river flooded the night and a strong but sweet warm, wind engulfed the entire company.

Valen looked up above him, where there soared a massive flock of majestic creatures garbed in shining, shimmering, dazzling white, with flaxen beaks, glowing like golden horns, and emerald eyes and chests of glory glowing.

# THE WITHERED KING

The mighty birds descended gracefully, their beautiful wings flapping warm air past their unsuspecting guests. Valen had the urge to ride one, though he knew them to be far more dangerous than they appeared. The birds formed in a line and walked to the middle of the field, away from the company. They stood, waiting as though they had been waiting for orders to march to war for thousands of years. The light of the moon shimmered off their feathers. Francis stepped beside Gawdspelle.

"They wait for you," said Gawdspelle.

"Yes, I know," said Francis downcast.

"Do not trouble yourself. I am sure all they want is to discuss things that have long been forgotten—things that need to be said."

"I hope you're right," said Francis looking away. Then, slowly, he began to walk down the hill. Gawdspelle watched him as he walked across the field, his head hanging down.

"Do you think he'll be okay?" said Henry watching, as Francis stood, dwarfed by the massive birds.

"I'm sure he'll be quite fine. Come, let's give him a moment."

Gawdspelle placed his long leathery hand on Henry's shoulder and went back to where the Rikrooturs and the other boys stood.

A good amount of time passed by before Francis and the creature he was speaking with finished their conversation. When it had come to an end, Francis made his way back to where the other Rikrooturs and the boys stood. Francis approached the group, slowly.

"They have agreed to take you."

"Oh?" said Gawdspelle, his eyebrows raising. "Do they indeed? Well, this is very good news."

"They leave at once," said Francis. "They will take you to the Fields of Cylvirstone. Gather your things. Come, quickly."

"Will you be coming?" said Gawdspelle.

"Yes. I will fly with you across the forest and then return here."

"Thank you very much," said Gawdspelle. "How can I ever repay you?"

"It is perhaps best that you never return. Rikrooturs want nothing to do with This Realm. Our time for fighting is over. My people have been scattered throughout this land for hundreds of years now, but this is preferable to enslavement by Our Adversary. No, we will remain hidden, away from the fading Light. We do not want to fight. We do not want any trouble and we do not want to be caught up in any journeys, especially ones with elves, and humans."

"You do not speak for all of us," chimed in Piddlefoot. The other Rikrooturs stayed silent. Ivan had a sympathetic eye.

"Quiet," snapped Francis. "I am captain of this land. Whether we are blood or not. I will not here of such treasonous talk."

"But you cannot say who will fight and who will not. I will fight if I must. I am no coward!"

"You do not know of war," said Francis gravely. "You do not know of the blood and misery, the cold hard hatred of the armies of our Adversary. They are merciless. They want This Realm and all in it to be cast forever into darkness."

"Which is why we should fight," said Piddlefoot placing a fist in his hand with a smack.

"Enough!" roared Francis. "We will not fight!"

"Yes," barked Piddlefoot. "We will." His eyes flashed with glory, waving his hand through the air as if he was talking to a ten thousand man army. "What if we united the Lost Armies—the remaining Rikrooturs? What if we—"

"SILENCE!" said Francis. "Not another word." He sighed, breathing deeply. He looked over at the birds. The morning light of the sun had crept over the land and had painted the far eastern sky. The birds stood, their majestic feathers glistening in the gray morning light.

"We do not have time," said Francis after a moment of silence. "The Falkose grow weary with waiting. Come." He turned and began walking over to where they stood. Piddlefoot tore off in the other direction, muttering to himself. Gawdspelle turned and made off for Piddlefoot. Francis watched from a distance, where he and Gawdspelle talked quietly under an old withering tree.

Valen, Veeps, Mr. Tiddle and the boys said goodbye to the other Rikrooturs then turned and walked across the meadow. The birds stooped down, like trained horses. Valen threw himself over the neck of its soft golden feathers flickering from the growing light. Gawdspelle joined them.

There were enough Falkose to carry all of them and many more to spare. Though some did not have passengers, they ascended into the morning sky, inseparable from their kin. It was a deep relief to the entire company that the Falkose agreed to carry them across Fogmoor. Now that they had, they soared high up above the black trees below.

Valen looked back down at the land and towards Piddlefoot, felt hoping that they would see one another again. Then, he thought he heard fell voices in the air as his bird flapped its mighty wings effortlessly along. He clutched the bird's feathers tightly as though he was riding a wild horse. It flapped and cawed, turning its head left, then right. Valen was up front, trailing Gawdspelle and Francis. Their birds were swift. They carved through the air powerfully, their giant wings sweeping huge gusts of wind. Night had passed. The sun finally poked its head over the horizon. Strips of purple and red now blotted the morning sky. Wispy clouds shrouded the birds and their passengers as they flew onward.

"Hang on!" shouted Gawdspelle behind him.

They floated effortlessly through the vast sky. Then, lush green fields that stretched for miles and miles appeared. The sun, danced on the surface of the Emerald Sea far in the east. They traveled for days like this until at last, Valen saw high upon a hill an exquisite castle, bulging with magestic white stone. Its turrets, reached high into the sky. Tiny windows sparkled as the sun began to set. The company descended rapidly, the talons of the mighty birds brushing the blades of grass as they approached what seemed to be an impossible landing. Valen hung on as the creature lifted its head, stretching out its wings and grabbed at the air as if they were giant parachutes. The landing took a few seconds. Valen could hardly believe it. They flew like shadows. How they were able to land so smoothly, as heavy as they were, Valen only wondered.

"Amazing!" said Henry, his hair standing wildly out of place, greeting Valen as he jumped down to the ground.

"Yes," said Valen. "Incredible." Feeling unworthy to have ridden on such a magnificent creature, he moved away, quickly. The creature flapped its wings. It looked for a moment, staring wild-eyed at Valen. Valen stared back.

"He will not forget you now," said Gawdspelle. "Falkose never forget."

"I wish I knew his name," said Valen.

"I am sure that one day you will know it," said Gawdspelle reassuringly. "For him to give you his name, means that you will be forever united to him until he dies. He will bear you and you will be his keeper. You do not choose them, though. They choose you. They give you *their* names. You can never ask them for theirs. Wait, for it will one day come."

Gawdspelle left Valen and Henry to themselves, and headed over to where Francis sat, mounted high upon his bird. Jack and Jude rushed over to Valen and Henry.

"What do you suppose they're talking about?" said Jude curiously.

"I don't know," said Valen. "What do you think, Jack?"

"I'm not sure either."

Francis stood, unflinching, staring off back into the forest. They concluded. Francis bowed. Gawdspelle nodded like an old wise king. Francis mounted his bird, then took off, disappearing into the cool morning. Gawdspelle returned.

"Is everything okay, sir?" said Jack.

"Quite. Come, we must not tarry. Cylvirstone awaits us."

They hiked for some time under the giant trees surrounding the castle, past a stream, over a stone bridge then up a steep flight of stairs.

"Where is he taking us?" said Henry nervously.

"We are going to visit the Kings and Queens of Cylvirstone," said Gawdspelle. "Do not fear, for this land is safer than any that I have ever been in. Your heart may rest here. But, do not get too comfortable for we leave soon. If we are granted permission, we will travel under that mountain just over there." Gawdspelle pointed beyond the castle where a tall mountain loomed. It rose up against the morning light. Giant mountains stretched to the north and south. The mountain which they had to go under was positioned right in the middle and broke up the range which now towered above them.

Mr. Tiddle lagged behind, dragging his bag up the steps.

"Why don't you lose that thing?" said Veeps scowling. "You'll never make it to the top if you don't drop some of that weight."

Mr. Tiddle sighed, "If you're so concerned, why don't you help me?"

Veeps was speechless.

"Help you?"

"Yes," said Mr. Tiddle. "It would be very humane you know?"

Veeps stammered. "Oh, all right! Give some of it here!"

Mr. Tiddle took off his hat, adjusted his tweed jacket and sat down.

"What are you breaking for?" demanded Veeps.

"Well," said Mr. Tiddle. "I need to get a second wind. You know, conserve my energy. Dysapiers are not used to walking long distances or upstairs mind you. We like flat things—you know—comfortable." He smiled and pulled out his pipe.

"Conserve your energy?! I'll see you at the top!" snapped Veeps. He grabbed half of Mr. Tiddle's belongings. He tore off up the remaining stairs. Mr. Tiddle watched, puffing his pipe quietly. Veeps hands were glowing, his knuckles wrapped tightly around the bag.

Once at the top, Gawdspelle made for the giant wooden doors. He rapped his wrinkled knuckles boldly. Minutes passed with nothing but silence. Then, a noise rose from behind the door. Mr. Tiddle finally made it to the top heaving heavily. The door crept open.

"Yes? Who is it?" A withered creature with gnarled hands pulled back a window in the door.

"I am Gawdspelle son of Guthenne of Dingilf the Great. And I am a friend of your King."

"What business do you have?"

"I cannot divulge that here," said Gawdspelle. He looked around, his eyes darted back over towards Fogmoor.

"Well then I am unable to help you," said the creature. He shut the slot he was peering out of.

Gawdspelle knocked again. The slot slid back open.

"It is urgent that I speak with your king," said Gawdspelle.

"On what business?"

"I *must* speak with your king. There isn't time to waste. Now please—"

"It is against the laws of this country to let anyone in that I do not recognize. I have been here for many centuries and I have never heard of your name before. Times are evil. Foul rumors ride the air."

"If what you say is true, then all the more reason that I see your king."

The creature eyed Gawdspelle suspiciously.

"Tell me," said the creature,"how did you get into this land?"

"The mighty Falkose—they have returned."

"Falkose, you say—" he threw the window shut. A loud cranking noise began and the door creaked slowly opened.

"You mean to say that the Southern Post has opened again?" he said, finally outside. "Our neighbors, the Rikrooturs, are active? They are at work?"

"I am afraid not. They—" Gawdspelle's sentence fell short.

"A dwundlegob, too?" The creature spoke in disbelief. He was short and squat, and dressed in silver chain mail. He wore a tall pointy silver helmet and on his side hung a sword that was much too big for him to carry. It dragged along the ground as he encircled the company. "These are *strange* times. A dysapier too and humans? Well, why didn't you say so?"

"A dwundlegob!" the creature said again. "Very rare creature indeed!" He looked at Veeps mesmerizingly. He bowed. "Welcome to the Cylvirstone." Veeps bowed too. The old disheveled creature's mouth gaped open. "I have only read of your kind in the Great Books, in legends told by my father, long ago." He circled Veeps curiously sizing him up and down. Valen hoped that the creature did not notice him, too.

"I am Gloosclap, a Guard of The Great City of Cylvirstone," then he came uncomfortably close to Veeps.

Veep's hands glowed. He stared back, relentlessly.

"Most inhospitable!" blurted Veeps. The short creature turned away.

"Come!" He darted back into the castle.

The door was made of a dark wood that was enormously heavy. The creature shut it behind them. The walls were like a great cathedral, towering above them. Valen looked up. Skilled crafstman had carved exquisite renditions of battle scenes that had spanned thousands of years of Eoorthe's history. He walked along the hall, following Gawdspelle and Gloosclap, amazed at the magnificent carvings on the walls.

"Hey," said Jude stopping at one of the carvings. "Look at this."

Valen, Jack and Henry came over to where he stood, while the rest of the company carried on, Gloosclap was talking so much to Mr. Tiddle that he neglected to notice his guests falling behind.

"This is the Son of Darkness," said Veeps who also had stopped. He was pointing to a shadowy figure carved into the mighty stone who was fleeing six men mounted on silver horses, their swords pointing towards him warding off some hideous monster.

"What are they doing?" asked Henry, his voice quivering.

"He betrayed them," said Veeps, "and he was banished from their kingdom."

"Legend mostly," said Veeps running his hand over the carving. But, when he did a darkness suddenly covered the hallway. The Light in his hand faded then reappeared lit as he withdrew it.

"What was that?" said Henry in a frightened voice.

"Do not worry, Master Henry," said Veeps. "It is only one of the Great Stories. A tale you'll hear soon enough I'm sure. Folks have troubled themselves long enough about it."

"About what?"said Henry.

"Yes, Veeps," said Jack. "What?"

"About the Silverfeather—the bow crafted long ago from the Hallowed Trees of Iddling. Remember the two items Gawdspelle mentioned? One from the Wragog and one from the Tremendous Tree. The Key and the Silverfeather." Veeps studied the picture further.

"Coming?" said Gawdspelle, unexpectedly.

Henry bolted up off the ground, terror in his eyes.

"Nothing to be afraid of," said Gawdspelle reassuringly as he patted Henry on the shoulder. "At least not yet." He glanced at the picture. "At least not today. Come, we must go see Solominn, King of the Cylvirstone."

The company moved along slowly, awestruck by the grandeur of the hall which was made of white silverish stone. A long argent carpet lined the floor as they quickened their pace. Giant torches lit up the long hallway. Light from the cracked windows above trickled into the corridor.

Finally they reached a giant open room. In the middle stood a mighty round table. Around it sat many chairs. Gloosclap led them along the edge of it, up to the other side. Once across, they came to where there stood another doorway that led into another section of the castle. "This is the Hall of Kings and Queens," said Gloosclap. They had made it to the heart of the castle. Here stood seven thrones; one of wood, one of stone, one of iron, one of silver, one of gold, one that looked like fire, and one of green that looked like the leaves of trees. Then a figure emerged. He sat there, alone, his hair long and white, with no beard to be found. His hand withered, clutching a rusty sword. An iron crown webbed in dust sat upon his head. In his eyes there was great sadness.

"Ahem—" said Gloosclap clearing his throat. "My King, guests from beyond the Dark Forest—Fogmoor—have arrived." The king stirred slightly.

"Your highness—" continued Gloosclap. "*Guests*—from beyond Fogmoor—."

"Why are you burdening an old man?" he interrupted. "Leave me, I do not want to be bothered."

"This is Gawdspelle, Son of Guthenne of Dingilf the Great and he desires to speak with you."

"Gawdspelle?" the King moved slightly. "The name sounds familiar."

"That is because I fought with you three thousand years ago in the Terrible Wars." Gawdspelle paused. "You do not look well, Solominn, Mighty King of Cylvirstone."

"My heart is weary," he sat up, his withering hands gripping the arms of his grand chair. "What brings you at this hour?"

"Do you have no news?" said Gawdspelle.

"News of what?"

"The Factories of Darkness are in operation, ships are sailing on the Doobglash. The Verustome has been stolen." Gawdspelle raised his brow.

"Verustome?" said the King. "Bah! I don't believe in such foolishness."

"And what about the *Serifym*, the Great War at Iddling? You do believe in that don't you?"

He laughed a deep laugh, clutching his side with his gnarled fingers.

"So, you are hear to persuade me to join you in some crusade?"

"Yes, that is why I've come," said Gawdspelle clutching the hilt of his sword tightly.

"Because you've heard that the Factories of Darkness have opened?"

"Yes."

"Well, let me tell you something." He leaned forward, his hand gripped the shaft of his sword. "The Kings of this City have long ago abandoned allegiance to This Realm. Our ties have been torn far too deep for them to be sewn back together with such ease, least of all on such an occasion as this. Did you really think, Gawdspelle, Son of Guthenne, that you could usher me off to some war of yours? You fool."

"You will be the fool if you do not listen!" At this point, Gawdspelle seemed to grow another two feet into the air.

"You do not startle me," the King sneered.

"Our Adversary is gathering armies now as we speak. He will attack, if you are not prepared. He is on the hunt. Othoritees are on the hunt, people all over are being betrayed and fooled into believing despicable things. A gloom is falling and we must resist him. The *Lightlessness* has begun and the *Long Lawlessness* will follow. A time such as this has not happened since the Beginning of the Elves and when the Silver Knights fell. Now more than ever, we need the Seven Kings to unite the Cities of Gold and of Wood and of Iron and of Stone—all of them, before it is too late."

"I am the only King left. The others have fled. Some have hidden in the mountains. Others have ventured across the Far Plains, beyond the desert. Some have traveled to other lands far beyond the Emerald Sea.

They have taken their warriors with them. They will never return."

"They still carry the Firelight with them. They will return if they are summoned," Gawdspelle retorted.

"Not so," said the King. "They must be sought out. They must be found. They have left of their own free will, weary and full of grief from this world. They have moved on, hoping to find a better land."

"There is no better land," Gawdspelle took a deep thoughtful breath.

"There is still a hope that you have and rightly so. For is that not why you have stayed all these long years?" concluded Gawdspelle.

"This is my home. I have been here since I was a boy. I still love the fields and orchards and lakes and the High Mountains. All of it is dear to my heart." The King's eyes flickered with memories which stirred his heart. Valen saw his eyes go glassy with tears.

"And what will you say when your high wall around your vast kingdom cannot be protected? What will you do when they are breached with stone and fire and Our Adversary's slaves, which are taught all sorts of despicable things from when they are young, bring destruction and death and pillage to all you hold dear?"

The King paused and looked out across the hall.

"Then I will die fighting them alone! No one has yet been able to take my life. I am the master of it! I will say when it is that I die!"

"So be it," said Gawdspelle. "Your pride will be your utter ruin. I can see that I have wasted my time here. Well, if you will not aid us in war, will you let us pass through the land of Cylvirstone? You protect the passage Where the Mountains Meet."

The King paused, looking contemplative. "What business do you have in the Netherwurld?"

"We must make it to the Forges of Bood."

"You mean to prepare for war?"

"We will not make a stand here. Though war is imminent we must eventually gather all who can pick up a weapon. Everywhere Light is fading."

"The People of Bood have left long ago. The Ruins of the Great Forges is all there is left. There is no use in going. You are wasting your time. There is no hope."

"We are passing through the Forges of Bood and should we meet more who will join us, then so be it, but we do not seek refuge there. But, you are wrong. There is always hope. I believe One is coming that will arise from the pages of the Sacred Books esteemed by the Creatures of the Golden Blood."

"You speak of that vile race as if it has contributed to the welfare of This Realm. Let me ask you this, where were they when my people needed them? They have promises of there being a King that will come, who will destroy Our Adversary forever. Have you seen that day? Times are dark indeed but I will not put my faith in a worthless race of creatures hidden away in their precious City of Dorodroos in the Great Trees."

At that moment, Veeps became infuriated, his heart raging inside, billowing over with a fiery anger. He stepped out from behind Jack, his hands all aglow

"What is this?" said the Solominn. "A dwundlegob in my very midst? I have offended you? I see that your hands glow silver. Rare indeed. Your powers have only been heard of in faded legends and memories, but they have no power here, nor over me." The king laughed.

"You have insulted my people," said Veeps trying to maintain his composure. "*You* are a King and yet you are fit to roam the fields with wild beasts!"

At this, the king stood up, trembling. He dwarfed Veeps who stood barely above the King's knees. "Do not think that because I am old that I would not run you through with my sword."

"Please!" pleaded Gawdspelle. "We have enough enemies. Now is not the time for insults or violence. Veeps—" he placed his hand on his shoulder. "Save your powers for when they are needed." Veeps obediently withdrew his glowing hands.

The king turned his face away from Gawdspelle. He went over to the distant wall, where there lay a charred, splintered shield.

Gawdspelle watched from a distance. The King knelt down, running his hands along the edge of stone that it sat on. He remained solemn for a few moments before returning with a fragment of it.

"This is the shield I bore when the warriors of Cylvirstone marched out into war many years ago. It was during battle that I saw the Great Giants—Giants of the South—whose smoke curls up from their mouth. They are terrifying. Their stench is horrid. Their gaze is piercing. Their skin is thick and the fire in their veins will surely consume you if you come across them." He paused gloomily. "The last I saw of those foul beasts was when my people waged war against them just beyond the other side of those mountains which you now desire to pass through. They had brutalized our lands with their stench, their metal boots, their hideous flaming wagons. They ripped up trees which were thousands of years old. They turned lovely streams into pools of filth."

"You are not alone in your dismay," said Gawdspelle generously.

"I too fought against them. We had chased them along the pass, down to the river Rizzenne. You were betrayed by one I know and you have significant cause for bitterness. But let not that be the epithet of your people, let it not be the thing which, like vines around a tombstone blots out your name and it at last takes over you. It was both our desire to rid our land of that hideous weapon, but it was lost through no fault of our own. It is the nature of any wicked thing or creature to cloak itself in riddles and half-truths."

"That is why I shall not fight. You do not understand the despair which I have long endured. My sons fell, my daughters taken from me. My beloved bride, dragged away in chains like a beast to some foul place. Who will right this wrong? How can such reckless evil be accounted for? I would like to campaign with you, if I had but a flicker of hope, but long have I endured the agony of grief and I have found no comfort." King Sollominn bowed his head. His weary hands shook as they gripped the sword which he was leaning on. Valen gazed at the old king and though he did not know him, his heart was stirred by what he said. "I have watched the Light begin to fade," continued King Sollominn. His words floated gently through the air. "The fields do not sparkle in the morning as they used to. I know in my heart things are changing. I have lost much Gawdspelle Son of Guthenne, too much." Sollominn paused again and a passing shadow fell across his face. "The weapon of which you speak, I have heard of it in much lore since it came to my land. My father spoke to me of its many riddles. When at last, I was face to face with it, I understood its power. The *Darkfeather* is maddening—"

"The Giants carried it for Murkus," said Gawdspelle. "In secret they tried bringing it to him and he still desires it. It was for that, that you went to war and surely it was not in vain. Rumors are in the air that it has yet again been rediscovered."

"If it has been found, as you say, then you should make your way to the White Kingdom to warn the White Tigers, but do not be deceived. I have heard that Toren has found something or is looking for something—I fear it may be the weapon of which we speak. Though, I do not know for certain. He knows about that battle which was fought at the Forges of Bood. He knows what the Giants were carrying. Make no mistake though. I do not know what has happened to Vorfynn, Toren's father. He has been gone for months. My armies were broken long ages ago and my men were scattered. They are warriors at heart and should you ever meet one on your journey, you will know it at once." Sollominn took a deep breath as he surveyed his quiet land. Birds fluttered and tree leaves turned upwards by a small breeze which blew all around. An apple fell and rolled down the hill in the distance near a stream which flowed down from the mountain. Valen heard it bounce into the water. "This is the only way through," continued Sollominn. "You may travel through Looming Mountains, but at your own peril. The creatures who live in the cliffs just up there, told me that Snogardz roam the mountains these days. Be on the watch! That is all the time I can spare for you. It has been good to see you Gawdspelle," said Sollominn. He bowed. "Now, I have things I must see to." Solominn looked up at a tower which grew up out of the ground. It was massive in size and made of stone that had a story all its own to tell. Its foundations lay firmly near a bubbling brook, which carved its way throughout the landscape. Huge clouds now formed and rose and swept through the sky. Sollominn looked up at the looming tower. "If we meet again, then I hope it is not on the eve of war. I have seen too many battles in my life."

Gawdspelle nodded. Sollominn gathered his robe and walked with surprising swiftness. The clouds blew ever quicker. It was mid-afternoon now. Valen watched the old withered king walk on until at last he disappeared into the arch of the tower. A drop of rain fell from above. But the clouds continued to restrain themselves. A breeze continued to churn up leaves and twigs.

"Come," said Gawdspelle. "The time is late. Night will soon fall. Let's make our way to the forest on the other side of the meadows, then up the mountain."

"Can we rest now?" said Jude sleepily. "I'm very hungry and tired."

"We all are," said Jack squinting through his glasses.

"I know you are all weary as I am, but we must make it to the forest, just beyond the edge of these fields. There we will head up the mountain and then under it where the River Rizzenne begins," said Gawdspelle. "We cannot delay. Othoritees are on the move. The Falkose told me before we parted. They have seen them on the move. Danger increases each day."

After crossing the fields, they began making their way through the trees when they were met by a creature which looked very much like a large rabbit, with red boots on and a white tricorn hat. He held a bow and arrow pointed at the group.

"Halt!" he shouted. "You are trespassing. Give me one reason why I should not shoot you through the heart."

"We have been given permission by your King," said Gawdspelle.

"Othoritees are on the hunt," said the creature, his eyes flickering.

"How can I trust you?"

"We are no trespassers," said Gawdspelle.

"Then what business are you on? Quick, speak!"

"We make for the White Kingdom, beyond the River Rizzenne," said Gawdspelle.

"You are going to see the King of the Great Tigers? Well, why didn't you say so? Only those with courage have attempted to go through the Netherwurld." He glanced up at a dark opening at the base of the mountain. "Many friends have gone in there, never to have been seen again. What is your name?"

"I am Gawdspelle Son of Guthenne."

"*The Gawdspelle*? A Legna beyond the Great Star? I am sorry, I did not know, excuse me. I am shocked that you are here. How did you arrive?" He gave a low bow.

"I was sent," said Gawdspelle solemnly.

"Sent?" said the little creature putting his arrow back in its quiver. "This is alarming. What for?"

"I cannot answer you now in full," said Gawdspelle. "You must speak with your King should you want to know more, but even he was unwilling to hear all."

"Very well," said the creature respectfully and turned and walked up the steep treed side of the mountain.

They followed their guide closely as he led them up. They traveled up a long road tucked into the rocks of the cliffs far above the trees. It wasn't visible from the fields below, but just beyond, hidden in the side of the mountains, was a tiny city. They reached the gate in a few hours. The gate to the city was made of a dark wood. From up above them, their guide heard one of the tower guards call down.

"Who goes there?" came a voice suddenly.

"It is I, Chalfin son of Adynnow of the Highest Guard. I am on watch this night. We have a guest from beyond. Open this gate at once." The door creaked open. Inside it was deathly quiet. They were greeted by an older looking creature who was a head taller than Chalfin, but hunched over. His face weary with war and time. Yet his eyes were refulgent. His hands, aged and frail, yet strength endured, seasoned by battle. His forehead stuck out over his eyes. His nose was long and slender and his hair was gray and braided, tied back by a golden ribbon.

"Welcome, I am Alexander, Captain of Westeree known to some as the Mouth of the Netherwurld, the city you have just entered. In accordance with the Seven Kings of Cylvirstone, you must have permission to go beyond this point." Alexander stepped forward. "Under *normal* circumstances—yet," he paused grinning. "Welcome Gawdspelle son of Guthenne of Dingilf the Great, friend and ally against the *Lightlessness* and his company of friends, to Westeree. We are deeply grateful for your contributions thus far in the preservation of This Realm. It has been many years since the people of Westeree have seen anyone come through its gates. For far too long, our world has been silent. But, I am sure your journey has not been an easy one. Follow me, please. Quick, everyone into the gate. Our Adversary has many agents who hunt after the light of the moon fades and our city is no longer safe—for it will not be out much longer." More clouds rushed above them like a swift river. He looked up at the dimming moon and sighed.

Wearily, Valen, Jack, Henry and Jude entered through the gate. Veeps and Mr. Tiddle followed. Inside, lights from various houses tucked into the round rocks began bursting into the night as they shone out through the windows. One by one they entered into the city. As the lights began to glow, creatures that looked to be the same kind as the one who greeted them at the gate opened their doors and glanced sleepily into the darkness of the night. They yawned, stretched their arms and then the city suddenly burst into life. Many creatures of all shapes and sizes began rushing the streets. A collection of voices rose. Alexander stepped out from behind the darkness.

"How did you know it was me?" said Gawdspelle squinting. Then, slowly, he looked further and saw that Alexander's right hand was missing.

"Fain—my old friend!" shouted Gawdspelle. "I did not know that you retired to the mountains."

"Retired? Men of war do not retire," laughed Alexander. "The day I retire is the day I rest in my grave."

Gawdspelle laughed, too.

"It has been many years since I saw you last," said Gawdspelle.

"And years since I have been called that, yes," said Fain. "It is good that you have found me at this hour."

Valen, Jack, Henry and Jude, listened intently.

"Humans?" said Fain turning to look at the boys. He noticed Valen immediately. "And an elf?"

"Yes," said Gawdspelle. "I found them, imprisoned in the Other World."

"Imprisoned?" said Fain. "What do you mean?"

"Only the elf, but it is late and my story is very long," said

Gawdspelle. "We need rest and food. Will you accommodate us?"

"Of course," said Fain adventure flashing across his eyes. "Chalfin, lead the way."

"Thank you dear friend. Then, I will tell you the tale when my friends have rested," said Gawdspelle.

Chalfin led them up several flights of stairs before they finally reached a house carved into the side of the cliffs. It had exquisite details of trees and the stars above engraved in them, for Westeree was close to the heavens and its people loved the forest and night sky. It looked out below to the fields of Cylvirstone. Miles beyond lay Fogmoor, the Dark Forest and further on was the Southern Post, only a small speck now.

They went inside, sat down, made a fire in a giant stone pit, where they ate cakes and bread and a bubbly apple drink which Valen remembered long afterwards. Gawdspelle shared with Fain and Chalfin that night all that he knew about Valen, Murkus, the Key and the Verustome. Halfway into the story, the boys had fallen asleep. Valen, though his eyes were shut, remained awake. For elves do not sleep. Gawdspelle's voice eventually faded like a song nearing its end, and though Valen could not fall asleep, he had seen Gawdspelle in his mind's eye urging him towards the White Kingdom should they be separated.

Hours passed and Gawdspelle's voice had long faded. As Valen lay there, he heard a sudden rustling nearby. Slowly, he opened his eyes. Valen couldn't remember if Gawdspelle had actually spoken to him or if he dreamed it all. Near the tall wall where he and his friends lay, a caped figure with a long hood on appeared. Valen rose to his feet. He looked where the figure stood. It beckoned Valen with a wave of its arm. Though Valen knew they were safe for the time, he did not know what or who was under the disguise. Curious and knowing full well that Othoritees were on the move, he felt it was safe enough where they were and was confident enough it wasn't one of them. Valen followed the figure down a stone path that wound its way past a small stream. Then the figure suddenly disappeared leaving behind a small brown bag. Valen picked up the bag quickly and followed the figure towards the sound of a trickling brook. The hooded figure ran and jumped up onto a black horse which appeared next to a tree. The figure guided the horse towards a bridge which spread over the small stream. It turned and snorted, then stood on its hind legs before disappearing over a small bridge.

Valen returned quietly to where he was before the figure had arrived. He settled back down onto the ground wondering who the mysterious figure was. Though he was quite tired from how far they had walked since leaving the Southern Post, he sat up.

"I saw you leave," said Mr. Tiddle, not paying any mind to the bag Valen now had slung over his shoulder. Gawdspelle was in the distance still speaking with Fain and Chalfin near a large crackling fire.

"Best not to wander these nights alone," said Mr. Tiddle who appeared out of thin air, looking down the end of his nose. His large eyes blinked through his bifocals. Then, he sat up and adjusted his tweed jacket. His whiskers twitched and he gave a sniff.

"Oh," said Valen. "I thought everyone was asleep. Did I wake you?"

"No," said Mr. Tiddle taking a sip of tea and handing a pot to Valen. Mr. Tiddle had constructed another fire where a kettle of steaming water hung. "Here, would you like some?"

"Yes," said Valen. "Thank you very much. The air is getting crisp."

"As I say," said Mr. Tiddle. "Tea is the thing which warms any heart or body. Though, I can scarcely do without cream and sugar. Lots of sugar and cream is the only proper way to drink it. I do hope that these folks have both since I am very nearly out."

Valen thought about telling him about the figure but then Mr. Tiddle spoke first.

"Just look at those stars," said Mr. Tiddle taking another sip. "Have you ever seen so much beauty?"

Valen looked up. He had seen stars in Had Wink before. But it was true, he had never seen so much beauty in the spans of the heavens above. They glowed like silver fireflies floating above long dark fields. Swirls and swirls of them whirled about their heads as though a great wind blew them from some distant part of the sky. Clusters of stars wheeled round and round till they made Valen nearly dizzy.

"It's beautiful," said Valen pointing. He paused for a minute and took a sip of tea. "Though, what is that black thing?"

"The Lonely Planet," said Mr. Tiddle. "A sad, sad, hideous place. A place where love no longer exists; a place where those who are there, only have themselves to love. A place where the proud of heart have chosen to live (if you can call it that). The King, in his goodness and love made it long ago; for he knew that there would be those who would not love him. Those who would deny he ever existed in the first place or, ever cared for them."

"Is that why the stars go around it?" said Valen.

"I would go around it if I was a star too," said Mr. Tiddle pouring more tea. "Wouldn't you?"

"I suppose I would," said Valen. "Have you been there?"

"I have not and I don't intend to ever go. I have other places I would rather be. Many have been rescued from there," said Mr. Tiddle. "It was long ago and I dare not tell the story now, for it should take the entire evening."

"You said the King made it. But how did it get there?" said Valen persistently. "I have never known of any king to make planets."

"That too is a long story and we shall have to tell it another time, perhaps maybe the King himself will tell you," said Mr. Tiddle. "But, be glad it is far, far away and for now we don't have to go there." Mr. Tiddle poured some more tea in his large cup. Valen stared up above him looking ever deeper into the sky.

Veeps was now awake and quietly sitting near the cliff's edge staring out towards the Southern Post, further on into the great gulf of darkness. Mr. Tiddle at last started to fade as he tried effortlessly to keep his large eyes open. Eventually, he gave up, took a final sip of his, 'Travel Tea' (one that he had made especially for their journey) and fell fast asleep.

Night had cloaked them quietly as they rested from their travels. It wasn't long before they awoke to the rustling of Veeps and his voice piercing their sleepy minds. It was still cloudy and the temperature had dropped.

"Quickly!" whispered Veeps to Henry, then to the others. "We must leave at once!"

"What? Where?"

"We have to *go*!" hissed Veeps again.

Jack, Henry and Jude opened their groggy eyes.

"It's early—still dark," said Henry.

"Hullo?" said Jude dumbly. "Who's there?"

"A messenger has arrived. Murkus has sent his Othoritees. Murkus knows Valen is here. Word arrived in the night that they have captured two of the Rikrooturs," hissed Veeps. "They are getting closer, though the Falkose won't bring them across Fogmoor. They will have to go through that hideous forest on foot. Though, more may be coming. We must head for the Netherwurld at once!"

"But why do we have to leave now?" said Henry sorely. "Can't we rest some more?"

"Haven't I just told you? They are all together evil. Lost their minds they have. Othoritees are on the hunt—come now. It isn't safe! Now, up! If you want to live, we have to go into the Netherwurld. Now!"

Jude mumbled something about his stomach rumbling. Gawdspelle was standing next to Chalfin and Fain along with Mr. Tiddle.

"The sun takes longer these days to rise," said Fain. He cast his eyes to the heavens. "I do not have weapons to give you, but these cloaks should keep you very warm. They were made from the White Wolf's hair—creatures rarely seen these days. You should not wait any longer. Othoritees hunt in packs. If they catch you, they will shackle you and make you travel on foot through the Land of Decay—a barren land of the Old Ocean where no living thing exists. Some say a place full of spiders, serpents and," he paused, "dragons, too. Though, I have never been there myself. I daresay, I have been close to its borders."

"It is full of those creatures and many more," said Gawdspelle. "You are quite right."

"Those cloaks should keep you warm in the Netherwurld," said Fain in admiration as Valen and Jude displayed theirs proudly. "Winter is coming at least where you're going, you may see Black Snow."

"It's a little big," said Valen.

Fain laughed.

"What is Black Snow?" said Jude.

"Snow that has lost its Light," said Fain.

"Yes," agreed Gawdspelle. "One more thing that is becoming Dark. That is the first desire of Murkus. The second is the *Long Lawlessness*."

"What is the *Long Lawlessness*?" said Henry.

"I fear we all will find out soon enough," said Gawdspelle. "We must march on."

He paused and looked thoughtful again.

"I do not know all that is in the Netherwurld," spoke Fain. "It has been hundreds of years since anyone has passed through here. Once you make it to the other side you will soon be at the edge of the River Rizzenne. Once you get through the forest on the other side of this great mountain, you will soon arrive at the Kingdom of White Tigers."

"Thank you for your hospitality," said Gawdspelle. "I hope we will meet again soon."

"I am sure that we will," said Fain bowing. "Though I do not think it will be on the occasion that we desire."

"I believe you are right," said Gawdspelle. "Take courage old friend. Eoorthe has seen black days before."

"Yes, but not like this." Fain mustered a smile. "Goodbye."

"We will see one another soon," said Gawdspelle and he and the rest of his company followed him down a long stone cavern. Beyond, at the end, several hundred yards away and up the side of a steep cliff sat the entrance. It was dark at the entry point, which is what Valen saw earlier. But a giant wooden door guarded the way. Once the company was inside, the ceiling reached high into the mountain. Gawdspelle drew his sword and held it up with two hands. Slowly, the edges of it began to glow a faint orange then the length of the sword began to spread with a smoldering fire. In a few more moments it was shining bright orangish white. The darkness of the cave crept back a little.

"Come," said Gawdspelle. "Stay close to me. It is a day's journey through this place. Hopefully, we won't come across anything too terrible, but there are many strange things in the unseen places of This Realm and none I wish to meet."

Henry gulped. Time passed and the company was silent. The darkness and silence settled around them like a tomb. The trail went from dirt to stairs which spiraled down and down till at last the reached a cobblestone road. Gawdspelle raised his sword. Massive stone statues, men which held swords spanned the rocky cliffs which they were carved out of. It was a city. A stone wall rose out of the dark. The entrance to this underground city lay nearly in ruins. A huge iron gate had nearly fallen off its hinges. Gawdspelle led the company on his flaming sword illuminating their way. Valen then heard running water. He looked down to the right of the path and saw a swiftly running stream. The city was in ruins and abandoned, but Valen sensed something peculiar about it. Then he thought he saw the figure who had left the bag, but he was not sure. Shadows moved all around him, but then he was sure he saw something move.

"They say dead things live here," said Mr. Tiddle suddenly. "I know, I've read about it."

Valen continued watching for the figure.

"What kind of *dead* things?" said Henry frightened.

"Men who walk on all fours," said Mr. Tiddle. "Man-beasts. They only eat dead things here, for they are dead themselves."

"Have you ever seen one?"

"Of course not! This is my first adventure. All I know are books. Books! But, stay close to me if you can't stay close to Gawdspelle—I'll protect you as best as I can." He pulled out a dagger. It glistened from the light of Gawdspelle's sword. Henry's eyes grew large and said, "You wouldn't happen to have an extra one would you?"

"Only one, I'm afraid. This was passed down to me by my great-great-great-great-great grandfather. It's widely believed by my ilk that his skills were used in the First Wars by the rulers of his time."

Henry stared blankly as he watched the faint shadowy outline of Mr.

Tiddle walking ahead of him.

"What did they use your grandfather for?"

"He could vanish in an instant without anyone noticing. He slipped behind enemy lines while no one was watching, undetected, unchecked."

"Oh," said Henry.

Mr. Tiddle stopped and turned around.

"Then he would cut their throats."

"Cut their throats? That's disgusting. I thought your people were lovers of tea and books?"

"Well, they were wolves if you want to know. Great and terrible wolves, that stole many a children. What else were they to do? Besides, we still love tea," said Mr. Tiddle turning to continue on the trail. "It was only that my ancestors cut so many throats that they retired to books and tea. We have given up on war and battles for the time. But, should the time come we will be the first at arms! The sword was long ago fashioned to keep evil at bay and those of good hearts should never render them to any ruler. For what should happen if their rulers became wicked. How then would they defend themselves against tyranny?"

Mr. Tiddle waddled up the path Gawdspelle led them down; he continued talking to Henry as they marched through the thick gloom of the Netherwurld. Gawdspelle found a small worn path through the rough stone of the cave. Valen looked behind them, and in the darkness, Wysteree, which he had seen a few hours ago, had faded. They had come to a path in the cliffs which were on either side of an old city under the mountain. Stone walls now appeared and they were in some sort of corridor. The light of Gawdspelle's sword burned bright. Twisted shadows danced on the nearby stone walls. Valen could also make out boulders that looked like they had been placed there by someone very large. Someone he didn't want to imagine. He saw that there were several of them. Suddenly, Gawdspelle came to an abrupt stop.

He held his sword high and its bright light was cast onto the walls.

"Stay close!" he said. "Valen, I need your ears. Veeps, I need your hands. Come, I do not know what we will encounter here—in the dark."

Valen rushed up to his side. Veeps followed.

"What do you hear?" said Gawdspelle.

Valen strained his ears.

"Nothing sir," said Valen."What am I listening for?"

"Nonsense!" said Gawdspelle. "You're an elf. Don't tell me you can't hear."

"Honestly, sir. I ca—wait! I can. I hear a voice!"

"Well, what does it say?" said Gawdspelle.

"It's calling us. It's telling us to follow her."

"Good," smiled Gawdspelle. "That is the Lady of the Nethurworld. A Princess from Cylvirstone who died long ago. She guides all those through the Lone Passage in this awful place. They say she came in here alone, looking for her beloved. She was lost for some time, before they found her horse trotting along the River Ryzenne just beyond. No one knows what happened to her. Some think she still lives in here. Some think she haunts it. Others think she protects it."

"You mean she disappeared?" asked Henry nervously looking around in the darkness.

"I do not know. All I know is that those who have followed her Voice, have made it safely to the other side. So, we will follow it and Valen shall be our guide, since I cannot hear it. But, mistake not her Voice for any other, for there is more than one voice under the mountain."

"We must hurry though. Light is leaving Eoorthe and I do not know how long we have before Murkus makes his first move. We must travel with stealth. Come, we make for the Forges of Bood just a night's journey through the mountain."

Gawdspelle held his sword high above Valen's head as they walked along, casting light along the narrow path. He listened closely as he heard the woman's voice penetrating the silence of the cold damp underground. She was singing. It was soothing and sweet, but sorrowful and heartbroken and it was in a language he had never heard before. But, the words flowed over his heart like an ocean. Valen could tell that she had lost something indeed. Perhaps it was the man she went out to find many years ago. He did not know.

He walked along, stepping over small stones that had fallen from the massive ceiling above. On either side of their path the hillsides rose higher and higher before meeting up with the ceiling. Veeps walked in between Gawdspelle and Valen, his hands glowing dimly. A soft silvery glow emanated from them, illuminating his tiny vest. His large eyes glowed with the orange of Gawdspelle's sword. Henry, Jack and Jude followed closely behind while Mr. Tiddle hummed quietly to himself as if he was waltzing through a quiet, sun filled forest without a care in the world. Though, in his hand he still held his dagger close to his side, unsure of what lay hidden in the blackness.

Hours had passed and nothing but the long darkness of the seemingly endless caves filled their eyes. Gawdspelle's sword seemed to get smaller as the gloom wore on. Valen continued to follow the voice of the Lady as they climbed up long narrow passageways. At times they had to stoop low to get through cramped sections of stone. Other times, the ceiling of the caves was so high that it felt like they were floating in a sea of ink, forever lost.

As they pressed on, Valen began to hear fell voices in the air. At first they were only whispers. Soon, they turned into voices that everyone could hear.

"What is that?" said Henry.

"They are Sools," said Gawdspelle. "Withstand their speech if you can, or you will find yourself bound to this place. Stay close to me."

"What are they saying?" said Henry again, his voice shaking violently.

"Do not try to understand them," said Gawdspelle. "Sools are mischievous, deceptive. Come, we are close to a resting place. The Spire of Cylvirstone, a place that we can take refuge in for a while."

"We're sleeping here?" said Henry. "It's terrible, too terrible. The darkness is unbearable."

"Not sleeping," said Gawdspelle. "Resting for a while."

Just then Jack slipped and fell.

"Heeeeelp!" he shouted as he tumbled down the face of a slope leading to the edge of a murky body of water at the bottom of the small ridge they were now on. He kicked out his feet and dug them into the ground as he slid faster and nearer to the bottom. "Gaaaaaaawdspelle!"

He crashed into something hard and crunchy as he came to a sudden stop. Bits of it tumbled onto him as he lay in a heap of it. He looked back up to where he was and he could see Gawdspelle's sword glowing brightly. He stood up and stepped backwards into the water, pulling his foot out quickly. He looked down and there on the ground sat his bag that he had been carrying. "Bones!" he muttered to himself. "These aren't rocks, these are bones!" He grabbed his bag and walked up the hill a few steps. He glanced a little farther down the shore of the lake. Then, he noticed the water moving. Gawdspelle's sword shined on what he thought was the surface, but instead of water he found a scaly beast rearing its head up out of the water like a giant crocodile, waiting cunningly. His teeth were white and dripping with blood and slime, his eyes a golden yellow.

Valen watched helplessly as Jack and the beast faced one another. Jack tried running back the way he came, his legs moving stealthily up the slope. Then he heard a force of water, looked back and saw the terrible beast bearing down upon him. Suddenly a violent flash of silver lit up the cave, smashing into the creature's face. Veeps was coming down the hill. Jack fell again, slipping closer to the creature's giant gaping mouth, his teeth hungry for Jack. Then, 'fooooom' Jack heard another one of Veeps silversluggz crash into the creature again. This time it howled violently, crashing back into the water, followed by a vicious hiss. The creatures eye burned hot with ball of dazzling silver light. It continued to glow after the creature had gone back under the surface of the water and armor of all shapes and sizes lay at the bottom of the small lagoon.

Jack fell down on the ground as Veeps came nearer. Without warning, the creature reared its ugly head again, lunging out of the water fully, dashing wildly up the banks tearing after Jack's legs.

"Hurry!" shouted Veeps grabbing Jack by the back of his coat. He fired another one into the beast. It moaned and growled ferociously.

Jack ran as fast as his legs could carry him. He tripped on rocks as he scrambled up the steep hill. He passed Gawdspelle on his way who now had his sword drawn as he ran down to battle with the creature.

Jack stood a top the hill, safely on the trail he fell from moments ago, breathing heavily. He looked on as Gawdspelle wielded his swift and terrible flaming sword at the foul creature. Veeps moved quickly in the darkness, firing comets of silver at a terrible speed.

"Flee you monster of death!" shouted Gawdspelle and he swung his sword and chopped off the creatures front leg, making it screech horribly. It withdrew into the water and disappeared at last, the water whirling around its ugly head. Gawdspelle and Veeps retreated back up the slope.

Back at the trail Gawdspelle continued to hold sword high above his head.

"Thank you for saving me," said Jack still breathing heavily. "How can I ever be of service to you?"

Gawdspelle grinned.

"Watch your footing," said Gawdspelle. "We are sure to meet more creatures in the this darkness."

"The elf!" shouted Veeps suddenly. "He's gone!"

"And the boys, too," added Mr. Tiddle.

"Impossible!" said Gawdspelle. "How did this happen?!"

Gawdspelle turned his head swiftly for any sign of him.

"They were here just a minute ago," said Mr. Tiddle. "I—" He looked around. "There!" He pointed. "Look—a passageway. They must have fallen below!" Gawdspelle turned and there, just beyond the trail to the right of where they stood, was a long narrow stone passageway which fell into a deep chasm.

"It's too small for me," said Gawdspelle. "Veeps, you must go with Jack."

He placed his hand on Veeps' shoulder.

"You must find the elf at whatever cost," Gawdspelle said.

"Wait!" said Mr. Tiddle. "I don't think Jude went with Valen and Henry."

"What do you mean?" asked Gawdspelle.

"I saw him go off in the other direction. He said he had dropped something," Mr. Tiddle said exuberantly.

"Alone? Dropped something? You have been fooled! Jude has dropped no such thing! He has been playing us as a fool! He has been up to mischief since he first came here," Veeps snapped. "I saw him long ago. He wandered into the Woods of Dorodroos when I was a young. Now I know it! He was looking for something. Asked if I could help him."

"Looking for something. Dropped something?" said Gawdspelle suspiciously. "When was Jude not with us?" Why didn't you mention this before?"

"It was a memory that I haven't been able to place since I first laid eyes on him in Had Wink; he is older now, but surely nothing has changed in him. He seems just as clever and deceptive as he was when I first saw him."

"Why did Valen and Henry *leave*?"

"I heard Henry yell amidst the clamor. He must have lost his footing and Valen tried to rescue him," said Mr. Tiddle frazzled. "I can think of no other explanation."

A hushing spell fell over the company.

"Jude—I didn't trust him in Had Wink and I don't trust him now!" Jack gathered himself. "The Southern Post! Do you remember? He was out doing something.Valen and Henry must have followed Jude!" shouted Jack, his heart racing. "I heard Jude mutter that he had someone to meet."

"I do not know who he could have to meet. Though, I believe Jude has been here more than Master Veeps knows, which is the reason for this riddle. There is no time to lose! Valen cannot be captured. I do not know if he is lost or not—yet. If Othoritees capture him, it will become darker yet! We must go and find him at once!"

"Been here before? What do you mean? We came here together over the Bridge in the Sky," said Jack.

"Long before I was sure Valen was an elf," began Gawdspelle."I visited Had Wink. I watched your island for a very long time. I discovered Jude one day on the shore late in the summer months getting off a hideous ship with black flags that had recently moored. He had been gone for days before he anchored. He has been caught up in a web of riddles that we must untangle. Do you remember Fin's leg and why it was in a hole? I fear Jude in haste had tried burying the horse. I had been looking for that horse ever since it went missing from the Horsekings. Fin was stolen. For what purpose I could only guess. Didn't you think it odd? A horse with its leg missing? Jude was hiding all his activities. I believe he has done something terrible, but we can only guess what that is. For good or evil I sense that these events are not entirely in our own hands. The days are treacherous. Wherever he has gone to and whomever it is he has gone to meet, we must accept it for now." Gawdspelle finished his thought and turned and looked up at the thick stone walls.

"Accept it!? Suppose he gives us up? Jude knows our plans." Jack breathed heavily. "What about the Key? What about Murkus and the Othoritees hunting for us—and Valen?" said Jack with a great sigh.

"Othoritees are frightening indeed. They are growing and are hunting down anyone who is not loyal to Murkus. The way of tyrants. Death and slavery as it has always been. It is all they care about. But death is never the end," Gawdspelle said with a heavy voice. "I think Jude is more foolish than any of us yet know. It is not the Key he will speak of, but only his desire for gold that he cares about. Murkus makes many promises and I am sure he has promised a position of power in his Kingdom. We will bear this Key for a time, though it terrifies me. No one knows what is behind the Door, but Murkus has been trying to get through it since he crept into Pestyphooris long ago. We will find out what to do with the Key soon enough. In the mean time, I have sent a warning to a friend should we have gotten separated. He'll know what to do should he meet Valen and hopefully he has received it already—though I am worried more than ever now that Valen is on his own. We will continue on towards Hyddenne—the Fair Princes will know what to do. Come, we must bear this Key's safe passage to The Festival of the Two Wandering Stars."

"We could use the remaining light from my lantern for our journey," suggested Jack.

"It won't last in this darkness," said Gawdspelle, the orange light from his sword illuminating the lines of his aged face. "There is no time to waste!"

"I'll go after Valen sir," suggested Veeps bravely. "The road may be dangerous, but I'll find a way. If I can intercept him or at least follow him to where he has set out to go, then it may save us all grief before our journeys' end. I will go alone."

"Alone?" said Mr. Tiddle. "You can't be serious?"

"It is quite alright. I had been planning on something happening such as this," said Gawdspelle placing his hand on Veeps' small but sturdy shoulder. "You cannot let the elf fall into the wrong hands—"

"You mean we are to separate?" asked Jack. "Wouldn't it be wiser to stick together?"

"We will meet again at the the White Kingdom," began Gawdspelle. "I believe it is safer and less conspicuous to have Veeps track him. I worry about the size of our company drawing too much attention. Now—there is no more time to lose," he said. "We must make it out of here and then soar as the bird's flight!" He paused. "Veeps?" Gawdspelle sighed deeply. "Do all you can."

"I'll meet you in Hyddenne," said Veeps bowing low to the ground.

"I'll go with you," said Mr. Tiddle suddenly and grabbing his pack. He slung it over his shoulder. He pulled his hat down hard, his ears sticking out.

Gawdspelle looked down at him with a raised brow.

"I'll go *alone*," said Veeps agitatedly ignoring Mr. Tiddle's uninvited company. "Thank you, but I do not need your help."

"Ah, but you do," said Mr. Tiddle. "I know a great deal about things and you'll need me, for—things like...protection." He grabbed his dagger. "Thank you," said Veeps trying to conceal his uncomfortableness. "I will go alone. I must go now."

"There is no time to delay," hurried Gawdspelle. "Valen! We must find him! Quickly!"

"Great!" said Mr. Tiddle ignoring Gawdspelle as he gathered up his teacups off the ground. "I'll just gather my things."

"I don't think you understand," said Veeps getting angry. "I'm going *alone*."

"There we go," said Mr. Tiddle placing the final one in his bag. "Ready."

Gawdspelle watched the two curiously.

"I can *go* without you," said Veeps emphatically. "Besides, I know of no other creature who drinks tea at such odd times. We are in the Tunnels of Cylvirstone, with Water Dragons,— and the threat of the Sools and you have time for tea?! What possible use could you be to me!?"

"Ahh," said Mr. Tiddle politely. "You see, it is tea that calms the heart. Where would we be if we did not drink tea in times of war, danger? You say that I shouldn't drink tea at a time like this? It is *because* I drink tea at this time that makes me your perfect companion."

"We do not have time for this!" replied Veeps perturbed.

"He's quite right, Mr. Tiddle," said Gawdspelle with a chuckle. "You'll need a companion."

"Great!" said Mr. Tiddle. "Let's go!"

"YOU ARE NOT COMING WITH ME!" shouted Veeps finally, his temper flaring up.

"Dee-light-ful," said Mr. Tiddle unmoved.

"Are you so stupid?" said Veeps.

"Actually, I have read a great many books. Books you would do well to read, too."

"That's it," spat Veeps. "No more, I cannot take another moment of this. We're wasting time. I'm off!"

"This is perfect," said Mr. Tiddle. "I have read about dwundlegobs in my many books and now I get to go on a grand adventure with one. Splendid!"

Veeps stomped down the path towards the narrow tunnel below angrily, his hands aglow. He slipped down the small trail that led in front of them towards a sharp edge. He jumped down over it and slipped into a small corridor that fell into blackness. In a few moments he was gone. Jack watched him as his silver hands faded into the blackness.

Mr. Tiddle waddled closely behind. Jack noticed the faint glow of his tobacco pipe fading as Mr. Tiddle sung merrily to himself with his bag of books and tea swung over his back.

"Well," said Gawdspelle after a moment of silence. "We make our way to Hyddenne. There isn't a moment to lose! Come, Jack! We cannot follow after Valen because the path is too small! It is very grim news that Valen has fallen out of my hands—for now—but I must leave his fate with Veeps. In my heart, I fear much—for should he fall into the hands of Murkus, fiendish beasts and creatures of all sorts which have not been seen in thousands of years shall arrive in This Realm. They will come like a hideous darkness to our already darkening world! Come! Quickly!"

With that, Gawdspelle threw his mighty sword high above his head and trudged on through the dense atmosphere of the cave. Jack followed quietly. He looked on at the back of Gawdspelle and was glad that he was not taken under the dark water.

# MIGHTY RUINS

"Are you sure about this!" said Henry hanging onto a large rock. A swift river was forcing him to hang onto the rock by his fingertips. "I mean, what if we get lost!?" Henry tried shouting over the raging water.

"We are lost now!" said Valen. "I have no idea where this river goes and it is dark, too. We may have lost Gawdspelle, but he found me once and I am sure he will find me again. If we pick up the Lady's Voice, once we get to the end of this river, then we'll make it through. We will wait there. The river must come to and end."

"But we *have* followed the Voice and now look where we have ended up. We have fallen down a long tunnel and we have no idea where we are," said Henry hopping over a small ledge where the trail fell off to the right. "What if Gawdspelle doesn't find us? Or worse, what if we meet someone we dare not want to? Gawdspelle clearly said that Murkus' Othoritees are on the hunt. Suppose we meet these Othoritees? What'll we do then?"

Valen came to an abrupt stop.

"That's the thing about getting lost, of course we shouldn't have gotten lost. But if Murkus is to find me," he began as his face stiffened. The sound of the river grew. "Then you are right. It is for the worse."

"But," interrupted Henry, "we can't just *wander* around Eoorthe forever. I mean where are we even going?"

"We are going to make it out of here is the first thing and hopefully to the White Kingdom. Though I am not at all sure I want to go there," Valen said. "Now, I don't know the way, just as much as you don't. But, suppose we just make it to the other side of the mountain and find that Gawdspelle is there waiting for us? Seems like the best thing to do. There is no going back where we came. It is too far a climb. We must float down the river as best we can. I think I see a light growing."

Henry shuddered, then gulped.

"Have you gone mad? You can't really be serious?"

"I *am* not crazy, but I am serious," said Valen resolutely. "We have no choice! The river is rising!"

"I cannot hold on anymore!" shouted Henry. Valen heard Henry let go and then his voice faded down the cavern. Then, Valen fell into the swift dark water too.

The river rushed on and on until at last it slowed and they came to a shore. Henry dragged himself onto the beach. Valen soon washed up. A faint light glowed all around them. A jagged doorway appeared. A long flight of stairs rose up into the mountain near the beachhead. The river flowed quietly behind them. A small light trickled down the stairs.

"This looks like the only way to go," said Valen. "Come on, I hear the voice again!"

Neither of them said anything to one another for the next few hours. They trudged along up the long stairs, when at last a path with white stones emerged. All around them felt as if they were in a graveyard. The Voice continued to grow and at first Valen could not tell if it was just one voice. He heard a host of voices which seemed to grow with each step.

Henry swatted spider webs out of his face and Valen, who could see much better, continued to lead the way.

"Do you suppose it's that way?" said Henry getting up and pointing up towards the stairs. "The trail goes no other way." He looked around to shore up his doubts.

"There's only one way to find out. Come on, let's go," said Valen stepping up.

They made their way up a few steps, but before they got any further they began to hear a strange voice again

"It's the lady's Voice," shouted Henry jubilantly. He hadn't been able to hear the Voice before. Just then the ground shook.

"What was that?" said Henry feeling as though it might be an earthquake or worse some horrifying creature which he imagined to have huge teeth and a large appetite.

"I do not know," said Valen. "But I do not like it whatever it is." The voices, which were beginning more and more to sound like growls, reached up into their hearts and ears.

“There are the voices again. I have been hearing them for some time,” said Valen. “I fear it is no Lady’s voice.”

“What if they’re—lions, bears—or worse, *giants*?” said Henry quivering.

“I do not like the sound of it either,” said Valen as the voices intensified in his ears.

“This is awful,” said Henry. “They could be trolls?”

“Shhhhhh!!!” said Valen putting his finger up to his lip. “I hear them again.”

“I think it’s coming closer,” said Valen looking around for a place to hide. “Come on. Whatever it is, I don’t want to be seen by it.”

“Me neither,” said Henry. “I don’t want to be eaten by a Troll or some strange animal in this awful place!”

They’re conversation fell off when they finally reached the end of the long steps and they felt things becoming warmer. They went right and then down another set of stairs, on into the long darkness, before they came to a cold stone wall at the bottom.

A curious glow of torches illuminated the end of the tunnel they were walking through and then it grew dark. All around them stood ancient trees. Valen stopped and listened. Above them loomed a massive stone ceiling. They had stepped into a large opening. The river which was on the other side of where they now stood appeared to the left of where the stairs were. A quiet stream of water came out from above a face of large lion’s mouth carved into the rock and cascaded onto the ground below, forming a small stream which wounds its away across the floor. Valen followed it along as the light flickered off the surface of it. The water wound its way around and down towards a cliff in the distance, disappearing into the blackness.

“Shhhh!” he hissed, placing his hand in front of Henry to keep him from going farther. They waited for what felt like an hour. “Do you hear that? There it is again. Look,” he hissed, pointing. “Those lights are moving. They are torches. Someone is in here too!”

“What is it?” said a gnarled voice out of the thick blackness.

“Animals,” said one dark figure, which stood as large as an old oak tree and standing practically in front of Valen. Valen felt something hot and hairy brush past his face. “I can’t see anything.”

The creature gave one last sniff, turned, then walked over to another creature roughly the same size as itself. The torches which the creatures had been carrying, stuck out of the wall and grew brighter as the creatures shouted and stomped.

Valen now saw their huge silhouettes. "Giants!" he thought. Some of them were leaning on giant **Y** shaped pieces of wood and had large leather type bags strapped over their shoulders. Torches which lined the walls, glowed brightly. Above them, where the creatures stood, hung thick iron chains. In the distance near the end of the river, which had turned into a tiny stream, fell over the edge of a huge cliff. Six of the creatures were now huddled together. Valen and Henry heard a rumble, when without warning, more of them in another adjoining cave flooded into into a huge circular area. Huge rocks formed a ring around them.

"What do you suppose they're doing," said Valen gripping the sides of the stone wall more firmly.

"Probably planning how to eat us," said Henry with a look of dismay. "Look at that pot they have."

A few of them were stomping on the ground, while others pulled giant stones from huge leathery pouches (Henry imagined them to be giant potatoes) that hung across their bare, gray chests, tossing them into the air as if they were about to go into a great big stew.

"Well that explains the ground shaking," said Henry trembling. Then he gasped. "Incredible," he said as if he had discovered for the first time an unknown species of animal. "Look how big they are!"

"Keep you're voice down," said Henry. "Otherwise we really are going to be eaten! But look, they're breaking up into sides," said Valen pointing.

On either end of the wooded arena stood two oddly shaped trees, with one on either side. The trees had vines wrapped tightly in between them forming a goal of sorts. Next to their trunks lay a small, shiny, polished green stone. Some of the creatures began tossing huge boulders back and forth to each other as if they were as light as cotton balls. The torchlight glistened off the green stone.

"It looks like they're about to begin some sort of game," observed Valen.

"A game?" said Henry sarcastically. "Do you think creatures like that play games? They are planning to eat us!"

Next, six of the giant beasts walked to one side and six of them to the other. A few of them were stretching, one grunted and turned his head side to side like a large angry bull rearing up for an attack. Another took what Valen thought to be a massive wooden slingshot and jammed it into the ground. Next, an old one came to the middle of the field and began talking. After a few more minutes he went back over to two oddly shaped trees.

"On my order," shouted the tallest one. His voice boomed

throughout the entire cave. Valen and Henry covered their ears. “FIGGGGHHHHTTT!” The ground shook, thunderously. At once, the creatures came crashing across the field like wild charging bears shaking the arena with destructive force. Then came boulders which flew through the air as fast as arrows. Some of the creatures had their slingshots out placing boulders in them as they ran, pulling back on the strap attached to it, pummeling their opponents mercilessly with them. Valen watched as they exploded on impact, knocking the creatures to the ground with tremendous force, while others missed entirely, crashing against the wall like massive meteors. The little green stone remained untouched.

Loads of rocks the size of small houses soared back and forth crushing the other creatures, while some lost complete balance, crashing heavily back to the ground. The game was over in less than an hour. While two of the biggest creatures were fighting, one of the smaller ones finally managed to move the green stone to the other end of the field. The winning team was shouting and cheering, torchlight and shadows danced off the stone walls. Though it sounded more like the roars of thunder smashing through the heavens. Valen cupped his hands and put them over his ears again. Henry did the same.

“Well, I guess that’s it,” said Henry with a startle. “We should be going now.”

“I think we should stay,” said Valen, “I mean what if they can help us? We are lost.”

“Eat us is more like it,” said Henry. “Come on.”

Henry turned around to walk up the stairs they had come down, when one of the creatures from the other side of the field seemed to be looking curiously at him.

“I don’t think we’re going anywhere,” said Valen gazing upwards into the face of one of them who appeared suddenly. “We’ve been spotted.”

Henry turned immediately and rushed back towards the stairs, as fear turned to beads of sweat which began pouring down the sides of his face. And just when Henry thought for sure the creatures would begin skewering them in preparation for a nightly roast over a hot fire or even possibly to boil them alive in a large iron pot, a most strange thing happened. The creature bowed as if to introduce himself.

“I am Mogus,” said the biggest one with a large welcoming grin.

“Valen, RUUUUNNNN!!!! They’re going to eat us!”

The creature turned around and picked Henry up by his waist.

“Please, don’t hurt him!” shouted Valen. “He’s my friend.”

Then the remaining creatures that were on the field, made their way over to the noise.

"What have you got there Mogus?" said the tall skinny one.

"Human," said Mogus twirling Henry around like a stick. "And an elf."

"Elf?" said the squat little chubby one who had won the game. He waddled over to get a closer look at Valen. "I thought elves were gone from This Realm?"

"Yes, I thought elves perished long ago," said another coming nearer.

"Strange animal," said Mogus. Henry tried to scream but found his mouth unable to open. After Mogus had finished his examination of Henry he placed him gently on the ground.

"I'm not an animal!" shouted Henry.

"Why does he yell?" said Mogus scratching his head, thoughtfully.

"He thinks you're going to eat him," said Valen.

"Eat you!" laughed Mogus his voice boomed off the walls. "Mightys don't eat living things."

"Did you call yourself a—*mighty*?" said Valen awkwardly.

"Indeed," said Mogus looking down at Valen and Henry like an enormous statue.

"You mean you're not *giants*?" said Henry gathering himself, his voice quivering.

"Giants?" said Mogus nodding his head. "No, no—we are mightys."

"So you're different than giants then?" said Henry with a relaxed look on his face.

"Much different," said Mogus. "Giants are cruel and violent. Mightys are kind and peaceful."

"You call the game you were just playing, *peaceful*?!" said Henry.

"It *is* something we enjoy," said the chubby one who was three times as tall as Henry.

"You enjoy being crushed by rocks the size of carriages?" said Henry flustered.

"What are carriages?" said the chubby one.

"They're things that horses pull in the Other World," said Henry.

"Ah, yes," said the chubby one again. "The Other World. Strange creatures come from that Realm."

"You mean you know where we're from?" said Henry inquisitively.

"Well, no, not exactly. I've never been there myself. I'm familiar with some things in the Other World, but not all."

"Well," said Henry returning to the previous subject again and finding himself relieved that he would not be their dinner. "How is it that you can handle being crushed by huge rocks?"

"Rocks don't harm us," said Mogus, chortling.

"Why's that?" said Henry.

"Because our bones *are* rocks—strong as Dragon's hide," said Mogus turning his focus to Valen. "Why does your friend ask so many questions? My head is beginning to hurt." Mogus turned, heading towards the little stream where the water went over the huge cliff.

"So why are you called mightys?" pressed Henry again, his heart racing fast as a rabbit as he looked on the tremendous girth of the creatures that sat all around him.

"We have descended from a mighty people," said the skinny one pulling a large slender pipe out of his belt and pressing it in between his lips to take a deep, concentrated drag. "Things should be given names according to the kind of thing that they are. We are only few in number now."

"Oh?" said Valen before Henry could ask another question.

"We left our home a long time ago," he began, "after the Terrible Day when Golden Blood had been spilt—*The Slaughter of the Dwundlegobs*." He took another drag. "That was when the Light began to fade. It was only then that we knew in our hearts that something was amiss. For we lived many days away from Dorodroos—the home of the dwundlegobs. When finally news had reached our ears, This Realm began to grow dim, and all that we held dear had fallen into a fading light. The Light began leaving our home, the trees, the sky—all good things. This Light we had come to love so dearly, had fled and we found ourselves alone in a sorry gray world. The quiet trickling waters of the River Rizzenne, which surround our vast city, and was once bright and clear, its waters too, had become murky. The sun itself had started to darken and all the mightys knew that we could no longer stay where we were. So, we became wanderers across the vastness of This Realm. We have not been home in thousands of years. But our adventures did not end with wandering. For Murkus launched a War."

Valen and Henry listened vigilantly, their ears hanging onto each word.

"Some of our people," continued the mighty, taking a drawl from his pipe, "were killed after a vicious battle ensued on the Fields of Fading, where several of our brothers, friends, and fathers had fallen. Few of us escaped. Those who did not, were captured by Murkus' henchmen and used to run his terrible war machines. Others were made to dig deep under the fortress of Pestyphooris, where miles below, our Adversary was constructing a terrible prison for all slaves brought back to his dominion. This was the very worst thing for a mighty and once we heard of what his plans were we groaned in our hearts. For we are creatures of the forest, sky and sun. The day is our friend. Night our enemy. To not see *any* Light at all— " The mighty couldn't finish his tale. Tears welled up within his large green eyes. "I'm sorry," he continued wiping them away. "I don't believe we even know one another's names. I am Lenny." He wiped away another large salty drop off his cheek.

"I'm Valen and this is my friend Henry."

"Hello," said Henry gulping.

"We are pleased to meet you," said Lenny with a giant respectful nod of his head. "Though I must say, we do not see many elves around here."

"The Elves existed long ago," began another. "In another time. It's very strange, I must confess, seeing an elf walk through there—" He nudged with his head towards the crack in the rock where Valen and Henry appeared.

"Well—what are *you* doing here?" said Valen curiously.

"We are prisoners," said Lenny fixated on some kind of dried plant he was cramming into the end of his pipe, then puffing it with a satisfactory look on his face as if he talked of these sorts of things regularly. "Been locked up here a long time now. Going on hundreds of years."

"Prisoners?" said Valen. "But how? Why?"

"Brought here by Murkus himself. That was what I was laboring to tell in my story. We were brought here after we lost the battle for our home just beyond these mountains. The siege was terrific, I recall. We were taken here against our wills and made to dig deep under this mountain. For it is said in much lore that somewhere in the heart of it is an item of such power that Murkus would do anything to find it." Lenny took another deep drawl. "The story is that a weapon used by the elves which could kill dragons was hidden here. Sometimes we hear the Lady's voice who is supposed to be the one who had taken it long, long ago."

"We were forced to work night after night for what has been hundreds of years. But, we never found it. Our captors soon gave up and left us here for dead, seeing we weren't finding it. They went over that bridge which was once made of stone." Mogus pointed to a massive chasm. "They destroyed it so we could never leave. We have been looking to escape for a very long time." Mogus paused, "It hasn't been asked yet," he said folding his great hands in front of him, "but where might you two be going?"

"If truth be told, we are lost and we are hoping to meet back up with

Gawdspelle," said Henry in a quivering voice.

As he said this, whispers fell, on the huddled creatures.

"Lost? Gawdspelle?" said Mogus surprised. "I knew him when I was a might-wee-bit. Long ago he would visit us in the summer by the sea. He would fish with us and sing songs."

"We set out from Hallowell and are headed to Hyddenne. Everything in between is too much to tell here. The story is long," said Valen. "Better let Gawdspelle tell it. What I will say is that Murkus has stolen the Verustome and everyone has been talking about it being in the Great Foreshadowings,"

"*Foreshadowings—Verustome—elves*?" murmured the chubby one. "What do you mean? There is something to this. All the elves are dead."

"Well, I am no ghost. I *was* a boy once, that is, an elf. I have to keep reminding myself that I was an elf all along. It was Murkus who had been trying to twist me into something else. Gawdspelle mentioned a legend from a long time ago," Valen concluded. "I don't remember it in full as he does. Something about the Tremendous Tree."

"The Tremendous Tree?" gasped Lenny. "I have heard of this, but my memory of this tale is a little gray too."

"We haven't heard any news of anything beyond this place for a very, very, very, long time," said the chubby one again. "If you are lost, where are you going?"

"For the time, we are trying to reach the other side of this mountain. After that we are headed to Hyddenne to meet with the Fair Princes to decide what to do about Murkus," said Valen. "We have to decide what to do about the Key and *the Door That Was Shut*."

The mightys murmured and whispered amongst themselves again.

"*The Door That Was Shut?* I do not believe this!" said Lenny. "This is the most wonderful news I have heard since I was a might-wee-bit too!"

"Yes," said all the mightys in unison.

"Yes, but if you do find it, have you fathomed the long journey? Have you considered that if you were to open the Door, what you might find?" asked Mogus doubtfully. "The distance is quite far, I know, though I never actually found it myself. It is a treacherous journey."

Valen and Henry remained quiet.

"Gawdspelle, should he find us, is leading us there," said Valen after some time.

"Maybe *you* can help us," suggested Henry with a letting down of his chest.

"Help? What can we do? There is no way out of this horrid place.

Besides, what will you do when you arrive?" said Lenny puffing his pipe. "Take on all of Murkus' hideous beasts by yourselves? His great Armies of Darcnis? You are going to need your own armies for that sort of thing, if you can even find anyone willing to go. All creatures in This Realm who are any good have been scattered or are lost just as we are."

"I do not know," retorted Valen who crossed his arms impertinently. "But we have to try."

"And how will get past the Blackbogs and the manwolves which prowl all around?" chimed in another mighty.

"And the Ancient Road? Do you know where it is?" said another.

"Murkus' kingdom is shrouded in a fog of stench. If you can even get close to it you go will go mad because of how lonely it is. It is terribly desolate. Nothing grows there."

"OKAY!" shouted Valen. "So, we don't know the way. Do you have the courage to go?"

"I do not think it is about courage," said Mogus calmly. "At least not for you. For you do not have fear—yet. It is when you have fear of something and you decide to act in spite of that fear that one possesses courage. Now, you are ambitious, I see that. But, let me tell you something, young elf. A time will come when you may have to cross the Mountains of Moori. They stretch for miles and miles around Pestyphooris, high into the sky, black jagged razor cliffs. But, before that you must find the Ancient Road, then you must be silent as a wolf. For you must sneak past the Dragons of Old and the Great Giants who never sleep. I have been there, long ago. It is far too evil a place for me to describe in full, though that is part of what I remember. It is a wicked tormenting place—an unimaginable, terrible darkness dwells there. Death itself, some say."

"What would you have me do, then?" said Valen.

"You must get beyond the River Rizzenne," said Mogus after a long pause. "There is no other way. From there you should make your way to the White Kingdom where the Great Tigers dwell. They are kind and fair and strong. I think they will help."

"Well," said Valen, "that is where Gawdspelle was supposed to be bringing us anyway—before we went to Hyddenne. So, it is good that you should mention it. Though, I don't know the way."

"I can't handle the dark any longer. I am ready to leave this horrid place," Henry said with a shudder.

"I agree. You cannot stay," said Mogus. "There is no way out for you in here. You must go back a little ways and hope that you find another exit."

"I don't know if we'll make our way through on our own," said Valen. "There are many roads to take in the Netherwurld and I don't know which way to go. That's how we ended up here to begin with."

"You need a guide," suggested the old mighty. "You *must* have a guide."

"We could all go with you," said Mogus turning to Valen.

"I'm not going anywhere," said the old mighty again. "This is home now." He turned and looked up at the flames dancing off the top of the cave roof.

"He's right," said Lenny. "We cannot all go."

"But, we can't stay *here*," said another flabby but wrinkly one. "I am tired of eating these fish. We have been here for too long. I miss the sun, the fields, the clear streams." He looked over at the other black stream which ran through the middle of the floor of the cave. Their houses they had built were fashioned out of rocks. Next to it lay piles of dead fish and bones. Old withered, dead trees lay on the ground, some still stood at the stream's edge.

"We must go. It is what we must do now," said Lenny pocketing his pipe.

"But—" began the chubby one again.

"Have you ever tried getting out?" said Henry shyly.

"We have been prisoners for a very long time" said Lenny solemnly. "We were barricaded in long ago on the other side of this deep chasm." He took a torch and threw it over the edge. With another one in his hand, he showed the bridge which was out. On the other side lay a stone road which wound around looming black cliffs before disappearing around a bend. "The only way out is down," said Mogus. "Only, it is too long a journey to the bottom."

"Suppose there *is* a way to climb down?" said Valen hopefully.

"It is time for all of us to leave this place," said Mogus' father placing his hand on his son. "You have longed to leave, ever since we came here. As we all have. The Elf's arrival is no accident. An elf in the High Heavens is not mere chance. He was meant to find us and we are meant to find our way out. Things are happening that have not happened since long ago. Valen is right. The cliff is the only way down."

"Then we will leave together," said Lenny turning to face him. "Once we go down this cliff, we must make it across the River Rizzenne, past the Forges of Bood. From there it will be through the forests as far as the eye can see—the forest which surrounds the White Kingdom, then up the mountain."

At last, they gathered their things. Valen walked over to the edge. Mogus and Henry followed him.

"Look," said Valen holding the torch high above his head. "Just there. Stairs carved right into the mountain."

"They are too far," said Mogus. "We have strong bones which can withstand most impacts, but even that is too far for me to jump. Besides, far, far below is a deep dark lake. You cannot swim it if you tried. Down there, is how we came to be here. They brought us on a ship and we ascended like beasts in a cage."

"Doesn't look like we're going anywhere," said Henry. "Valen, what should we do?"

All at once Valen knelt down and set the bag down which he had been carrying.

"Here," he said to Mogus. "Hold this." Valen gave Mogus the torch. All the other mightys gathered around to see what he was doing.

"This isn't going to work," said Lenny loudly. "When we were put here they made it impossible for us to escape. We have tried countless times."

"Yes," said Valen. "I am sure you have, but you've got to have the right tools is all. Here—" He reached into his bag and pulled out a shimmering golden coil of rope.

"Rope? Where did you acquire such a gift?" said Mogus. "Of all the things you could be carrying! Your finding us is no mistake!"

"Wysteree," said Valen. "Someone gave it to me before I left. I didn't meet them, but it is as if they knew this would be my road." Valen cast the long rope over the edge and tied it off to a tree.

"How will we get it off?" said Mogus.

"A special fisherman's knot my father showed me," said Henry. "It's tight when you climb on it, then you give the rope a good whip and it comes right undone. Here, let me tie it."

Henry took the rope and made his knot and then gave it a good pull.

"I'll go first," said Valen. "But we need to see where we are going." He threw a torch over the edge and it bounced and fell headlong and disappeared into the darkness. He tried again, and it too bounced off the landing where the stairs were and disappeared.

"We only have one more," said Henry. "Better let me try."

Henry dropped it, and as they watched the flaming torch fall the light of it faded. In the distance a thud rang out. The flame had disappeared at first, then all at once it grew and the landing slowly became illuminated.

Cheers rang out and Henry grinned.

Valen was the first one down, then Henry who was quite nervous at first, but he had climbed much on the vines near Had's cliff and so it came quite naturally. The darkness was still stifling, until he made it to where the torch was. Soon, all the mightys had made their way over the edge of the cliff. Valen held the torch high above his head.

The stairs were long and wound around the long cliff before disappearing. Henry gave the rope a snap and at first it did not come down, then he did it again and again.

"Now, what'll we do," sighed Valen. "What if we need it again?"

"It's stuck on something," said Henry sheepishly.

"Here," said Mogus. "Let me try." Mogus gave it a similar snap and it came down immediately. Just then, fell foul voices rang out.

"Sools," hissed Lenny. "Man-beasts. They have been watching us for some time. We mustn't let them follow us. Soon they will start their horrible howls and laughs."

The company gathered their things and followed the stairs as quickly as they could. Hideous laughs and screams rang out, just as Lenny said. Valen looked back occasionally and saw eyes gleaming in the dark. Then a whole host of them appeared above the looming cliff which they had just descended. Before long the stairs had brought them to a dead end or so it seemed. Valen held the torch and moved it all around to see what they were up against.

"It's a door!" he shouted. "Look!" Sure enough, up close it looked just like plain rock, but stepping further back it was obvious. The door was made of thick stone and there was no getting through it. They were trapped if they didn't get through. The laughs and screams they had heard a moment ago rang out again. Valen was comforted for the time, knowing that the Sools couldn't just jump down the long cliffs, but it didn't give him too much confidence because, from the looks of it, they were quite trapped.

"What do we do?" said Henry. "It's obviously a door and we obviously can't get through it."

"There must be a way through!" shouted Valen. The voices gathered in the distance. They seemed to be getting closer, but in this darkness it was impossible to see beyond the light of the torch which now was fading.

A strange odor suddenly arose. Valen moved the torch all around. In the face of the cliffs he saw at first several carved figures and out of their mouths poured forth a black liquid. Some appeared to be wolves, snakes, crows, some bears, some foxes, some vultures, some boar, some horned goats. Their mouths were all open. It poured down the cliffs like a thick black waterfall. A small ember floated up into the air from one of the torches and landed on the liquid. It immediately turned the liquid into an inferno as it spread all around like a massive fiery snake. Out of all the mouths came flames which grew and grew. The figures started to move and break free from the rocks which they were grafted into. Valen, Mogus, Henry and all the other mightys looked all around. They were in a huge underground cavern. By the looks of it, they were near the bottom. Each creature took its fiery tongue and lit a stone torch that laid next to it on a small ledge. Then the fire suddenly turned into a long fiery chain began to come alive. Valen watched as it bound the creature to the ledge. The chain strapped the wolf and goats and boars individually to the stone wall. Behind each creature stood a door. Each creature was bound to a ledge which jutted out from the massive stone walls which stretched high underneath the mountain. The laughter and screams rose steadily. They were trapped. The noise of the flames grew rapidly. Valen felt as though he were in a furnace. Then all at once, a great hammer rang out from below the pit. It sounded as though an anvil were being pounded. Valen heard it again and again. Thick chains began to descend from the dark roof above and a thick stone platform with it. Valen watched it go down into the darkness as the hammer fell again, and again. Soon the chains started to go in the other direction and the platform returned. The hammering stopped and then it grew deathly quiet, but only for a brief moment. Then, the roars, screams and chants rang out again.

"What's happening?" said Henry at last.

"Shhhh!" said Mogus. "They do not know we are here yet. These creatures cannot see nearly as well as you or I. We have seen this before. Do you see that empty door up there, where there is no flame?" Mogus pointed. "The platform which descended moments ago, is on its way back up. It is bringing up a new prisoner."

"This has happened before. It has been happening lately with increasing intensity. A new prisoner is brought here often. It seems every few days, though I do not truly know if it is a day or not, for it has been too long since I have seen the sun. I have lost my sense of time," said Mogus. "The guard ascends on that platform from the bottom where there is a lake. For this is how we came to be here. They bring you in by the River Rizzenne. This is our only chance to escape. The platform is a far jump and we will have to wait until it begins to go back down, but once it does we have only one chance. I will overpower the guard and stop the platform from descending farther. We will take Valen's rope and tie it to the platform and all of us will climb onto it. But, be prepared for a fight. There will be a skirmish at the bottom too, and the guards of the ship which brought the prisoner, will not be expecting us."

Mogus was right. The creaking chains rolled on and on and out of the darkness below rose a thick wooden platform. On it stood an ogre. A roll of fat hung over his stomach and a thick chain hung about his neck. In his one hand he clutched a club with large spikes in it. In another he moved a wheel which housed the chain that connected to the top of the ceiling which held the platform. The ogre moved the handle around and around until at last it came to a stop.

Valen looked over to the figure which he could scarcely make out. The sound of the chains creaked and crunched as the platform moved up. Flames flickered all over the cavern. More screams, laughs and roars rang out. Cheers ascended. Then, all at once Mogus leaped from the ridge where the company stood. He flew through the air like a grizzly bear. It looked as though he was about to miss it completely, when he struck the platform with such force that it swung back and forth like a giant pendulum. The ogre lost his balance, but regained it with a bewildered look. He turned around and all at once, Mogus gripped him with such strength that it hardly had a chance. Mogus took the ogre and threw him over the side. A splash as though a boulder had fallen off a mountain and plummeted head long into a lake and echoed of the rock walls. The prisoner lay on the platform apparently unconscious. The platform continued to sway like a church bell. Their screams, roars and chants stopped.

"Throw the rope!" Mogus shouted.

Lenny, who had the best throw, tied a small rock around Valen's rope and sent it flying. Mogus caught it with ease. The platform came to a rest. Mogus stooped down to see the prisoner and to his great surprise it was a woman.

"Come! roared Mogus. "We must go now! Prepare yourselves for battle mightys!"

The other mightys and Valen had pulled the massive platform towards the cliff. Everyone boarded quickly. The platform regained its center of gravity and they ascended into the abyss.

"Who is she?" said Valen.

"I do not know," said Mogus. "We will find out soon enough though. For now we must focus on the task at hand." Mogus paused. "Mightys! It has been hundreds of years since you have seen battle, but you trained for this when you were young and so all your skill, though rusty, must be used now. I hope will find you at the moment you need it most. We must destroy the ship which awaits us. We do not know how many of them there are, but we are soon about to find out."

The platform fell farther and farther until at last it reached the bottom. A sea of dark water spread out around them. Valen saw flames which rose up growing brighter and a tall ship with gray wood and hundreds of beasts much like the ogre which Mogus had killed moments ago. Mogus and his fellow mightys were three times their size, if not more.

"Who are they?" said Valen.

"Will they capture us?" said Henry in a trembling voice.

"Do not fear," said Mogus with a large grin. "Prepare yourselves. Valen, Henry, stay here."

"We will not," said Valen. "If those creatures are associated with Murkus, then I will do my part to kill them if I must. I am an elf of the highest order, then I certainly will not stay here while you go off to fight on our behalf."

"Very well," said Mogus. "Stay near me. Henry?"

"I'm not going to deny that I am afraid, but will fight too if I must," said Henry with a gulp. "I will not leave Valen or you in your hour of need."

"Grab the oars!" said Mogus had already gotten in the large rowboat which the ogre had left behind before bringing his prisoner above. The other mightys joined in and rowed towards the ship. Valen and Henry were sandwiched between them.

The torches on the ship grew brighter and brighter as they rowed along. In moments they were right at the hull of the ship. A long rope ladder of sorts was cast over the side.

"We must move with speed!" said Mogus in a low voice so as not to give away their position. "They know something has happened because of that ogre that I threw over. Be prepared." Mogus climbed up the ladder. His father, Lenny and the others followed. Valen and Henry were last up.

The ogres were at the back of the ship speaking with what looked to be the captain.

"Whatappenz?" said one of them.

"I don't know," said the tall fat one, with a ridiculously tall sprout of hair coming sideways out of his head. He had a massive sword slung across his back and and a thick belt on. He wore no shoes.

"That wretch couldn't have thrown our best guard over! The prisoner, she's weak." The captain spit on the deck of the ship. Valen saw now that he had long dark hair and glaring yellow eyes. One wouldn't stand still and the other kept looking off in one direction. The flames of the torches grew brighter by the minute.

"How long until we attack?" said Valen anxiously.

"On my order," said Mogus. "I am waiting to see what their plans are."

They were hiding behind several large barrels.

The captain continued, "Find out if she is alive, something's goin' on. She couldn'tve overpowered Garf if she wanted to. If she ain't chained properly, then how am I gonna report back? What if she escapes? She's one of them special creatures which is why she was brought here. It took us too long to see her slip through our hands now. Where is she?"

"Still on the platform," said the sprouted-headed one. "If I may say so, you underestimate these creatures. She is stronger than we are in some ways."

"Shutup!" said the captain. "I don't want to hear your weak talk."

"Sir, it isn't weak, she's—"

The captain drew out his sword and suddenly cutoff his head.

"Anyone else want to argue?" said the captain.

"Now!" said Mogus.

Mogus rushed out from behind the barrels. He was three times the captain's size and the ship rocked as Mogus moved forward. The captain could not believe what he was seeing. Mogus' father joined in. Lenny and the other mightys, Valen and Henry followed at the rear. The battle was over in a minute. Mogus had found a club and was whacking all of the creatures one by one on the head. It wasn't much of a battle. Mogus and Lenny gathered up all their bodies and threw them into the lake.

Mogus shouted, "Go and grab the prisoner. We will sail this ship out of here."

Lenny and another Mighty climbed back down the side of the boat and into the small rowboat. They were back in a few moments from the platform and Lenny held the woman prisoner in his arms.

"It's a woman!" shouted Lenny.

"Bring her up here," said Mogus from above.

Lenny grabbed up on to the ladder and held the woman on one shoulder as he scaled the side of the ship.

Valen lit torches and lanterns all over and the ship was soon aglow with light. Valen and Henry peered over the edge where the ogres had sunk below the surface. Then, they went over to where Mogus and the other mightys stood. The mightys were hovering around the prisoner who lay unmoving on the deck of the ship. Suddenly, she stirred.

"Where do you come from?" said Mogus.

The woman stirred again. Valen could see now that she had on a dark green cape. She had on high boots and on her neck she wore a wooden pendant shaped in the form of half a moon. Her hair was long and dark. She slowly sat up and looked around.

"Oh, hello," she said. "I am looking for my horse. Have you seen my horse? Where am I? Who are you?"

"You are underneath Where the Mountains Meet," said Mogus. "You are on a ship—"

"I lost my horse," she said again. "I was walking under the trees when I was attacked. I was on my way to—"

"Are you a Princess?" said Henry staring at her.

"A princess would not ride alone, would she?" said the woman. "Wild bands of hideous creatures are capturing all fair folk. I was fleeing them and was overtaken by them when I fell off my horse suddenly and then I remembered no more. When I woke up I found myself in darkness." The woman paused. "I left my home long ago, for rumors were all about that Our Adversary would be waging war against our Great Walls—never before breached—then—" She abruptly stopped and looked up. "I was on my way to find help, I fled in secret; because my father, whom I love, has gone mad. He has been deceived." She now stood up, moving her hair to the side for she had much of it and it flowed all around. "Who are you?"

"I am Valen Vanderbolt and these are my companions, Mogus, his father, Lenny and his friends. . . "What is your name?"

"I am Ela," said the woman. "Have you freed me?" She looked at Valen with intensity. The orange light flickered off of her green eyes.

"Yes," said Mogus. "We have taken over this ship and I must say," he continued, "we did not expect to find a lady such as you being taken up to the prisons above." He bowed. "What crime did you commit that would give you such a fate?"

"I have committed no crime," said Ela.

Valen now saw that she was tall and fair and lovely to look upon.

"There is a growing malevolency that has taken over all fair things in my land," continued Ela." "All around, small villages and towns by the sea and rivers and in the mountains are falling to Murkus' treachery; he is deceiving folk all over. Fathers and mothers, brothers and sisters—friends of every age are betraying one another. A maddening disease of heart and mind is spreading. Murkus is behind it, I am sure of it; Do you know his name?"

"Yes," said Mogus, "He is also the reason why I and my people are here. Long ago his thugs brought us here to die, but we have endured in this oppressive darkness."

"I have had too much of it already," said Ela. "Shall we leave? This lake goes on for a few leagues. Then the River Rizzenne flows out through the mountain. There is a bridge just beyond, but soon we shall see the blue skies and feel the wind on our faces and hear birds again." Ela paused. "I believe we are better off taking the smaller vessels that hang just over the edge of the ship, don't you?"

"Yes," said Mogus and Valen in unison.

"Then, let us go at once," said Ela. "I cannot bear this foul place any longer."

They lowered the boats, got inside and were soon sailing across the dark waters under the mountain. After some time they came to a gently lapping shore and moored.

Valen and his band of companions climbed out of the boats and stepped into the water. The shore was dimly lit by the torches which flickered upon the ship. Everyone was soon out of the water and they began walking along the sand to higher ground. The lake had a tiny breach in the end of it, where its waters flowed continually over and down, forming into a stream. The cave became narrower and the company scrambled down the rocky hill below where the lake was. The roof of the cave got narrower and narrower as the stream got bigger and wider. It wasn't long before they finally reached the bottom of the inside of the cave. Before them, the mouth of the cave appeared and they stepped out of it. The swift water of Rizzenne flowed past their feet. Light came rushing in at once. Valen squinted hard; as did the mightys, Henry and Ela. The wind rustled. Large, full trees lined the river. Valen's eyes followed Mogus as he stepped into the river and knelt down in its clear lapping water at the bank. It was high noon. Then Mogus' father wept quietly.

"How terrible it was to see no light for so long. I always remembered the goodness of the skies and sounds the birds and rivers made," he continued. "But one does not know truly how immeasurably healing they are if you have not had them for so long a time."

Valen noticed that all of the mightys had great tears in their kind eyes. He noticed other things too as he looked on at Mogus. Mogus was truly massive. He stood was much larger in the daylight. His arms and legs were as thick as a trunk of one, too. He was bald and his skin was gray because he had not seen any light for so long. Upon his face sat a large thick beard. Around his waist he wore a thick belt and from his neck hung leather bags in which he carried rocks of all shapes and sizes. He had a sling which he carried like a sash over his shoulder. Valen stood in awe of such a large creature.Though in prison for so long, he had maintained his strength.

"Enjoy the light of the sun while you can," said Ela. "If Murkus has his way he will take it down from the sky and bury it forever." She paused. "All the golden fields are beginning to turn gray. The green in the fields and leaves are beginning to brown. The clear waters are becoming murky. Even the sky has begun to loose its deep blue. It feels as though a fog, mist and winter will begin to lay heavy upon This Realm for I do not know how long. Commoners I know have said the animals that used to play under the trees and in the tall grass are no more. Boars and wolves and bear now roam free. Tall mountains have begun to crack at their foundations. A black rot has spread through the tall, fair trees of my homeland that have been there for thousands of years. Murkus is up to some foul thing. What, I do not know. My heart is broken and not easily mended. But, let us not despair; the goodness of Eoorthe has not left."

Valen now looked at Ela with mesmerization. She was more fair than he could tell under the mountain. She had freckles all about her face and bright greenish blue eyes, deeper than the sea. She had black hair, but now it looked as though it was the night sky itself. He thought she must have come from a land that was more lovely than was capable of imagining, for never did he see such a wonderful and fair face. It seemed all goodness and kindness lay upon her. He smiled, feeling that even though the world he was now in felt grim, Ela still remained and that was enough for his heart.

"I am sorry," said Ela, "Who are you?" She looked curiously at Valen. "How does—" her words fell. "How does an elf appear out of the mountain? This is stranger than I have yet imagined my journey to be. Though, I know the stories of my people and it has been said in stories long ago spoken and those which remain, that when Light begins to fade, that another fairer light shall appear." Ela gazed at Valen and his moon colored hair. "From where do you come?"

"Through the Bridge in the Sky on the Western Edge of Hallowell," said Valen.

"Oh," said Ela. "That is far away and I do not know the road. I have only ever been as far as the Southern Post. Tell me, where are you headed, under these great mountains?"

"We were headed to the White Kingdom," said Valen. "Though, we lost our way briefly. Gawdspelle, our friend, and guide was leading us, but then we were separated and found our way to these mightys here."

"If you have come from over the Bridge in the Sky on the Western Edge of Hallowell," began Ela, "for what reason do you travel so far? It is not custom for anyone to travel out here all alone, even if you are descended from such a line of beings as you. Though, I do meet many who journey to different cities for different reasons."

"You seem fair enough," said Valen, "and I trust you all very well. Our journey is further up towards the Hyddenne City. The Key has been found, the Key to *The Door That Was Shut.*"

Ela gasped.

"Is it so?" she said. "I have been there with my father and brothers long ago. It is a Door unlike any you have ever seen and you say you have *the Key*?"

"I do not have it with me, no" said Valen. "Gawdspelle has it. It is better that way, at least for now. I brought it here, though. I found it in the light house near Had's Coast."

"I don't know where such a place as that is either," said Ela tossing her hair to one side because the wind had blown it all over. Valen looked up at the sky.

"It is lovely, isn't it?" he said. "I have never really seen the sky. But, here it is more than the sky, it is as though you are actually in it."

The light was now changing the landscape and a golden blanket of light lay upon it. Wind blew through the trees and flocks of birds rushed out of the tall grass in the distance. Trees swayed and the River Rizzenne twinkled in the light.

"The Key being found has been long discussed by many, many people all about this land and lands beyond," continued Ela. "What will you do with it now that you have it?"

"It is not for me to decide," said Valen.

"Do you know how long and how many terrible battles have been waged on account of finding it?" said Ela. "Murkus has long wanted to take the World Beyond This Realm and take all its Light forevermore. My people have fought him and his legions many times. Some of them are near impossible to kill. They fly as fast as birds and are equally as fiendish. They are masters at deception and when you wage war against them, they are all around you and you soon find yourself under a great and terrible weight as though someone steals your wits and all that you thought and believed about fair and good things slips away from you at once." Ela looked up at the sky too.

"But do not let fear or lies grip your hearts," said Ela. "Your journey is long and I will help you as I can, but I must go now."

"Go?" said Mogus suddenly. "And risk being captured again?"

"I am going to a faraway land," said Ela solemnly. "I must go. It is the only way."

"What?" said Valen. "What is the only way?"

"I cannot tell you all that is in my heart at this hour," she said, "but I make for the Barrows by the Sea if you should know my road. Many of us and those in Eoorthe are journeying there. I have seen many travelers all about making for that land."

"Well," said Mogus' father sternly. "I will go with you and so shall the rest of us, save Valen, Henry and Mogus. I have been to the Barrows myself and they are quite near where our homeland is too. If my lovely queen is still living, then I shall journey to see her before it is too late. Hyddenne is a farther road. Should you like the company?"

"You would go with me?" said Ela in disbelief. "I have never traveled with such strange folk. Forgive me."

"If you will have me," he said. "We are strange in appearance, but our hearts are good; you remind me of my daughter who fell asleep long ago, and I should protect you should you run into any other foul thing."

"I don't know what to say," said Ela. "It was my plan to go alone, but it is more dangerous than I thought. And, if your road is the same as mine, then we shall travel together. So it is."

"It is settled then," said Mogus' father. "We leave at once."

Valen looked at Mogus' crestfallen face.

"I know I am not a might-wee-bit any longer," said Mogus sadly. "But, you shall ever be near to my heart." He reached out, towering over his father and embraced him.

"Lenny, friends," continued Mogus bowing his head. "We shall meet again."

"Well," said Ela bowing, "farewell, Valen, Henry and Mogus—until we meet again. There is mystery in the air I feel. Things which have never happened are happening. The Key and its destiny will soon be revealed I am certain. Stay off the road if you can and watch out for strange folk. Not all are as they seem."

Everyone embraced one another and said their farewells. Valen watched as Ela and the other mightys walked down near the shore and then into the fading light. Dusk now lay heavy on the land. Mogus, Valen and Henry walked into the trees which poured down into the valley where they now stood. The mountains and the mouth of the cave and the River Rizzenne lay behind them. Soon they were standing under a grove of old trees with large thick trunks.

Mogus led the way through the thick forests which swept down from the land that bordered the Mountains they had passed under. Massive trees with trunks so thick it took minutes to get around them, jutted up out of the ground. Valen looked up and saw clusters of stars all around.

"We'll camp here," said Mogus. Without any objections, Valen and Henry followed suit. "It's best not to have any fires." Mogus looked around. "Though fire can protect us, it also may draw beasts to us that we do not want in our company. There are terrible creatures in here and I do not want to meet any of them in my sleep."

They sat down and made comfortable places for the night. Valen took off his coat and rolled it up into a pillow to rest his mind. Though morning came quickly, they never saw the light of the sun. Valen was disgruntled to be surrounded again by nearly the same amount of darkness they went to sleep with. Dark clouds hung above them. Mogus snored like a giant elephant before he stirred.

"Breath the sweet air," he said. A smile spread across his face. Valen watched him as he took deep breaths. "This forest is a good place, but long ago, before I was put in that prison, rumors were in the air that strange creatures have taken up residence here."

"Henry!" shouted Valen loudly. "Where's Henry?!"

"Gone!" bellowed Mogus with a despairing look as he looked frantically around.

"Look! Are those Othoritees!?" hissed Valen. Suddenly, his eyes adjusted to the gray forest and it was if he could see everything in it perfectly clear. He felt his eyes surge, then focusing harder he caught sight of five dark figures, and their pale skin. He watched them approach a distant meadow, which lay deeper in the forest. They were riding on what looked to be wolves and Valen noticed how quickly they were leaving. He pointed. "Look! Henry!"

"Kidnapped!" said Mogus crestfallen. "This is terrible. Come, quickly! We must not waste another moment. It isn't safe," roared Mogus. "I will protect you as sure as the sun rises in the morning. Stay close to me. Quickly!"

"What should we do?"

"We will alert the White Tigers as soon as we arrive. They're speed is far greater than mine. They will be able to find your friend. My job now is to bring you to The City of White Tigers. We cannot stay here long. He reached into his large bag and pulled out what looked to be a large cookie. "Gather your strength little elf."

Valen took some and quickly devoured it.

"Mmmm, it's sweet and salty and," he smiled, "excellent. What is it?"

"It is a mighty food, fit for traveling. I have been saving it for a very, very long time. It never spoils," Mogus said. "My people call it, stam."

"Well," said Valen helping himself to another piece. "I think I like stam very much."

"Don't eat too much," chuckled Mogus. "It is meant for creatures of my size. You have just consumed enough for two mightys. I think you will soon see that you will be unable to move."

Valen laughed then clutched his stomach. He already felt as though he had swallowed a huge stone. After a long time they traveled deeper into the forest before at long last coming to hill which rose up out of the forest suddenly. Below them lay a ruined stone city. It had been a whole day of traveling since Henry had been taken. The clouds had given way to twilight and stars now glimmered in the sky.

"Where are we?" said Valen.

"We are in the Old City of Rizzenne," said Mogus. "One of the last cities of the mightys, home to some of my people. It is a place far more fair than you could imagine, a place of splendor and majestic spires, placid rivers which after their long journey pour into the sea. It was a place that you could rest when you were weary from travels. But, even in all its glory, it too, was not out of reach from the might of Murkus' hand. It has fallen. Its kingdoms laid bare. Its strong stone crushed by the armies of Darcnis."

Valen stared out onto the barren city below, as Mogus continued his tale. "I once was not the size I am now. And, when a mighty is young it is his duty to learn to fight and protect in the company of older seasoned veterans of war. It is a terrible thing, war. But, our size is no excuse. We must learn to fight when we are small. For when we are grown it is our obligation to protect those who are weak. But, the heavy burden of war, is, at times, too much to bear. It is peace that we long for. But, we do not have the luxury of deciding when war will come. No, it is not in our hands. Even now, in this age— I believe a War is coming whether we want it to or not."

Mogus continued talking about the long history of his race, and how and when he had finished his training as a young soldier, and how the army of Darcnis had invaded the once impenetrable borders of the

Mighty Kingdom; betrayed by the deceptive Slytongue. Secretly, he told Valen, they had made a deal with the Giants of the South, which numbered many thousands and though the brave mightys fought valiantly, the battle was eventually lost and the remaining ones were captured and taken as slaves, chained in the dark tunnels of the never-ending Factories of Darkness, far away in the land of Pestyphooris.

He finished his long story and looked out at the vast barrenness below him as night at last descended. Stars gleamed and shooting stars traveled across the sky. Valen could see the Lonely Planet far away on the horizon, a dark sphere. He turned and looked upon Mogus' crestfallen face as they surveyed the abandoned city from the cleft of the rock where they now stood.

"What happened?" said Valen sympathetically.

"Murkus," sighed Mogus. "It was only a few hundred years after Murkus finally seized the city. He razed it to the ground, took the mighty wives and children and made them slaves as he had done to our people near the Barrows, where my father and Ela are going. It is doubtful that any of them now live, but there is always hope, so long as we do." Mogus looked up at the night sky. "I should like to find the mighty wives and rebuild our home. But, I do not know if that will last either, so long as there is Murkus. Valen looked up at his solemn face. "It has been far too long," he said holding back a large tear. "Just look at it," Mogus lamented. "Left it all to rot and ruin. It's a terrible thing taking someone's home. The mightys are good creatures, gentle, merciful and hospitable, too. We don't like war or unsettled times. But, if it's war we have to go to, then so be it. You don't want to make us too angry—no. One can only bear so much." Mogus' face was overcome with anger and a deep sorrow hung over him. Then, tiny tears spilled down the sides of his cheek.

"What is it?" said Valen consolingly.

"It's nothing?" said Mogus. "Come, we must be going."

But Valen knew, that there was a deeper history associated with his new friend than he was telling.

"Where are we headed?" he said following along.

"We must make our way to the forest just beyond those crumbling walls."

He pointed in the distance where there once stood a sturdy wall with a twisted gate, covered with vines. This was the entrance into the city. An old cobbled road crept its way into the forest beyond, disappearing under stone and dirt.

The moon broke through the clouds at last and the forest below glistened in the new glimmer of light as it illuminated the rich green of the trees. They descended from the cliff onto a narrow pass that led its way down into the ruins of the city below. They found the main road that wound its way through columns and arches and eventually to the gate they saw on top of the cliff, where they had stood only a little while ago. Hours had passed as they traveled through the long city. Animals had taken up residence all over. They slipped through the gate into the starless forest ahead and disappeared into the ocean of night unaware that someone was watching them from a distance, creeping quietly along, its feet silent as snowfall.

CHAPTER TWELVE

# TRAVELERS ON THE CLIFFS

"We make our way along this road," said Mogus as he trotted on. "We must travel through the night. The forest is safest, but we should still remain unseen for we must be on the watch. If we continue through the night, we'll arrive at the White Kingdom in a few days."

Valen thought of what Gawdspelle had said of Toren and what he had found. He also wondered about the Great Tigers. He hadn't been able to get them out of his mind as hard as he tried. Most of the tigers he had ever read about, ate nearly any living thing and now he was to go, without Gawdspelle to see them. He focused on their teeth for a while before finally getting the image out of his mind.

He swallowed hard and they hiked into the thick of the forest, unaware of the strange shape following them. Gnarled looking trees with twisted branches and thick trunks took up the majority of the forest floor. A warm wind blew through the forest. Valen breathed in the sweetness of the old trees as he reached out to touch the bark. Once his eyes adjusted to the dark, he began to make out giant shapes. The trees seemed to be living. Their leaves glistened with a soft silverish glow. At points he thought they whispered words to one another. He walked onwards thinking of Murrin. He remembered how beautiful she was and how sad it was to see her leave. Where, he wondered, was she now? Would he ever see her again? He came to a large tree which had a very wide trunk and looked to be at least a few centuries old. The forest became stranger and he felt someone was following him, though when he turned around and focused in on the odd shaped things moving under cover of darkness, he saw only animals.

He walked on for hours in complete silence. He became hungry and tired, but he pressed on, not wanting to complain. It was getting cold, too. He threw his hood over his head. His mind wandered a while, thinking of his friends. Where were Jack and Jude? He thought of how he had been brought to Eoorthe by the Voors, then to Hallowell where he met Gawdspelle, but he didn't feel at all sure that things were going the way they were supposed to. Gawdspelle was gone, along with Mr. Tiddle and Veeps. Now that he was in a forest with trees he swore kept moving he was also being led by a giant of sorts to the White Kingdom where there dwelt tigers. None of this comforted him. Where was Gawdspelle? How could he have led him here only to have abandoned him? Perhaps worst of all was Henry being kidnapped. Where was he? Would he ever see him again? Now that Gawdspelle wasn't near to protect him and Henry was taken, Valen was sure the Othoritees Gawdspelle had kept mentioning would find him. Though, despite Valen's fears he tried to take courage that Mogus was friendly and huge. Should anything try to harm them, Valen was sure Mogus would smash them to bits.

"The forest is alive," interrupted Mogus, "in This Realm, as in all Realms, in stories long passed, familiar to those who have read of Trees going to war. But, these are not fighting Trees. They are givers of life, protectors of those who pass through their land." Mogus stopped and looked around. "They are aware that we have come into their domain." He blinked. "And I believe there is someone else on our trail, too." He sniffed the air. "Come, there is a place in the distance where we can rest for a while. It is best we get off the road. I am not sure who our guest is, but if it is the same kind of creature who snatched Henry, then I should like to get you into safety."

In the distance emerged a small quaint stone house with a wooden roof, nestled atop a tiny knoll. The road they walked on which wound its way from Rizzenne through Meerdorf all the way to the White Kingdom, passed now in front of the house that stood before them before descending deep into a valley tucked far away in the heart of the Magnificent Meerdorf.

They continued up the road towards the house. Mogus and Valen approached the wooden door. The house it seemed was asleep. The mighty forest, hushed by the fall of night. Mogus rapped his knuckles gently on it and the entire house rattled. Birds flew out of the chimney above. Valen opened the door and walked in.

"You rest inside for a while and I'll stay out here and keep watch."

Mogus tightened his grip on his weapon and patted Valen on his back as gingerly as he could. The weight of Mogus' hand threw him forward. "Sorry," said Mogus with a chuckle.

Valen laughed as he caught himself.

"Get an hour's rest and then we'll be on our way," said Mogus. Turning, he grabbed the doorknob with his massive fingers and closed it tight. The frame of the door buckled for a moment, then relaxed. Mogus sat down in the grass and rested his back up against the house.

Valen entered the room and took off his jacket. He found a large stone chair that stood in the corner. He looked around. Aside from a few books on the mantle above the fire place, there was nothing else in the room. The chair suddenly became very enticing as Valen's mind became clouded. It was an unusual chair for such a small house. Valen gazed at it curiously. Looking at it, he began to feel drawn to it. It was as if the chair *wanted* him to sit in it. He walked over to it slowly, when he felt a spell come upon him suddenly.

"I wouldn't sit in that chair if I were you," came a voice from the darkness.

"Who's there?" said Valen.

"This house looks innocent," said the voice, "but do not be deceived. There are *mooldwarts*—all around. I have been hunting them. They may have followed you and your giant friend here. Just look out there." A figure moved into the moonlight which poured in through the window and pointed to the trees in the distance. Shadowy figures moved across the darkening forest floor. Valen saw them too. He shuddered, gazing at the back of the figure's ragged clothes and torn hood.

"What are you? Who are you?" said Valen nervously now seeing that it was a man, but not just any sort of man. Valen looked upon him and thought surely the man was of nobility—a King perhaps. Valen saw he had on a long tattered cape which had seen much travel for upon it lay mud and dirt, but just underneath it lay an image he could scarcely make out. At that moment Valen heard Mogus' voice booming in the night.

"VALEN!"

"I am here" he shouted as Mogus ripped the house up suddenly from its foundation and over his head.

"Your friend has strength. Good we may need it yet!"

"Who are you?" demanded Mogus suspiciously.

"Who are you is the better question?" said the man. He grasped his spear and adjusted the long rectangular shield on his back. "There isn't time to waste. Mooldwarts and hoarmen infest these woods, too.

Othoritees are on the move. They have spotted you. Choose to stay if you wish, but it would be a swift end. Murkus is drawiong them; they are gathering in full force."

Valen looked at Mogus and Mogus, Valen.

"Where will you lead us?" said Valen.

"I am headed to the Kingdom of the White Tigers," said the man.

"That is *our* way, too," said Mogus gripping his weapon. The figure's eyes flickered with a wildness that Valen could not interpret.

"What is your business in a place like this?" said the man.

"Henry," said Valen, "my friend. He's been taken."

"Taken?" the man scanned the trees.

"Yes," said Valen. "Aways back."

The figure stood up.

"You don't mean to harm my friend do you?" said Mogus, his knuckles nearly piercing his thick skin. Valen was sure Mogus could pound the stranger into the ground if he had to.

"If I desired to harm you I would have succeeded already."

Mogus gripped his weapon. "Not if I have anything to say about it."

"It is not *I* that should worry you." He glanced at the trees again. "What do you say?"

"How do we know we can trust you," said Valen looking at Mogus uncertainly.

"I cannot tell you whether to trust me or not. I know the road you would take," said the man. "But it is too dangerous. This forest is corrupted. Meerdorf has many paths through it and I shall take you on one that is not known to many. It is a few days journey to the White Kingdom. Which way has your friend been taken?"

"He was—" Valen began to answer when he was cut off.

"Shhhh!" hissed the man. "In the trees. Hide! Hurry!" He darted down the hill. Valen and Mogus followed. Valen looked down. The man was gone!

"He's disappeared?" said Mogus. "I worry, Elf. There are strange men in the wild places of Eoorthe."

"Here!" came a voice suddenly to Valen's ears.

Valen looked.

"Hurry! Behind these rocks," said the man whose voice came from a cluster of boulders nestled to the right of a large tree. Valen and Mogus moved closer.

"We cannot see you!" said Valen moving in between the rocks.

In a moment Valen could see only the giant stones surrounding him and Mogus as they moved closer to the trees. Then they both disappeared behind a thin veil that they saw once on the other side of it. The man was sitting on a rock, hurriedly building a fire.

"Magic?" said Mogus in awe. "A true Wanderer."

"I thought you wanted us to leave?" said Valen. "And you think it's a good idea to make a fire at this moment? Won't they see us now?" Suddenly a giant flame burst into the darkness.

"The heat will keep them away," said the man. "Do not worry! They cannot see us—Quickly! Gather some branches."

"Who? I don't see them," said Valen as he frantically followed orders.

"The Hoarmen."

"The who?" said Valen throwing an armful of wood he gathered onto the roaring flames.

"There," said the man pointing. "Dead beings. They have infested this beautiful wood. They are wicked beings who've moved into Meerdorf long ago. They are destroying this forest. They capture, hunt, mame and kill all fair creatures that come into this land. Some they use for eating, some as slaves to build their ugly Infested Cities. They are workers of mischief."

At that moment, a few of the hoarmen came up over the hill and stood right in front of where they were.

"There'ss a nassty glow here. Only I can't see it," snarled one of them.

"Yesss! We can't see Light, idiot! We need an enemy to help us. Help us sspot them!"

"You're right my liege! Nasty, enemiesss. We need to capture one!"

"These travelersss come more frequently. We will find the sssource of this devilry. It infesstz our land like a diseaze."

"Yess, they musst be nearby," hissed the other.

"Are you sure they went thisss way?"

"Yesss, fool!"

"Ever ssince you losst that eye in that battle, you've been uselesss during patrols."

"And you, with your hand missssing?"

"Don't joke," said the one with a twisted iron sword in his other hand, blood stains at the hilt. "Or we'll be eating you tonight? Come on, thersss nuthin here. It's these cursed treess I tell you. Always playing trickss on the eyesss."

"I know I sssaw sumethin," spat the other. Then he gurgled, hacking up what looked to Valen to be a leg bone of some poor animal.

"Yes, well itsss not here anymore isssit? Come on, I'm gettin' hungry."

"What about the elf?" said one.

"Elf?" said the other.

"You know—there's supposed to be a reward for it. Its been losst," snarled the uglier one. "We're suppossed to check thiss house."

"We're not supposed to discusss it in the open."

"Yess, but do you think it's whereabouts are known?"

"Shhh! Don't bring it up again." The taller one turned, revealing a giant gouge in his face.

Valen recoiled. He watched as they walked away continuing in their discussion. They disappeared through the trees.

"They are gone now," said the man putting out the fire. "Clearly, they know about you. We must still be quiet as mice. We will be safe for a few minutes. Time enough to escape."

"Who are you? What is your name? What were those creatures talking about," demanded Valen scanning the figure closely.

"So it is as they say," ignored the man. "The *Great Foreshadowings* are coming to pass. Strange Omens have been happening lately, that have not happened before. All my calculations were correct, though I did not expect to find you here. It has been thought that the elves have disappeared." The man glared pensively at Valen for a moment, mesmerized. "And yet, here is one of them, right before my very eyes."

"Find me? You've been following us?" said Valen.

"I have paid careful attention to the signs," said Ansel.

"Signs?" said Valen confused. "What are you talking about?"

"You didn't expect to just enter our world undetected?"

"I—"

"You are not just being followed by me. A decree has been sent out—by the Othoritees. Murkus wants you. But, I know the way to safety if you should follow me. Where are you from?"

"I'm from Had Wink—a place just beyond the—" Valen's sentence fell off. "It is not in This Realm." He paused. "Where would you take us?"

The man knelt. "My name is Ansel and I am a Wanderer of Noroth." He placed his spears in his belt. "I am at your service."

"I'm Valen Vanderbolt—and this is my friend, Mogus." Valen paused and thought for a moment, gazing at Ansel. "Have you been there before—to my world?"

Mogus looked at the man suspiciously.

"No, no. We cannot go there. There are too many battles that must be fought here. We must stay in This Realm."

"We?" said Valen.

"Yes," said Ansel. "There are many of us."

"Oh?" Valen said curiously.

"Many of us protect This Realm and the Other World," said Ansel.

"Why do you travel alone?" asked Valen.

"Traveling with others of my kind is forbidden," said Ansel.

"Forbidden?" said Mogus. His forehead crinkled with more suspicion.

"Yes, for only when there are wars and battles are we summoned together. That is when we join ranks. Though, the Light is fading and I fear that war is coming for us soon. My heart wishes that it does not come to that, but I sense some ghastly thing descending that has not come upon us ever before." Ansel looked to the sky. "As to what they are looking for I do not know. There are many cherished artifacts that are lost in This Realm. Othoritees are on the hunt. They will be inspecting travelers, wanderers of every kind, rounding them up and imprisoning them."

"Right," said Valen. "Wait, what? Mogus are you ready to—Mogus? Ansel, where is he? Mooogusssss!" he whispered in a silent yell under his breath, careful not to draw attention."I found these two heading back towards their lair," said Mogus appearing suddenly gripping two creatures. "Hoooarmens! I have seen these before, before I was taken prisoner. They still infest this forest. I heard them saying they thought they'd seen the faint shadows of us." His voice was guttural. "They meant to come back with more of their beastly friends. We cannot let them escape. Valen's life is in danger!"

"*Elf*?"spat the one looking at Valen's silvery hair that hung out through the edge of his hood.

"I knew I ssmelled something foul!" gurgled one.

Valen tried concealing himself by stepping behind Ansel. Mogus had caught two of the hoarmen and had them clutched tightly, one in each hand, their eyes bulging out of their heads.

"I don't like them. They stink." Mogus gave them a sniff with his giant nose. "What should we do with them?"

"We must kill them," said Ansel.

"Mogus does not like to kill living things—unless—" His sentence fell.

"If we let them live then we will have a whole host of them on our trail. We must do it at once!" commanded Ansel.

Mogus dropped them to the ground. They squirmed and writhed their pale bodies like trapped snakes.

"Don't kill us!" they said in unison.

Ansel stood over them with his spear.

"Wretched creatures," he said then lunged a spear into each of them. Their blood smelled awful. Valen wedged his nose in the crevice of his arm.

"Foul beasts," said Mogus.

"Come," said Ansel. "We leave at once. This time we must flee. Soon, more patrols will come and they will surely hunt for us. Gather your things and we'll be on our way. If you want to find your friend, then we must hurry. I know all the trees from here to the White Kingdom."

"As do I," said Mogus. "You may have just killed those creatures, but you still do not give us good reason to join your company, small though it is."

"You may know some roads, it is true," Ansel said, "but I know a road which you do not and I if you would let me, I would lead you by safe passage there. Othoritees are out in numbers, they are rounding up all who oppose them and are taking them away."

"I do not fear you, but if you have some other foul thing which guides your heart, then you should part now for you will not like what happens; but you are right, I do not know all ways through Meerdorf. If there is another road, then it would be best to travel it."

"You have my word, that I will lead you safely to the White Kingdom." Ansel bowed.

Mogus towered over Ansel. Valen watched Mogus as he stared down at Ansel.

"We should eat," said Valen awkwardly.

"Eat on the way. There isn't time now," Ansel said gathering his dirty tattered cloak and throwing it behind him. Valen studied the cloak closely. The moonlight glistened on it. At first it looked to be brown, but then he noticed that near the border bits of golden thread and a pattern of leaves were imprinted upon it. "We will eat on our journey," continued Ansel as Valen stared on, lost in thought. There was something curious about Ansel that Valen couldn't quite make out, but whatever Ansel's intentions were, they had to trust him for the moment.

"Quickly!" said Ansel again, finally capturing Valen's attention. "We need to make it up to the that hilltop!" Ansel pointed through the trees, where there stood, towering under the moonlight, a large dark hill. The moon passed behind a giant dark cloud and then it reappeared exposing a tower which grew up into the night. "There marks the beginning of our road. Ready?" Ansel threw his hood up over his head, turning to face the path that led away from the house in the opposite direction of the way

Valen and Mogus had come. Before either of them could respond, he left abruptly.

Valen and Mogus followed. The three of them trudged onward with the moon glowing above them softly. Valen watched darting shadows move all about the forest floor, running up trees, diving into holes in the ground and peering out from behind rocks.

"I know many of the animals in the forests of This Realm," said Ansel. "But some of them are devious. It is best to keep silent until we are in safer lands."

Valen noticed a tiny fox sitting on its hind legs curiously gazing at the three of them as they made their way down the myriad trails that crisscrossed back and forth, winding their way higher and higher into the dark mountains above. Soon they were out from under the trees into a meadow, with rocks which lay all about. Valen thought some of them moved. They continued on as the meadow turned into a slight hill. Soon it turned into a steep slope and the forest reemerged. They passed under the trees which had branches that looked like gnarled arms grabbing and reaching down towards the ground.

Hours and hours passed as they continued higher and higher through the thick tundra up the long mountain side. Soon, they came upon a large precipice. Valen was in front of Mogus and Ansel as they stood at the edge of a looming cliff where they gazed upon another ruined city.

"A city taken up by a foul queen long ago," said Ansel. "Once, families and children played in the streets. They are long gone now having fled to the sea. They have gone to the Barrows."

"Will they ever come back?" said Valen.

"We wait the arrival of the King," said Ansel hopefully. "But, he has been gone for a long, long time. There has been rumors that he is on the move, but none have seen Him. He hides himself quite well."

Suddenly, howls rang out below and Valen saw dark shapes moving through the city ruins. Valen felt the cliff shake.

"We are not alone," said Ansel. "Othoritees are swift, but they do not know the land as I and we will outwit and outrun them. We cannot stay. Come, let us go higher."

The temperature plummeted. The giant trees swayed in the wind. The moon still hung high in the sky, but the light that it now cast, soon disappeared in the shadows of the trees. Then suddenly, the moon faded and thick black pieces of what looked to be ash, began to fall upon them. Valen looked at the one that landed on his shoulder. It felt cold as frosted metal. It blinded the three of them as they tried to make their way down the now fleeting trail. All at once, a light appeared and they could see each other. Valen looked forward and Ansel had a sort of lantern in his hand. Light shown brightly out of it and it was soon overwhelmed by the snow, but it remained true, continuing to shine.

"We're in a Black Blizzard!" he shouted over the howling wind. "Be on your guard! We are now in the heart of Meerdorf!"

"Can't we go another way!?" shouted Valen back through the wind. But Ansel did not hear him. In an instant he was gone, sucked into darkness. Mogus was more obvious to see because of his size. Valen followed him. Together they followed the fading light of Ansel's lamp.

Time passed and the black snow continued to hammer them. Valen struggled, clutching his cloak closely to himself. He pulled the hood tightly around his face. They moved on through the thick forest as he stumbled up and over rocks and fallen trees grabbing at anything he could. Then suddenly a piercing silence fell over them and the black snow immediately stopped falling.

"Be on guard," hissed Ansel clutching his two spears. "We're not alone."

Valen looked around him. It was still somewhat dark but much lighter than before. Then, he began to see and hear movement. Nasty creatures with rusty armor and half rotten shields began slipping in all around them. Soon there were too many to count and Valen had moved closer to the safety of Mogus.

In an instant the three of them were surrounded. A moment later the black snow ensued and all sight was lost. What followed the darkness were screams and growls of which Valen had never heard before. At one point he felt a huge hand grab him, nearly squeezing the life out of him. Minutes passed and all that was heard were clanks of metal hitting together, groans, grunts and yelps. Ten more minutes went by of this and then another piercing silence fell.

Ansel's lantern was relit, revealing his face. It was then that Valen realized it was Mogus' hand that grabbed him and put him on his back while he fought off the attackers.

"What were those things?" shouted Valen who seemed to forget that he was right next to Mogus' ear.

"Mfff!" roared Mogus, as he held his ears. "Careful!"

"Sorry," said Valen.

"Those were Dark Bears," said Ansel holding up his lantern a little higher to see Valen. Around him, large mounds of fur, heads, and arms, laid strewn about. "This is their forest and they do not want any unwanted guests." He walked over to a bear still breathing and pulled his spear out of his chest then drove it into it again.

"They smell awful!" said Valen covering his nose.

"They smell because they eat all living things," said Mogus.

"Who do they fight for? Are they part of Murkus' army?" said Valen in a softer voice as Mogus placed him back on the ground.

"No, they fight and care only for themselves. They kill and mame all who enter their forest. It is gold they seek. They are slaves to thievery and murder. Come, let us go."

They walked a good while and then in the distance an old, unused, trail rose before them. " At last! A Wanderer's trail!" said Ansel stepping over a log with a grin. "Hoarmen and Dark Bears don't know about it. It saves a Wanderer months of travel, using this path."

He turned about with his lantern hanging limberly in his hand and faced the darkness. Then the snow began to fall again. Mogus picked Valen up and threw him on his back and trudged forward through the blizzard following Ansel into the night. It was so dark that Valen's eyes barely made out anything other than the soft orange light emanating from Ansel's lamp and the back of Ansel's cloak.

After a very long time the three of them made it to the edge of the forest. They were covered in sopping wet black snow, their faces weary and worn. Though Valen did not walk, he was terribly exhausted from hanging on to Mogus' neck. Mogus placed Valen on the ground and then Valen turned around and looked up above the canopy of trees where there still hung a thick dark cloud furiously pouring its black snow down. Valen sighed.

"It is late," said Ansel who began walking towards a large pile of boulders several feet away. Valen and Mogus followed."We're nearly there," said Ansel again placing his bag and his spears down. "We'll make a quick fire to warm ourselves, but then we must be going. It is a few more hours journey up beyond that cliff over there." Ansel was facing the opposite way that they had come, pointing to a jagged rock shaped face that seemed several miles high to Valen.

"How do we climb *that*?" asked Valen skeptically looking up it the immensity of the rock face.

"There is a way," said Ansel. "You cannot see it now, but it is there. Stairs carved out of the rock long ago."

The three of them sat down on the cold ground. It wasn't long before the black snow tapered off and a soft white snow started to fall instead, cleansing their stained clothes. The tiny fire Ansel made was popping and fizzing as it encountered the new falling snow. Behind them the Meerdorf Forest still raged mad with its blinding snow.

"The snow; it's changed!" cheered Valen.

"Getting past the Dark bears was no easy task. The snow changing is evidence that they have admitted defeat. It is their sign of surrender! Now, they must travel somewhere else and commit their crimes! For they no longer have this forest under their spell," said Ansel. "Defeating them is not done easily and most of them time, those who get caught in their foul weather, never come out again. But, we have succeeded!"

Valen moved closer in between Mogus and Ansel to shield himself from the fresh biting wind. He wiped the snow from his head then reached out in front of him to warm his hands. Ansel in the meantime had taken out a little black pot and was stirring up some type of stew. Valen gazed intently as he watched him stir it. Ansel was now in a lively conversation with Mogus. Valen clutched himself tightly trying to warm himself further, but it was no use. The cold stabbed at him like daggers.

Soon the fire died because of the whipping wind and they ventured upwards towards the face of a precipice where a carved set of stone stairs made its way behind the tall cliff, climbing high into the sky. The wind pounded them like a boxer as they struggled to make their way up the steep slope. Mogus jumped from boulder to boulder, shaking the ground around him as he went. Before long they finally reached the base of a behemoth white cliff. Valen saw something out of the corner of his eye. The ledge they were on was long and narrow, but to the east lay a mound of rocks. A fire flickered out of the top of it. It glowed like a tiny volcano. The wind carried voices with it.

"Did you see or hear that?" said Valen.

"Yes," Ansel said, drawing his spears. Mogus was on guard too. He placed a rock in his sling. The three of them neared the small outcropping. The voices grew more clear. The creatures continued on in their discussion as their voices rose in intensity. Valen climbed the rocks and peered over the edge. Mogus was to his left kneeling. Ansel knelt to the right side of Mogus.

"No, no, no, we can't be eating those," said the skinny one.

"I'm telling you I've done it before," said the fat one, squinting, through what looked to be crooked glasses made from twigs and some kind of strange colored glass, which also had one lens missing as they rapidly slipped off his face. His eye bulged as if under a microscope and it moved about his lens oddly.

"CAN'T WE JUST EAT?!!!!" said another angry impatient one who had his arms crossed tightly as if this was a common occurrence for him and his friends regularly did not listen.

"AAAAHHHH," screamed the fat one knocking over the pan of meat he was cooking.

"See I told you it was jinxed," said the skinny one. "No one ever listens to me."

"No, no, l-l-look behind you," said the fat one pointing his chubby finger at Mogus with one hand and trying to grab is sword with the other. Mogus' head hovered above the rocks. "Swords, swords, quickly grab your swords. Atttack! Attack! We are being attacked!"

"Put your swords away!" commanded Ansel. "We are not here to rob you."

"Who are you??" said the fat one clamoring, looking at the sheer size of Mogus. "Giants!?"

Gasps, and whispers floated into the sky.

"I am Ansel of Noroth. Mogus the Mighty and this is Valen from the Bridge Through the Sky."

"Bridge Through the Sky?" said one putting his sword away.

"Is it a way that connects the Two Worlds, Eoorthe and the Other World?" said another.

"It is as you say, yes," Ansel replied.

"But, who is the boy?" they said curiously gazing at Valen who was concealing himself under his hood.

"We are on our way to the White Kingdom," said Valen. "I am trying to get to the Glass Boot eventually, where my father is. After that we are going to—" his sentence fell off.

"I wouldn't tell anyone where were going," said Mogus suddenly. "We don't know who they are." He glared at the creatures.

"Well, what's in the Glass Boot? No one has been to the Glass boot in ages," said another suspiciously. "What might you be doing there?"

"We were just going to ask you the same thing? What are four dwundlegobs doing away from their homes in the Trees?" asked Ansel rising to his feet.

"It's no secret," started the fat one, "we're instructed to meet up at the City of Secrets; the Festival of the Two Wandering Stars."

"Sssshhhhh!" hissed the temperamental one smacking him. "It's a secret!"

"Well, it isn't anymore," said the skinny one with a sigh.

"Thanks to Barty the big mouth," said the temperamental one again. "I knew we should've left you at home"

"And how would you have gotten this far?" retorted Barty.

"Now we aren't going to get any farther," sighed the skinny one somberly.

"Barty, we can't have you telling strangers our plans," said the cross-armed one.

"Sorry," said Barty in a drawly voice.

Valen laughed quietly to himself. Then as the dwundlegobs's conversation continued to progress he could not contain himself anymore and began laughing out loud.

"You shouldn't be laughing," said the female one who was stirring soup over a quiet fire. She looked peculiarly at Valen. This silenced everyone for her voice was a beautiful pleasant sound that gave Valen a fresh batch of goosebumps. He had never heard a voice so pure before, save Ela's.

"Who are you and what is your name?" said Ansel coming up over the rocks. A tall, large, ring of rocks surrounded them.

"I'm Fiarella," she said pointing to herself. "This is Bartholomew or Barty if you like," she said, wagging her finger at the porky one. Barty bit into what looked to be a large link of meat and it shot out a hot stream of juice into the fire making it roar momentarily. "And this is Fitzwell, also known as Fitz," she continued moving her giant, yet slender hand around to the skinny one. "And this is Chester," she concluded, pointing to the hot-tempered one.

"Why are you here?" pried Ansel again. "This is a long way from home for dwundlegobs and much too cold." He adjusted his cloak around his neck as the wind picked up.

"It was an old, wise man who visited Stump, some time ago," began Fiarella. "He said the dwundlegobs would not be safe if we did not leave."

"When did you see him?" said Ansel.

"I didn't," said Fiarella." I only heard about it the morning after he arrived, as did the others. The man had apparently snuck into Dorodroos sometime during the night."

"Well, where are the rest of you?" asked Ansel.

Mogus and Valen climbed over the edge of where they had come up and took a seat up against the cliff wall as Ansel proceeded to ask questions. The fire blazed bright.

"We were told to go in secret," said Barty.

"*Don't* listen to him,"said Fiarella angrily.

"I told you we shouldn't have brought him," said Chester in a pompous voice, crossing his arms again. "You really are stupid aren't you? And a prattling idiot, if I might say so myself. I can't believe I must call you *my* brother."

Barty turned his face away and picked up a branch, poking it at the fire. Valen thought he heard him mumble. "Sorry."

"Leave em' be," said Fitzwell. "He wanted to get out of Dorodroos just like you and me."

"Well, he's still an idiot," said Chester taking a pot that sat over the fire and pouring a cold drink from his flask into it. Valen watched the steam billow up.

"Why in secret?" proceeded Ansel.

"I don't know," said Fiarella. Her eyes began to glitter under the remaining light of the dying fire.

"We are going where there—" began Barty, who was quickly swatted by Fiarella.

Ansel raised his eye brows. "Go on," he said suspiciously. "What is it?"

"It's nothing," said Fiarella awkwardly.

"I am no enemy," said Ansel. "The Wanderers of Noroth have always had an alliance with your people."

The dwundlegobs murmured amongst themselves while they sat staring at the last of the coals which glowed cooly against the incoming darkness of a distant storm. Fiarella gathered her things calmly and beckoned the others to follow her.

"You are leaving?" said Ansel.

"Yes," said Fiarella. "We must go now."

"But you haven't told me all you know," said Ansel. He watched as she gathered her things. She was about to put out the fire when Ansel spoke again.

"Stop," he said. "We will use it. If you must go, then I understand."

He sat down and reached into his bag. He pulled out cakes, sausages, cheese, bread, beer and apples.

Then he heard a great rumbling that nearly shook the ground.

"Do we have to go?" said Barty desperately clutching his stomach. "We haven't eatin' anythin' for days. Except for this lousy sausage."

"You're hungry?" said Ansel loading the dying fire with fresh wood.

"Starving."

"Yes," said Fitzwell sitting down. "Quite hungry, actually."

"Help yourselves." They began munching away. "You are welcome," said Ansel. "Will you be staying too?" His eyes moved over to where Fiarella and Chester stood.

"We aren't to trust strangers," she said squinting her eyes.

"I see," said Ansel. "And how did you plan on surviving?"

"We lost our food at the Mouth of the Doobglash where the rapids form," began Fiarella. "Our vessel capsized in the night, when it ran up against a rock."

"Oh," said Ansel. "I'm sorry. How long has it been since you've eaten?"

"Barty just ate the last sausage—which he had hidden away in his pocket."

"I found it!" retorted Barty. "You're just jealous you're not as clever. It's been over a week," he continued looking intensely at another fat sausage Ansel was now frying up.

"Much too long," said Ansel. "Won't you stay a while, eat a hot meal and then go on your way? We mean only to befriend you."

"I've heard Othoritees are on the hunt. On the hunt for spies and all those not loyal to Murkus," said Chester suspiciously snatching an apple from Ansel. "I heard they pass themselves off as commoners."

"And what about Elves?" said Valen in an attempt to rescue Ansel and nervous of the news they just shared. "Are they hunting elves?"

All the dwundlegobs became suddenly still. All Valen could hear was the rumble of Barty's stomach.

"That's a very odd question," said Fiarella. "Very odd indeed." She looked at Valen curiously.

"Yes, why do you say 'elves'?" mumbled Fitzwell, his big squishy eyes popping out of his head.

"I don't think so," said Chester suspiciously. "Elves are extinct, you know."

"Are they hunting them or aren't they?" said Valen.

"Who did you say you are?" said Fiarella becoming more curious.

"I didn't," said Valen sharply. "It's only that—"

"*Who* are you?" said Fiarella again now coming closer to him. "I am no fool. I know when there is something strange going on."

Valen felt her come closer—too close. She peered up into his face as his hood concealed him.

"Impossible," gasped Fiarella in disbelief, barely making out Valen's eyes. She stepped away. "I cannot believe what we have found."

"What haf we fund?" said Barty stupidly.

Chester grunted.

"The Othoritees are hunting for an elf," she said at last. "That is why he asked. We have found an elf!"

"I am—" Valen's words fell before he slowly took down his hood revealing his argent hair and bright shining eyes.

"Marvelous, quite marvelous," said Fitzwell as he stopped eating his sausage halfway through.

"Elthfes," said Barty stupidly. "Ur an elfth?"

"Yes," said Valen. "I am."

"But—how'd you—where did you come from?" said Fitzwell. "Elves left This Realm a very long time ago. They're only known in legends."

"Well, what kind of an elf are you?" said Chester. "A good one or an evil one?"

"He is descendant of the Luminous Elves," said Mogus.

The four dwundlegobs gasped.

"The *Loooominous Elves*!?" they all said in unison with both fear and trembling.

"How did this happen?" said Fiarella. "Why have our people not heard of this news?"

"Perhaps they have," said Ansel. "The dwundlegobs have higher councils, do they not?"

"Yes, we do," said Fiarella. "And my father has told me, that there are many secrets and foreshadowings of things that are yet to come to pass and that none but the very wise understand."

"Well," said Fitzwell. "Surely, this is one of them. I mean—*Luminous Elves*! This is impossible! And fantastic, too. My mind must be playing tricks on me. I have only heard of elves in legends and stories that have faded long ago into distant memories."

"But I *am* an elf," said Valen confidently. "I am not a memory."

"Hmm," said Fitzwell. "You do have a point."

"Not a memery!" blabbered Barty.

"Oh, shut up!" said Chester.

Barty mumbled something under his breath that no one heard. Though Valen seemed to think he heard him say something along the lines of wanting to send him flying over the edge of the nearest cliff with a—

'BOOM!' That's when it happened. Chester went flying through the air with a golden comet pressing down on his chest and his arms and legs dangling like threads of a well worn jacket through the air.

"BAARRTYYY!" yelled Fiarella.

Chester landed with a loud thud on a distant rocky slope at the edge of the nearby cliff Barty aimed for. Chester got up and dusted off his pants. Then suddenly, his hands glowed a bright amber color and he too sent another silver comet through the air in retaliation. Soon, silver comets were soaring all through the air, dashing against rocks, exploding against trees. Valen managed to find safety behind a large boulder until the small battle had finally ceased after Fiarella began yelling.

"ENOUGH!" she roared. "WE DIDN'T COME HERE TO FIGHT WITH ONE ANOTHER!"

"Apollow-gize!" stammered Barty.

"Apologize?" spat Chester.

"Yes," intervened Fiarella to defend Barty. "*Apologize*." She gritted her teeth.

"Me?" said Chester mockingly. "You've got to be joking."

Fiarella glared at him.

"Oh, all right. Fine! But, it's his fault you know."

"Apologize—now!" she said tapping her foot.

"I'm sorry," Chester said.

"I'm sorry . . . ?" mumbled Barty chewing up the rest of his sausage.

"Barty, Barty! I'm sorry, Barty!" said Chester, unsympathetically.

"For?" urged Fiarella.

"For your having been so irritating, that I had to tell you to shut up."

"That's good enough," said Fiarella.

"You can hawdly call that'n apollowgee," said Barty.

"It'll do," said Fiarella. She turned and looked back at Valen again. "I simply cannot believe my eyes." Then suddenly, a memory of something her father had read to her long, long ago came rushing back into her mind—yet, it was a broken memory, but one that gave her pause.

After some time she said, "It is true. No, it cannot be. Oh, but it is! You are the beginning of the One who will come to put things back in order," Fiarella gazed into the fire as if she was searching back through time. "My father told me of one—your kind—who would come here and bring The Light back to Eoorthe and the Other World. You are of the lost line of elves."

"I am not who you think I am," said Valen uncomfortably. "I mean I know that I am descended from the *Luminous* Elves—Gawdspelle told me the story—but I am not here for any special mission—whatever it is, you have in your mind."

"You see," said Fitzwell, "That is where you are wrong. You *are one of the One* who is written about in the books and oracles that were spoken of many ages past," he continued. "*The Great Foreshadowings*! We have waited for you for one of you for a very, very long time. You have come to help destroy Murkus and give us all back our lands and our homes."

"I don't mean to disappoint," said Valen. "But—" his sentence fell off when Ansel interrupted.

"It is late," he said gazing up at the sparks from the fire as they swirled into the night sky seeming to add stars to the dark canopy shrouded above them. "We have a long journey ahead—we must be going."

"As must we," said Fiarella gathering her things.

"You are going alone then?" asked Mogus.

"Yes, we go alone," said Fiarella. "That is our road. We are very resourceful creatures and do not need help from anyone." She glared at Ansel momentarily.

"We should travel together," he said staring back with a wooden gaze.

"We go alone," said Fiarella again with the three of her companions waiting behind her, blinking their large eyes thoughtfully.

"Very well. Go alone, if you must," said Ansel stepping around a small rock and looking up towards the ever darkening sky. His eyes scanned the horizon. "Should you need anything, we will not be far off." And without another word from any of the four creatures they set out at once, rounding their way up the rest of a seeminlgy undending amount of stairs which reached high into the cliff above. Ansel stood and watched as the creatures slipped out of sight."There is no time to waste. A storm is upon us," said Ansel. "We must get through this pass quickly."

They set out at once up a different route opposite the dwundlegobs, for Ansel spoke of a shorter way through the giant cliffs. Mogus led the way with lantern in hand until he extinguished it for fear of Othoritees. They scrambled around boulders and fallen rocks. Then the wind picked up a bit making it hard to hear anything. The storm descended upon them swiftly. In a little while they reached the top of the mountain which was filled with a thick forest of trees at the top. The wind blew through the trees.

Ansel slipped into the forest followed by Mogus and Valen. Mogus got stuck when his sling got hung up on a large branch. He managed to get it out fast and they continued on into another thick, murky, vast sea of gnarled, twisted trees. The wind whistled as the trees rustled about bending and snapping under the weight of a powerful wind. Though the canyon below brought a biting wind, the trees provided much protection from the elements. It wasn't long until they came upon a well worn path. Ansel looked left and right quickly, before going left. Shortly after turning he came to a halt.

"What is it?" asked Valen. Ansel relit their lanterns.

"This forest is not as I once knew it to be," said Ansel. "Something terrible has happened to it, just as it has in Meerdorf." Mogus clutched his weapon watchfully.

"Come, we must move with caution," said Ansel taking the lantern from Mogus and putting it out. "Valen you can see best so you must go first. I'll be right behind you and Mogus will protect the rear."

Immediately they got off the road and ventured back into another part of the forest. The trees and brush kept getting thicker and thicker. Suddenly Valen heard voices. "Look!" he said pointing to a bright glowing spot. Then, it disappeared.

Slowly and cautiously they started moving themselves further into the forest. Valen got the chills as he pulled his collar up around his neck. It was an eerie place. Large birds with big yellow eyes sat up above them hooting—much like owls, but darker, bigger. Twigs broke underneath his feet.

"Quiet! Get down," said Ansel commandingly. "We're being followed."

Valen crouched down at Ansel's orders and peered around the nearby tree to get a better look. He waited next to Mogus who breathed loudly. Ansel watched patiently, his eyes gleaming with watchfulness under the brim of the hood of his cloak. It suddenly became deathly quiet. *Someone* was out there. Someone had been following them, just as Valen suspected. He watched intently as a shadow moved across the forest floor.

"What is that?" he said pointing.

The shadow disappeared for a few more seconds, then a bright ball of golden light lit up the forest with bits of glittery dust settling around a dark moving shape. One small figure that Valen could not make out, attacked the darker figure who was now moving away. The creature turned and suddenly was coming closer towards Valen! Then he disappeared again. Moments passed as an eerie silence surrounded them.

Suddenly, several winged creatures emerged twice the size of Mogus and surrounded them. Ansel seized his spears. Valen was unable to distinguish between them and the darkness. Mogus grabbed his weapon and a nearby boulder and placed it in, ready to attack. Clouds shifted in front of the moon snuffing out any available light. Then Ansel launched his spear through the air like a missile and Valen watched, his elf like eyes, suddenly coming into full focus. The spear soared past his head and hit one of the creatures in the throat, who was right upon Valen. It made a gurgling noise and fell to the ground, hobbling away before going airborne again. Everything happened quickly and in a moment Valen found himself on the forest floor looking up into the face of a hideous creature. Bright, yellow, cracked teeth, dripped a bloody drool onto his face. Then, when he was sure the creature was going to eat him or kill him, another unexpected golden ball of light exploded like a meteor and knocked it back a hundred feet, making him unconscious for a moment; before it flew up into the air with a roar and disappeared. Mogus fired his rock and blasted three of them to pieces, along with several trees. Ansel attacked two more, before finally they flew into the night.

"What were those?" said Valen trying to make out the tiny figure before him.

"I do not know," said Ansel. He paused and looked Valen's way.

"An elf and a mighty traveling together?" said the voice suddenly which Valen recognized immediately.

Ansel relit his lamp.

"And how often is it that someone of your countenance travels alone?" said Ansel holding the lamp closer to the creature's face. The little fellow chuckled.

"Good to see you, friend."

"And you," bowed Ansel as if he had been expecting the creature all along.

"Veeps!" shouted Valen with excitement. "It was you following us?"

"Yes, elf," said Veeps whom also bowed.

"I meant to find you once we had lost you under the mountains, but it was so dark and the path back was impossible," said Valen.

"Did you see a group of your kind?" said Ansel.

"My kind? What on Eoorthe do you mean?"

"We just met four of your kind," said Ansel.

"Dwundlegobs?" said Veeps in disbelief.

"Yes," said Ansel. "That's right."

"That's impossible."

"It's true," said Valen.

"These *are* strange times," said Veeps. "No one of my kind, except for our ancestors, have left the Woods of Dorodroos to journey beyond. We don't go beyond our borders." He looked befuddled. "Who were they?"

"A skinny arrogant fellow, a sassy female, a simple minded but very fat one and a rather talkative one who liked to eat."

"Hmm," said Veeps. "I don't recall anyone by that description."

"There names are Chester, Fiarella, Barty and Fitzwell."

"Hmmm—nope. Still don't know the names," said Veeps. "It is very strange that they are here though. Did they say where they are going?"

"The Festival of the Two Wandering Stars," said Mogus.

"I don't see why they would go to that. Yet, many things have happened that I never thought I would see in my life! Times are strange indeed and my people have never had any dealings whatsoever with those in the Hyddenne City. I suppose we shall find out soon enough what they are up to."

"How did you find us?" said Valen.

"I've been on your trail for a few days now," said Veeps.

"Have you seen Gawdspelle, Jack—Jude? Do you have any news? Where is Mr. Tiddle?" pried Valen.

"I looked everywhere for Jude, but I do not know where he is. Gawdspelle and Jack have gone on to Hyddenne. I went as far as Waxynne along the River Rizzenne, then up the mighty Doobglash." Veeps paused. "Mr. Tiddle's gone off—said he had some business to attend to."

Ansel eyed him suspiciously. "Business?"

"Yes," Veeps said. "I do not know what. He said he aimed to find something."

Valen looked at him again, this time even more troubled. "Find *something*?"

"Struck me as odd," said Veeps. "Mr. Tiddle seemed—well—uneasy—said he had to find it—kept mumbling how he was sure of its location. Kept saying it was there, all along, in his books, but that he hadn't been able to decipher it. I had no idea what he was talking about. I care not about dysapiers, though. They weary me from too much talking." Veeps paused before continuing. I met the Eegols from the West who carried me far, far over Cathedral Rocks. Once I passed through, we landed on the Fields of War. They only took me because they knew my father from long ago. I went to the land on the other side that borders the White Kingdom where the Eegols took me to their Lord."

"What news do you have from them?" said Ansel.

"I could not meet him, for I do not think it is good. Foul beasts have begun traveling along the roads that border their Kingdom. They protect their lands with the greatest of security and yet those who have been sneaking into their country lately—their numbers have grown. There is no solution but to kill them. Their enemies are growing. Their Lord cannot be reached and the High Guards do not know what to make of it, for it has been a very long time since they have seen any movement in their lands. These are not the first rumors that I have heard. Something tells me that some horrible thing is at play. I fear a terrible war is coming. Just as Gawdspelle fears."

"Have you spoken to Gawdspelle about this?" said Ansel.

"No," said Veeps. "We have not seen one another since our departing under the mountain."

"Why did he journey to Hyddenne?" Ansel said.

"He has gone to meet with the Three Princes where The Festival of the Two Wandering Stars is taking place."

"For what reason?"

"I'm not sure," said Veeps.

"Surely he said something—"

Veeps turned to look at Valen. "Murkus *is* hunting for you as you know, and a war will come such a destructive war that has never been waged before," Veeps lamented.

"I know. Gawdspelle mentioned this before," said Valen. "He said that Murkus seeks to murder me." Valen shuddered. "Gawdspelle assured me that his plan had been thwarted. You were there, Veeps?"

Veeps nodded sadly. "It is darker still. You are right—were right." Veeps looked down at the ground with sorrow. "Gawdspelle's hope was that Murkus had not grown in power, but he has become darker and more hideous than any creature you can imagine and he *is* hunting you. He will not stop until he has found you—until he murders you."

"But this is terrible," said Valen. "I don't think I like this story very much. I don't want to die. All my life I have been sick and now Murkus wants to murder me? Are you sure he wants *me*?" But, just then, the forest became heavy with a darkness and there was a long silence.

"There is something which Murkus has his will set on," said Veeps. "I can scarcely see it in my mind's eye. Long, long ago something was hidden from him by those very wise and Murkus has never possessed it since. There are many, many things in This Realm, which many have sought and never found. But, this—this is different. I sense it in the air and wood. Something which has never happened is about to happen. Some deeper mystery is about to unravel." Veeps paused and took in the sweet scent of trees. "There is much we do not know," he continued, trying to reassure Valen. The fire in the lantern Ansel held began to fade. "Whatever it is, it is not all merely in our own hands to change the course of whatever is happening. Yet we can do our small part and that can change mighty things. We should not tarry. It is late and Othoritees are on the hunt and they are the ones which will bring you to Murkus, should they capture you. Once we arrive at the White

Kingdom we will be safe for a while. From there we will make our way to Hyddenne. Whatever the reason Murkus wants you, he will not yet, not on my watch! Mogus—friends. We must bring him safely to the White Kingdom! I do not know what evil will come out of Pestyphooris, but it will not come for you yet. At least not this night."

"Come then, there is no time to waste," said Ansel. "We must go and try to ally ourselves with the White Kingdom."

The four of them set off into the dark forest. Stars barely illumined the forest floor. They traveled for a few more days under the trees. Night and day came and went. The trees were so thick that they could scarcely tell at points what hour of the day it was. Valen heard growls when they rested and he thought he saw hideous faces and creatures moving under the trees. One night it snowed heavily and he thought he heard a sleigh with bells and the hammering of hooves on the forest floor. Though they were days away from the dwundlegobs they met recently, he sensed that they were following at a distance.

When Ansel and Mogus lay deep in sleep and it was Valen's turn to be on watch, a distant ringing, like little bells arose. Clamoring voices too, rung out across the craggy area where he was. Trees rose up out of rocks. The wind whistled. A cold, quiet water cascaded down a little rock face just opposite a tiny path Valen meandered through. He snuck down a small cliff, then around a trail which wound its way up a high towering rock. A small faint light began to grow above a distant wall which he now stood at the base of. He climbed up to where he thought the voices were coming from and poked his head over to see who it was. Valen thought it must be Fiarella and her small band of dwundlegobs. When he reached the top of the cliff and peered his head over he saw something he had not quite expected. It was snowing now and the bells he heard jingled from giant gray foxes which lay beneath him. About a dozen or so of them were sitting around a fire. Snow began to fall. Valen looked closer. Other creatures soon emerged from behind the foxes. They looked like corpses. They had on high leather boots and Valen saw their terrible possessed eyes. The creatures carried chains and shackles around their thick ghoulish necks and bore large axes with pikes on one end. Upon their legs they wore spiked greaves. Valen saw them to be part wolf, part man and he trembled upon seeing them. As Valen focused in they were passing a paper around to one another with a drawing on it which looked like—him! Othoritees! How did they know what he looked like? Dr. Grimm! But, what if it was Jude? For the moment he took relief in knowing that his appearance had changed drastically since Mr. Tiddle's bookshop. He took one last look at them and saw they were cooking some poor creature over a hot fire, alive. It squealed and Valen thought it looked at him and said something, but he could not make out what. He quickly turned to flee and climbed silently down the edge of the cliff back up to his camp. He woke Ansel and Mogus at once and spoke as softly as he could to warn them of the danger. They got up from their sleep and escaped under the remaining darkness.

Night wore off and they continued to climb higher up. They covered miles that night. Soon, the land flattened out and eventually, a gray sky hung over them and Valen came to a sweeping view. A long valley swept away below them. The Looming Mountains were now southeast. Cylvirstone lay just beyond and the Doobglash and Rizzenne rivers lay through a pass where the valley split. They had traveled days and they were low on food and Valen was hungry. Ansel insisted that they ration it until they arrive at the White Kingdom. Mogus gave Valen a small piece of stam. Valen was weary, but he knew how important it was to find Henry and meet up with Gawdspelle and Jack and so he pressed on.

Ansel was a gifted woodsman for they had lost the Othoritees through grueling climbs and passages which their assailants could not travel. Through Ansel's long years living in the trees helped them to elude capture. Their scent was now only on the wind and soon that too would dwindle. The wind whipped hard against the sloped mountain and thick tundra. They traveled on and on until at last twilight was upon them. Valen followed Ansel, who led the way. Veeps trailed closely behind. Mogus was at the rear.

Ansel walked along the trail that wound its way out of the forest. They reached the top at long last. The wind had stopped. At last it felt as though spring lay upon the land. Though the weather was erratic. Earlier, when Valen had seen the Othoritees it had been snowing. Now, a gentle breeze rustled through the trees which stood at the entrance of a long sweeping field. In the distance a towering city with thick stone walls and turrets with lion faces carved out of them, stared out across the field. A rich golden light and crimson sunset had fallen all around the castle, the trees, the grass the rocks and their faces. The land was drenched in a golden light which turned to a rich, deep red. Valen followed behind Ansel sleepily. It had been some time since he'd had any real sleep and his stomach was making all sorts of different noises.

They crossed the meadow quietly. The warm breeze continued to blow now that they were off the cliffs. In a few more moments they were looking up at a large wooden gate that spanned the stone towers above.

Mogus raised his gigantic fist to announce their arrival and yet before he did, there came a young, stout looking white tiger striding gently towards them through the grass. Valen saw him first and gave away the cat's silent approach.

"Ansel! Look!" he blurted.

Mogus, Veeps and Ansel all turned at once. A cat approached slowly, turning, making his way to them. Then Valen noticed he was not alone. For he carried another on his back. The large powerful animal slumped to the ground. The wind picked up and rustled the grass below. Ansel moved cautiously towards the cat. In moments a thick fog rolled in. Ansel bent down to see if the cat was still breathing. Valen turned his focus towards a new spectacle. Out of the fog walked twenty or so tigers dressed in dazzling green and gold armor. Their massive white paws pressing into the earth below. Valen swallowed hard. The tigers flowed like mighty ocean waves. Their muscles, shaking the ground with thunder. Their eyes, fierce, burning as the sun and black blood had stained their white manes. The largest one was carrying a dead, large, gray fox in its mouth.

# A MYSTERIOUS FINDING

Like a flash of lightning they surrounded Valen and his companions. Valen tried to be brave as he moved nearer to Mogus who stood towering above the company of cats. Veeps watched, resolute, as more behemoth tigers made their way towards them. Valen's hands shook. He had never seen real tigers before, for he had only read about them. Yet, they were more real than he could have ever imagined.

"What happened?" said Ansel.

"Foul Foxes of Fingbad!" shouted one. "They've invaded our land and we are hunting them down!"

"Bring this one into the city! He is our prisoner now!" shouted the largest one, who looked to Valen to be the leader. "Find out what he knows, who he knows and where he is headed! I want to know where he has been. Put him in the dungeons!"

"Who are you?" said the tiger abruptly circling them. "Tell me—where do you come from?"

"I am Ansel, a Wanderer of Noroth and these are my friends. Valen Vanderbolt of Had Wink. Mogus a Mighty of Rizzenne and Veeps, a Dwundlegob from the Land of Dorodroos."

"A mighty and a dwundlegob?" the tiger said curiously looking at Valen."We've been looking for humans who've made it into our world. What business do you have coming to the White Kingdom?"

"We've come to seek Vorfynn's counsel," said Ansel strongly.

"For what purpose?" said the tiger, his giant golden eyes gazed commandingly.

"I cannot discuss it here," said Ansel.

"You will discuss it now or you will be torn to pieces."

Ansel did not blink at this threat. Valen was awestruck at the sheer size of them as he sat gazing at their massive manes and dark green and gold armor. Ansel remained steadfast.

"Very well," he said gripping his spears. "I will tell you the answers you seek, but not for fear of you. First, you must tell me who *you* are."

The tiger growled. Valen shuddered again, for these tigers were no normal tigers. They were twice as large, and their heads were so terrifying they looked as though they could snap an elephant's leg in half with one crushing movement of their razor teeth. Valen stared at them, his heart hammering inside his chest. He continued to be as brave as he could. As he watched the tiger talk, Valen paid particular attention to his fangs; certain they had crushed many legs or even worse, necks.

"I am Toren the Strong."

Ansel bowed respectfully. He stood back up and looked at the tiger determinedly.

"The Othoritees are on the hunt," said Ansel.

"Othoritees? Murkus' filth?" said Toren with a rumble in his voice. Toren circled him. "I have heard this rumor. Tell me, do you know this to be true?"

"Yes, it is not just a rumor," said Ansel. "I have seen them in my travels. More and more are showing up everywhere. They travel here and there stopping, checking travelers, as they journey from city to city. Yes, I've heard that they are capturing and taking anyone who utters a word in opposition to Murkus."

"He has forgotten the Armies of Gold and Green!" said Toren with a confident snarl.

"I think it is best we get inside the city." Ansel looked at the dark woods they had just come through. "We have come to speak with your King," Ansel said at last.

"My City? Do I detect fear?" said Toren.

"Othoritees are on the move in these forests," said Ansel turning and looking back to the forest. "Valen saw them yestereve on the high rocks with their sleighs and foxes."

"I know they are near too," spat Toren. "Can you not see we have captured one?"

"We have met many dangerous enemies on our patrols," snarled Toren as he circled Ansel; his mighty claws piercing the ground. "There is nothing that frightens me!"

"There may not be," said Ansel. "Nevertheless, Othoritees are vile creatures. They do not fight with sword or teeth, spear or bows. They do not fight against the strength of arms. No, they fight in ways that are deceptive, deadly, destructive and poisonous. Many have been tricked by these foul creatures. They can deceive even the strongest.

"You say they are capturing people, going about checking travelers?" said Toren in a lower voice.

"They are," said Ansel. "But, you can't always tell who they are nor where they've come from. Horrible things are not always as they seem. No, sometimes the darkest thing imaginable is right before our eyes, before we had the sense to see it."

"Never mind all this talk," said Toren at last. "I'll ask you once more? What reason do you seek the King!?"

"I only seek his council."

Toren looked at him suspiciously. "Many come to seek the King's council. His wisdom is deep and yet—" His sentence fell off and he turned his mighty head, looking away.

"And yet?" said Ansel.

"He is not here!" roared Toren

"Not here?" pried Ansel.

"He left some time ago," snapped Toren.

"Where did he go?" inquired Ansel.

"I do not know the answers to all your questions," roared Toren again.

"A king roaming Eoorthe at a time such as this?" Ansel looked gravely concerned. "Did he go with anyone?"

"No," said Toren.

"This is not good news," said Ansel. "I fear him traveling on his own."

"Do you doubt the king's strength," growled Toren.

"No—"

"Then what is it Wanderer? Speak!"

"I have seen much. And your king, mighty as he is, is not enough to ward off the evil that lurks beyond your borders."

"Silence!"

"I—"

"You have blasphemed the King! Soldiers! Seize them at once!"

Within moments, giant blurs of white soared through the air. Most of them, attempted to try and seize Mogus because he was the largest and most threatening. Valen saw about ten of them wrestle him to the ground. Mogus grabbed them with his massive hands and sent them crashing into the side of the thick stone wall that surrounded the city. Valen barely had any time to react and before he knew what had happened he was bound hand and foot. Veeps fired, knocking two tigers unconscious. Soon, several tigers pounced on him and he too was captured. Realizing he was no match for so many powerful creatures at once, Ansel surrendered. Though Ansel had been bound, Valen thought he had given himself over. Secretly, Valen thought there was something much more powerful to Ansel than he led on, but Valen could only keep suspecting.

"Take them to the dungeons!" said Toren and he roared louder than ever shaking the very stones in the wall.

After all of them were bound, Toren called for the giant wooden gates to be opened again and his soldiers marched them through.

Valen trudged along at the rear. He looked over at Mogus, his hands fastened together with a giant rope, his face resolute. Veeps held his head high, staring forward, a sense of purpose on his face. Ansel looked poised, and kingly.

As they walked along, Valen saw giant turrets reaching far into the crimson sky. They were fashioned out of impenetrable hard stone, worn and whitewashed from the sun, but smooth as glass from years of rain hammering away at its surface. As they got closer, Valen noticed that these turrets were hewn into tall muscular battle ready cats standing on their hind legs. One had his mouth open as if he wanted to swallow the now rising moon. One had its eyes shut as if it didn't want to see its light. Or maybe, thought Valen, it was sleeping and that at any moment it would wake. A terror shuddered through him. The other two stood, fearless, ready it seemed, for war. One with its claws sharp as knives, its hackles raised high. More tigers walked upon the mighty walls looking out over the distance forests, their armor flickering from tall torches which lit up the shroud darkness, ready for an invasion from some lurking enemy in the old forests below their colossal kingdom.

Toren's soldiers led them down a long flight of stairs. Valen felt the cold damp air coming up from the dungeons. He crossed his arms, stiffly. His bones chattered as they journeyed down deep into the earth. Valen felt an eerie silence close in on them before at last they came to a long tunnel where at the end stood mighty iron doors. Torches illuminated the cold dark. The door slammed shut.

Out of the darkness emerged a soft glowing light. It flickered for a moment before becoming constant. Slowly the light grew and Valen could see Mogus, Ansel and Veeps.

"They didn't account for the power of the dwundlegobs," said Veeps with a smile.

"Neither did I," said Ansel relieved.

"Veeps' hands! We can blast our way out!" said Valen excitedly.

"No, you won't," came an unfamiliar voice. "The walls—they're too thick."

"Who's there?" said Veeps turning.

A pair of eyes reflected the light from Veeps' hands. Then, slowly, a dirty, decrepit, skinny and sickly tiger approached them.

"It is been a very long time since I have seen any light," said the tiger enjoying it as it swept over his sagging whiskers.

"Who are you?" said Ansel.

"Trumfis," said the cat heavily.

"I am Ansel and these are my friends, Mogus, Valen and Veeps."

The tiger sat down studying his new guests. His tail twitched.

"It's a great comfort seeing faces again, even if they are foreign to me." said Trumfis. "What brings you here?"

"I came to seek your King's council."

"Ah—so do many."

"What council do you wish to receive?"

"Oh," said Ansel surprised. "It is no matter now, because I cannot meet with him."

"No matter?" sighed Trumfis. "No one troubles themselves with the King of the White Kingdom unless he is seriously in need of something. So, do not guard yourself. I am a friend."

Ansel looked thoughtful.

"Come," said Trumfis, "what is it?"

"Do you know much of the history of Eoorthe?" said Ansel finally.

"Which piece of Eoorthian history are you interested in knowing?" said Trumfis.

"Before I answer you," said Ansel, "tell me, how did you arrive here?"

"You mean Toren did not tell you?"

"He only mentioned that the King is gone."

"And yet he failed to mention that he seized the throne in my father's absence?"

"You're his brother?" asked Valen.

The cat nodded.

"Toren has betrayed the King?" said Ansel quietly. "Now I know why he never responded to my letter I sent many moons ago."

"Almost two moons ago," said Trumfis. "I was with my father when it arrived. Toren has assumed my father is dead because he has been gone for many years now." The cat sighed again. "My brother is a fool. He is intemperate, reckless, ruthless and cruel. He desires power, to rule. My brother has always sought the throne. But, my father would not give it to him. Before my father left, he entrusted the kingdom to me and now it has fallen into my brother's hands. But, I must find a way out before he brings the White Kingdom to ruin."

"How do you plan on escaping?" asked Valen.

"In one months time, there is set to be a battle," began Trumfis. "It is an annual festivity of my people where the greatest warriors fight. Though, because my brother thinks that no creature that lacks in strength or power is worthy of life, he has pitted himself against me to fight him. And he has starved me for the occasion. The winner will take the King's Seat. If I lose, death awaits me and that will be my escape."

Valen looked at him with great pity.

"That's not right," said Valen. "You're his brother. He can't do that to you."

"I am weak," said Trumfis. "But, I am not dead. I can still fight."

"You can't fight him looking like that," said Mogus concernedly.

"He's right," said Ansel. "You can't fight him in this condition."

Trumfis grinned.

"My brother is much stronger than I am, yes. But secretly he fears me. He knows that I am the better fighter. He knows that he has never before won in a match against me and this will occupy his mind. I am a frail veteran of war. He is powerful, yet inexperienced."

"But what if he does?" said Valen. "What if he *really* does, kill you?"

"I guess we shall wait and see," said Trumfis casually. "Now, why have you journeyed here? My father only mentioned that I should expect to see you. He would not tell me of your letter."

"Perhaps we should wait," said Ansel.

"Until what?" said Trumfis.

Valen watched him curiously for he also didn't know what Ansel wanted Vorfynn for.

"I—" began Ansel. He leaned forward. "I've been searching for something. . ." His sentence fell off. He sat down on the ground and began rummaging through his sack. He pulled out a tiny strange looking log. Then he began gathering stones. He formed a ring, then placed the log in the middle of it and poured a bit of golden colored dust onto it. Immediately it erupted into flames.

"Amazing," said Valen staring in disbelief. "What is that?"

"Wanderer's Dust," said Ansel.

"But the log," said Valen. "Won't the log go out shortly?"

"No," said Ansel. "This is rare wood from my country. It will burn at least through the night."

"What about smoke?" said Valen moving closer. "We're in a confined space."

"It does not have any," said Ansel.

After that, there were no more questions and, feeling that it was safe, Valen moved closer to it excited about its warmth. He was shivering.

"I am fortunate we have met," said Trumfis moving closer to the flames. He paced back and forth slowly, warming his fur. He grinned widely. After shifting several times he settled down quietly. "I haven't felt this warm in ages. You were saying that you were looking for something?"

"Ah, yes," said Ansel lowering his voice. "I came here to—"

"Find out if it's true?" said Trumfis finishing his sentence.

"If what's true?" recoiled Ansel.

"The legend of the Silverfeather," said Trumfis as if he had been expecting this conversation for a very long time.

"How did you know?" said Ansel.

"Rumors fly as the bird flies," said Trumfis as he wiggled his nose, sniffing the air. "Messengers of the White Kingdom made known to me that you left Noroth many moons ago. Tigers conceal themselves just as well as your kind. My father did not tell me of your letter as I have said, but I am not fool. I knew your reasons."

"The Silverfeather," said Valen trying to recollect. "We saw it engraved in the halls of the Withered King—Solominn of Cylvirstone."

"The Withered King was there, when the bow string released its volley of arrows. The Silverfeather," began Trumfis, "is a weapon of immense power. It was made by the Iddling Elves before the First Dark War of the Elves."

"Why didn't Gawdspelle mention this to us?" said Valen looking at Veeps.

"Potus Gawdspelle?" said Trumfis. "*The* Gawdspelle—son of Guthenne the Great of Dingilf? This is impossible." He shook his head in disbelief.

"What do you mean?" said Ansel.

"He must be an impostor," said Trumfis.

"You cannot say that," said Valen trying to feel courageous. "I will not let you." Valen felt himself become angry, but quickly realized that he was speaking with a battle-worn tiger many times bigger than he, even if he was frail.

"Are you sure he is whom you say he is?" said Trumfis.

"Yes," interjected Veeps at last. "I know it is him. Why are you questioning this?"

"Because I saw Gawdspelle slain before my eyes thousands of years ago."

"Slain?" said Valen doubtfully.

"Yes," said Trumfis. "Quite."

"If he died, then who is . . ." Valen's sentence fell off.

"He did not die," said Ansel. "Gawdspelle is one of the Myraris."

"The what?" said Valen.

"They are close in kind to wizards," said Ansel. "Very rare indeed. Though their companionship broke a long time ago. When I was younger, I read of them in the long halls of the library of Noroth. And it was at that battle you spoke of, Trumfis, where Gawdspelle was betrayed."

"Betrayed?" said Valen aghast. "Who betrayed him?"

"The other Myraris,"said Ansel.

"But why?" said Valen.

"Because he picked up a sword during that battle and killed another."

"Isn't that what you're supposed to do in battle?" said Valen.

"Not Myraris," said Ansel. "No, their kind is never to shed the blood of another. It is forbidden. They are to dedicate themselves to lore and wisdom. Picking up a weapon of any kind is forbidden and going to war or slaying another is treasonous."

"This news, that Gawdspelle has appeared, is the most surprising news I have heard in some time," said Trumfis who began pacing. "It is most extraordinary news."

"I don't understand," said Valen.

"Ah," said Trumfis, his mind racing. "Our world grows darker, and Potus Gawdspelle, thought to be dead, has suddenly reappeared? There is something to this. Something that I cannot quite see. These events are not coincidence. No, it is much deeper than that. It is as if it was intended to be this way all along."

Valen looked at him, curiously.

Trumfis turned, and looking at Valen from a different angle saw what he hadn't seen before.

"Magnificent," said Trumfis; suddenly noticing Valen's strange features. "And an elf, too, right in my very midst? This must be a dream, a mistake. Elves are extinct. There has been no word of them since long ago. And yet, I have one here, before my very eyes? How is this possible? Where do you come from?"

"I am from Had Wink," said Valen. "And I have come through a bridge in the sky through a barn in the forest behind my house. I ended up in Sorothgar in the Western Kingdom near the town of Hallowell."

"Had-win . . . road, barn—*behind your house*?"

"Wink," corrected Valen.

"Where is that?"

"The Other World," said Ansel, "just beyond."

"And Gawdspelle? Where did you meet him?"

"We stayed with him at Hallowell," said Valen. "And with Thomas Tiddle."

"*Tiddle*?" said Trumfis thoughtfully. "I don't know the name."

"And what of you Ansel, Wanderer of Noroth?" Trumfis asked.

"I joined company with Mogus and Valen near the Forges of Bood just inside the forest of Meerdorf after they had parted company with Gawdspelle under the Looming Mountains, just beyond the River Rizzenne."

"The Hoarmen have taken over," said Trumfis looking at Ansel.

"Yes," said Ansel. "They've taken over the remnants of the city and the forest."

"I'm afraid it will only get worse," said Trumfis. "I've been watching the Light fade for some time; since before I came here. Good kings throughout our world have sensed that Something is Deepening."

"Yes, the Light began fading many moons ago," Ansel said, raising an eye. "But now, because it is fading faster, it has many worried. Some are saying *the Long Lawlessness* is coming. And, I have traveled far North to meet with Notswin Lord of the Golden Horses in the Land of Rowmyn. His mind grows heavy, for he has spoken to me of Morgs and Lorgs traveling near his border, heading south from the City of Nogkz. And, of course, Othoritees have begun capturing, innocent lawful creatures all over. And there are Dark bears, too. Yes, I have seen many strange things begin to happen, all troubling to me."

Valen watched Ansel as he spoke, and felt for the moment that there was something much more mysterious to him than when they first met.

"Yes," continued Trumfis. "It worries me just as much, for I cannot see what lay upon the horizon and yet; I sense a War coming that has not yet been seen. The Second Darker war—the worst war."

"The Darker War?" said Ansel with a troubled voice.

"It is only my guess," Trumfis said who looked to Valen to be thousands of years old now, "but, yes. For rumor has reached my ears that terrible beasts have come down from their hiding places in the deep parts of the Koratik and Ormuc Mountains which border Koratikoom and Pestyphooris. And strange men, who walk on all fours as animals, have begun mobilizing. But, for what purpose, I do not know."

"Do you know the legend of the Silverfeather?" Ansel said returning to the subject

"Ah, yes," said Trumfis thoughtfully. "There are many legends and sacred stories that have nearly been forgotten, but the one of the lost Silverfeather has endured."

"Will you tell us the story?" said Valen.

At that point they heard keys jingling and suddenly the giant door creaked open and a tiger walked in. But before that happened Ansel had extinguished the fire he had made and the company sat in darkness again. Following behind the massive tiger was an animal that looked much like a wolverine. Valen watched its fangs hanging in its mouth like sharp icicles in a cave. His claws were razor sharp and he wore a grayish colored breastplate of armor. His fur was dark like tree bark and his eyes were black as ebony. The orange light of the torch flickered in his eyes.

"Dinner," spat the little beast with a nasty snarl, as he threw a bucket of moldy apples and rancid meat over to them. "Eat." It turned and walked back to the door where the tiger stood. The little creature slammed the door behind and Valen and his friends stood engulfed by darkness again.

Ansel relit his fire which brought immediate warmth to everyone. Valen stared at the bucket angrily.

"How do they expect us to eat this?" Valen protested kicking the bucket over.

"We don't have to," said Ansel. "And I wouldn't anyway."

"Stam!" said Valen remembering excitedly. "Mogus, you have stam don't you?"

"Enough for a few days. Beyond that, I don't know what we'll eat." He reached into his pouch that he had slung over his shoulder and pulled it out.

"I've brought some provisions too," said Ansel he pulled out a concealed bag from under his cloak. "I believe we'll be okay for a few more days."

"We won't be here that long," said Trumfis. "Today is a day far better than I could have ever imagined."

"What do you mean?" said Ansel taking a seat.

"There *is* a way out," said Trumfis walking away from the fire.

"Well, why haven't you left yet?" said Valen.

"I cannot do it on my own," said Trumfis.

"I am weak, though a fight I can wage against Toren," said Trumfis, "but I will need the strength of your friend to open it." He looked at Mogus. "Teeth and claws are no match for the doors of the White Kingdom." Trumfis looked at Mogus. "Come, let us go to the other side and rest for a while. Ansel, I want to hear of your travels."

"I have traveled thousands of miles, over mountains and through rivers and forests in hopes that I would find a clue to its whereabouts," said Ansel once they had settled in. He relit the fire. He got back to the topic of the Silverfeather with great concern in his voice. "If you knew where it was, it should bring us all great hope."

"I have heard of the Silverfeather's power," said Toren sitting down, "but I do not want to raise any hope for anyone. If it was found, it may usher in a darkness which none of us have ever yet seen. We do not know all its powers. My lands and people certainly know your people are not foreign to war. I fear, Ansel of Noroth, that, that is our destiny should it be found. Besides, the Dragon is gone and it is good enough not to be terrified by him any longer. Its Hide was hidden, long, long ago and hopefully it shall never return to it."

"Yes," said Ansel, "but something is growing in the lands of Pestyphooris. On its borders, hideous things have been seen passing over them. I do not know what it means, but I have heard rumors that a giant pale slithering creature was seen moving through the forest. Whatever it is, it is weak and has barely any strength. Dark clouds and carrion crows are flocking to Koratikoom and Ormuc Mountains. Thick trees have begun to split. Raging rivers have begun to slow. Mists have gathered on mountain tops. I believe the time has come. We are about to enter the Darker War."

Ansel moved in front of the great, but sickly cat.

"I must know if you know where it is," Ansel said, pausing. "It was said that the Great Cats found it long ago."

Trumfis looked into Ansel's eyes with an iron gaze.

"We shall all know soon enough. The Silverfeather is but one relic from the long past of Eoorthe. There has always been a great mystery surrounding it, but there are other great mysteries surrounding other items too and while I know some of the Silverfeather's story, I do not want to raise any hope in your heart of its location—for all we know it could be lost forever."

"It is not lost forever," said Ansel. "Have you not paid any attention to the heavens of late? When the Silverfeather first appeared a Great

Comet drew near to Eoorthe and that is precisely what is happening now. The skies are full of strange signs, which have not been seen in many ages past."

"I have seen the Comet, yes," said Trumfis. "You are a Wanderer whose people study the heavens." Trumfis now looked quite contemplative. "Do you think the riddle of the Dragon and the Lance is coming to pass?"

"What is the riddle of the Dragon and the Lance?" Valen interjected.

***"The Dragon that went away, shall never again come to stay. Yet, in the Dragon's heart lay, forever Spring and Day."***

Trumfis uttered the words solemnly.

"With all my heart I believe it," said Ansel.

"Then you must head to Hyddenne," said Trumfis. "But first, you must rest—get some sleep for you will need it."

There were no more protests or traded words after that and Ansel became quiet of heart and tongue as they all fell asleep for a good many hours. Soon Valen heard the sound of Trumfis's voice.

Trumfis was walking through to the other side of the dungeon where there stood a large arched doorway. The light from the fire barely illuminated it and the tiger's shadow crept up the wall as he moved closer to the doorway.

"Follow me," he said looking back. Then, he slipped down the stairwell and disappeared into the blackness. Mogus, Ansel, Veeps and Valen followed closely behind.

As they descended deeper into the dungeon, Valen felt like he had been back under the Looming Mountains as he could barely see his hand in front of him. The stairs seemed to go on forever before at last they reached the bottom. As Valen did he felt he stepped on something.

"What was that?" Valen said with a startle.

"Groll bones," said Trumfis.

"Grolls?" it rolled off Valen's tongue oddly.

"Some time ago they found this entrance over here," said Trumfis pointing to what looked to be plain stone wall.

"I can't see anything," said Valen and as he said that Veeps hands slowly started glowing. He walked over to Trumfis and cast the light of his hands onto the wall.

With the help of Veeps, Trumfis lunged forward, pressing his shoulder into one of the larger stones.

Valen watched as he pushed hard.

"I could help," said Mogus thoughtfully. he pushed it out of the way.

"This way." The tiger turned and headed into the tunnel leading them down a dirt path to a set of stairs which led up now. Valen could feel warm air on his face as they began to climb them. He looked around. The tunnel they were in seemed enormous and open. It didn't feel like a dungeon at all.

"What is this place?" said Valen as they made their way through.

"It is the entrance of a mining shaft," said Trumfis following Veeps. "It was built by creatures who dwelled here long ago."

"What were they mining for?"

"Silatrommi," said Trumfis.

"Sila—what?" said Valen.

"Unending life," said Trumfis.

"There's such a thing?"

"Legends and myths," said Trumfis. "Perhaps."

"So this silatrom stuff, what does it look like?" asked Valen ignorantly.

"Silatrommi is deceptive and bares many faces," said Trumfis walking along. "Gold, jewels, power, cities, love. It comes in many forms. Many races, creatures, men, countries, nations have searched for it. Yet, they have been unable to find it. Do you know how to find it?"

"Me?" said Valen laughing nervously. "I wouldn't even know where to begin."

Trumfis grinned at him.

They continued walking through the long dark stone tunnels. The air became warmer and warmer as they went along. Valen followed Trumfis and Veeps who led the way. Ansel and Mogus walked closely behind with Valen in the middle.

Valen looked around. Veeps moved his hands here and there, shining light on what looked to be a plain small circular stone room with no exit.

"Where are we?" said Valen thinking he saw the light of Veeps' hands reveal a shape of a face in the stone wall. He looked again. As he studied it closer, it *was* a face which emerged out of the wall into the shape of a giant stone tiger head. The rock suddenly popped and cracked, crunched and crumbled and the mouth of it began to open wide nearly as tall as Mogus. As it opened, Valen noticed that a wooden door sealed the entrance of the tiger's throat.

"Long ago," began the tiger. "There were those who searched for *silatrommi* and could not find it, but one day after many thousand of years they found something, hidden, deep within the rock beneath the White Kingdom. It was hidden so deep that the Council of Tigers thought that they had discovered something that was not supposed to be discovered—a knowledge. Some kind of secret language. They believed they had awakened something. And so it was decided that it should be disposed of, that it should be taken somewhere safe, that it needed to be hidden. Something strange began to happen amongst our people. It was thought that they disturbed some lost prophecy. Cursed, they believed. Vorfynn ordered the Council of Tigers to gather and there they decided what to do with it. They decided to have it taken, and nailed shut, by the Carpenters of old. No, they never opened it for fear of it. Soon, word began to spread that something very mysterious and yet very powerful had been found. Kings of other kingdoms came here wanting to know what had been discovered. The Council knew that to safeguard the White Kingdom something had to be done with it. But, they delayed and soon wars broke out and the White Kingdom found itself vulnerable. I tried to leave with it, but each time I did, violent storms engulfed the city and the very foundations shook. Terrified of its power, it was decided that it should be hidden again here, never to leave. After this was decided, my father decided to seek the council of Stump of Dorodroos. In the *Great Foreshadowings* there is something written that speaks of this and Stump feared that what we had unearthed may be it. So, when my father returned, he entrusted it to me—it was our secret. Yes, I have been its keeper for an age. Toren knew that I had met with my father, but he did not know what we had discussed. All this time, Toren has not known that I had this in my possession. And yet, I knew that when my father left that things would grow dark here. Though, I did not know that I would be betrayed. On the eve of my father's departure, Toren began to act strange and I knew at once that he could no longer be trusted; so I took the box and hid it for safe keeping. I hid it here, in the hopes that the one was destined for would come to claim it, and here you are."

"My father?" said Veeps. "He knew of this?"

"I am not sure what they discussed," said Trumfis. "All I know is what Stump said, 'Hide again what has been found, hide it deep in the ground until One will come again to bring to light what was once hidden.'"

"So, it's still here? And you still do not know what it is?" said Valen.

"Yes—," said Trumfis. "That is what I was waiting for you to ask me. Long ago—a stranger arrived and tried stealing it in the hopes of breaking into the heart of our Kingdom. He came through the dungeon and tried leaving through the dungeons down into the mines and just before he escaped, he turned into stone. He could not take from here, what only one was foretold to."

"I am the one to take it?" said Valen awkwardly.

"Elves *are* powerful," said Trumfis. "What is in this box is a rare weapon, I believe; though I do not know for sure. It is this weapon, that Toren obsesses over. It is why I am in here. He is going mad over it."

"It is the Silverfeather, no?" said Ansel.

"I do not know," said Trumfis solemnly. "But if it is, it is not something to be used. It would be like the Hammer Deep when Horothgoor lay it at the base of the mountain before smashing that fiend, that monster's head—that blood thirsty dweller by the fens. It is not something to meddle in. Items have their keepers, as in all worlds."

Trumfis dug deeper into the ground with his matted paws before at last he came to a long dark brown colored, wooden box. He reached into the hole with his mouth and grabbed it gently. Then, he placed the box on the ground at Valen's feet.

"Is it safe to open?" said Valen.

"You cannot open it here! No one can open it here. The safest place that I know for it to be opened is the *Old City—Hyddenne, the Great City of Secrets and Mysteries*—which is where you are going."

Valen looked at the box curiously. It seemed too plain to be anything of special significance. He studied it carefully and as he did he saw that it bore a dark engraving and the faint outline of what looked to be a gryphon. He twirled it in his hands, contemplatively.

"But what do I do with it?" said Valen who now was running his hands over the length of it.

"Bring it to Gawdspelle," said Trumfis at last. "He will know what to do."

At that moment, they heard voices coming down the passage back from where they came.

"Quickly," said Trumfis. "It is Toren! You must leave at once! No one has ever been able to get through this door until now and it is up to you to bring this box safely to the *Old City.* Do you understand? You cannot let this fall into anyone's hands."

Valen nodded with understanding.

"I know the way," said Ansel. "At least to the borders of Hyddenne."

"Then I will follow you," said Valen humbly.

"Quickly then!" said Ansel. "We must get through that door before Toren arrives!"

Valen ran over to the door as quickly as he could with the box clutched tightly under his arm. He grabbed the doorknob and tried turning it hard, but the door would not budge.

"It's not working!" he shouted.

Suddenly, a company of tigers came charging down the tunnel, their giant legs shook the ground like a thousands of thunderous horses. The walls shook.

"I'll do my best to hold them back!" roared Trumfis. "But you must go! Quickly!"

"I'm trying," shouted Valen. "It's not working!"

Ansel, Mogus and Veeps rushed over to where Valen stood; frantically trying to open the door. The sound of the tiger's legs rolled towards them.

Valen grabbed the knob again, turning it, desperately; then he dropped the box. Forgetting it for a moment, he seized the knob with both hands as hard as he could and then thrust his shoulder into the door, but nothing happened. The tigers descended upon them with greater speed. He looked back, then bent down quickly to pick up the box. Out of the corner of his eye he saw Veeps, who fired a *silverslugg* up the tunnel past Trumfis, sending several of them soaring through the air, where they landed in a heap of gold, green and white. Valen watched Veeps' missiles travel like flaming meteors through the darkness. He fired them again and again. Veeps' hands, powerful though they were, deterred the power of the White Tigers for only a moment. Yet he managed to kill one tiger where it lay dead upon the ground. It's green and silver armor knew battle no more. Veeps turned and ran as swiftly as he could while he had a chance.

Trumfis turned bravely, standing his ground, fighting skillfully, until at last he was overtaken by ten others. Valen gave the door knob one last turn when at last he heard a click. The door was open, but there was something blocking it on the other side. A little light streamed in. Then Mogus threw his massive weight into it and smashed through the door with such force the earth shook; the light of early day poured in through the dim, dank, dungeon. The company fled, teeth and thunderous muscle at their heels. Valen looked back one final time in great relief, for now he saw that the rocks on the outer walls came crumbling down. A deep noise rang though the air and Valen's heart sank for he could hear a great roar and he knew at once it was Toren's. And then more great roars rang out and the rocks in the mountains that stood above them shook with a low rumble. The company had made it.

# VOYAGE TO THE SECRET ENTRANCE

The doorway led into a tiny gulley and soon to an old gate which spanned the width of it. The gulley opened up and soon gave way to a hilltop in the distance. They climbed it swiftly. Behind them stood rock and mountain. The way they had exited was a secret entrance into the tiger's powerful fortress. Valen looked below into the valley where, spread out before them was a long, forest which went on for miles and miles. It reached beyond the horizon. The trees spoke of a time that seemed to stretch back to an age far out of memory. Valen took in the landscape. The sun crept up over the horizon, painting the sky with a rich purple and blue. Bits of golden light dripped from the trees and rocks and streams. Late summer had arrived and the first signs of cold arrived as a gust of wind whipped across the land. Colossal clouds rose up out of the west to greet the morning sky.

"We cannot waste a moment," said Ansel ducking under a low hanging branch. He was moving swiftly. "I did not see Toren in the tunnels, but I am certain he will begin his hunt for us. The only thing that aids us now, is that he cannot pass through the door because of the collapse. He has to go around the Long White Mountains, then over the pass; which is very treacherous. But, we should not underestimate his speed. The White Tigers are swift as a river and falling into their hands is not something I wish for any of us again. Though, the darker fear now is for Valen. I believe Toren has betrayed his people and he seeks Valen at Murkus' request. He sought to hand him over. But, we have more to fear than the White Tigers of this land. The Othoritees and their devilry travels on the winds and the birds above have spotted them. I have many friends in the skies and they have clever ways of warning me of many dangers. See just there, a Fair Falcon—" Ansel pointed to a swift passing bird as it rung out a call which only Ansel understood. "There are ten foxes and their sleighs, with Othoritees pushing them onwards," continued Ansel. "I do not know where they are headed, but wherever it is they too may soon be upon us. The Light fades just as my father warned. We must get this and you," he looked at Valen seriously, "into the Land of Hyddenne at once. There is no more time to lose. There will be questions,"Ansel continued. "And with questions, come answers—answers, I do not want to give. Toren will soon discover that what he desires in this box has has been taken. Once he does, he will be furious. I do not know what he is capable of, but my heart does not trust that he will have any mercy on us if we meet him again. We must keep the box out of his hands; even if all else fails. He wants it, but for what purpose, I do not know."

"The box!" Valen said suddenly. "I've lost it!" He looked around frantically. "Veeps! Ansel! Did you see it? It must have fallen out of my bag!"

"Gone?" said Ansel in disbelief, scanning the ground. His eyes shot towards Valen.

"I don't know how—" began Valen.

Then quietly, Mogus stepped forward and stretched out his huge hand. It was bound in a tight fist. He uncurled his fingers slowly and there, to everyone's surprise it sat, unharmed and intact.

"How did you—what?" said Valen, shocked. "You have it? How?" Mogus smiled.

"I do not think whatever is in this box—whatever tale it is to tell, wants us to know its story or the secret it possesses—or anyone for that matter. And, I don't know if *I* want to know either. There are many evils, some hidden and some plainly before us—this box may be one yet—but we must be on guard! We must bring this to Gawdspelle, with great speed and care. We are being hunted now. We must move faster!" Ansel scanned the trees.

"Do you think Toren will do something terrible to Trumfis?" said Valen.

"I do not know," said Ansel seeming to recall a distant memory as he moved along. "But we cannot control all things that happen. For the moment, we must move with stealth. If we delay any longer then we will find ourselves back in that dungeon. Now, come! Follow me! We make for the Old City—Hyddenne, the City of Secrets and Mysteries!"

Mogus reached down and gave the box to Valen.

"You can be its keeper," smiled Mogus, with a slight pat on Valen's head.

"I'll do my best." Valen reached for it, then placed it again in the sack he had slung over his back. This time, he tied the top to conceal it.

Hours passed as they marched on through the trees and along narrow paths which wrapped around high lakes, nestled deep in the forest. Valen thought he heard roars on the wind as they climbed higher and higher until at last they came to a rocky ridge. Spread behind them, lay the other side of the forest they had come through where they had reunited with Veeps. The The Looming Mountains rose up out of the southwest stretching high into the sky. Between the ridge where they stood and the Looming Mountains lay a sea of trees. They continued on for a while as the ridge climbed down. Soon they came to a clearing and bright golden light poured into a break in the branches and all around them lay pools and pools of clear golden water. "Drink from these," said Ansel. "It will quench your thirst until we reach Hyddenne. These are the Healing Waters of the kingdom which used to be here." Everyone stopped to rest and took long deep drinks and felt refreshed enough to carry on for days even weeks. It was the most refreshing water that Valen had ever tasted. They continued on for hours more and soon, night had fallen. Valen, Mogus and Veeps ran as fast as deer, trailing behind Ansel in the dense overgrown forest. Valen could not believe how fast Ansel could run. His legs sped along like a wild horse. Valen struggled to keep up with him, at first. Though, as he followed along, he felt his legs become lighter and his feet swifter. He remembered that not too long ago he was falling downstairs, unable to walk. Now he was right on Ansel's heels, his legs moving ever faster. His confidence heightened as he looked behind where Veeps trailed. Though, as small as his legs were, Valen could not believe how quickly Veeps moved. He ran, quick as a fox and his hands were clenched tightly into fists as he focused seriously on his pace.

Though night had long ago fallen, they continued on, running at a steady speed. The forest opened up to long flatlands and suddenly there rose, under the light of the moon, a solid rock tower which was abandoned. It appeared closer than it was like the base of the mountain that seemed unable to be reached no matter how much one traveled.

Valen gazed at it with curiosity. After an hour they came to it. Near the edge of the base was a cliff which was a sharp drop down into a ravine which disappeared into darkness. Valen looked up and saw it had a window in the top and it looked just like the lighthouse in Had Wink. But deep in the forest on the edge of a cliff?

"What is this place?" Valen asked.

"It once served the Kings and Queens of Lorsegood and their armies of Lorsings. They guarded all the land between Cylvirstone and Hyddenne. Once upon a time, from the Forges of Bood and the edge of the White Kingdom, there used to be the Singing Sea. But then, Grendagsoor and his maggoty warriors came across from those boggy wastelands where rot and stench rise always up from the ground," said Ansel. "They came and conquered that good king and there was much weeping. But, then another hero rose and slew that foul imposter Gren and his head was thrown into the sea and eaten up by the monster of the deep. Though, it has not been used since ages ago. It was once used to warn ships. I believe those in the Other World, would call it a lighthouse. Here they are called Flameguards. Come . . . we must flee," said Ansel. "Toren grows closer. They are gaining on us."

Occasionally they heard the mighty roars of the tigers behind them. At times it seemed they lost them, partly because of the wind which ripped across the land. Days and nights passed and no one had slept. The sun rose and set and then night came upon them again. At last they all became fatigued—except Valen—for elves did not grow tired, though his mind was weary from thinking. And he desired a little water, for his mouth felt parched and he longed for the cool taste of it. It had been days since the Healing Waters.

They rested for an hour and everyone slept deep before waking. Valen realized that they had come to rest on a precipice and far below a swift black river raged making its way through a long deep stony canyon. Valen woke Ansel because he thought he heard growls and armor clanking. Then, Valen thought he saw shapes moving down near the river banks. He peered over the edge to get a closer look.

"Ansel," he said, pointing. "Look! Do you see them?"

"Yes," he said.

"Are they tigers?" said Valen.

"It is most likely," said Ansel clutching his arms as the incoming night air grabbed at his skin. "But there are many kinds of creatures in these parts."

"What do we do?" thought Valen aloud.

"There is a cave up there," said Ansel pointing way up above them. "Let's make our way around the side of this mountain. We will be safe there."

He grabbed his cloak and pushed some of the excess cloth around his neck to keep him warm. A cold gust of wind ripped up the face of the cliff below, howling. They walked up the side of the mountain, keeping close watch where they stepped. Valen glanced over the edge again. The fall was a long one, he thought, stepping back. Rocks lay scattered all around as the light of the moon faded. Valen could not see much ,as he tried focusing. He walked along cautiously, watching his footing. He tripped once, nearly plunging into the chasm below. He looked over the edge as rocks disappeared into the darkness. After some time, he looked up and saw the mouth of the old cave. He could see the silhouette of Ansel standing in the moonlight.

"We'll sleep here tonight," he said and walked into it.

Valen and Veeps went up the rest of the way and Mogus followed behind.

It didn't take them long to settle in and though it was late none of them were very hungry. A cold air came uninvited into the cave as they sat, resting for the longest time since they had left the White Kingdom.

"We are safe for the time being—enough to warm ourselves," said Ansel. In a moment the noise and wind became muffled at the mouth of the cave.

"It will not last long," said Ansel lighting a fire. "But long enough to rest and get warm."

Soon, the cave felt warmer and safer to Valen as he laid down to rest his mind. The wind was out of his face at last and he bundled himself up as tightly as he could to counter the chill in the air. He lay awake, his mind racing with thoughts of Jack, Henry and Jude. It had been some time since he had thought of any of them, but he wondered now where they were. Valen was sure Henry must have died or had been put into chains by some wicked creatures in a distant dungeon. But, it was Jude who had worried him the most. Who did he meet at the Southernpost? What was he up to now and where did he go when he left them under the Looming Mountains? Valen couldn't answer any of these questions as he watched his friends fall fast asleep. Hours past and after a long while, Ansel stirred.

In the middle of the night, Valen thought he had heard something. At night the forest was eerie and full of strange noises and though he could barely see anything but the outline of the mouth of the cave, he thought he had seen things moving from time to time. He was certain they were not animals. Then, suddenly he saw the shape move again. He tried to make it out as he watched it pass in front of the cave a few times. Then the creature stopped, turned and headed into it. Valen wasn't sure if the creature could see him, but he dared not move. His heart pounded against the inside of his chest.

He heard the creature moving closer. What was it? Could it see him? Wild thoughts raced through his mind. Valen moved over to the wall. Then, suddenly, a small golden light began to glow.

"Veeps?" he said frightened. "Is that you? Hello?"

The light slowly began to illuminate the cave. He listened closely, but the wind was the only thing his ears found.

"Veeps?" he said again."Hello?"

"Who's there?" said Mogus waking up suddenly.

"What?" said Veeps coming out of his sleep.

Suddenly, a white light burst forth, illuminating the cave where a strange creature stood; a glass orb dangling from a rope, hung around his neck. "Tell me your names!" said the creature, his sword drawn, his face unflinching. "Swiftly!"

Ansel had his spears at the ready. Veeps hands glowed a cool silver. Mogus made a low grunting noise. Valen looked at the creature. It was a head taller than Veeps. His skin was a golden color and his eyes were a deep blue. He had on high boots and a traveling cloak. Around his waist he wore a large belt with a sheath for his sword. The creature looked to be human, but he had seven fingers instead of five. Valen decided, that judging by the looks of his hands, that he must have worked with them, for they were rough and leathery looking. All over his body was a fine golden hair, that sparkled like the sun glistening on the surface of the sea. And in him, Valen saw a bit of wildness but also, kindness.

"Do not delay or I shall run you through with my sword!" He pointed it at Valen.

"Put your sword away friend. We are not your enemies. I am Ansel of Noroth. These are my comrades and we are trying to get to Hyddenne."

"*Hyddenne*? *The Old City?* How do you know of this place?" said the creature looking at them skeptically. "Tell me, what business are you on?"

Ansel hesitated, glanced at Valen, then back at the creature.

"We must hide. For the rest, I cannot say."

"Hide? Cannot say?" The creature focused on Ansel, tightening the grip on his sword.

"You will tell me now or I will seize all of you at once! Do not think that because I am outnumbered, that I am unable to arrest all four of you!"

Ansel planted his feet firm in the dirt, his eyes fierce. The creature stood fixed, stout as a brazen warrior; his sword calm, like stone. "Do you know that there is a pack of one hundred battle hardened tigers thundering towards you this very moment?" said the creature unmoved by the spear pointing directly in his face. Ansel tightened his grip.

"They cannot climb these heights," said Ansel.

"I assure you they can," said the creature. "They are climbing these rocks as we speak."

"One hundred?" said Valen gulping. "That's too many."

"That *is* too many," agreed Ansel. "How do you know this?"

"Haven't you listened? I have seen them, for it is my duty to know what goes on in my lands," said the creature. "Besides, it's no secret that Toren the Brave has lost his mind. Traitor!"

"So you know too?" said Valen.

"Of course, I know," said the creature. "It will be a stain on the White Kingdom for a very long time. He has betrayed his father and brother. The Green and Gold flag will never fly again. No, now what we have is one more enemy!" He paused, looking greatly surprised. "You are an elf?"

"I suppose it is not secret anymore," began Valen.

"Yes," said Ansel. "And a *dwundlegob, along with a mighty*."

"A mighty!?" said the creature. "Tell me, Ansel of Noroth, is this some sort of trick? Some devilry? Surely, elves do not exist. And the mightys went into captivity long ago. And you say you have a dwundlegob, too? Now, all of them are here traveling under the Wild Trees on the borders of the White Kingdom? This has never been seen before! Something strange is afoot! Either this is all some great hoax, or it is true and we are at the dawn of something extraordinary!" He paused and a sour grin spread across his face. "Dwundlegobs have never left Dorodroos, not even when their lands came close to burning. They do not care about anyone but themselves."

"You had better take that back," said Veeps, the silver in his hands glowing cooly as embers in a fire just catching flame, "or I will send you off this cliff." Valen watched his silver veins pulsing as bright white trees shimmering in the darkness.

"I meant no harm," said the creature gripping his sword. "Please, forgive me."

Veeps stepped away into the shadows.

"I assure you, it is no joke," said Ansel. "Though we are not evil and things may become dark or evil yet, I do not know."

"Well, whatever path you take, the road to the *Old City* is hidden and you cannot find it on your own."

"I am a Wanderer of Noroth," said Ansel defiantly, again. "I know these lands."

"Well, Ansel, Wanderer of Noroth, I tell you the truth. The way to the city you seek is invisible from all eyes and you cannot find it without my help."

"How do we know you are not a *Mooldwarp*?"said Ansel. "I have killed two already and will not hesitate to do it again."

"A what?" asked Valen curiously. "There are far too many creatures in this world!"

"And how do I know you are not one?" he retorted. "If you want to reach the Old City soon, follow me."

Ansel stared at him suspiciously.

"Come, tell us your name," said Ansel growing impatient. "I will not ask you again—what sort of creature are you? I have never seen your kind before."

"That is because there are only a few of us that remain. We are the Timms, we possess this name because we are afraid of much. Afraid because we unlocked the door to a terrible Deemonwitch—but my family had no hand in this. We are known to be fearful creatures, cowardly some say, but I am not..." He tightened his hand on his hilt. "I am Gobbins and I have come from the Land of Timmoris." He bowed low, then stood back up.

"You are a descendant of the creatures that unlocked the door to the Deemonwitch?" said Ansel with a great shudder.

"Yes," said Gobbins. "They were searching for the *Lost Books*—knowledge of secret designs, plans—plans to build cities that would last beyond time. My people have never believed in the *Great Foreshadowings*—no—they did not. Yet," he looked at Valen and Veeps in disbelief. "You say you have an *elf*. And, a creature with golden blood—a dwundlegob has left Dorodroos? Still, a mighty?"

"Yes, I am Valen Vanderbolt of Had Wink." Valen stepped forward revealing his argent hair.

"And I am Veeps, Son of Stump the Stouthearted, a dwundlegob." Veeps said formally introducing himself and returned from where he stood cloaked in the shadow of the cave's walls, his powerful hands still glowing faintly from his anger before.

"And I am Mogus, a mighty—from the land near the Barrows on the edge of Monstrous Deep, far beyond the River Rizzenne. Though I grew up in the City of Rizzenne."

"It is very, very, pleasant to meet you," Gobbins spoke and bowed quietly. "My people refused to believe in the *Great Foreshadowings*, but I always have—" he gathered himself; "I knew that when the elves arose again, things would change forever in this horrid place—*This Realm*." Gobbins sighed. "My heart is glad you are here." He smiled at Valen, but Valen did not return the smile. His heart felt heavy, because he knew that the hope or burden, as he saw it was a fading flame on an already smoldering fire. He turned away.

"There is no more time to talk, if what you say is true of the White Tigers," began Ansel. "There isn't a moment to delay. We must move with speed as we have never done before."

"I will show you the way," said Gobbins. "Only, I need your help first."

Ansel's eyes raised with suspicion.

"If you help me," said the creature, "then I shall help you."

"There isn't time for bargaining," said Ansel. "The Great Cats are descending upon us as we speak."

Then suddenly, a great thunderous growl, rose up from the valley below.

"What do you say?" said the creature.

"I am sorry, but I am their guide—for now," said Ansel. "We cannot help you, whatever it is, you may need."

"I only ask for help with my brother!" said Gobbins angrily. "He has been taken by the Othoritees. Taken from his bed, while asleep; only a few days ago." Gobbins became choked up. "He is my dearest friend in this world, and I fear something dreadful has happened to him. Othoritees all over Eoorthe are abducting good folk," he concluded solemnly. Ansel, stood silently, gazing at the creature thoughtfully. Then, after what seemed to be a full hour, even though it was only a minute, he moved towards Gobbins and placed his hand on his shoulder. "I know what it is like to have someone you love snatched from you."

The creature had been holding his sword out the entire time when at last he lowered it.

"You have lightened my heart," said Gobbins. "There is one way—an escape route that was built long ago in the event the city was sacked; it goes far underneath the Old City. It hasn't been used for ages."

"How do you know of it?" said Ansel.

"I found it long ago when the Timmoris sought their treasures. My light is dimming," said Gobbins, clutching his orb as it flickered out. "It is a warning. Enemies are upon us. It will flicker, but it will never die. The Light is leaving all things and the *Long Lawlessness* I fear is beginning. Though, as evil as things become there is the King far away that bears a Light which will never fade, even if all else goes dark." Gobbins smiled. "Move your feet!"

A cold wind blew into the cave, bringing with it the murderous roars of the approaching tigers. The cave filled with darkness and Gobbins stood at the mouth of the cave gazing down into the black valley beneath them. "Follow me," he said. "Quickly! To the tunnel that leads to the Old City."

Valen, Veeps, Ansel and Mogus at once followed Gobbins out of the cave and up through to the top of a small hill where the trees became thick again. They wasted no time and fled under the shadows of oak, ash, elm and beech trees. The howls of the tigers grew stronger and came closer. The company ran as fast as they could. Valen looked up at the trees and saw the trees silhouetted by the light of the misty moon. Clouds rushed in, sending the remaining light fleeing. It began to rain.

"How much longer?" called out Ansel.

"It is just beyond those trees!" shouted Gobbins through the rain. "Near the edge of the cliff."

"There is nothing there!" shouted Ansel again. "Where are you leading us?"

Gobbins scurried along, unable to hear Ansel through the heavy wind.

Then at last they came to the edge of a small lagoon surrounded by massive white cliffs. A tiny waterfall cascaded down out of the mouth of a cave above them.

"There!" shouted Gobbins as they heard over the winds, the low growls of the tigers who had been following them. "Quickly—into the lagoon! If you do not want captured, then you must dive!"

"Mightys do not swim," said Mogus roughly. "I will stay and fight!"

"No," said Ansel. "Save your strength! We will need it another time!"

The wind snapped and pushed against them. The rain fell violently.

"The mouth to the tunnel is down there?" said Ansel trying to look into the deep water.

"Yes," said the creature. "It is the only way!"

"If we drown or are torn to pieces because of any—" but Ansel's words stopped as the sound of branches cracked in the distance. The tigers were upon them, Toren at the lead.

"They have our scent!" shouted Gobbins. "Quickly, go!"

Straightaway, Veeps jumped into the cold, but clear water. Valen could see Veeps' hands glowing under the water. He jumped in next, his head disappearing under the surface for a moment. Gobbins waded in after them followed by Mogus and Ansel. Ansel glanced behind, his spears drawn, fearing an attack.

"Put your weapons away! There isn't time! Dim your hands!" hissed Gobbins, his head just barely above the surface. "We must travel to the entrance of Hyddenne through the darkness. Do it now! When it is safe again, I will signal to you with my orb! I shall leave a rope for you to follow through the water." With that he dove down beneath the surface and disappeared. Valen and Veeps slipped below at the same moment. Then, all at once, the rain stopped and the wind settled. Ansel saw Mogus' head go under next and in the distance, near the shore, he could see white blurs sniffing the edge of the water.

Quietly, Ansel took a breath, grabbed the rope and swam down deep into the lagoon. The rope led them through the water around a towering column of rock that stuck up from below. Then, it went around to the edge of a cliff, before at last, they came to the entrance of the tunnel. Out of the blackness Gobbins' light shown forth. Valen saw the light and followed it. Gobbins swam quickly up into a long wide rocky cavern that carved its way deep into the rock at a sharp angle towards the surface, past the level of the water in the lagoon. At the edge were crumbling stone steps that jutted up out of the water. Gobbins' head had breached the surface of the water. He gasped for air, then Valen and Veeps appeared next, followed by Ansel and Mogus.

"Light your hands," Gobbins called to Veeps as his orb began to glow. He started up the stairs. "We are safe—for a while for tigers cannot swim and even if they could, the water is too dark to see the entrance."

The light of Veeps' hands and of Gobbins' orb shown brightly in the dark tunnel. They were all now cold, tired, hungry and sopping wet. They walked for a while, before coming at last to another small climb. The ground rose slowly as they ascended into a long passageway. It was large, but Mogus found himself constantly ducking or hitting his head on the ceiling. After hours and hours and several twists and turns, the ground flattened out again. Valen felt he had been in there for days, when at last they came to the end. A comforting breeze grazed Valen's cheek.

"The air of the Old City," sighed Gobbins. "A place safe from all foul things," he concluded with a smile. "Men of renown and wise kings and queens from far away have come here to seek the council of those wiser—the Fair Princes. And a rumor has reached my ears that the King who left has now come near."

"What King?" said Valen.

"The King of all This Realm has gone away—" sighed Ansel. "I will only believe it when I lay my eyes upon Him."

"Do you mean the King of the Golden Land? The King whose people make all fair things and come from the *Country That Cannot be Reached*? The King who lost his Beloved and did all he could to find her?" Mogus said all these things solemnly yet also with joy.

"Yes," said Gobbins. "I believe He has arrived at last. Come, let us go. We haven't time to lose. We are close. We can rest and find comfort there." No one said another word and the company moved forward, then upwards towards a shining stone door engraved with bright rich gold on its hinges. The land had the feel of spring after a long, brutal winter. They approached the door at last and it opened on its own. Valen felt it had been waiting for them. It opened slowly, as if the city had been expecting them all along.

And there before them stood a city of such beauty that it nearly took everyone's breath away. It stuck up out of the ground on top of a small knoll, like a giant glowing moon. Spires reached high into the night sky. Glowing candles slowly flickered on, illuminating the tall slender arched windows. Creatures from all over were gathering into the city, pitching tents. Valen saw creatures too many to count. Animals and all sorts of shadows moved over the hills. Valen saw the Great Comet rising in the Eastern sky. It soared above them and lit up the countryside surrounding the Old City. Tiny boats and canals lay all around. Huge, thick, oak trees stood here and there and tiny cottages covered the small hills that rested near a calm stream that wound its way through the valley below and away beyond the horizon. Separated by all this lay a large pristine lake with high walls, which fed itself into a small stream and gave way to a lovely waterfall. A little further on it turned into the Silver River. It was named the Silver river because it was clear and bright and it captured the moon's light and illuminated the entirety of its flowing water which was held back by bright green rolling hills. All along the river and coming out of the hills were beautiful, pure white waterfalls which all fed into the lake and river too. The moon was full and the light she shined spread out across the land creeping slowly around thick birch forests which spread all around the perimeter of the land.

"So this is Hyddenne?" asked Valen who was standing next to Veeps now.

"That's right," said Veeps, "The Old City—*City of Secrets and Mysteries*. The Festival of the Two Wandering Stars is about to begin. It has not happened in a very long time." Veeps looked on longingly.

They rested for the night and soon the sun was up. The company moved down a small, dirt path. They neared a long flight of beautiful white stone stairs. Valen smiled. The warm air was soothing. Their journey had been long and exhausting since Valen first entered the Western Edge of Hallowell. He looked down, where stretched out before them, near the bottom, was a long stone dock made centuries ago and many boats that were going in and out across the water. On either side of them stretched walls of pure gray granite. Lanterns with soft lights glowing in them hung from shiny silver rope which was mounted onto either side of the cliffs above. When they at last reached the bottom there was a long empty ship waiting for them to board.

Mogus approached the ship cautiously. Once he boarded the ship it nearly sank. Mogus quickly made his way to the rear where he sat to avoid hitting his head on the masts and sails. Everyone else sat up front to distribute the weight of the boat; yet still, it looked as if it would capsize at any moment. Valen gazed over at Mogus who was looking at his reflection in the water, blinking slowly as the ship pulled away from the shore. Then Valen made his way over to him as the ship glided smoothly over the placid water. They looked out over the deep yet clear lake as the ripples from the ship went out from beneath its wooden hull. After a short sail, they finally made it to the other side.

Everyone slowly got off the boat and stepped onto the sandy cove. Valen followed Ansel and the company up a long and winding path to the top of a small hill that overlooked the lake below. A tiny breeze blew quietly across the water. At the top of the hill sat a tiny house. It had old shudders and a dark slate roof. A small light trickled through the foggy window panes as the company approached the house. Soon they passed it and walked farther on. It was late afternoon. The Comet above grew in intensity.

No one talked for a while, for they were too busy trying to keep up with Gobbins's pace. The forest faded and eventually turned into a long lush green field that rose higher and higher. Large grey boulders were scattered throughout the field. In less than an hour they reached the base and right before their eyes stood the Old City tucked away on top of the small hill. The company moved forward.

They moved forward towards the city gate and there upon a high wall were sentries of soldiers. Their armor dazzled white with crimson pieces interwoven throughout. They were handsome men with rough looking beards. They were tough and battle worn. At the base of the white walls stood a thick, ancient, impenetrable gate. Then two came forward. One had sandy blonde hair and the other dark and sooty.

"Halt!" they said synonymously. "Tell us quickly, how did you get into the city! No one dares enter it until morning. I should say that you are up to some treachery if I didn't think better of this situation."

"The tunnel that runs into Hyddenne on the edge of the forest," spoke Gobbins quickly.

"Tunnel?" spat one of them pointing his sword at Gobbins' throat. "Tell me, foul thing from the forest, why do I not know of this and my family has guarded this city for thousands of years?"

"You do not know of it, because it has fallen out of knowledge," said Gobbins.

"And I'm to trust you, trespasser?"

"We are no criminals," said Ansel. "We are here to meet Gawdspelle," he continued, standing tall, taller it seemed to Valen than he had yet seen. As though he was a mighty prince who had left home long ago never to be remembered. Valen watched him as his hands clutched tightly on his spears.

"Gawdspelle?" said the blonde soldier suspiciously. He circled around them. "Forgive me, but, I do not know the name."

"We must speak to your king," said Ansel calmly watching the soldier closely.

"King?" sneered the men in unison. "We have no King. We have waited for ages for a king. My father, my father's, father's, father. King—"

"Surely there is someone you give an account to?" said Ansel.

"The Fair Princes," said the dark haired one. "Our allegiance is to them. We have abandoned the idea of any *king* for a long while. Enough of Kings and the past." Then suddenly a small band of soldiers on white horses approached with tall lances piercing the night sky. A giant man jumped down and Valen felt the ground tremble slightly. His tall head nearly touched the sky, though he was not nearly as large as Mogus, but nearly twice as big as Ansel.

"What business are you on?" he said in an unexpectedly kind voice as the rest of his men became immediately hushed.

"Mine and my friends' matters are our own," said Ansel.

"Forgive my men," said the man. "We mean you no harm."

Ansel's hands relaxed suddenly.

"We have been expecting you," said the man, his fierce blue eyes glistening off the rising moon. "I am Brayce son of Doog."

"But, sir!" shouted the man who had greeted them initially. "They are enemies! They have snuck into our city like thieves come to rob a poor old woman in the night!"

"Thieves? They are travelers, who have come for the Festival. And this, is no ordinary festival. Have you not seen the Great Comet draw near? You should have studied the stars when you were young, as I did. Your courage is needed," said the tall man. "But save it, for what may yet befall our beloved city. These are friends of Gawdspelle son of Guthenne the Great and he has just arrived not long before them." The man got back up on his horse. "Take them to the cottages by the stream near the mouth of the Arsan. Give them rest and food and lodging; they will be staying with us for a time.

"Gawdspelle has made it?" said Ansel surprised.

"Yes," said the man with a troubled face. "He has been worried of your arrival. Yet, I am afraid now that you have arrived safely, our fears have truly just begun. He has returned with someone—two of them—one by the name of—"

"Jack?" chimed Valen. "Henry? Jude?"

"That's right," said Brayce trying to gather control of his horse's bridle. Jack has been injured I am afraid. It is worse concerning Jude."

"Injured!?" blurted Valen. "How? Who? What of Henry? What has happened to Jude?"

"Jack will be fine and can tell you the story," smiled the man again. "Henry is fine too; though he has come to us much less a boy than he was. He has been to places ruled by Murkus. Awful, hideous places. For now, they are both resting under the Healing Trees. We will see them in the morning." Brayce took in a deep breath. "I have known Gawdspelle for an age and we have been to war together. We met on the road to Hyddenne. I thought I could help him track Jude; but it was not to be so." Brayce paused. "I did not want to be the one to tell you this; Jude has betrayed us. He has gone to Pestyphooris. Gawdspelle looked everywhere for him, yet he is slyer than a fox. Word has reached us that Jude has been to This Realm before."

"Betrayed us?" said Valen in disbelief.

"Yes," said Brayce. "That is all I know and forgive me for saying so at this moment."

"But, I thought he was our friend?" said Valen.

"It is more tragic that he was your friend and he betrayed you," said

Brayce solemnly. "Gawdspelle will tell you more, I am sure."

Valen remained silent for a long minute.

"What of me sire?" said Gobbins suddenly.

"Thank you for your services," said the man, "but they are no longer needed."

"No longer needed? But, what about my brother!?" said Gobbins with gritted teeth. "He's been taken!"

"Taken?" said Brayce suspiciously. "By whom?"

"The Othoritees," said Ansel. "Just the other night. I promised Gobbins we would get him back."

Brayce stroked the mane of his horse."Then you must stay. We have plenty of room for you." He gazed down at Gobbins. "I am sorry for your loss. I hope nothing foul befalls him. You may stay as long as you like."

"Long enough to gather a small band of brave warriors to track him down?" said Gobbins with clenched fists.

"I do not know if we can spare any soldiers," said Brayce. "Our armies are weak—thin. The Othoritees are many in number, violent, organized, well trained and they mame and capture indiscriminately and other enemies and cruel folk are on the move." He paused. Night had fallen. "Enough talk. Come, let us find rest for the evening." He looked at the men who had first greeted Valen and his friends. "I have changed my mind. I will lead them to the cottages. Good evening men." And they departed swiftly, obediently.

Beautiful white trees with wonderful red smelling flowers lined the road they walked down. A cool wind began to blow and some of the petals, fell from their long arched branches twirling up into the night sky. The company moved past the heavy wooden gate. It creaked slowly shut. They traveled down a tiny stone path which Mogus could not fit on. Instead he walked in a field that ran along the path his friends were on. Valen listened to the sound of his footsteps swishing through the tall grass. Then Mogus sneezed. The sound of it echoed off the old stone and a light slowly emerged in one of the castle windows. Shortly after the end of the path they were on they came at last to a tiny bank that dipped down into a low lying field which made its way over to a swift stream traveling under the city. Once they arrived, they came to a mighty looking ship, that had one large sail which sat across it. The boat was long and made of thick, dark wood. Everyone got on. Valen watched the water moving swiftly beneath them as it wrapped itself around the rocks that stuck up out of the water.

Soon they were off, gliding quickly down the stream. In a moment they were under the castle. Small lanterns hung along the wall, sparkling off the water. Mogus' head nearly hit the top of it as they wound their way through. A few minutes later they arrived at a set of stairs, that rose up out of the water. Brayce guided the boat to the nearby ledge. They quietly exited the ship as the hull ran softly ashore. Then they walked up a few flight of stairs. At the top of them stood an impressive wooden door. Torches lit up the entry way. Brayce opened it.

CHAPTER FIFTEEN

# THE FESTIVAL OF THE TWO WANDERING STARS

They traveled up more long flights of stairs. More guards and soldiers, like the ones they had first encountered, walked about the city; their bright silver and red armor glistening from the Comet and Moon grew brighter. Valen was right behind Ansel now, as they marched further and further up. Veeps, Gobbins, and Mogus lingered at the rear.

At last they entered a small swath of green grass. They were high up now and Valen looked out at the land. The forest lay in the distance and the river looked like a tiny glinting thread below. Brayce led them to their quarters for a night's rest, refreshment and food and said he would return in the morning. They all settled in quietly, with Mogus having to sleep under the stars. They thanked Brayce for his hospitality and then did not utter another word. They were all quite exhausted having traveled so far. They all retired to a pair of small thatched cottages.

Valen was awake. He stepped into the entry way of the tallest house. The room was dark and his heart flooded with questions and he hoped Gawdspelle had answers. He clutched the wooden box that Trumfis had given him and reached his hand in his pocket to see if the book left by Gawdspelle remained. He hadn't thought of the book in quite some time. His mind was weary from travel. His thoughts weighed heavy on him and for a moment they shifted to Murkus' desire to murder him and he suddenly shuddered; but that all seemed so far away, like a dream that long ago faded. Brayce had told him that Gawdspelle was in a secret meeting with the Three Princes and that Valen could see him soon. What he wondered were they discussing and when would he find out? It would be a long time before Valen knew.

He lay the box on the bed. Then, he went over to a seat that was built into a window that overlooked the land below. Valen peered out. He opened the window. It seemed he was floating, lost in an endless galaxy and Murkus was just one horrible nightmare. He sat down and propped his feet against the side of the window. A warm breeze rustled through his room and his argent hair danced liked a tree's branches before an oncoming storm. He thought of Henry, Jude, Jack, the Voors and then Mr. Tiddle, all gone on different adventures. He thought back to when he lay sick in bed in Had Wink and it seemed to be ages ago. He looked down at his hands and legs and he seemed to have grown some since he reached Hallowell with Veeps. He still tried hard to believe he was an elf—and a Luminous elf at that. Descendant of one of the most powerful beings ever to have existed, thought to be gone. Yet . . . his thought ended. His mind went into a place where his thoughts froze solid, no dreams, only pure tranquility. It was not long before he heard the sound of Mogus' deep breathing. Mogus lay asleep beneath the window Valen sat in.

Morning came before long. Valen still sat perched on the ledge of the window sill and looked down where Mogus laid the previous night and saw an impression the size of an elephant in the lush grass. Mogus was awake. Slowly, Valen got up from where he sat and went over to the bed where the box lay. He picked it up and made his way to the door. Once outside, his mind became suddenly engulfed by the richness of the towering walls which were laced with ivy that looked to be thousands of years old. The turrets and mighty ivory colored towers Valen had seen earlier, were now right in front of them. Huge walls of white stone brick stood all around him. The castle gleamed brightly in the sun. It boasted huge columns. Hyddenne seemed to Valen a formidable, unknown guard to all of Eoorthe. It was dug out of old eternal stone. The mountain it sat upon was rooted deep into the ground, immovable. Ansel and Veeps joined the company of Mogus underneath Valen's window.

A few days of rest had passed by them, nearly unnoticed. Valen heard birds tweeting and the Silver River lapping below in the distance. At night when the Comet appeared, it lit up the countryside in between the river and the forests, which now lay in the far horizon; though they were still huge, and looked quite close. Valen learned later, from Brayce, that the trees were guardians—guardians which had been planted by the King long ago. It was impossible to pass through them, unless they had given permission. As it was, this is what was happening now, for more and more creatures walked through it under their branches.

Now at last, night had come upon them again. Valen looked up and could see that the Comet was brighter than ever. All around the water sparkled and a sea of lanterns lay about the hills. Banners and tents were now raised. Food of all kinds went out from the city gates day and night. Drink in large barrels sat under every tent. If winter lay beyond Hyddenne, spring was certainly all around the Old City. Valen heard birds chirping, even as night had fallen and flowers bloomed and the creatures below were singing and dancing all over the hillside.

Soon, they heard Brayce greeting them. Moments later they gathered in the courtyard which bordered the backs of the tiny cottages they slept in.

"I spoke with Gawdspelle last evening," began Brayce. "The Festival and Gathering begins soon. Follow me."

The wind blew lightly and pleasantly, but with it came a dark canopy of clouds. Soon, they passed like a flock of birds which passed swiftly into the horizon. The company set off at once and before long they reached the place Brayce had been laboring to bring them to. It was at the top of the mountain, but not quite the very top. Valen looked out across a small grove, where in the distance a walkway with a small stone wall wound its way around to the summit. He clutched the box tightly. Though it seemed quite ordinary, he felt he carried something, that was far too powerful for him alone to contain; should it by chance be opened—even if he was a Luminous elf. They followed Brayce at a hurried pace across a bewitching garden and at last came to a large oval stone table with two thick and long stone steps which encompassed it. It sat upon a small hill which sat above the entire city. There before Valen stood several bent, twisted and stooping trees scattered around the tiny courtyard and garden which surrounded the table. The trees looked as though they had died long ago, but still possessed a beauty and magnificence unlike any Valen had yet seen. There were several large kingly carved wooden chairs that appeared to keep guard, roots and ivy had grown over them.

Valen heard a noise. There stood Gawdspelle looking out over Hyddenne at the edge of the meeting place. Gawdspelle looked as though he had a large stone upon his back. For as he began to walk he looked hunched, ruminating over something of deep concern, sorrow even.

Mogus had become fixated on the trees that hung gracefully over the table, which created an arch. The end of their branches were locked together to form a wooden roof. Hanging below their branches sat soft whitish, golden colored globes that looked like giant apples waiting to be picked. They carried a light that had only recently faded, for they flickered bright then faded, then flickered bright again. The globes floated through the air as though lost in a small sea. The Comet cast a bright golden light upon the land. The Moon also floated above, in a starry sky.

Brayce, Gobbins, Veeps and Mogus stood quietly; waiting for Gawdspelle to greet them. Valen held the box he carried close to his chest. The band of them stared up at the Comet for a long moment. Gawdspelle turned slowly, before making his way over to one of the tall majestic wooden chairs. As he turned the globes flickered again with a dim light for a small moment.

"Oh, Gawdspelle! You are here!" said Valen. "I have wanted to see you since we were under the mountains!"

Gawdspelle smiled wide and deep.

"It is good to see you, Valen," he said.

"Please, tell me," said Valen. "Brayce said Jude has betrayed us? Tell me it isn't so."

"It is," said Gawdspelle sadly. "It was he who first came over the Bridge in the Sky. He appeared by the Iron Candle last Summer's Eve. I had been near the Ormuc Mountains as I traveled near Hallowell. I was with my horse near the lake fetching water, when he fallen down out of the sky. I followed him. He was working with Bendy I believe, yet I could never prove it. Unwittingly, he led me to Had Wink and to you. Whatever part Jude is to play before the end, is not clear to me. Though, for some purpose, I believe, it is because of his betrayal that brought us here." Gawdspelle paused. "For now, Jude is gone. I believe he has gone to Pestyphooris to tell Murkus of our meeting. What's in it for him, I can only wonder. Yet, before Murkus knows we are here, we shall already be gone." He paused again. "Now, I see you have made some friends on your journey from the Looming Mountains," said Gawdspelle looking towards Mogus and Gobbins and Ansel.

"At your service," said Gobbins with a slight bow, the light glistening off his golden hair.

"And I," said Mogus with a small snort.

"I know both of your kind," began Gawdspelle. "But, tell me, are you indeed a mighty?"

"I am," said Mogus crossing his powerful arms. "Not to be confused with a giant, of course." He grinned.

Gawdspelle nodded.

"When did you come across the elf?" he said.

"It was the other way round. I was in prison for a long time," Mogus began. "Valen and his friend came across me, under the Looming Mountains, near the Forges of Bood at the mouth of the Doobglash and the river Rizzenne just south of the Forest of Meerdorf."

"And who are you?" he said at last turning to Gobbins.

"I am Gobbins of the Timmoris."

"What business do you have here?" said Gawdspelle.

"My brother," said Gobbins with a slight stomp of his boot. "It is my mission to find him."

"Oh?" said Gawdspelle his forehead raised.

"He's been kidnapped by the Othoritees. I won't leave him to their evil ways. It wouldn't be right. There is some saying about friends sticking closer than honey-brothers, but that's not how I read it. I take it to mean that brothers should be the way that best of friends are to one another."

"So you are going to find him?"

"If I have to die doing it—"

"If I can help find him," said Gawdspelle solemnly, "then you shall have my help."

Gobbins bowed again with deep gratitude.

"The Festival begins this evening," Gawdspelle said looking up at the bright Comet which illuminated the sky with such brilliance that even the very blades of grass were aglow. "A great feast will be served and we shall meet the Three Princes soon. They are on their way at this very moment."

A set of long stairs fell away, down the side of the hill where the long table sat. Everyone took their seats and soon murmurs and voices and footsteps rose up out of the night. Torches illuminated the stairs. A procession of men and women carrying trays of food and barrels of drink arrived. Food and drink lay before them in such abundance. The grass rustled and songs and dance floated up from below. Then, three hooded figures appeared on the stairs, and Valen stared at the three empty chairs, which waited to receive them. At last they came closer and the orbs which hung from the branches began to flicker on and grew to a steady glow. Then the trees started to grow leaves. As they got closer Valen saw that they wore long robes. Large hoods shrouded their heads. Long white beards hung from their faces. Valen was expecting them to be younger and though they looked quite old, they moved as quick as young stags.

"Welcome travelers from the Other World," said one who had a round beard. "I am Thrind of Thryldon and these are my brothers, Leif and Wynd. Please, eat, drink. Tonight, we celebrate the Binding of the Great Dragon from long ago. The Festival of the Two Wandering Stars, when they came near so long ago and when we captured Murkus, unhided him, bound him and brought him, with the help of the Falkose, to the Lonely Planet beyond. Do not fear, for now you are in the Old City in the Land of Hyddenne. You have traveled through the High Heavens and you are in the Land of the Stars as it is also known. This Realm is the World which men cannot see. We have waited for this moment for a very, very, very long time. Valen of Had Wink on the Western Edge of Hallowell, welcome." The Three Princes nodded. "And Mogus of Rizzenne, Ansel of Noroth, Gobbins of Timmoris, Veeps of Dorodroos and Brayce of Doog and Jack of Had Wink." The Princes smiled. "We have been acquainted with Jack for some time now since he arrived with Gawdspelle many evenings ago and we are happy for his company."

Valen listened quietly, as he ate and drank as much as he could. Soon everyone was content to listen to what the Three Princes had to say, though Thrind said the most.

"We knew that something strange was afoot; when the Great Comet appeared. We knew when Valen entered This Realm. We saw the sky and leaves and colors changing in the grass. It was just as the King had said it would be all along. Many, many have looked for Him; yet, none have found Him. A little girl had seen him walking along the ridge, yestereve." Thrind paused again. "But, I do not know when He shall aid us. He has much work to do, I know. Long, long ago," labored Thrind, "the elves went away. The Great Exodus of the Elves as it is known. Elves no longer could live amongst men in the Other World, for their hearts grew evil, their imaginations twisted and the King became weary, for Murkus, who sought to corrupt all living things wanted more than anything to rule and to also be King. He wanted nothing to do with being a prince. But, we are getting ahead in our story and the evening is only beginning! Though, this is an occasion for celebration, the time that is upon us is grim." Thrind paused. "Murkus was bound long ago, but Gawdspelle tells us that the Key to *The Door That Was Shut* has been found at last and he is hunting for it. Murkus had sought all along to find it and yet; it lay right beneath him when he captured Had Wink and he didn't have the sense to see it."

"Othoritees were looking for Valen, I knew, but I lead them off your trail for awhile, after the Looming Mountains. I knew they would be looking for me and for you for they had followed me for many months when I left my home, long ago. Should they have found us together, they would have surely known we had the Key. They knew of my love for elves and they knew I too, cared for finding the Key; though of course, they did not know I had found it. What they did not expect was an elf traveling virtually alone in the wider world, much less with the Key that Murkus had been looking for, for thousands of years. I hoped to draw them to me; though, I much preferred the company of Ansel who knows all the lands between Noroth and Hallowell, a full years travel as the crow flies. I am sorry that I left you, but it was for your own good. More meets the eye than one can see." Gawdspelle looked at Mogus and grinned. "As it was, the Othoritees were fooled. I was hoping you would find Ansel and you did. I was eager for him to find you and so I asked him to leave at once. That was just after last winter had passed. I had been looking for you, it is true. If we had gone on together, they would have hunted us like dogs."

"But now what do we do with the Key and this?" Valen set the long dark wooden box upon the table.

"That is a weapon of immensity," came a sudden, deep and powerful voice.

"Vorfynn, King of the White Tigers," said Wynd. "Welcome."

"Late it is though," Vorfynn said. He was sitting upon a large stump which was at the opposite end of the long table. "I have heard the horrid sleighs and foxes hissing and their bells piercing the land day and night. I can avoid being seen if I want to, but what are you to do with this and the Key—send the elf away with it? Then what?"

"Are you the King they have been speaking of?" said Gobbins sheepishly interrupting.

"No, the King of which you speak," said Gawdspelle, "is the High King, the King above all other kings. He is near."

"This item which was brought from the White Kingdom," began Wynd, "do you know what is?"

"I have my guesses," said Vorfynn.

"As do I," said Gawdspelle. "I believe it is the Lance which pierced the King, long ago. The Lance that was the King's which he gave up to win back his Love; when he and Murkus battled. It was found high on the mountain where Murkus slew him."

"Do you mean when the King was looking for his bride?" said Veeps. "The Lance? Great lore surrounds that box if that is so, as has never been told of anything in all This Realm."

"How did you come upon such a thing," said Leif, "if it is the thing which you say it is?"

"Trumfis," began Valen. "He gave it to me."

"Trumfis is alive!?" said Vorfynn with great glee. "My son! He was taken—betrayed by his own brother," said Vorfynn solemnly. "But this is news that lifts my heart as no such thing has before."

"Do not let it lift your heart too soon," said Ansel. "Trumfis helped us to escape. The last we saw of him, he was fighting to free us."

"So it is," said Vorfynn sorrowfully. "It is just like him to sacrifice himself for others. If only more were like him. Since I do not know his fate and you also do not know, we shall focus on this item at hand."

"Is it not the Silverfeather?" said Ansel. Then the wind blew mightily and the Comet dimmed.

"Do not utter the name of such a weapon in this Hallowed Place," said Thrind. "If it is such a thing, we shall surely usher in an end which none of us can escape."

"I am sorry," said Ansel. "I only thought it was the bow which was lost."

"Forgive me," said Gawdspelle humbly, "but it is worth mentioning what Ansel is concerned about. Toren believed that weapon would save the White Kingdom at last. But I know, as you have said Thrind; that it is a terrible weapon."

"It is treacherous," said Thrind. "Should it ever be found, it should be broken once and for all. What would we do if Murkus had it? We should all be on our knees, slaves to vile things, our minds and hearts darkened by the madness it brought forth. Yet, should it be found, if anyone were to ever use it, and there is only one who could; he must speak with the King about all its mysteries and powers."

"Trumfis said that it was I that should take this weapon," said Valen gazing at Vorfynn for a brief moment and looking down at the box. "But, what shall I do with it?" He looked at the long mysterious box which sat quietly on the table. It seemed so ordinary, but there was something peculiar about it too.

"There is only one way to find out of its significance," said Leif. "Do you see these trees here?" He glanced all around.

Valen surveyed all the trees.

"They look as though they are dead, but it is because they poured their life into that weapon of which now you speak. The box and the Lance are made from these trees, they are trees which grew in Hallowell ages long past. They are elvish trees and only an elf can place *the Wood That Was Cut*, back into the the tree it was taken from."

"Come, now," said Leif. "I will show you where it was taken from."

Valen got up and went to the other side of the table. Near the entrance at the bottom of one of the trees lay a deep gouge. Valen looked closely at it and near the sapwood it sparkled and glowed silver. It pulsated and twinkled gently, like a star.

"Place it in the tree," said Leif.

Valen did not hesitate. He walked over to the tree and placed it inside the tree and it disappeared. Nothing happened for a long while as everyone looked on, waiting to see what would happen. Minutes passed before finally the tree moved a little. At first Valen thought he heard a song. Then, the tree's gouge healed and disappeared and all the orbs which hung from the branches flickered and then went out. The Comet above shined even brighter and illumined all the trees. It seemed as though it was snowing starlight. Then suddenly, the orbs began to glow again even brighter than they had before and right there in front of Valen stood, the Lance. Everyone gasped. It was exquisite. It was made of such detail and craftsmanship. The handle was fashioned of wood as dark as ebony. The tip was argent and seemed to glow. Everyone murmured and whispered as they gazed upon it.

"So, it is true?" said Vorfynn mesmerized. "Things are coming to pass, which I never thought I would see. Light is gathering above us, but This Realm grows dark. An elf and the King draw near and now we have the *Lance That Pierced the King*, thought to have been lost and now Gawdspelle has the Key, too?"

The Three Princes, Gawdspelle, Ansel, Mogus, Veeps, Gobbins and Brayce began whispering amongst themselves.

"It was not the Silverfeather, as Trumfis, Toren and Ansel thought. Rather, this is *the Lance That Pierced the King*?" said Mogus with great inquisitiveness. "Well, there is no doubt now, is there?" He looked over at Valen.

"We should bring it to Dorodroos," said Veeps. "And we should bring it at once!"

"We can do no such thing!" said Thrind. "This is the one thing that Murkus fears, more than all other crafted items in This Realm. Unless you forget the story when the King and Murkus waged war on each other. It was the King who gave up his life for his beloved when Murkus drove it deep into his heart. He had no power over the King and he never will. It was the King giving up all his power which stripped Murkus of his hide and power. And though he has been bound for some time now, Murkus seeks to regain the power he had lost. His fetters have worn thin, he is hunting for his Hide and should he find it; we will see such a War, the Darker War, as has never been seen before, but there is always hope."

"Hope?" said Gobbins. "They are rounding up good, decent folk all over This Realm! What hope do we have? My brother is among them! He will be murdered!"

The wind rustled the globes and trees. The Comet above them flickered as it finally passed by. Valen watched as it floated towards the horizon.

"This is our hope," said Gawdspelle humbly laying the Key upon the table. "If we stand any chance of slaying Murkus once and for all, we must open the Door. It is our great hour which now is before us—the Key to *The Door That Was Shut*."

"Hope?" said Ansel despairingly. "This Key has only gloom and sorrow written upon it. I want nothing to do with it."

"Nor I," said Mogus. "The Door was shut for reasons none of us know."

"Murkus is looking to unlock the Door and he believes if he murders the last elf, then he can go on to unlock it himself," said Leif solemnly. "He will stop at nothing to kill the elf. Murkus believes that if there *is* one elf which remains, then it will stand in the way of the Door being opened. Though, he does not know, that the Key has been found and so we must keep its discovery from him."

"Many strange things are afoot; the *Lightlessness* and the *Long Lawlessness* have begun, the Lance and the Key have been found and the elf has arrived," said Gawdspelle. "I do not think we have any other choice but to go into that hideous land. Perhaps, there is something beyond our own imaginings that we may see something not more foul, but more beautiful than any of us here can imagine yet."

"Foul things lay behind that door," said Ansel with certainty. "Horrifying, monstrous things."

"You do not know this!" said Thrind. "I was there when it was shut, though I do not know what lay behind it. I do know what lay near it and it is still like that to this day. Bogs and moors, stench and dead things and graves which go on and on for miles and miles. That is where the Door lay, deep in the Land of Deth near Pestyphooris."

"My father was there!" shouted Ansel. "The things which came out of that place infected the Golden Wood of Noroth; the trees, plants, birds, fish—all living things. It is not up to us to open *the Door*. We do not know what lay beyond it and so, I shall not be apart of any fool's errand."

"Let us throw the Key into the sea and invade Murkus' realm," said Brayce forcefully. "We can crush them with our armies if we must and hew down the Door. We need no key. What we need are axes, swords and steeds, which ride upon the wind!"

"Are you a fool?" said Veeps his hands beginning to glow; his mind seeming to change. "We can do no such thing. It must be opened. There is no other way. It is our only chance to defeat Murkus."

"Supposing you are right?" said Brayce. "Then what? What if what is behind that Door is more monstrous than Murkus himself? We shall all be pitied and every song and tale told of the fools who brought the Key to the Land of Deth and forever cast This Realm and the Other World into utter despair."

There was a long deep silence for awhile after this as the debate subsided like a smoldering fire. All around the festivities continued. Valen looked on the ground where mice scurried here and there. Squirrels snickered in the trees. A tent of stars glittered above them. Valen looked over at the Lance which stood up against one of the trees. He felt it beckoning him for a brief moment. Then, he turned and looked down at the Key.

"If Murkus seeks to murder me, then it does no one any good waiting for him to find me here," said Valen solemnly. "If this Key opens *The*

*Door That Was Shut*, then we must try and open it. It was not by chance the Key came into my hands."

"Then, I shall take it," said Veeps standing up. "Someone must take the Key and someone must take the Lance. Should Murkus discover the Key, then we must do everything to protect Valen and the Lance. Murkus desires to destroy the Lance, because he fears its power. The Lance is the thing which can slay him. After he murdered the King, he thought he could take the Lance as his own, but it fell and was lost to him. It was on that mountain that he lost his hide. Now, he wants nothing more than to become a dragon again. Yet, he knows that if the Lance is found and wielded against him, he shall come to his end. The King hid is hide and none of us knows what lies behind the Door, but should it be his hide, and Murkus captures the Lance to destroy it, then there is nothing that will save us from utter destruction. Valen must take the Lance to the safest place in this Realm and use it for his defense against Murkus; should the elf be found—"

"He is sure to be caught!" said Gobbins. "It is a treacherous journey!"

"We shall go together. There is no other way," said Gawdspelle, at last agreeing. "I will aid Veeps and Valen as I am able to. We shall head west to the Golden Trees of Noroth. Murkus knows we are here, but he does not yet know the Key is here, nor does he know about the Lance being found, at least not yet. But, once he does, he will send all his foul creatures to us and he will not stop until he retrieves it; so we must travel the secret roads and paths of This Realm."

"Then I shall go too," said Ansel. "I have traveled for a year, but what is another?" He grinned, but Valen knew Ansel's heart was heavy.

"And I," said Brayce gripping the thick hilt of his sword, which was shaped as a tree. He bowed his head.

"Well, you're not going without the mightys!" Mogus said suddenly, standing and hitting his head on an orb.

"Nor us," came two voices which Valen immediately recognized.

"Murrin! Henry!" Valen shouted. "When did you arrive? Where did you come from?"

Henry looked at Gawdspelle and smiled, and Valen looked at Henry and saw a great change about him. Henry no longer looked entirely like a boy. Valen thought he looked more like a man than ever. He had on princely clothes and a sword hung across his back. There was something more grown up about him. Murrin still had her long golden hair, but now she seemed like a young princess. Across her forehead sparkled a twisted silver band. Large, dark red boots and a flowing bluish cape flapped behind her. Her eyes twinkled.

"I left mother and father a month ago," began Murrin. "I heard Henry's scream from my lands far away. My father would not come and so I escaped as soon as I could."

"It will bring trouble upon us," said Leif. "A daughter of the Voors escaping his care and eye. I do not like it."

"Forgive me, but things are not as they seem," said Murrin as she stepped into the moonlight. "My father is a kind and good king, but he is not himself of late. Traders have come up from the South and have laid many cares upon him, such that he is not himself anymore." Valen saw tears well up in her eyes. "It was my mother who asked me to come. It is her desire to free him from the clutch of that beastly wicked man who is the leader among those traders. He is a robber, a pirate of some sort. He goes back and forth between Eoorthe and the Other World in secret. His pirating, which yields much treasure, is then brought to the Screaming Sea. All he cares about is gold and my father is foolishly auctioning off our lands and even our home under this man's meddling. He has cast a horrible spell upon my country and my father. When mother heard that the Festival was to happen, she sent me immediately in the hopes that someone would dispatch a Healer of Minds from Hyddenne."

"You heard Murrin. That pirate is bringing things to the High Heavens. He is connected to what Murkus is up to. There are evil things," agreed Henry speaking, as though he were her brother and wanted just the same to rescue him. "Terrible things lie about in This Realm which I never want to see again." He swallowed hard.

"But what happened to you when you were taken in the forest?" said Valen. "Where did you go?"

"I was taken to a place that I never wish to see again. The Screaming Sea is a place you do not want to go either. I was taken on a ship to a lone little island surrounded by storms which never stop. On the way, all you see are great swells of the sea and monsters in the deep waters and flying machines which patrol every which way. On the island, it is desolate. Nothing lives there, or so it seems. It is only barren rock and some dead trees. I then met a woman who at first appeared beautiful and lovely. You at once fall in love with her. Her skin is fair and her eyes a deep green with yellow. She greeted me in a white dress and offered me food and shelter when I was tired."

"Why were you brought there?" asked Valen suddenly.

"The island in the Screaming Sea is a hidden place where Murkus operates," Henry said. "It is a place, where the pirate Murrin spoke of transports things to Murkus' kingdom that I do not want to name. The only time I will ever set foot there again is to destroy it. That is what I vowed when I left."

"But," Valen pried. "What are they doing there?"

"It is only part of what Murkus is up to," Henry said. "As we all know, Murkus is capturing every good thing in This Realm and he is using his Othoritees to abduct defenseless creatures all over. Now, he has gone into the Other World, too. The woman is under his spell, doing terrible, horrible things to some of those same creatures."

"What?" said Veeps angrily. "What are they doing!?"

"I cannot say," said Henry. "I will not say, not now."

"I too have seen things which have grown dark on our borders," said Wynd suddenly.

"And I," said Leif certainly. "You need not utter what you have seen, but let it be known that what these two speak of is true. The Light is dimming, and the *Long Lawlessness* has begun. It is what has been spoken of in the *Great Foreshadowings* and we would be fools not to heed what they say!"

No one said anything for awhile and even though everyone felt quite gloomy, a tranquility settled in, despite Henry and Murrin's news. Valen looked up. The Comet still lit up the sky. The trees and their globes glowed brightly all around. Mogus was still eating. He looked up at Valen and grinned. Then Thrind began to speak again.

"So this is where the Key and the Lance bring us to?" he began. "I will rally all good creatures to our aid should we be in need of them." He glanced around. "Let the journey to Pestyphooris and the Golden Trees of Noroth begin. I implore all blessings from this City and all goodness and joy to be upon your roads. This Realm has seen war since its beginnings long ago, and I daresay we are about to enter *the Last Great War—the Darker War*. Do not fail in your passage of the Key, my dear Veeps of Dorodroos, for if you do and Murkus has his way, then he may usher in something of such horror that we will only long for rescue," continued Thrind solemnly. Though his eyes were meek, a look of great concern was writ across his deep blue eyes which now sparkled against the stars. "But do not fear. Evil will not always be so. True, pure love conquers all things in the end and when your heart fails and you are surrounded by shadows and sorrow, remember the great songs and stories of your youth. Even I know the great songs of Dorodroos." Thrind smiled this time. He then turned his wise face toward Valen. He picked up the long dark Lance. Valen felt it had a long story to tell, all its own. It weighed heavy in his hand. "Take this Lance and keep it near you at all times. Do not let it out of your care. None of us can carry this weapon except for one such as you. It will slay more than a dragon. I do not know all that is before you, but until we see one another again, and I hope that we do; do not be too burdened. This Realm and the Other World will soon be freed forever from tyranny and sorrow. And do not lose heart. Your father loves you very much and he will find you. Of that I am sure. The King is on the move too, and if he has anything to say of where we now find ourselves, I am sure He will bring Spring and songs which will never fade."

Valen had not thought of his father much until that point, but he wondered very much what he was like and if he would ever see him. But he forgot all about that for the time as his mind shifted at last to what now lay before him.

"In the morning, you will leave in ships which will be prepared for you this evening. The Silver River is long, but it is best you travel on it. Othoritees are sly and quick, and they will stop at nothing to find the elf." Thrind paused. "Do not let your hearts be troubled! Tonight is a celebration that began when Murkus, the dragon from long ago, lost his hide. And a dragon which does not have his hide is no longer a dragon at all. He has lost all his power for he knows he is but a little while to deceive! Though your journey and road before you is dark, the King is near. He has come again and will show himself soon enough. Let the evening and Festival of the Two Wandering Stars last until morning. But, sleep if you must!"

Everyone departed after that and went down the long stairs and back through the city and out under the trees. Lanterns hung about on thick trees. Tents glowed and food and song rose up into the night. Valen took the Lance and found one of the trees which sat high up on a hill. He sat alone, his back pressed up against it. He wasn't much in the mood for food, song or dance or journeying anywhere; despite Thrind's encouragement that the King was near. He didn't know the King and so what did he care? He looked down at the Lance and then up at the Comet which still glowed brightly. It seemed to be moving and staying in the same place at the same time. He was gazing long and hard it, when Gawdspelle appeared without warning. Valen watched him as he walked up the long steep hill towards the trees. A figure appeared in the forest and all at once, the diary that Valen had been carrying all this time and had completely forgotten about, began to glow a silvery blue again. A strong wind swept down the hillside and shook the tops of the tents. It was a strong wind, but not overpowering. The lanterns shook gently in the trees. The Festivities stopped for a moment and the songs became silent as the wind blew all around. The figure, Valen noticed, rode a mighty, powerful horse. It whinnied loudly and snorted and shook the very trees that were near. Thrind, Leif and Wynd had said they had seen the King lately. Was that Him? Gawdspelle neared the trees. The Comet flashed brightly and a sudden meteor shower of such magnitude soared down upon Hyddenne as though the very stars had fallen from the sky above. The whole land lit up. The grass sparkled with starlight. The trees shimmered and Valen just caught sight of a large man, a man he had never quite seen before, sitting on top of a white battle ready horse. Armor wrapped the horse's sides. White greaves lay upon its legs. Valen saw a shield long and rectangular which hung upon the man's back. As soon as the man arrived, he slipped back over the hill and disappeared. Valen turned his gaze towards Gawdspelle where he stood. The meteor shower continued and a tree which Valen had not seen before, emerged. Gawdspelle reached up and picked some of its fruit. Valen was not sure if Gawdspelle had seen the man or not, but whatever the case, something strange was happening.

"The *Lightlessness* has begun and the *Long Lawlessness* will follow," Gawdspelle said suddenly appearing next to Valen, much to his surprise. "I have never seen such a Great Comet and all at the hour of our meeting and before our journey. There is much I do not know. Though, I wish with all my heart I could unlock the riddles which surround us." He paused. "Here, this fruit will give you nourishment that nothing else will. It will heal any wound."

Valen wanted to ask him about the man, but if Gawdspelle had seen him then surely he would have mentioned it.

"Did you see—" Valen began.

"The stars falling?" said Gawdspelle looking up. Valen then knew, that only he had seen the man on the horse. But, who was he and why did he not come down the hillside? He certainly did not seem an enemy. And, after all, Thrind, Wynd and Leif said that they had seen the King on their borders. Was it the King? Could he see things which Gawdspelle did not? Valen's mind shifted to the diary, but when he looked down it only looked plain and ordinary again. He decided not to say anything about it for the time being. He would tell him once their journey began. He was tired and wanted to rest and soak up the spring time air, which lay thick upon the land.

"Come," Gawdspelle said. "Let us rest. We have a long way to go, down the River. We leave at the crack of dawn."

Before long, rich golden sunlight poured over the fields. Creatures of all sorts were taking tents down and rolling large barrels onto wagons. Horses dragged them back into the city gates. Brayce appeared, waving near the shore of the river which sparkled brightly. Valen had rested the previous night near the large tree. He looked back at the hillside where he had seen the man on the horse. There were trees now which swayed back and forth. Leaves rustled and swirled up into the morning sky.

When Valen arrived at the bank of the Silver River he was greeted by his friends. Mogus looked larger than usual. The sun glistened off his head. Around his neck hung his bags which he had carried his stones in. Around his chest he displayed his sling. It was a terrifying thing, thought Valen; seeing one of those stones flying through the air. Mogus smiled and ate some stam. Ansel looked more kinglier than ever. His spears lay crisscrossed upon his back. He stood taller. Ansel got into one of the large boats. Then down the hill came Jack, Henry and Murrin. Jack and Henry had swords on their sides. Small, square shields lay across their backs.

"We're readier than ever," said Henry getting into the boat. Valen didn't mean to, but he was ignoring Henry. He was looking at Murrin. Her hair glistened in the sun. She did not look like a warrior of any sort, or at least it seemed that if she was, in her eyes she did not want to go to fight anything. But, she hid it well. She smiled, nodded politely and stepped into the boat. Gawdspelle, Gobbins, Brayce, and Vorfynn followed. Jack and Henry had already joined them. In all they would take three boats, Mogus nearly taking a full one himself.

The boats bobbed up and down. There was a horse in each boat, one gray one, one brown one and one black. They stood calmly, their necks hung over the edge of the ship drinking quietly. The water was clear and shallow as it lapped up against the hulls. Beautiful fish swam all around. Otters played with one another as they chased and pulled one another's tails. They darted back and forth. The anchors were unmoored when at last Leif, Wynd and Thrind appeared. They stood on the shore and Thrind began to speak.

"We prepared every provision for you that will aid you on your long journey," began Thrind. His white beard was large and bushy and his eyes were wise and full of kindness. Valen liked him very much. "Where you are going and what you are doing is something which no one has ever attempted. Do not be deceived! Murkus is cunning! Be on guard. Do not let your hearts be troubled! There will come a day when Murkus is bound up forever and all the deep sadness and suffering which troubles us, will go away forevermore. The King will come again. I am sure of it. I do believe, he has heard what we are up to. Good tidings from Hyddenne." And with that he waved. The ships had launched and were floating gently down the river.

They all waved to the Three Princes. Valen felt the warm wind on his face. The River wound through large lush hills. Huge white stone outcrops lay all around. The sun was getting higher above them. Warm breezes pushed the sails of the ships down the quiet current. Valen sat with the Lance at his feet and the diary in his pocket. Veeps stood in front of him, quietly gazing out over the glistening river. The Key was tucked in a tiny bag he had slung across his chest. They both, nearly at the same time, looked back at the beautiful city in awe. It stuck up above the hill it laid nestled on and shone like the crown of a fair queen. Its white rocks glistened against the sun. The green rolling hills rose all around them and then slowly began to fade. Valen looked long and hard at the lovely landscape. His heart was light and without care. He smiled and kicked up his feet. Mogus began to sing a slow, rich song. Veeps and Ansel joined in, then Gawdspelle and even Veeps and Murrin. Valen did not know the song, but it washed over him like a warm wave and he was at peace. It would be the last peace he would know for a very long time.

~ So Ends Part One~

# THE ILLUSTRATOR

## JUSTIN GERARD

From the moment that Justin Gerard first learned that the crayons were meant for coloring and not for eating, he has been drawing.

He began painting later in life after he found a Step-by-Step Graphics guide on Peter de Sève. Armed with this and inspiration from the works of Arthur Rackham and the Golden Age illustrators he began creating narrative-driven images to inspire himself and others.

Justin has a special love for the Golden Age illustrators. He has made a long and detailed study of their brains in an effort to distill their collective genius into a drink, which he might sell for millions.

While Justin has always derived a great deal of inspiration from nature and human history, his favorite source of inspiration is story. The works of J.R.R. Tolkien and C.S. Lewis have remained constant sources of inspiration for him throughout his career.

Justin gave up a life of gambling, piracy and horse-thieving in 2013 to marry Annie Stegg.

Justin's work can be found at www.gallerygerard.com

# THE AUTHOR

## B.D. SUTFIN

The writer of this story grew up in Western Pennsylvania just outside of Pittsburgh on the Ohio River. He is one of six children, five of which were boys and all of which are now men. His sister was happy about her lot. Some children grow up on television-sadly. His father promptly threw the T.V. out of the window at his mother's prompting because she wanted her children to grow up in the woods. He thinks this is one of the greatest educational decisions of his life. Barges and trains, rafts and forts, fishing, fighting, hockey, tackle football and all around wildness accompanied him as he grew. After he "grew up" he studied philosophy, history and literature. One of his best memories is his father coming home and the smell of sawdust and winter clinging to his thick flannel shirt. He has four children of his own, which he and his wife take full responsibility for, loves America, woodworking, design, reads widely and will soon be getting a motorcycle. He is set to release Book Two in the series of *The Chronicles of Eoorthe* (as long as it doesn't take *another* ten years), amongst his other writings, once he gets his pilot license and jumps out of some more airplanes.

His work can be found at www.eoorthe.com

NORTHERNNESS PRESS

PITTSBURGH, PENNSYLVANIA

WWW.NORTHERNNESSPRESS.COM

www.ingramcontent.com/pod-product-compliance
Lightning Source LLC
Chambersburg PA
CBHW020936310726
48980CB00007B/791/J
*9780692988244*